DEATH'S STING

He hit another ledge, still some twenty feet above the floor of the forest, legs flexing to absorb the jolt, taking a step back to keep his balance as he dropped into a crouch. Bullets shrieked and howled from the boulder down from which he'd been sliding a moment before. Scrambling forward again, he clattered down on a loose pile of scree and talus, then rolled behind a sheltering boulder.

One thing was instantly clear: there were a hell of a lot more than five bad guys down there, and they were not "lightly armed" as he had been led to believe. He could hear the bullets as they snapped and whined, and they were coming from several different directions. Damn! There must be ten or twenty of them down there at least, and not just in the base camp either. He could hear them running in the woods now, coming from the direction of the barracks.

And his missed step had just stirred up the whole damned hornet's nest, bringing the enemy out in angry swarms . . .

SEALS
THE WARRIOR BREED

MEDAL OF HONOR

H. JAY RIKER

AVON BOOKS ◆ NEW YORK

AVON BOOKS
A division of
The Hearst Corporation
1350 Avenue of the Americas
New York, New York 10019

Copyright © 1997 by Bill Fawcett & Associates
Published by arrangement with Bill Fawcett & Associates
Visit our website at http://www.AvonBooks.com
Library of Congress Catalog Card Number: 97-93750
ISBN: 0-380-78556-0

First Avon Books Printing: December 1997

AVON TRADEMARK REG. U.S. PAT. OFF. AND IN OTHER COUNTRIES, MARCA REGISTRADA, HECHO EN U.S.A.

Printed in the U.S.A.

WCD   10 9 8 7 6 5 4 3 2 1

Author's Note

This is a work of fiction. As with other books in this series, however, *Medal Of Honor* is based on actual events. Names and certain specifics of the various operations described in these pages have been changed, some episodes have been invented from whole cloth or translated into fictional form from actual records or from the stories of men who were there, and most of the characters are either completely fictional or composites based on the experiences of several real people. This was done partly for dramatic purposes and partly out of respect for those living comrades and families of the SEALS who didn't come back who might not care to see those names used in a work of fiction.

This fictionalization of the historical record should not be misconstrued as disrespect for the very real heroes of the true SEAL story, the brave men, living and dead, who did what they had to do in a time when the nation was being torn apart by the horror and the stupidities of the war in Vietnam. Many of the stories in this book are based closely on fact; in general the more unbelievable an account, the likelier it is to be essentially true.

In particular, the Navy's policy of having the first award of the Congressional Medal of Honor for a SEAL go to an officer, as described in this book, is fact. The raid in which the action resulting in that award occurred has been fictionalized but is accurate in certain details of geography and operational history. Those interested in what *really* happened are invited to military history shelves of most bookstores . . .

or the exhibits at the excellent SEAL/UDT Museum in Fort Pierce, Florida.

It is to those whose exploits and valor are the solid reality from which this book presents its pale reflections that this work is respectfully dedicated.

—H. Jay Riker
December 1995

Chapter Prologue

Early March, Year of the Sheep

On the Ho Chi Minh Trail, near Station T-38
Ratanakiri Province, Cambodia
1520 hours

Phan Nhu Hung dropped into a ditch on the side of the road as the aircraft howled low above the jungle at treetop level. Explosions rocked the earth, sending billowing plumes of black and oily smoke roiling into the sky up ahead. A Russian-made truck was burning nearby, and as he watched, horrified, a rocket hissed down out of the sky and slammed into a second truck trying to pass the first. The vehicle's cab was enveloped in orange-and-yellow flame; the driver spilled out of the side, his entire body wreathed in fire as he writhed and twisted on the muddy ground.

Hung tried to worm his way deeper into the water-filled ditch, praying desperately that the flying death would pass him by. More explosions savaged the column, shredding the jungle vegetation and whirling the fragments about in cyclonic fury. Someone was shrieking in agony nearby . . . the truck driver, he thought, but he didn't want to raise his head above the level of the ditch to find out.

As suddenly as it had started, the bombing and rocketing ceased. The only sounds now were the crackle of flames and the continued shrieking of the wounded. A single loud gunshot interrupted the screaming in mid-quaver, silencing it abruptly.

"It's all right!" one of the cadres said, walking past. "It's all right! They are gone!" Somebody nudged Hung in the

1

back with the butt of a rifle. "On your feet, comrade. We have a long way yet to go!"

A long way yet to go . . .

Reluctantly Hung left the illusory shelter of the ditch, his green uniform muddy and dripping wet . . . which was just as well, since he found only now that he'd soiled himself during the attack. His face burned with shame at the realization. He was glad that none of his comrades could see his disgrace.

More than ever, Hung knew that he was not worthy material for a soldier. This was all a terrible mistake, and all he wanted in the whole world right now was to be allowed to return to his home in An Hai, a town on the outskirts of the port city of Haiphong. He hated this life, hated the stomach-squeezing terror, hated the boredom, hated the constant hunger and exhaustion and sickness.

He felt something on the back of his hand, looked down, and saw a four-centimeter-long leech clinging to his skin. Convulsively, he ripped it off, then rubbed the thin smear of blood the disgusting little creature had left behind. He shuddered. Most of all he hated the jungle, with its myriad ways of killing a man, of making him sick, of wearing him down. Blood-sucking leeches, spiders the size of a man's hand, stinging ants and poisonous scorpions, deadly snakes and clouds of disease-carrying flies and mosquitoes, the wet that turned a cold into pneumonia . . . the list of dangers and discomforts was endless.

A month ago, he'd asked the cadre in charge of his platoon if he could go home, and been bluntly refused. He was a volunteer, they'd told him, fighting to liberate his cousins in the South who'd been suffering for years under the invading Americans and their corrupt and vicious puppets in Saigon. There was no way to go back, not now. *No* one who'd volunteered for service in the South returned, not until the final victory that united North and South under Hanoi's victorious banner.

And if he didn't want to serve in the glorious liberation, perhaps it would be necessary to examine him and his revolutionary fervor more closely, in order to determine whether reeducation might be necessary.

That threat had been enough, but sometimes Hung wondered how he was going to keep going. Still, he questioned the fact of his "volunteering." About two hundred young men, from his town and from other towns in the Haiphong area, had attended a huge rally one night, where cadres and political officers had described with passionate drama the sufferings of their countrymen in the South, and the horrors of the American occupation, and the need for every young man in the North to support the revolutionary struggle. "Who here supports the struggle of our suffering and oppressed cousins?" an officer had demanded. Hung and his friends had surged to their feet, shouting, "Me! Me! Me!"

And the next thing he'd known, he was at the main NVA training center at Xuan Mai, southwest of Hanoi, learning to shoot, learning basic tactics, learning how to care for himself in the field by keeping dry and taking his antimalarial pills every day.

He'd hated the regimentation and the drill, the callousness of his instructors and the privations endured by the recruits. He'd actually run away once, slipping under a barbed-wire fence and walking or begging rides all the way back to An Hai . . . but the girls had scorned him and the neighbors had complained to the authorities and his father had bluntly refused to speak to him. Within a day or two of his return home, the soldiers had come to take him back to Xuan Mai. His punishment had been relatively light—extra duty for the rest of his training period, and a public confession of wrongdoing in front of his comrades. Worse had been the certain knowledge that a bridge had been crossed, that he would never be able to go home again until the war in the South was over. Eventually, training had been over, and he'd been told that he was going South.

It felt as though he'd been walking forever. His load was light; in his pack he carried only an extra uniform and a set of civilian black pajamas, an entrenching tool, five loaded clips of 7.62mm ammo, and some personal effects. On his head he wore a cork sun helmet covered with cloth. His feet were shod with *binh tri thien*, sandals cut from old truck-tire treads; he'd heard that the Americans referred to them derisively as "Ho Chi Minh sandals," though he didn't understand why that name should be considered insulting. "Uncle Ho," after all, cared for the needs of all his people, however slight or seemingly insignificant, and it was not impossible that he would have had a hand in the invention of this most practical item of worker-soldier's footwear. His weapon was a Type 56 rifle, the Chinese version of the SKS, though if he proved himself worthy, he could hope one day to be issued the redoubtable AK-47.

How long had he been on the trail so far? A month? Two? He'd long since lost count of the days, and he wasn't entirely certain of when they'd crossed the border into Laos and, later, into Cambodia. Progress was measured by the numbered *Trams*, or stations, along the way, each about a day's march apart—ten to twenty kilometers, depending on the terrain. He'd lost a week or so at T-22, when he'd developed malaria despite the pills and had been incapacitated by fever. When he'd recovered, he'd started off again with another southbound group, since his friends and companions with his original group had long since gone on ahead.

As he resumed his march, he felt very much alone and afraid.

Hung dreaded the time when he would actually reach the South and be expected to fight against the Americans. Americans, the new recruits had been told, ate their prisoners, or disemboweled them, or shipped them as slaves to far-off South Korea, where they replaced the ROK soldiers who'd come to South Vietnam to fight against the revolutionary forces. Strangest of all were the stories of an American machine that somehow turned Vietnamese prisoners into *blacks* ... a fate worse than death for a people who believed blacks to be subhuman barbarians or worse.

By now, Hung was learning to accept the pronouncements both of the political cadres and of his fellow soldiers with a certain amount of skepticism. He didn't really believe the story about a machine that changed people into blacks, for example. American machines tended to be far more brutal, indiscriminate, and direct ... like the aircraft that spread flaming napalm across the jungle in their constant efforts to interdict the Ho Chi Minh Trail.

Still, some of the stories were spoken in whispers and with

a knowing fear that indicated the whisperers were telling the truth. Some Americans, at least, were as monstrous as any barbarian cannibal. They were at home in the jungle as Hung and his comrades could never be. They were savage in their cunning and murderous in their disposition, creatures of the night that came out of nowhere, vanished into emptiness, and fed on human flesh. They were invisible, powerful, and deadly, walking nightmares in human guise. Some called them the Men With Green Faces.

Others called them SEALs. . . .

Chapter 1

Friday, 17 March 1967

San Francisco State University
1215 hours

How the hell am I going to tell her?

Greg Halstead trudged across campus, head bowed, arms wrapped around his textbooks. He'd gotten used to San Francisco fog, but today it seemed oppressive, closing in on him, and he longed for a sight of the open ocean. He'd always loved the sea, ever since he was a kid. Back home in Jenner, some seventy miles up the coast, he'd spent most of his free time—when he wasn't working at Halstead Drugs, that is—either on the Russian River or on the coast, swimming off Goat Rock, running along the beach, climbing the cliffs, or just standing and staring out at the vast gray expanse of the Pacific. It thrilled him to think that the way he felt was probably the same way Balboa had felt, the first time he gazed on that seemingly endless sea four centuries before. He stood still for a moment, facing west, imagining Lake Merced and the ocean that lay beyond it. There was such serene power there . . . with no hint of the conflict raging on the other side, half a world away.

Is there any chance that she'll understand?

He turned and started off again. He was headed for the Student Union and his regular Friday afternoon date with Marci Cochran, a Berkeley student his sister Pat had introduced him to well over a year ago. He'd been a sophomore at the time and Pat just a freshman, but she'd always been more social than her brother, more outgoing, quicker to become intimate with people. Within a week of arriving on campus, she'd made dozens of new friends, while he was still something of a loner. After almost three years now, there weren't more than three or four guys that he could say he knew well. Even his roommates—there were six of them crammed into a tiny two-bedroom apartment—were more acquaintances than friends. Somehow he just didn't seem to have much in common with them.

But Pat knew everyone, not only here at State, but across the bay in Oakland as well. She'd met Marci at a Berkeley peace rally, and they'd quickly become fast friends. Since Marci had her own car, she would frequently drive over to see Pat, and on one of those visits Greg had run into the two of them on their way to the Student Union. Pat had asked him to join them, and he did, he still wasn't sure why. The three of them had talked for hours. Then Pat left, and he and Marci had talked for hours more.

He'd long since forgotten the specifics of what they'd talked about. He'd never known anyone like Marci. She was so . . . so alive, so interested in everyone and everything. He didn't agree with a lot of what she said, but arguing with her was exciting, stimulating. At first he wondered if she was hanging around him just to try to convert him to her free-speech, antiwar ideas, but soon their relationship deepened. She was bright and witty. Sex with her was spectacular, but they had so much more in common as well. This past fall she'd gotten an apartment by herself out in Oakland, and Greg had been spending most of his weekends there. They would meet here at State after Greg's last class, have a late lunch at the Student Union, and then drive back across the bay.

But not this weekend.

Greg came to a stop outside the tall, rough stone building. He hadn't yet figured out how much of Marci's activist talk was motivated by deep conviction and how much by an eagerness to be involved in something that seemed exciting, with people who were doing exciting things. He'd felt the lure himself, and certainly it explained Pat's involvement. When he'd first met Marci, he'd assumed that she was just a spoiled rich kid kind of playing at being an activist. He wasn't so sure anymore.

He had a feeling he'd be finding out pretty soon.

Taking a deep breath, he pushed open the door of the Student Union, crossed the main lounge, and trotted down the steps to the snack bar in the basement. As he entered the snack bar, he could hear that new Beatles tune "Penny Lane" playing on the college radio. A quick glance around the room told him he'd beaten Marci there, so he grabbed a tray and got in line. A couple of hamburgers, some French fries, a Coke—typical college fare. It didn't matter what he got; he didn't think he'd even notice the taste. He found a free table and sat down facing the entrance so he could see Marci when she came in. *Somehow,* he thought, *I've got to be able to make her understand.*

He'd become more and more fed up with college over the past two years. His first year had been pretty exciting, the heady experience of being away from home for the first time, being in a big city, the thrill of large university classes ... but after a while he felt that most of the other students weren't there to get an education at all. It was like they were just playing at being adults, without accepting any of the responsibilities. Some of the guys, he was sure, were only there to avoid the draft. And more and more of them lately had been getting into the free-speech movement, carrying the First Amendment to ridiculous extremes.

The worst of it was, he no longer felt that he was getting a good education. So many of the professors seemed to be knuckling under to student protests and watering down their courses. Even his history profs seemed more concerned with what their students *felt* about what they were studying than with the facts . . . or the truth. Just a little over a year from now he would have to be thinking about what he was going to do *after* college, and he had suddenly realized that he had no idea.

He had gotten through both hamburgers and most of his fries before he spotted Marci just getting into line. She saw him and waved, a smile lighting up her oval face. *God*, how he loved her. He watched her carefully select her food, probably a salad and a sandwich that she'd eat without the bread. She was big into healthy eating. He was very much aware of the admiring looks her long lanky frame drew as she strolled toward his table with her eyes fixed on him. He found himself grinning idiotically as she approached and placed her tray down opposite his.

"So. Have you decided yet?" she asked, as she began to dismember her sandwich.

What? How did she know? "Decided?" He repeated her word, stalling for time.

"About the rally."

"The rally." He was confused.

"Where *are* you this afternoon, Greg? Still back in the fifth century?" She smiled. "You really are an absentminded professor, you know." She cut up the chicken from her sandwich and tossed it into her salad. "The big rally in New York next month, remember? April 15. Martin Luther King's going to be there. Pete Seeger. Carmichael. Dr. Spock. Everybody. You've got to decide soon if you want me to reserve space for you. We don't have that many cars."

"Oh, yeah, the rally. I'd forgotten about it." He'd never intended to go, though he'd always put Marci off when she asked him. It seemed to mean so much to her. Now it felt as though he'd been deceiving her.

"So. Are you going or not? Pat's already signed up."

Damn. He wondered what Dad would have to say about that, the daughter of a World War II veteran marching in an antiwar protest rally.

"No, I'm not going to go." He finished his fries and tried to figure out how to say what he had to say.

"Come on, what's your excuse?" she demanded. "You're

doing well in all your classes. This won't take more than a couple of days around the weekend. It'll be easy to make up the work when we get back.''

He loved looking at her, her dark eyes flashing with excitement, her long wavy dark hair framing her face. He realized it wasn't going to get any easier the longer he put it off. ''Marci, I . . .'' The words stuck in his throat.

Now she looked worried. ''Greg, what is it? Is something wrong?''

''I'm leaving,'' he blurted out. ''I'm dropping out.''

''You're what? Dropping out of college? You've got to be kidding. I mean I know you haven't been exactly thrilled with all your profs, but . . .'' She reached out and touched his hand. ''Look, Greg, it's not money, is it? 'Cause if that's it, I could—''

''No, it's not money,'' he interrupted. ''That's not it at all. It's just . . . it's like there's no point to being here. I have no idea where I'm going, why I'm studying what I'm studying. I mean, what's a history major good for?''

It was a rhetorical question, but she answered it anyway. ''Same thing my poli sci major's good for—preparation for law school.'' She grinned. ''In fact, that's a great idea. Let's both go to Harvard Law, and then together we'll change the world! How about it? Hey, we could even start up our own law firm. What do you think—should it be Cochran and Halstead, or Halstead and Cochran?''

Greg picked up her hand and held it briefly to his lips. ''I'm serious, sweetie,'' he said. ''I've got to leave. And I'm leaving today.''

In the silence that followed, ''California Dreamin' '' by the Mamas and the Papas floated out of the radio. One line hung in the air like an echo—''I could leave today.''

''You're leaving.'' Her face looked stunned. ''You're leaving today. You've already decided all this, and you didn't even think to ask how I felt about it. *God*, I don't believe this! Where am I in this picture, huh? Am I even *in* the picture? I thought we meant something to each other. So when did you make this momentous decision, anyway? It doesn't take more than an hour for me to drive over here, even in rush hour. You couldn't have taken two minutes to call me, say you wanted to talk, something like that? Damn, I could use a drink right now.''

Greg looked up in astonishment. "You don't drink."

"Well, I'm ready to start drinking after this bombshell. So what are you going to do? What are your plans? Do you even *have* any plans?" Suddenly her eyes grew wide. "Canada, that's it, isn't it? You're going to Canada, aren't you, and you didn't want me to know so I wouldn't have to lie if anybody asked until you were across the border. Did you get a draft notice? I know they killed the blanket deferments, but I thought your grades were high enough——"

"Marci!" His voice was louder and sharper than he intended, and several people turned to look at their table. He continued more quietly. "Marci, I am not going to Canada. This afternoon I'm going to drive up to Jenner to see my folks, and then next week I'm going to enlist. I'm joining the Navy."

She just stared at Greg for a long moment. "California Dreamin' " finished, and the DJ put on another new Beatles song, "Strawberry Fields Forever."

"Hi, guys. Okay if I join you?" A petite blonde pulled up a chair and plunked herself down between them. "Mmm, I just love this song. The Beatles are so cool."

Greg managed a small smile. "Hi, Pat."

Pat looked back and forth between Marci and her brother and shivered. "Brrrr, the atmosphere is distinctly chilly in here. What gives?"

Marci turned to her, arms folded belligerently in front of her chest. "Ah, so he didn't tell you either. That makes me feel a little better. At least I wasn't the last person to find out." She glared at Greg.

"Find out what?" Pat asked. "What's going on here?"

"My dear Pat, your brother here has just informed me that he is dropping out of school and that he's going to enlist!"

"Dropping out? No, he didn't tell me." Pat looked at Greg. "Navy?" she asked.

He nodded.

"You don't sound surprised," Marci accused.

"I guess I'm not," Pat said, thoughtfully. "I mean, not about the Navy part of it, at any rate. Our dad was in the

Navy. World War II. Grandpap, too.'' She turned to Greg. "So did you get a draft notice? Is that why you're enlisting?"

"I don't believe what I'm hearing!" Marci said. "I mean I knew Greg was waffling, but, Pat, I thought you were as committed to the movement as me."

"I am, Marci, I'm totally against the war in Vietnam. But Greg's not joining the Army, he's joining the Navy. He won't be in the war."

"He's still supporting the military-industrial complex," Marci countered. "And if you think the Navy's not in the war, you haven't been doing your research. Hell, you haven't even been watching the news! Who do think started this damned war in the first place? It was the U.S. Navy that fired on North Vietnamese ships in the Gulf of Tonkin and blew them up. And what about all the *Navy* aircraft flying off *Navy* carriers carrying out air strikes against North Vietnam? And not even restricting them to military targets—they're bombing the hell out of civilians! Don't tell me the Navy's not involved in this war, Pat. I won't buy it!"

"If you two would let me get a word in edgewise," Greg said, "I'd like to know why you both think the only reason I would join the Navy is to avoid getting drafted into the Army! There is such a thing as patriotism, you know."

"Patriotism!" Marci made it sound like a swear word.

"Yes, patriotism! I *believe* in this country, in the flag and everything it stands for. Freedom. Democracy—"

"Damn it, Greg!" She shook her head. "You're talking about going over there and killing innocent civilians, women and children and babies and . . . and everything! Supporting a butcher government that doesn't give a damn about its own people! It's monstrous! No, don't give me that garbage about patriotism! It's nothing but a sham, a way for the pigs to excuse their policies over there, and dupes like you to avoid taking some *real* responsibility! By ending this stupid bullshit once and for all!"

There was no point in continuing. Greg stood up, towering over the two girls. "And I obviously made a big mistake in believing that you could possibly understand, that you would even *want* to try to understand. Good-bye, Marci. I'm sure you'll make an excellent lawyer." He picked up his books and turned to Pat. "Anything you'd like me to tell Dad this afternoon, Sis? Like about how the daughter of a decorated veteran is going to be marching in an antiwar protest rally? I'm sure he'll be thrilled to hear that."

He left his tray on the table and walked off. When he got to the door, he turned and looked back. Marci had her head down on the table, and Pat was leaning over her. For one brief moment he allowed himself to believe that she was sorry. Maybe he should go back, maybe he could reason with her. Just then she raised her head and turned to look at him. The coldness, the *bitterness* in her eyes shocked him. He realized that no, it wasn't Greg Halstead she was crying over, it was the man she'd thought he was . . . or at least the man she'd thought she could turn him into. Well, he wasn't about to be manipulated, by her or by anybody else. He was going to do what he believed in, even if he didn't know where that would lead him.

He started running as soon as he got out of the Student Union. It wasn't that far to his apartment on Pinto Avenue, but by the time he got there, he was breathing hard. Damn, but he was out of shape! He'd been a cross-country runner in high school, but he hadn't had much time for running since he went to college. He'd have to get a lot of runs in over the next few days, or else boot camp was going to be murder. His dad had told him that the boots—that's what they called the new recruits—ran everywhere. Deliberately he ran up the stairs to his third-floor apartment. Panting, he opened the door to what had been his home for almost three years. *Good, no one's here.*

It didn't take him long to pack; he just jammed his clothes into two suitcases and stuffed his towels and bedding into an old seabag of his dad's. Books were a problem, though. He decided to leave most of them for his roommates to divvy up among themselves, just taking a few of his favorite paperbacks. He glanced around the room he'd shared with Bobby Emmons and Ted Mason. He didn't have many personal things—there wasn't room for much in this tiny apartment—but there was one item he needed to deal with. He strode across the room to his bedside table and picked up the framed photograph that rested there. Carefully prying the back open, he extracted the photograph and methodically tore it to shreds.

"Hey, Greg, what gives? What's with the suitcases, man?"

Greg whirled. It was Ted, leaning against the bedroom doorframe with a puzzled look on his face. His eyes grew wide as he saw the torn remnants of the photograph in Greg's hands.

"Hey, you and Marci have a fight? I thought you two were like this." Ted brought his forefingers together.

"I'm leaving, Ted," Greg said as he walked over to the wastebasket and tossed the scraps in it. "I've dropped out."

"You're kidding, right? C'mon, no chick is worth that. I mean, you've been getting As and Bs. What the hell would you drop out for? You'll lose your deferment!"

"Damn it!" Greg exploded. "I am sick and tired of people thinking that the only reason I was in college was to stay out of Vietnam!"

Ted raised his hands in front of his face, as though to ward off Greg's anger. "Hey, sorry, Greg. Didn't mean to tick you off." He backed up into the living room. "So, you're really leaving, huh?"

"Yup. Talked to the dean this morning."

"All official, huh?" Ted whistled. "So where to now? Do you know?"

Greg looked at his roommate somewhat defiantly. "The Navy."

"No shit. You're enlisting?"

He nodded.

"Man, you've got more guts than me, I can tell you. Your folks know?"

"No, that's where I'm headed now." Greg took a deep breath. *Take it easy, stupid! Ted's not Marci!* "How about giving me a hand with these things?"

Ted grinned. "Be glad to."

Together they got everything downstairs in one trip and quickly stuffed inside his ancient, bright blue VW beetle, Babe, parked out back.

"Think Babe'll make it?" Ted asked.

"If she doesn't, I'll get out and push her the rest of the way."

"Push, hell, just pick her up and carry her on your back." Ted laughed. "I never could see what a big guy like you would want with such an itty-bitty little car!"

"She's economical. I don't need a hose to give her a bath, just a watering can. And besides, she's very versatile. She's so watertight, I can use her as a boat."

"Ah, so that's why you're joining the Navy, so you can take Babe along with you!"

Suddenly Greg realized he was going to miss Ted and his other roommates. He reached out and grabbed Ted's arm. "So long, Ted. It's been good to know you."

"Hey, man, don't go talking like we're never going to see each other again. I expect to see you at my graduation next year, wearing your spiffy sailor suit with all your pretty ribbons."

Greg chuckled. "Right. Oh, I almost forgot." He pulled some bills out of his wallet. "This is for my share of the rent and stuff for the rest of the semester. And I'm leaving a lot of my books. Split them up any way you like. Well, that's it, I guess. So long."

"Write if you find work."

Greg folded his large frame into the tiny car and started her up. *Come on, Babe,* he thought. *Just hold together for a little bit longer.* He pulled out of the lot, waved to Ted, and soon was heading north on Nineteenth Avenue—Route 1. *It's really happening,* he thought. *I'm doing it.* Suddenly he felt a sense of relief, *knowing* that he had made the right decision. This time next week, he'd be a sailor.

And proud of it.

Chapter 2

Friday, 17 March 1967

Jenner, California
1610 hours

It was a little after four by the time Greg turned into the parking lot behind Halstead Drugs. His dad's gray Chevy was there, in its usual spot. And Molly's flaming red Dodge. *Babe'll feel right at home,* he thought as he pulled up next to his father's car. He got out and walked around to the front of the drugstore, thinking about the many hours he'd spent working there, after school, weekends, summers. It was a family business, started by his grandfather back in the twenties. He wondered if he'd be there today. Grandpap had been slowing down the past few years—after all, he'd be seventy-two next month—but he still liked to put in an appearance, more for public relations than anything else. His older customers liked to see him there, even though they knew that Dad was the one really doing the work these days.

Both elder Halsteads had hoped that Greg would carry on the tradition, that there would be a third generation of Halstead pharmacists. He shook his head. He liked science—he'd always enjoyed electronics, for instance—but chemistry had been a real problem for him in high school; he knew there'd be no way he could make it through pharmacy school. So what *was* he going to do with his life? Damned if he knew. But he had a pretty good idea that the Navy would help him figure it out.

He pushed open the door and walked in. Still the same.

The same orderly look of stacked shelves, the same mingled smells of perfumes, medicines, and hamburgers. What had he expected? It'd only been a couple of months since he'd been here last. He checked out the Pez candy dispensers next to the cash register in front. He used to get a real kick out of those when he was a kid; it was the dispenser, more than the candy, that was fun. Just then the rather stocky woman behind the register turned around and saw him. Her eyes grew wide. "Greg!" She pushed her way out from behind the counter and gave him a big hug.

"Hi, Molly." He grinned. Molly Jorgensen had been part of Halstead Drugs for, well, forever, it seemed. She'd been working here since long before he was born. When he'd first started coming by the store after school, she would find some chore for him to do, straightening shelves or checking stock. And she would always have a little treat for him before he left.

"What are you *doing* here?" she asked. "No, never mind. I'll hear about it in good time. Doc! Doc Halstead! Look who's here!" She held him at arm's length for a moment, then hugged him again. "My gracious, it's good to see you, Greg. You're looking more like your daddy every day!"

"How's everybody doing, Molly? You keeping yourself fit?" he asked.

"Well, I'm just fine, Greg. I'm always fine. Your granddaddy, though . . ." A crease appeared in her forehead. "He just doesn't have the spunk he used to, you know what I mean? He's not sick, exactly, he's just . . . kind of tired. He only comes in, maybe once, maybe twice a week. Your daddy now, it seems like he's never going to slow down. Sometimes I have to remind him to take the time to eat a bite now and again."

"You telling tales on me, Molly?" a strong bass voice interrupted.

Greg turned and watched his father walk down the aisle toward him. A strong, ruggedly attractive man, tall and blond like his son, David Halstead had a commanding presence. Greg had always looked up to him; it suddenly struck him how very much he wanted his father to approve of his decision.

"Greg! This is a delightful surprise!" David grabbed his son's hand in both of his. "Come on, let's sit down and have a little smackerel of something." He put his arm around Greg's shoulders, and they walked toward the soda fountain. "Jerry!" he called to the boy behind the counter. "We have a special guest today. Come meet my son Greg."

They sat down at one of the tables while Jerry wiped his hands and came around from behind the counter. He was about thirteen or fourteen, it looked like, medium height, skinny, energetic. "Pleased to meet you, sir," he said, shaking Greg's hand. "Your dad's told me a lot about you."

"Aw, come on, Jerry, don't call me 'sir.' 'Sir' is for old relics like this one," he said, pointing at his dad. "The name's Greg. I was a soda jerk, too, remember. Tell me, are your banana splits as good as mine?"

Jerry's grin spread from ear to ear. "The best, sir. I mean, Greg."

"And one of your spectacular chocolate marshmallow creations for this 'old relic,' Jerry."

"Yes, sir!"

David watched as Jerry went back behind the counter. "Jerry's a good boy," he said. "Been working here since September. Picks things up fast. He shows a real interest in pharmacology, too."

"I don't remember him here Christmas," Greg said.

"No, his grandmother was ill. The family went up to Oregon to visit her."

"How old is he? He looks kind of young for the job."

"Turned sixteen a few months ago, would you believe it? He just got his license. He's looking to buy a car, but he says everybody laughs at him, all the used car dealers, 'cause he looks like he's barely out of grade school."

Greg tried to figure out how to break the news. His father with his usual tact was carefully refraining from asking any questions, but he must be wondering. Greg never came home without calling first.

"Here you are, gentlemen," Jerry announced, arriving with a tray. "One Chocolate Marshmallow Spectacular for

you, Doc, and for you, Greg, the Halstead Special Banana
Split Extraordinaire!''

"Jerry, you have outdone yourself!" David said. "Mrs.
Halstead is going to be upset with you when she finds out
you're the reason I can't eat any dinner tonight!"

"Hey, Jerry," Greg said. "Would you be interested in
buying a used VW bug?"

"Would I!" His eyes lit up.

"Her name's Babe, after Paul Bunyan's big blue ox. She's
old, but mostly reliable. She's out back, if you want to take
a look at her."

Jerry looked pleadingly at his boss. "Can I, Doc? Just for
a minute?"

"Go right ahead, Jerry. We'll watch the fountain."

Jerry dropped the tray on the counter, whipped his apron
off, and charged out the back.

The elder Halstead looked at his son. "So. You're selling
Babe?"

The moment had come. "I . . . I've dropped out, Dad."

His father pursed his lips and nodded. "I wondered," he
said finally, "when you came in. Coming home unexpect-
edly. And there was something in your face . . ." He looked
searchingly at his son. "I was aware at Christmas, of course,
that . . . well, that you were not entirely satisfied with your
college experience. This doesn't come as a total shock." He
plucked the cherry off the top of his sundae. "I will not insult
you by asking the obvious questions. Whether you realize
how close you are to getting a degree. Whether you would
consider even finishing out the semester. Whether you are
aware of how many doors you are closing by taking this
action. I assume you've given this careful thought. You're
not one to do things impulsively."

The tense knot in Greg's stomach began to dissolve.
"You're . . . you're not disappointed in me?"

"I'm disappointed, yes. But not in you. I had hopes and
dreams for you, I'll not deny it. But they were *my* hopes, *my*
dreams. Not yours. You paid for college yourself with your
own hard-earned money. I've no right to tell you how to live
your life."

"Thanks, Dad," Greg said. *Maybe now I can enjoy this banana split.* He took a bite. "Mmm, you're right, Dad, the kid's good."

David chuckled, gesturing with his spoon at the mound of whipped cream in front of him. "Far too good for my waist-line. I'm having to watch what I eat more carefully these days."

"Molly says you don't eat unless she reminds you."

"Molly is an old worrywart. I'm surprised she doesn't remind me to put on a sweater when it gets chilly."

"How's Mom?"

"Doing well. Switching to the Visiting Nurses was a good move for her. She has to do a lot of driving, but the work itself is easier and more varied. Better hours, too. The most important thing, she feels she's performing a real service."

"Molly said Grandpap was . . . not doing so well."

"He's doing magnificently for a man who's seventy-one. I think he's just finally realized that I'm competent to run Halstead Drugs without him, so he's letting himself take a well-earned rest." He put his spoon down. "I'm afraid I can't finish this. You're welcome to have some, if you'd like."

Greg took a spoonful of his dad's sundae. "Mmm, that is good."

Just then Jerry reappeared. "Greg, she's beautiful!"

"You like her, huh?"

Jerry nodded enthusiastically.

Greg grinned. "Well, I want to make sure Babe's going to a good home. We'll talk price later, okay?"

"Okay, Greg. I'll be here at the store all day tomorrow. And thanks!"

Jerry whistled, not very expertly, as he went back to work.

"That was a kind thought, Greg. Jerry will be in seventh heaven for weeks."

"How much do you think he could afford, Dad, a couple hundred?"

David shrugged. "I'm not sure how much he's saved. I know he gives a good deal of his pay to his mother. But I can help him out if necessary. He's a good boy."

They sat in silence for a few minutes. "So," his dad said finally. "Where do you go from here? Do you have any plans?"

"I'm going to enlist, Dad. I want to join the Navy."

Greg saw a smile creep onto his father's face.

"I'd been wondering whether you would adopt any radical ideas down there in San Francisco. I'm glad to see you have not. Unlike your sister, who, I'm afraid, is quite entranced by well-intentioned but misguided idealism."

"Did you know she's going to New York next month? For the antiwar rally?"

David's mouth grew taut, and his fingers drummed the table. "That I had not heard. But, Greg, I trust Pat's integrity. Her basic values are sound, and at some point I believe those values will prevail. In the meantime we must let her . . . experiment with these new ideas, we must let her find out for herself what is right and what is wrong." His smile returned, only a little strained. "Now. I've got to get back to work. So why don't you go home, talk to your mother, to Grandpap. I'll be home in an hour or so, and we'll discuss your future after dinner. All right?"

"Okay, Dad," Greg said with a grin.

"Don't worry about Pat. She's sound. She'll be all right."

"I hope so."

"I *know* so. I know my children. Now go on, get out of here, and let me get back to work."

"Okay, Dad. See you later."

Greg waved to Jerry, who grinned back at him. He went out the front door so he could say good-bye to Molly, then he drove home. In less than ten minutes, he was parked in front of a familiar white frame house with the name Halstead on the mailbox. It struck him as he sat there that it might be quite a while before he saw that house again. He didn't know how time off worked in the Navy, but he was sure he wouldn't be able to simply leave for a weekend whenever he felt like it. And if he got stationed overseas, well, it could be a long time between visits.

He was still sitting and thinking when the front door opened and his mother walked hesitantly out onto the porch.

Slim, petite, at this distance she looked just like Pat. Her eyes lit up when she recognized Babe. "Greg? Is that you?" She ran out to the curb while he got out and came around to the car to give her a hug. "What a marvelous surprise! Does your father know? Did you stop by the store? Grandpap will be so pleased. He's taking a nap right now, but when he wakes up . . . Here, let me help you with your things."

"Whoa, whoa, slow down a minute, Mom," Greg said, laughing as he slung his seabag over his shoulder. "I'll get the rest of my stuff later. Right now I want some time with you . . . and maybe a cup of your marvelous coffee."

Ellie Halstead peered inside the VW. "That looks like more than a weekend's worth, Greg." Her eyes looked the question, but she didn't ask it.

"I'll tell all in a minute, Mom. Right now, let's get inside."

Inside of five minutes they were sitting down in the living room in front of a couple of cups of coffee and a plate of Ellie's famous oatmeal cookies. Not surprisingly, her first question after Greg told her his news was about Marci's reaction.

Greg grimaced. "I told her I was leaving college, and she immediately decided that I must be going to run away to Canada with the rest of the draft dodgers." He laughed, but there was no humor in it. "Then I told her I was going to enlist. Mom, it . . . it was like she became a different person. I mean I knew she was against the war and all, I knew she didn't particularly like the military, but I had no idea she could be so . . . *vicious*."

Ellie nodded, as though she wasn't at all surprised. "The Mortons down the street? Their daughter Joanie goes to Stanford. Beth was telling me just the other day that Joanie has been writing them the most awful letters, saying that if they support the war in Vietnam, then they're pigs and fascists! Can you imagine? Saying something like that to your own parents!" She shook her head in disbelief, then passed Greg the plate of cookies. "So how you do feel about Marci now? You love her, don't you?"

"Loved, past tense. I can't love someone who scorns

everything I believe in." He wished he could believe those
words.

"That's your head talking, son. Your heart's going to take
a bit longer to come around."

Greg looked up at his mom, saw the understanding pity
in her eyes, and almost broke down. He got a grip on himself
and said, "Well, then, I'll just have to make sure my head
stays in charge, won't I?"

Grandpap woke up soon after that, and he was delighted
to see his grandson. The three of them migrated to the
kitchen while Ellie made dinner, and before long David was
home. Conversation over dinner revolved around local
events, especially Ellie's new job with the Visiting Nurses.

"I'm not doing much real nursing now," she said, "but
I feel that what I'm doing is almost more important. Most
of my patients are chronically ill, so there's not that much I
can do other than make them more comfortable, but the people I'm really helping are the families. There's no time in a
hospital setting for the doctors or nurses to sit with the families and talk. Or listen. And that's what I do. I help the
families adjust to the idea of their loved ones being ill and
eventually dying, and I help them cope with the emotional
turmoil, as well as the practical problems involved in caring
for a very sick person. It's very rewarding."

"You picked a gem when you picked this one, David,"
Grandpap put in. He reached over and patted his daughter-
in-law on the hand. "If you do half as well, Greg, well,
you'll be all right."

Ellie smiled at Grandpap and squeezed his hand. "You're
prejudiced, old man. You just think I'm wonderful because
I spoil you."

"And rightly so," he retorted. "A man works hard all
day, he's got a right to expect to get spoiled when he gets
home."

"Oh? And how long's it been since you put in a full day's
work? Lazing around all day, reading the newspaper, taking
walks?"

"I worked hard enough in my seventy-some years to earn
me a little slack time now, woman!"

David sat back and grinned, looking greatly amused by this bantering between his wife and his father. Greg watched the three of them and thought to himself how lucky he was to have such a good family. He tried to picture Marci in the midst of this gathering . . . and failed. It was like hearing a foghorn in the middle of a beautiful melody—harsh and out of place. He was glad, he told himself, that he found out when he did what Marci was really like. He would have to keep telling himself that for quite a while.

After dinner David and Greg found themselves alone in the living room. "Man, I'm going to need a long run tomorrow to work off all this good food!" Greg said as he settled down in the green armchair opposite the sofa. "Jerry's banana split didn't help either."

"And just who was it that asked for a banana split, may I ask?" David said with a grin.

"Guilty on all counts, Dad. But I'll have to get in good shape for the Navy."

"Oh, don't worry about that. By the time you're through boot camp, you'll be in great shape, I promise you that." David rested an arm on the back of the sofa and looked at Greg. "So. Have any ideas about what you want to do in the Navy?"

Greg shrugged. "Hadn't gotten that far, I guess. What are my options? Do I get a chance to say what I'd like, or do they just say, 'Well, recruit, we need fifty thousand bottle washers this week so you're off to bottle-washing school'?"

David chuckled. "It's not quite that bad. You can say what rating you want, and usually you get a chance to strike for it. Of course, they'll run you through a battery of tests while you're in boot camp, and the results of those tests may narrow your choices somewhat. You wouldn't do very well as a sonar tech, for example, if you were tone-deaf."

"That makes sense." Greg leaned back in his chair and put his feet up on the coffee table.

"I don't suppose you would consider the Hospital Corps?" David asked wistfully.

"Aw, Dad, you know how bad I was at chem. I'd never make it."

"Hmm. There's not that much chemistry . . . at least, there

wasn't back in my day. Still, I suppose you're right."

"What are the different, um, ratings?" Greg asked.

"Well, they're grouped into categories according to where you would be working or what kind of work you'd do. The most important ones are the Deck division—that's mostly boatswain's mates and quartermasters. Radar and sonar, too."

Greg laughed. "Keep me away from sonar! Remember back in junior high when I tried to learn the trumpet?"

"That was a month I'll never forget, son," David said, wincing. "You were very, ah, diligent in your practicing."

"So, what else is there?"

"Engineering and Hull—that would be machinist's mates, enginemen, damage controlmen, that sort of thing. They're the one who like to get their hands dirty. We called 'em snipes. Aviation, Medical, Dental, they're obvious. Let's see. Ordnance—that's gunner's mates, fire controlmen, minemen, torpedoman's mates. They man the big guns aboard ship. Oh, and Electronics." David tapped his chin with a finger. "That might work for you. Remember that Heathkit radio you put together in, what was it, tenth grade?"

Greg grinned. "Yeah, that was a blast. So what would I do, basically run electronics equipment?"

David nodded. "That, plus maintenance and repair. It'd give you a good skill you could use later, too. After you get out."

"That's true. I hadn't thought of that."

"Greg, I've got a question for you."

"Yes, sir?"

"Why?"

"Um, why what, Dad?"

"Why join the Navy?"

"But . . . I thought you . . . I mean, do you think I shouldn't?"

David shook his head. "Not at all. I'm pleased that you're joining up and very proud that you're choosing the Navy. But I'm serious. This question is one you're going to be asking yourself a lot during your first few months, and probably after that, when things get hard . . . or boring. It helps if you've already thought about the answer."

"Why? Do you think I might quit if it gets tough?"

"Greg, you will have some physical challenges to face, that's true, but the toughest challenge of all will be mental. I know you're not a quitter. I'm just trying to help you prepare to meet that challenge."

Greg sat up and stared across the room. "I guess . . . well, it sounds kind of corny, but I . . . I wanted to serve my country. Like you did. And Grandpap. I wanted to do something that *meant* something. Something I could be proud of."

"And if you're sent to Vietnam? There're not many Navy men there, but it's possible. It's a scary thing to be operating in a combat zone, but back when I was in, it helped a lot to know that the whole country was behind the war effort, that we were fighting a definite, demonstrable evil. Things are different with this war. Pat is not alone in thinking that we don't belong in Southeast Asia."

"Yeah, I know," Greg said, with a bitter edge to his voice.

"You're thinking of Marci."

Greg looked up, startled.

"Your mother filled me in. Not that her reaction was surprising, of course."

"Dad, I . . . I just couldn't believe how, how *vicious* she was."

"You'll run into a lot of that, Greg. There's a sizable minority of people in this country who are violently opposed to the war. And that's why it's important for you to know where you stand and why."

Greg stood up and walked over to a table displaying a number of framed photographs. There was one blown-up snapshot of his dad and three other sailors on the deck of a ship. "I'm not sure I believe we should be in Vietnam, either, Dad. Some of what the protesters say is valid; it's their methods I don't like, the way they tear down their country and attack people who are just doing what they think is right. Shoot, even if they're right about the war, I thought that deciding stuff like that was the president's responsibility. He's got to know more about it than we possibly could. If I'm sent over there, well, I guess I'll just try to do my duty, and the hell with what anyone back here thinks." He looked at the photograph again. "Which ship was this, Dad? The *Blessman*?"

David joined him next to the table. "Mmm-hmm. That's Joe Matthews there on the left, Ralph Jensen between me and Joe, and Tod Ringold on the other side. Best bunch of buddies a man ever had."

"One of them was killed, wasn't he? When you were bombed?"

"Ralph Jensen." David pointed to the sailor on his right. "Ralph was in the mess hall the night the bomb hit. Died instantly."

"A Japanese Betty, wasn't it, Dad?" Greg had heard the story many times, but he wanted to hear it again. Next Monday he was going to go sign enlistment papers, a step that could lead to his going into combat. Always before when he'd listened to his father tell war stories, he'd just been thinking about his father, being proud of him. This time he'd be putting himself in his father's place . . . or in the place of Ralph Jensen. The thought sent a small, cold shiver down his spine. He couldn't tell if it was fear . . . or excitement.

David made a sound that might have been a chuckle, but there was no humor in his face. "It was funny in a way. We'd all just been congratulating ourselves that we'd missed the kamikazes, and then that damn plane comes and drops a bomb on us! Punched straight through the overhead and into the starboard mess hall.

"By the time I got on deck, the bucket brigades had already started. I found out later that all our hoses and pumps had been ruined in the blast. I patched up people the best I could . . . those that weren't already beyond help. You wouldn't believe how hot it was. And noisy. As the fire spread, it began cooking off stored ammo. But the worse thing was the explosives on board. We were carrying a UDT team that had just reconned the beaches at Iwo Jima. There was forty tons of their tetrytol below decks. If the flames had reached that, well, it would've been all over.

"The *Gilmer* was the only ship close enough to help. She was an APD, just like the *Blessman*. She began evacking the wounded, and then she came close enough to hose us down. David looked at Greg and grinned. "It was a sight to be hold—the bucket brigades singing 'Anchors Aweigh' at the top of their lungs, the *Gilmer* close aboard hosing us down, and that stored ammo shooting off like giant firecrackers.

"It took about four or five hours to contain the fire. When it was all over, we were a mess, but we were still afloat. Thirty-eight dead, including Ralph Jensen. And there were thirty wounded."

"That's sounds pretty bad," Greg said.

"Well, war is war," David said, "and war means killing. It's not glamorous. It's not *glorious*, no matter what you see in the movies."

"Isn't that when you got your Distinguished Service Medal?"

"Mmm-hmm." David nodded. "That's the Navy for you. There were lots of men who deserved a medal more than I did that night. Those UDT men, for instance. Some of them actually went into the burning troop compartments to fight the fire! Those guys are fearless! And the men who came over from the *Gilmer*, they were all UDT, too."

David chuckled, and it was genuine this time. "You know what those idiots did one time?" He walked back to the sofa and sat down again. "They were getting ready to recon Iwo, and I'd just downchecked one of them with a cold. So his buddies came in to sick bay and began hassling me. Said that since I'd made them a man short, I had to take his place. Said they'd get me outfitted in mask and fins. Told me I'd look real good in cocoa butter and camo grease."

"Cocoa butter!"

"Mmm-hmm. It was February, and that water was *cold*. The cocoa butter was supposed to keep them warm, or at least keep them from freezing to death." He chuckled. "When they were all greased up, they really did look just like giant silver frogs."

"So did you go with them, Dad?"

"Go ashore with those lunatic frogmen? Are you kidding? Son, I know sometimes you think I'm crazy, but I was *never* that crazy!"

Greg shrugged. "I don't know." He was thinking of his swims off Goat Rock. He loved swimming . . . and sometimes the Pacific could be *cold.* "Sounds like fun to me. Is the UDT still around?"

"Sure is. Got a letter from Tod a few weeks back. Seems his son is just about to head off for UDT/SEAL training."

"UDT stands for Underwater Demolition something, right?"

"Team. Underwater Demolition Team."

"What's the other thing you said, 'seal' ?"

"It's another acronym. Get used to 'em, son. The Navy loves 'em. This one stands for SEa, Air, and Land. The way I hear it, they're super-duper Navy commandos, like the UDT, only more so. And like the name says, they can go anywhere. One thing the old UDT guys griped about a lot, they were restricted to the high-water mark. They couldn't go up onto the beaches past the high-tide line. But this new outfit, the SEALs, well, they get parachute training as well as SCUBA training. They do everything."

"They get to jump out of airplanes? Like in *The Longest Day?*" Greg had been thrilled by that movie about the Normandy invasion in World War II when he'd seen it a few years back.

"Mmm. Just make sure you don't get your chute snagged on a church steeple, like the guy in the movie! Or drop down a well!"

Greg grinned. "Hey, that's no problem. You said they get SCUBA training too. Man, that sounds cool. So they train together—the UDT and the SEALs?"

"Sounds like it."

"Is that something I could do instead of electronics?"

"No, you'd still need a rating. This would be a special program you'd apply for later. Like submarines. Though you could let your recruiter know you're interested when you sign up."

David went up to bed soon after that, and Greg went out for a walk. The sky was so clear, so unlike San Francisco. He strolled down to the Russian River and stood on the docks, looking at the water. Less than a mile downstream, it flowed into the Pacific. In a few months—he wasn't sure exactly how long he would be in training—he might be sailing on that ocean. He might even be on the other side of that ocean . . . in Vietnam.

He thought about the question his father had asked him. As long as he could remember, he'd been patriotic; he'd never really thought about it, it was just a part of his life. Maybe now was a good time to start thinking about it.

Being an American was something he'd always been proud of. Marci had told him a lot about communism, and he'd enjoyed arguing about it with her. But he hadn't been arguing just for argument's sake; he'd meant what he'd said . . . about freedom, about democracy, about the American way of life. And if his going to Vietnam could in some small way help stop the advance of communism, help promote freedom and democracy in Southeast Asia, well, then he'd be willing to do that. Maybe as one of these super frogmen his dad was telling him about.

Greg Halstead, Navy SEAL.

He liked the sound of that.

Chapter 3

Bravo Platoon, SEAL Team One
Fifteen kilometers south of Nha Be
Rung Sat Special Zone, Republic of Vietnam
0445 hours

Torpedoman Second Class Christopher Luciano—"Lucky" to his friends—froze in place, not moving, scarcely daring to breathe. His right hand came up, clenched in a fist, and he sensed the other U.S. Navy SEALs following in his footsteps freezing as well.

Pure chance had saved him and the seven men with him. The sky was growing light now with the promise of a tropical dawn, and already it was light enough to see the encircling jungle, but the floor of the forest was still murk-dark and shadowed. A shaft of silver light, however, from a last-quarter moon had lanced down through a gap in the forest canopy and touched the trail just ahead, revealing the gossamer-slender length of black fishing line stretched across the trail.

Luciano had been avoiding the trail proper, of course, moving silently through the brush well to its right, but as he traced the near-invisible length of thread to its source he saw that another two steps would have taken him across its taut demarcation, strung across the forest floor ahead just at knee height. Maybe, *maybe* he would have felt the line before he'd applied pressure enough to tug it free . . . but in the dark, with his senses already stretched to their limit to embrace, if possible, the entire jungle night surrounding them, he might not have noticed the obstacle until too late. Well, Nhung had said there would be booby traps.

Flat on his belly, now, Luciano reached out and lightly touched the line, tracing it by feel away from the trail and into the inky blackness of shadowed ground at the base of an enormous tree several yards to his right. The trip wire, he estimated, must reach across over twenty yards from a similar tree on the far side of the trail, and that suggested that the device connected to it had one hell of a kick. Moving with all of the care and patience drummed into him by both his SEAL training and years of experience, he began searching for the package that must rest somewhere near the end of that line.

There it was. God, it *was* big, a two-pound block of C4 stuffed into a hollow among the tree's tangled roots. The lump of gray-white, high-explosive clay was about the size of a man's head . . . and its surface was thickly studded with bolts, pieces of wire, washers, rusty nails, and bits of scrap metal embedded in the claylike plastique, a poor man's claymore mine set to hurl a scything sheet of limb-mangling shrapnel across the trail at waist height. The massive trunk of the tree itself would have served to focus the blast, aiming it precisely where it would do the most damage.

With a surgeon's care and precision, Luciano found the detonator, an American-made M26 grenade partly buried in the white explosive, its pin pulled, its arming lever tied in place by several loops of fishing line held by a granny knot. Tug hard on the trip wire, and the arming lever would fly off; three seconds later, the grenade would explode and take the C4 with it . . . along with anyone standing downrange for a distance of fifty yards or more. Slick. And nasty.

So far in the Navy SEAL deployment to the Republic of Vietnam, booby traps like this one had accounted for more casualties among the SEALs than all other causes put together, including direct enemy action. Just four weeks ago, a kid who'd recently joined Bravo Platoon had tripped a booby trap much like this one, when Luciano had been right next to him. The kid, a newbie SEAL named Bill Tangretti, had thrown himself on top of Luciano and taken the blast himself. The last Lucky had heard, Tangretti was recovering nicely at the naval hospital at Bethesda, stateside, with a Purple Heart and a Bronze Star with combat "V" to show for his efforts.

Not that medals counted for much. SEALs just did their jobs, for the most part, without much concern about who'd won what, and colored ribbons didn't mean a hill of beans when it came to paying a man back for the shrapnel he'd absorbed saving your life. Shit, a VC booby trap like this one could ruin your whole *day*. . . .

Before safing the homemade device, Luciano took a long, hard look around, studying the surrounding forest with an intensity and a sensitivity that was part experience and part sixth sense. Traps like this one frequently were set to initiate an ambush, and it was possible that the shadowed night of the jungle held enemy troops, silently waiting for the blast that would signal the start of their attack.

Nothing. The steady chirrup of insects and the peep-peeping of frogs was steady and unbroken, and Luciano could sense nothing out of the ordinary. More than once he'd *felt* an enemy waiting in the jungle nearby, a heavy, watchful presence somehow picked out of the welter of sensory impressions, sight, sound, and smell, that filled the forest, but this time there was nothing.

Most likely, this booby trap had been set to warn the village up ahead of the approach of trespassers. Reaching into a breast pocket of his combat vest, Luciano extracted one of several spare grenade cotter pins he always carried there and, working more by feel than by sight, slipped the slender, double-bled-over strip of metal attached to the pull ring through the hole in the arming lever's base, safing the grenade. Turning then, he caught the eye of the man in line behind him, Chief Mike Spencer, and signaled OK. Spencer, in turn, raised his hand and passed the hand signal on to the men behind him. Slowly, silently, the line began snaking forward once more. Spencer moved up to Luciano's side and, after Lucky had showed him the trip wire, stayed there to guide the others past it. Luciano, who had point for this op, slithered quietly beneath the trip wire and kept crawling ahead.

The rest of Bravo's First Squad, guided past the wire by Spencer, followed. Bam-bam, MM1 Barry Chavez, lugging the squad's M60 machine gun, was first, followed closely by Lieutenant Edward Charles Baxter, Bravo Platoon's CO. Next was RM2 Phil Pettigrew, the squad's radio operator, his bulky PRC-77 just clearing beneath the fishing line as Spencer held it up and out of the way, and the Doc, HM2 John Randolph. Bringing up the rear were the Hoi Chanh traveling with First Squad this night, Nguyen Din Nhung, and the squad's rear guard, GM1 Paul Jenkins.

The Men With Green Faces, the enemy called them. All save the VC turncoat were nearly invisible in the jungle night, their faces heavily painted in shades of green and black greasepaint, the outlines of their heads broken either by green bandanas tied pirate-fashion over their scalps or by floppy-brimmed boonie hats. They'd come ashore from a SEAL patrol boat four hours earlier and had been winding their way through the jungle and mangrove swamps south of Nha Be ever since, with only brief periods of rest for the squad's "guest" for the evening. In all, Luciano guessed that the squad had covered less than three kilometers. Parts of the jungle in this area were so thick that a man could only proceed at all by crawling on his hands and knees; the need to avoid trails as obvious magnets for ambushes, and the need to examine each step ahead for booby traps or signs that the enemy might be near, with only a faint light filtering through from the sky as illumination, could make progress a painstakingly slow evolution at best.

Forty yards beyond the booby trap, the forest opened suddenly onto a small clearing embracing a couple of dozen huts and hooches, most of them up on low stilts, a typical South Vietnamese village nestled between the jungle and a broad, open rice paddy gleaming in the moonlight. Calling another halt, Luciano twisted his head back, looking over his shoulder at the Hoi Chanh. Two weeks ago, Nhung had been a dedicated Viet Cong guerrilla, fighting to overthrow the corrupt American-puppet government and the Western-imperialist invaders. Then he'd decided his real sympathies didn't lie with the National Liberation Front after all, and he'd turned himself in to government forces under the Chieu Hoi program. Chieu Hoi meant "open arms" and was the centerpiece of Saigon's campaign to break the back of the

Communist revolution by enticing VC to rally to the South
Vietnamese government. A Hoi Chanh was a Vietnamese
who'd turned himself in, someone who'd "Chieu Hoied,"
as the lieutenant liked to phrase it; those who helped run
missions against their former comrades in the National Liberation Front were sometimes called Kit Carson Scouts, or
KCS.

Luciano wasn't sure how he felt about the idea of using
turncoats yet. It was hard enough telling the good guys from
the bad guys in this fucking war, and so far as Lucky was
concerned, anyone who'd turned on his friends couldn't be
trusted to take a crap. The word was that Nhung's father had
been killed by the VC, by one VC in particular. Now he was
leading them back to his own village, a nothing little hamlet
called Phu Thit on the maps. Luciano watched the little Vietnamese with an intensity approaching that of his study of the
jungle moments earlier. Could the man be trusted? Shit, *no*
one in this godforsaken place could be trusted, no one except
your buddies, though some sources of military intelligence
were a damned sight more reliable than others. What, Lucky
wondered, was going on behind those dark and enigmatic
eyes?

Spencer crawled up to a vantage point at Luciano's side.
Lightly, he touched the corner of his eye, then pointed at the
hooches. *The gook says that's the place* was the unvoiced
statement. Luciano nodded, then crawled a little closer, bel-
lying down a soft embankment to a point where he could lie
among the tangle of ferns and vegetation that walled off the
north side of the clearing.

He took his time sizing up the target. The village was
quiet, the entire population still sound asleep as far as he
could tell. The only visible motion was the jerky strut of
several chickens and the snuffling meander of a small, black
pig rooting in the garbage beneath one of the ramshackle
houses.

There were two men in sight, however, a pair of tough-
looking Vietnamese flanking the door to one of the raised
hooches about twenty yards from the edge of the forest. One
wore the VC's trademark black pajamas, while the other
wore black trousers and a white shirt; both carried AK-47s,

so there was damned little room for doubt about their political alignments. Better still, the fact that two well-armed bodyguards were out at this hour of the early morning confirmed both that the Number One target was in, and that he was as important as the Hoi Chanh had said he was.

Turning again, he caught Lieutenant Baxter's gaze, touching two fingers to his eyes, then holding the fingers up. *Enemy in sight. Two of them.* Baxter signaled understanding, then began giving silent hand orders to the squad, which filtered out to either side, taking up firing positions along the edge of the clearing. Luciano began readying his weapon.

The men of Bravo Platoon had been holding ongoing competitions on the pistol range back at the Nha Be compound. The current two best shots were Jenkins and Luciano, though rivalries were fierce, and individual standings shifted almost day by day.

Luciano's usual weapon was the M-16 with the new M203 grenade launcher slung beneath the barrel—the final and official version of the experimental XM-148 which SEALs had been testing in Nam for several years now. Until recently, Lucky had preferred the M79, the breech-loading "thump gun" or "blooper" that fired 40mm munitions ranging from high-explosive grenades to enormous canister rounds that discharged deadly clouds of buckshot like shotgun shells. The new 203s were better, though, since once you'd fired a grenade, you still had the comforting full-auto melody of the M-16 to rely on; bloop guns were one-shot affairs that had to be reloaded after each round, and that reload delay could be deadly in combat.

This time out, Lucky was ready with a second weapon, a Smith & Wesson Mark 22 Model O pistol. The eight-shot, 9mm weapon was a spin-off from the S&W M39, a pistol that had recently begun service with the Teams who'd requested it to silence guard dogs on stealthy sneak-and-peeks . . . hence its popular name, "Hush Puppy." Carefully, he screwed the pipelike length of the weapon's sound suppresser onto the muzzle, then chambered the first round, taking care not to let the slide *snick-snack* forward loudly enough to give the squad away. At his side, Jenkins prepared his Hush Puppy as well. Together, the two green-painted SEALs settled down farther into the mud and vegetation, using an arm-thick dead branch as a bench rest to steady their weapons.

For this kind of sniper work, a rifle would definitely have been the weapon of choice, Luciano thought, one with a nightscope or at least a telescopic sight. Contrary to the images of war and gunplay presented by Hollywood, it was damned tough to hit a target at any range over a few yards with something as short-barreled and hard to steady as a pistol. This op definitely required a silenced weapon, however, and all Bravo had available this time out was the Mark 22. There were sound suppressers designed for the M-16, of course—the SEALs had been testing some of those in Nam as well—but they were harder to come by, and the ammunition wasn't subsonic. The Hush Puppy's specially modified, subsonic round eliminated the sharp crack that was the sonic boom of faster bullets, and if Bravo was going to get away with this, they needed the initial shots to be as quiet as possible. No sound-suppressed weapon had ever been developed that could mimic the near-silent chuff of the spy pistols beloved of Hollywood, but the Hush Puppy came damned close. Better still, the suppresser could handle up to thirty shots before it was reamed out and useless . . . as opposed to the six rounds or so possible for most other so-called silencers.

Carefully, Luciano took aim, bracing the pistol's five-inch barrel across the log, bringing his eye as close to the rear sight as the slide action would permit. By unspoken agreement—the SEALs had worked this kind of takedown often enough before that preliminary discussion wasn't necessary—Jenkins would take the man on the right; Luciano's target was the one on the left, the one with the white shirt. Across the weapon's open sight, when he focused his gaze on the target, Luciano could see that the man was younger than he'd guessed at first, a kid of perhaps eighteen or twenty.

Too bad. He was old enough to carry an assault rifle, though that didn't make shooting them any easier. Luciano had heard that kids of nine and ten were recruited by the VC cadres, sometimes. It was a fucked-up war. Letting out some of his breath, then holding it, he drew down on the trigger, bringing it just short of the pressure necessary to fire.

"All set?" PJ asked to his right, a soft whisper.

"Let's do it."

"Okay. Ready, three . . . two . . . one . . . *now!*"

The two pistols spoke together, a close-paired double thud, like cloth-covered mallets hitting a soft wooden block. The suppressers couldn't rob the shots of all sound, but they deadened them enough to disguise them, muffling them into near anonymity.

Both targets staggered, Jenkins's man spinning all the way around as birds and other jungle songsters continued their predawn chorus uninterrupted by the sudden bloody drama below. Swiftly, Luciano reacquired his target above his pistol's rear sights, finding the kid just in time to see his face going slack-jawed and stunned above a spreading red stain on his shirt. Luciano held on the target, picking up the head as it sagged forward, then squeezing off a second be-sure round that poked a hole through the boy's forehead just above the bridge of his nose and shattered the back of his head in a black spray.

Luciano's heart was hammering in his chest now, and he could feel beads of sweat trickling down the sides of his green-painted face. This was the moment when it could all go wrong at once—a guard's involuntary twitch of a trigger finger, a groan loud enough to carry to the people sleeping in those huts, a suddenly barking dog . . .

This time, at least, the universe was less than totally perverse, and that damned meddler Murphy, it seemed, had stayed back in the SEAL barracks at Nha Be to catch some extra rack time. There were no gunshots, no cries of alarm. Both VC guards were down, sad-looking sprawls of rag-doll clothing in the dirt in front of the hooch. Luciano signaled the other SEALs at his back.

Sliding down the embankment, Baxter dropped prone between them. "Looked clean, guys," he said, his voice a whisper almost drowned by the peeping amphibians of the surrounding forest. "Good shooting, both of you."

"Two up, two down," Luciano replied quietly, trying to sound calmer than he felt. This sort of thing never became routine, no matter how often he repeated it. He nodded toward the silent hooch just behind the two bodies. "I think we got the son of a bitch dead to rights."

"We'll see. Let's go."

Like shadows, the other SEALs rose and began slipping silently into the moon-bathed clearing.

0453 hours

The war and the SEALs both had changed a hell of a lot since Lieutenant Edward Charles Baxter had first arrived in-country. That had been two years ago in February of 1966, when he'd come to Nha Be to take command of Detachment Delta, SEAL Team One. The SEALs he'd commanded then had been a disorganized and demoralized lot, unappreciated by both the Army and Navy commands they answered to. No one, it seemed, had known what to do with the SEALs.

Perhaps the problems had been inevitable, a result of the unit's odd mission. Called into being by an executive order issued by President Kennedy, the SEALs had been conceived as a commando unit that could operate in any medium, anywhere in the world. Drawn from the Navy's Underwater Demolition Teams, SEALs not only trained in the explosives and undersea-warfare techniques of the frogmen, they trained for ops inland as well. SEALs could go anywhere, do anything to accomplish their mission.

It was a philosophy that Baxter heartily approved of. He'd heard the story about one colossal screwup in World War II, when a UDT had reconnoitered the beach of an enemy-held island in the Pacific. They'd noticed—even photographed—the extensive Japanese fortifications and preparations inland, up off the beach and into the jungle, and reported them, but their report had been disregarded for the simple fact that the UDTs were supposed to be responsible for checking out obstacles and emplacements below the high-tide mark only, not above it.

The island's name was Peleliu, a name still written in blood in the history of the U.S. Marine Corps, and the horror was that the place could easily have been bypassed, indeed *would* have been bypassed had the planners paid attention to that crucial bit of intel. SEALs operated under the belief that they could gather their own intelligence and plan operations based on it, a far more practical and direct way of doing things than waiting for the word to trickle down the chain of command from bureaucrats who wouldn't know the business end of a weapon if it bit them.

Silently, the squad moved into the open. This was always the tough part of an op, for Baxter, at least, when he had to leave the comfortable shelter of night and forest and emerge into the open with a feeling not unlike being stark naked in the middle of a football stadium at halftime. If any enemy troops had the area under observation from the shelter of one of those hooches, this was the moment when the squad would find out about it, probably with a burst of machine-gun and full-auto assault-rifle fire.

No shots sounded, however, and the village remained death-silent, save for the clucking of the chickens. With a few swift strides, they reached the hooch that had been guarded by the two VC, taking up positions with well-rehearsed teamwork. Baxter, Nhung, and Spencer headed for the doorway between the two bodies, while Luciano, Pettigrew, and Randolph dropped into position in front of the bamboo-and-nipa-palm building, setting up a perimeter defense. Chavez—with the 60—and Jenkins maintained a silent overwatch from the edge of the forest, ready to nail anything moving that wasn't a SEAL . . . or to lay down a curtain of death and violence to cover the SEAL squad's retreat.

Baxter was carrying a CAR15, the baby-brother version of the M-16, but for close work in the dark and with need of silence, he was packing a Hush Puppy as well. His carbine slung muzzle down where it was easily accessible, he walked across the clearing with the Hush Puppy in his right hand. As they reached the rickety-looking three-step ladder beneath the door, he dropped his left hand to the Hoi Chanh's shoulder. "Just remember," Baxter said, hardening the whisper with menace. "If this is some kind of trick, you're the first one going through that door. You've got your friends in front of you, but you have *me* right behind you. *Hieu?* Understand?"

Nhung looked up at the SEAL with wide and fear-filled

eyes. He opened his mouth as though to reply, but Baxter tightened his grip on the man's shoulder, shook his head slightly, and touched the elongated muzzle of the Hush Puppy to his lips, warning the man to keep silent. Nhung hesitated, then nodded, hard, squared his shoulders, took the three steps up the ladder, and pushed open the thin nipa-palm door.

Baxter followed him up and in, close on his heels, the heavy muzzle of his weapon probing the darkness. Reaching up to his combat vest, Baxter pulled out a small pencil flash with a red plastic shield over the bulb, but he didn't turn it on just yet. Inside the hooch it was close and thick with the stink of fermented fish—the spicy-sour and pungent *nuoc mam* that accompanied every Vietnamese meal. It was too dark to make out details, but he knew his eyes would adjust to the dark in a moment or two.

However he didn't have a moment or two. He sensed movement to the left, a bulky shadow rising from a tangle of bedding.

"*Ong la ai?*" a sharp, nasal voice called out.

Baxter had no time to speak, no time even to think, not when another instant could bring a shouted alarm, or a volley of full-automatic fire. Whipping the Hush Puppy around, he aimed at the center of the shadow and squeezed the trigger once . . . twice . . . a third time, tapping off three quick rounds in half that many seconds. The shadow gave a grunt, a lone syllable carrying more surprise than pain, then collapsed to the floor. Switching on the pencil flash, he cast its beam toward the pile of bedding. A naked man lay there with three closely spaced holes high in his chest, hard, round, and black in the red light. Beyond, a woman, small, dark, and very nude, blinked up sleepily at the light.

Shit! This was unexpected . . . and it damn well could be disastrous if the woman screamed. Instead, though, she groped for a black shirt lying beside the sleeping mat, clutching it against her tiny breasts as she stared up past the light, trying to see Baxter's face. "*Ong la ai?*" she asked, repeating the dead man's question. "*Lon?*"

Muzzy with sleep, blinded by the light, she probably

hadn't recognized the shots for what they were and didn't yet know what was going on.

"*Im di!*" Baxter snapped, his whispered command harsh. He pressed the muzzle of the pistol against the side of her head for added emphasis. "Silence!"

Jerkily, her eyes glazing, she nodded. "*Dieng . . . dieng giet toi!*" she said, her voice soft. She hesitated, then repeated in thickly accented English. "Please. No kill me!"

The woman sounded terrified . . . and as Baxter put himself in her place, he could easily understand why. Her use of English suggested that she'd finally caught on that the raiders who'd burst in on her in the night were Americans. The VC often told civilian villagers that the Americans routinely disemboweled their captives, that they tortured the women and ate their babies; Baxter had heard the stories repeated back to him often enough to feel sympathy for what must be racing through this woman's mind.

"I won't hurt you," he said. "Just do what you're told and you'll be all right." Baxter had no idea how much she understood. He was also angry. The woman was probably a civilian. Maybe she'd been sleeping with the VC honcho out of patriotism, or maybe the guy had demanded her sexual services as part of the hamlet's taxes; it didn't matter, really, one way or the other. The question was what the hell he was going to do with her now.

Her presence could jeopardize the entire operation, and that was one thing no SEAL officer could allow. They were too far out in the bush for considerations of chivalry or even mercy, not when all of their lives depended on Baxter being right with every decision he made.

Yet he didn't want to put his pistol to her head and pull the trigger, not if he wanted to live with himself afterward.

Shit! The op had just become damned complicated, and Baxter didn't like that one bit.

Chapter 4

Friday, 23 February 1968

Bravo Platoon, SEAL Team One
Fifteen kilometers south of Nha Be
Rung Sat Special Zone
0456 hours

As Baxter wondered what to do, Spencer pulled back the nipa-palm door far enough that the growing sky light from outside spilled into the hooch. The woman saw then the body of the man lying on the floor next to her and gave a violent start. Baxter leaned closer, his hideously green-painted face inches from hers, the Hush Puppy brushing the angle of her jaw. "*Im di!* Keep quiet! *Hieu?*"

Trembling, she began fumbling with her shirt, trying to pull it on. Her eyes flicked from him to Spencer, fully visible now in all of his nightmare, war-painted glory. He hoped she wasn't going into shock.

Baxter picked up the rest of her clothes, squeezed through the fabric in an automatic check for weapons, then handed them to her. He was damned if he was going to run through the jungle with a naked woman in tow.

Only then did it sink in that he'd made his decision, that he wasn't going to kill her any more than he was going to leave her behind to warn any VC in the area. She was still a complete unknown; she could be a civilian caught in the wrong place at the wrong time, or she could be VC, a member of the VC security element known to be operating in Phu Thit and the surrounding villages. Either way, she might have

42

information that would be useful to future SEAL ops in the region.

Besides, Baxter drew a hard, personal line at slaughtering prisoners, whether they were civilians or military. "Doc!" he rasped out, his voice low. "Get in here."

When Randolph entered the room, Baxter nodded at the woman. "Take care of her. We're bringing her along."

The SEAL medic's eyes widened through the greasepaint, but he said nothing. Producing one of the plastic binders they carried for handling prisoners, he pushed her down and began tying her hands behind her back. Kneeling, Baxter shined the light on the face of the dead man, illuminating the features in a bloodlike glow that contrasted with the cold blue light of the dawn streaming in from outside. "Nhung?"

"That is him," the former VC said, nodding enthusiastically. "Nol Van Lon. He big man. Big VC."

In fact, Nol Van Lon had been chief of security for one of the local VC militias . . . and something of a bully, according to Nhung, even with his own men. He'd shot Nhung's father in a village not far from here over some slight or insult, and in reply Nhung had turned Hoi Chanh. Nhung's information had suggested that Nol would stop here at Phu Thit for this night, as he made a sweep through the district, helping the local VC tax collector raise money, rice, and recruits for the VC.

Apparently, he'd stopped here for other reasons as well. The woman sat quietly now, securely gagged and tied, with Doc standing guard over her. She was breathing hard but seemed more defiant now than afraid, her dark eyes alert and watchful above the tape covering her mouth.

"You know her?" Baxter asked Nhung, pointing at the woman.

The man nodded. "She Thu Thi Dinh," he said. "*Captain* Dinh." He mimed holding a handset to his ear and made a cranking motion with his hand. "She talk-talk for VC."

"Talk?" Baxter's eyes widened. "What, radio? A communications officer?"

Nhung nodded. "Radio officer, yes. For my old regiment."

The woman struggled to say something behind her gag.

"Spence," Baxter said sharply. "Take the place apart. The woman's a commo officer. There might be code books, papers."

"I think I got 'em," Spencer replied from the other side of the room. He held up a bulging knapsack. "Right here. We've got a shortwave here, too."

"Interesting," Baxter said, eyeing the woman speculatively. South Vietnamese civilians were forbidden by law to have such equipment, but the VC used them to eavesdrop on government and U.S. radio transmissions. Baxter hadn't been quite willing to accept everything Nhung said at face value, but the radio was definitely confirmation. She was VC.

A prisoner. They hadn't planned on that, this time out, but the SEALs were opportunists supreme, and a prisoner was always worth a hell of a lot more than a corpse. The rest of the U.S. military had been so wrapped up in the obscene notion of body counts lately that they'd forgotten the value of good, hard intel.

"Hey, Lieutenant?" Spence called. "We should be watching the time. It's gonna be full, kick-in-the-ass daylight pretty damned quick, and we have a long way to go."

"You're right. Okay, gather up the goodies and let's *di-di*."

Doc helped the woman to her feet and propelled her outside. With Spencer's help, Baxter dragged the two dead sentries up the steps and into the hut and, in a sudden bit of morbid inspiration, propped the three corpses up on the bedding, the still naked Nol sitting between the two dead guards, his arms draped around their necks, their heads nestled against his shoulders. As a final gesture, Spencer reached up and scraped some of the green paint from his face with his finger, then transferred the smear of dark color to the foreheads of each of the dead VC . . . although in the case of one of the corpses, he had to put the mark pretty high up beneath the hairline to avoid the entry wound of a 9mm subsonic round.

The mark was nothing fancy—just a streak of paint—but it would certainly capture the attention of the VC who found these three. Some SEALs—and some Army personnel as well—routinely left the ace of spades on enemy bodies as a kind of business card, knowing that the Vietnamese held the symbol in superstitious awe. For quite a while now, though, the SEALs had been creating their own symbols and leaving them within the enemy camp. It was part of the game . . . and part of the SEAL mystique to promote their own aura of invulnerability and deadliness. Men who operated in the night and the jungle more efficiently than any Viet Cong, who targeted specific officers and Communist officials and made them disappear right out from within a heavily armed and guarded camp or visit, who wore nightmare green faces that personified Death itself—these were warriors of an especially dreadful and terrifying aspect, men to be feared, respected, and avoided at all costs. Simply worrying about them could reduce a unit's military effectiveness.

It was Baxter's job to keep pushing that rep . . . and convince every VC he could that the only way to avoid the Men With Green Faces was to give up the fight and turn Hoi Chanh.

The SEALs made their exit silently, with Doc and Pettigrew marching the woman along in the center of the column. As they reached the treeline, Chavez and Jenkins, who'd been maintaining overwatch for the squad since the rest had gone in, separated from the shadows and joined the column.

They slipped out of Phu Thit as silently as they'd entered.

0508 hours

Luciano had come into Phu Thit as point; he was going out as rear guard, walking backward with his M-16/M203 combo held at hip level, the deadly twin muzzles sweeping the silent buildings at the squad's rear.

Pettigrew was still just this side of the jungle and Luciano a handful of steps farther out when a man appeared at the door of another hooch, bare-chested, stretching, and scratching himself. For a frozen instant, he stared at the SEALs still in the clearing . . . and then he nearly fell over himself diving back inside the building. "*Cuu toi voi!*" the man shrilled, his voice high and wavering. "*Cuu toi voi!*"

That fucks it, Luciano thought viciously. That bastard Murphy might have been asleep before, but he'd just woken up, big time, and decided to make trouble for the SEALs.

"Make for the trees!" he snapped. At his back, Pettigrew broke into a run, and Luciano followed, still keeping the column covered.

An instant later, the villager reappeared, holding a Chinese-made SKS rifle. Luciano pivoted, bringing the M-16 to his shoulder and squeezing off a single round.

The shot rang unnaturally loud and sharp in the early-morning air; the round caught the VC in the chest and shoved him back into the hut. More men were appearing in the village, but now the hard, deep-throated rattle of Chavez's 60-gun opened up from the wall of vegetation bordering the clearing. Luciano hunched over and broke into a full run, as men shouted, women screamed, and the village came fully awake behind him.

"What's up?" Baxter called as Luciano plunged into the forest.

"They just sounded reveille," Lucky replied. "I think they want to party."

"Shit. Let's hustle, then."

"I'm with you, boss."

Luciano did take the time, however, a matter of a few seconds, to return to the tree where he'd discovered the booby trap. When the last SEAL had crossed the trip wire, Luciano went to work on the block of plastique still hidden at the base of the tree, checking carefully to see that it could be moved safely, then adding a flourish of his own. It was part of the mind game the SEALs had been playing with Charlie for years, now. The VC in Phu Thit would have no idea which way the infiltrators had gone, though they might suspect. If they found the trip wire intact, they would assume the SEALs had missed it, and sooner or later they would recover the explosive device to use somewhere else . . . sooner if they decided that their base of operations here had been compromised, and they packed up to move somewhere else. When they lifted the plastique from its resting place, however, they would find an added twist; carefully, Luciano embedded a second M26 grenade deep in the bottom of the plastique block, opposite from the grenade already tied to the trip wire, its pin pulled, its arming lever held in place only by the weight of the plastique itself as he nestled the device back into its nest at the base of the tree. The VC engineers would safe the first grenade and lift the block, the arming lever on the second would fly free, and, with a little luck, there would be several fewer VC engineers to plant other booby traps where they might catch unwary Americans.

This gimmicking of booby traps was all part of the on-going operation to spread terror within the VC ranks, and something that Luciano took an intense personal pride in. For several years now, the American SEALs had been making a name for themselves among the Vietnamese. "The Men With Green Faces . . ." Sometimes the phrase was rendered as "the *Devils* With Green Faces," and Charlie never knew where these half-magical creatures would strike next. For years, the VC and their NVA sponsors from the North had pretty much had their own way in South Vietnam. "Charlie rules the night" ran the old adage, a warning that although the South Vietnamese and U.S. forces might control the cities and even much of the countryside during the hours of daylight, by dark Victor Charlie, the Viet Cong, was very much in control. Lately, the SEALs had reversed that old balance of power, however; it turned out that Charlie was as helpless as the conventional ARVN and U.S. forces in the jungle at night when he was brought face-to-green-face with the elite Teams trained to hunt him on his own ground. The Rung Sat Special Zone along the Soi Rap River south of Saigon had become a special SEAL hunting preserve, with the VC as game. The name Rung Sat meant "Forest of Assassins," an allusion to the fact that it had provided shelter to pirates, bandits, and murderers for centuries. The VC had claimed it for their own . . . but were learning now that the Navy SEALs could use their own tactics on them, and with enormous success.

In Luciano's experience, the Cong actually had considerable difficulty carrying out night operations, with poor fire discipline and poorer communications. When they were caught in an ambush, instead of the other way around, they often froze . . . or threw down their weapons and fled.

They weren't used to fighting an enemy that used night, cover, and terror even more effectively than they did.

Luciano finished rerigging the booby trap, then picked up his M-16 and hurried after the retreating SEALs. He could hear sounds of pursuit now, Vietnamese calling to one another in high, singsong voices, and there was a heavy crashing in the undergrowth to his right, on the far side of the trail.

He stepped up his pace, hurrying to catch up with the others.

0515 hours

Baxter halted the column once, swinging it into ambush position, a precaution in case the VC were coming in hard on their tails and spoiling for a fight. It took only a few minutes, though, to determine that the VC were trying a different strategy, throwing large groups of men into the jungle to either side of the SEAL squad, possibly in an attempt to cut them off.

"What do you think, Spence?" Baxter asked his senior NCO. "How many?"

"Hard to tell, sir. Two groups, at least. Ten, maybe fifteen in each. I'd say we have ourselves a situation here."

"You got that right." Baxter threw Nhung a hard look. "Our Hoi Chanh there didn't mention thirty VC in this group."

"No, sir, he didn't. You think it was a setup?"

Baxter shook his head. "If it was, it was piss-poor planning. Only two sentries, and no outlying perimeter defenses at all except for booby traps. My guess is there were five or ten in that security element with Nol, just like Nhung told us, but there was another, larger force that happened to be in the area."

"Just plain bad luck, huh, Lieutenant?"

" 'No plan of battle survives contact with the enemy,' " Baxter replied.

"Who said that? Napoleon?"

Baxter shook his head. "The guy who worked out Imperial German war strategy before World War I."

"Yeah, well, he should know, right?"

Obviously, the VC hadn't sent a column directly after the

SEALs. They'd tried that more than once in the past and had the column wiped out when the SEALs reversed course and set up an ambush on their own tracks. Moving once more, the SEAL column traveled quickly and with a sure knowledge both of the ground they were covering and of their destination. Having to avoid the two groups of Vietnamese was slowing them somewhat, however.

"Shit, Lieutenant," Pettigrew said, as Baxter called another halt several minutes later. "If I didn't know better, I'd say this bitch is trying to slow us up."

"She might be at that." Baxter signaled Chavez, the biggest, brawniest man in the squad. "Bam-bam! Give Spence your sixty. You carry our new friend here."

Chavez grinned, his teeth and eyes startlingly white against the dark face paint. "Hey, no problem!" Handing his bulky light machine gun to Spencer, he scooped the woman up and slung her head-down across his shoulder, then reached up with his free hand and slapped her fanny. "Come to Bam-bam, baby," he said as she twisted in his grip.

"None of that shit," Baxter snapped. "Just carry her ass out of here." He turned on Nhung, who was standing nearby, leaning against a palm trunk, panting. "And you, Mr. Nhung, had better keep up, or I'll detail someone to carry you."

The Hoi Chanh nodded, obviously stung. Keeping up with a pack of SEALs in their natural element wasn't easy, but Baxter thought the man's pride—he was the product of a male-dominated culture no matter what the Communists might say about the matter—would spur him on a bit harder. God knew, he didn't want the man captured by his former comrades now.

In the distance, a savage blast muffled by the dense jungle shattered the early-morning stillness. "All right!" Jenkins said.

Chavez grinned gave Luciano a thumbs-up. "Outa sight, man."

"I think our friends back there just tried to reclaim their booby trap," Spencer said.

"Hey, Lieutenant!" Pettigrew called. "How do we figure that one for our body count, man?"

"Fuck the body count," Baxter said, tired. "Let's just get the hell out of here."

It was fully light by the time the little column reached its first navigation point following their withdrawal from Phu Thit. The spot was a clearing with a low, bamboo-thicket–covered hill just west of the Soi Rap River. From there, they turned west, heading inland toward their primary extraction point, a hill rising nearly twenty meters above the surrounding marshland. After reconning the hill for enemy troops, the SEAL squad climbed to the top and set up a defensive perimeter.

Baxter lay down on the ground, studying the jungle that encircled the knob. "Better get on the horn, Pet," he told the team's radioman. "Haul your Prick over here and let's call the cavalry."

"Roger that, Lieutenant," Pettigrew said. Dropping to the ground next to Baxter, he held the PRC-77's handset to his ear and mouth and hit the transmit key. "Whiskey One-six, this is Highball, Whiskey One-six, Highball. Do you copy, over?"

After a moment's burst of static, a voice sounded over the handset speaker, just loud enough that Baxter could hear. "Highball, Whiskey One-six. We read you. Go ahead."

"One-six, we are ready for extraction at LZ Sierra-Tango. Be advised that we do have Indians in the immediate vicinity, over."

"Ah, roger that, Highball. Hang tight. The guns will be over your position ASAP."

Guns—helicopter gunships. Those would be the Seawolf helicopters tasked with fire support and extraction for the mission this day. This unnamed hilltop, treeless and exposed, had been selected as the primary extraction LZ for the team; Baxter had been over the entire area the previous afternoon in a C&C helo out of Nha Be, checking out the land from the air. There was room here to set down one chopper at a time, and to spare.

Briefly—very briefly, as Pet continued speaking with the inbound helos—Baxter's mind wandered far from the stinking hell of the Vietnamese jungle. A mental picture of his fiancée flashed through his mind, so sharp and so vivid he almost imagined he could reach out and touch her. He'd met Jeannie Nalder at Kent State, while she was an economics student and he'd been attending under the ROTC program. She was blond, blue-eyed, had legs that went on forever, and was quite frankly the best thing that had ever happened to him . . . except, just possibly, his making the Teams. They planned to marry just as soon as he was through with this rotation in Nam. Three more months to go. . . .

Angrily, he wrenched his thoughts back to the here and now. The Vietnam bush was no place for daydreaming, not when one small mistake could put you smack in a body bag. He could hear gunshots now, scattered and still pretty far off. It sounded as though the VC groups hunting for them were relying on the time-honored technique of reconning by fire, shooting more or less at random in an attempt to get their quarry to shoot back and reveal their position.

Fat chance of that. Shooting blindly in the jungle was a good way to hurt your own people, and the SEALs had better fire discipline than that. Baxter had been briefed about one encounter where a SEAL squad had actually managed to plant itself between two searching VC units, loosed a few rounds at both of them, then kissed the mud while the two enemy parties opened up on one another with everything they had. Eventually, the SEALs had slipped away while the VC units continued their savage firefight with each other.

"Pretty good haul, I'd say," Chief Spencer said. He was thumbing through some of the documents and cardboard-bound books in the canvas satchel from the hooch. "Ray Cole's gonna get that humped-the-neighbor's-dog grin on his face when he sees this shit." Captain Raymond Cole was Bravo Platoon's Naval Intelligence Liaison Officer—their NILO in Navyspeak—back at Nha Be, and he was the man responsible for coordinating their operations, as well as both the intelligence they uncovered in the field and the intelligence coming down from various sources in the MACV chain of command.

"Well, maybe it'll keep him from having to make the stuff up," Baxter replied. Cole, for his money, was a little too young, a little too eager . . . and a little too willing to wing it on guesswork and statistical probabilities when men's lives were at stake. "The question is whether anybody in Saigon'll get to see this stuff before it's gone cold, gray, and moldy."

"Or have it rewritten to fit some REMF's master vision of how the war's going," Spencer added, nodding. "I hear you."

"Det Bravo's got the right idea," Spencer said. "Get the shit yourself, and then go do something about it."

The SEALs in Vietnam were organized into specific detachments. Det Golf consisted of all SEAL Team One direct-action platoons, including Bravo Platoon, while Det Alfa included the Team Two direct-action platoons. Det Echo advised and trained the LDNN—the South Vietnamese equivalents of the SEALs—while Det Bravo took men from both Team One and Team Two to work with the PRUs. Det Bravo, for the most part, had to handle all of their own intel, but the bonus was that they got to act on it, often right away, while it was still hot. The direct-action platoons, though they'd been taking more and more of a hand in determining where and how the intel they uncovered was used, were still tied down to the MACV chain of command and the specific intelligence they decided to release. It was not always a smoothly operating process; Baxter still remembered an incident from his first tour with Det Delta two years before, when a SEAL ambush had taken out a VC agent . . . who'd turned out to be a double agent working for someone in Saigon.

This was one war where it was damned tough telling the good guys from the bad guys, and the challenge had been getting tougher lately.

The rotor noise, a distinctive, flat *whop-whop-whop*, sounded in the distance. Moments later, the first of the Navy Seawolf helicopters roared low over the jungle canopy, followed closely by a second aircraft, following the north–south line of the Soi Rap about five kilometers to the west. Acquired secondhand from the Army, the Seawolves were standard Huey UH-1Bs modified to Navy SEAL specs. Each gunship mounted an M-16 weapons system, a complicated-looking tangle of hardpoints extending from either side of the aircraft and aimed forward. The weapons load-out included four M60C machine guns, two to a side, with three thousand rounds of ammo for each gun, plus two M158 rocket pods, each loaded with seven 2.75-inch rockets fired in pairs. In addition, the helo mounted two M60 machine guns in the doors, and the door gunners were further armed with M79 grenade launchers, along with a supply of ammo that included both high-explosive and fragmentation grenades, canister, and colored smoke for marking targets. Seawolves operated in pairs and could always be counted on to provide a free ride or to pile on the firepower whenever a SEAL op started to go sour.

"Highball, Highball, this is Whiskey One-three," a new voice called over the radio. "We are in the general LZ area. Give us your posit, over."

"Whiskey One-three, we have you in sight," Pettigrew said. "Watch for smoke." He nodded to Jenkins, who yanked the pin out of an M18 smoke grenade. As the two Seawolves clattered lazily past, circling around to the south, he tossed the grenade, immediately releasing a dense red cloud.

"Highball, One-three. I see red smoke. I say again, red smoke."

"Affirmative, One-three. Red smoke. That's us. Come on in."

As one of the Huey Seawolves continued circling, the other angled in toward the hilltop, flaring nose-high at the last moment and gentling its runners down onto the ground, as its rotor wash lashed at the nearby trees.

First on the helo was the bundle of documents and code books found in the hooch back in Phu Thit, followed by the female radio operator, still bound and gagged. Chavez carried her across the hilltop and slung her into the Huey's aft compartment like a sack of meal. The mission—and the fruits of the mission—always came first.

Nhung was next aboard, bolting from cover and racing across the hilltop to scramble aboard before anyone could stop him. Baxter let him go, signaling instead to the circle of SEALs now formed up in a ring about the helicopter. *Close up! First three, get aboard!* Words would never carry against the thunder of the spinning rotors, but the team was well trained and rehearsed. Jenkins, Chavez, and Spencer climbed onto the aircraft. Baxter pumped his fist up and down hard, signaling the pilot to haul tail out of there. The Huey's pilot replied, touching his hand to the visor of his helmet, then lifted the bird a yard off the ground, dipped the nose sharply forward, and sent his clattering steed howling off at treetop height. One Huey could carry seven men—and more in a pinch—but Baxter didn't like crowding the aircraft's safety margins, and if one of the machines was shot down, half of the squad would survive at least, to rescue the others or to make it back to base and file a report.

Gunfire banged and cracked steadily now from the jungle. The VC would know exactly where the SEALs were now and be racing ahead to catch them before they could be extracted. Luciano's M203 spoke, a deep-throated, hollow thump followed seconds later by a shrill crash in the jungle, marked by a whiff of smoke drifting above the trees. More gunfire sounded, and this time, Baxter could see the twinkling of muzzle flashes to the southwest. Pet and Lucky both returned fire, emptying their magazines at the treeline, reloading, and opening up again with short, sharp bursts.

Baxter reached for Pet's radio handset. "Whiskey One-one, this is Highball," he said. "We're taking heavy fire at . . . I make it bearing two-three-five off the smoke, range two zero zero. They're right in there at the treeline."

"Ah, copy, Highball. Cavalry's on the way. Keep your heads down!"

Moments later, the first helo returned, roaring low overhead. Smoke puffed from the aft ends of the rocket launchers to port and starboard, sending paired contrails streaking into the jungle. The explosions followed two by two, harsh bangs that ripped through tropical foliage and hurled spinning fragments of palm fronds high into the air. The Huey circled back and around, pouring full-auto machine-gun fire into the treeline, shredding trees and vegetation already savaged by the rockets. Gunfire from the treeline ceased with the suddenness of a thrown switch.

As the first Seawolf laid down a savage curtain of fire, the second banked in toward the naked hilltop, making its approach. Baxter watched with an undisguised and unrestrained admiration. Lots of helo pilots—lots of *Army* helo pilots—

would point-blank refuse to fly their aircraft into a hot LZ. Helicopters were magnets for automatic weapons fire, as well as for larger, nastier things like RPGs and B40 rockets, and even a relatively minor hit by a single round could snick through a hydraulic line and cripple the bird. The Navy Seawolf pilots, however, flew with a single-minded dedication to the SEALs and PBR crews depending on them. Baxter had never known a Seawolf crew to refuse an LZ . . . and he'd never known them to abandon a team on the ground. Depending on how far they were operating from base, two-bird Seawolf units had a loiter time of about ninety minutes, but he'd known crews who'd stretched that time to the limit and well beyond to see a team through its mission or to hand them off to a relief gunship pair.

The second Seawolf touched down seconds later, its rotor wash lashing the grass on the hilltop and spitting grit in the SEALs' faces. "Go!" Baxter yelled. "Go! Go!"

Luciano, Randolph, Pettigrew, and Baxter dashed for the open door; a door gunner leaned out past his weapon to offer a helping hand, all but dragging Baxter up off the hill and dropping him on the Huey's deck. Then the deck was tilting beneath him as the pilot gunned the Seawolf's engine and dropped the nose, hauling tail as it clawed for altitude. The door gunner leaned into his weapon, firing wildly at the brown-and-green blur outside as empty shell casings avalanched from the breech of his weapon. Looking past his legs, Baxter saw a number of running figures already far below, black-clad men charging into the clearing, firing up at the slick. Even above the thunder of the engine, Baxter could hear the sharp ping and thump of bullets hitting the UH-1's fuselage.

Then the UH-1 gained more altitude, leaving the running figures far behind.

"Welcome aboard, Lieutenant!" the pilot called back over his shoulder from the aircraft's right seat forward. "Man, it looks like those people were right on your ass!"

"Not even close, sir," Baxter replied. As always happened after combat, he could feel the strength draining from him, leaving him limp and weak. "We had all kinds of time. I am damned glad to see you guys, though."

"Hey, all part of our complete and friendly service, Lieutenant. Courteous and with a smile."

"Yeah," the copilot added from the left seat. "Just wait till you get our bill!"

"Never mind the fucking bill," Baxter replied with feeling. "After that dust-off you just pulled, the drinks are on me!"

"Hey, sounds like a winner," the pilot said. "Make mine a Singapore Sling."

Looking through the Huey's windscreen between the pilot and copilot, Baxter could already see the untidy sprawl of Quonset huts, warehouses, and docking facilities that marked Nha Be . . . and beyond, a vast and ugly sprawl across the horizon, the buildings of Saigon. It was one of the many ironies of this supremely ironic war that a life-and-death struggle with the enemy in the middle of dense jungle could be waged less than thirty miles from the heart of South Vietnam's capital. Sometimes, going on patrols in the Rung Sat Special Zone was eerily like commuting to war.

And sometimes that commute could be murder.

Chapter 5

Saturday, 24 February 1968

Saigon, Republic of Vietnam
1745 hours

"Where the hell are we, Lieutenant?" Chavez wanted to know. "This don't feel right, somehow."

"I'm beginning to get the same feeling, Bam-bam."

The ancient taxi swerved, narrowly missing a gaggle of Vietnamese schoolgirls in matching blue-and-white outfits, like sailor suits. An ARVN truck loomed ahead, and the driver stood on his brakes and leaned on the horn, delivering a stream of auto-fire invective from his window. The Vietnamese soldiers in the back of the truck stared back at him with complete detachment and disinterest.

Baxter, Luciano, and Jenkins were wedged into the backseat of the taxi, while Bam-bam Chavez's impressive bulk occupied the front seat, next to the driver. They'd ridden one of the gray U.S. Navy buses up from Nha Be, then caught a cab at the bus stop just north of the Ben Nghe Channel. The drive had started out peacefully enough—for a Saigon taxicab, at any rate—but Baxter was growing worried now.

He was lost. As many times as he'd been in Saigon, he still found the tangle of crowded, oddly angled streets confusing, and it was easy to become completely disoriented. Still, he had the feeling that the driver of the cab was circling way too far to the northeast.

Hell, they must be north of the Saigon Zoo by now, and, damn it, even though the sky was a thick and oily gray overcast, the sun was in *that* direction . . . which meant *that* was west, so the Sai Gon River was *that* way, to the east.

They were headed in the wrong direction and had been for the past fifteen minutes.

Baxter didn't mind being lost so much as he minded being literally taken for a ride. The cab driver was a small, intense-looking Vietnamese man with deep creases in his face at the corners of his mouth and ebony eyes. When the SEALs had climbed into the cab and Baxter had told him "downtown, Victoria Hotel," the driver had smiled, ducked his head several times, and said happily, "Sure! Sure! You bet! I take, twenty thousand *dong*! Flat rate!" His grin had broadened. "Or just five dollar, American!"

"Nice try," Baxter had told him, shaking his head. U.S. servicemen were not supposed to spend American money in Vietnam; the idea was to keep U.S. dollars from destroying the South Vietnamese economy. Despite the precaution, plenty of dollars found their way into the local shops, markets, bars, and whorehouses, not to mention the ever-present and fast-growing black market. "Make it ten thousand dong."

After several moments of haggling, they'd settled on six- teen. Now, though, Baxter was wondering if the cabby was taking the long way around because he was mad at being rebuffed. Another real possibility, though, was that he had friends somewhere, and this was the prelude to a mugging.

And it was always possible that the guy was VC, and that the four SEALs had been fingered as Americans and targeted for assassination.

All four SEALs were wearing civvies, which were per- mitted now for men ashore on liberty. Baxter honestly wasn't sure yet whether that was a plus or a minus in this city; four tall, hard, muscular men in civilian clothing running around in Saigon could hardly be anything else but military, and therefore targets, either to enemy agents within the populace . . . or to unscrupulous local civilians looking for a fast buck U.S.

The neighborhood was definitely becoming less than de- sirable. There were still plenty of people around, but fewer soldiers, and the buildings here were dingier, closer together. In the distance to the right and up ahead, Baxter could see a clutter of huge fuel-storage tanks and what looked like warehouses. This was not familiar territory. In fact, it was beginning to look a lot like the shoreside view of the Saigon waterfront, which Baxter had previously only seen from PBRs in the Sai Gon River. The structures here were older than they were downtown and more dilapidated. Some of the structures were make-do affairs of concrete block and sheet tin. Wherever they were going, it didn't look like downtown.

The taxi pulled up to a traffic light, nearly standing on its nose as a mob of people surged past in front of its bumper.

"Excuse me," Baxter said, leaning forward. "Driver? Where the hell are you taking us?"

For answer, the man switched on his radio, which blared out with a deafening blast of rock music. "You boy like music?" he yelled over the beat.

"I don't think this turkey wants to talk to us, L-T," Bam- bam said darkly.

Exchanging a glance with the other SEALs in the vehicle, Baxter reached around behind his back and slipped his hold- out from the holster he wore clipped to his belt, concealed bene<del>ath</del> the long tail of his shirt. Few SEALs went into Saigon unarmed anymore, even on liberty—especially on liberty, when almost anything could happen, and often did.

The driver's eyes widened in the mirror as Baxter ostentatiously pointed his weapon at the cab's roof, dragged the slide back, then released it with a noisy *snick*, chambering a round. It was a sleek and beautiful little pistol, a Walther PPK, less than seven inches long overall, firing 9x17mm rounds from a seven-round box magazine. The PPK had originally been designed as a personal sidearm for high-ranking German officers who'd not wanted to bother packing a heavier and bulkier pistol, but it had rapidly become a favorite among Gestapo agents and operatives with other intelligence services. In point of fact, Baxter had originally chosen the PPK because of its association with James Bond; the movie versions of the superspy stories were just plain silly, but Ian Fleming had worked with British Naval Intelligence during World War II and knew something about what he was writing about. The cartridge—the PPK chambered both 9mm short or .380 ACP—was underpowered, especially for combat, but at point-blank range that scarcely mattered.

As the taxi driver's eyes widened further, Baxter pressed the PPK's muzzle against the man's right temple, letting him feel the cold, slick metal of the barrel. "Just what do you think you're you trying to pull on us?" he demanded.

Luciano produced his backup weapon with a flourish . . . a Navy Mark I diver's knife, but with its seven-inch blade razor-edged and parkerized in dull black. Bam-bam smoothly drew his sidearm, a snub-nosed Smith & Wesson Chief's Special revolver, while Jenkins produced a Swiss-made SIG P-210-2 automatic.

Confronted by that kind of firepower, the driver dissolved in a singsong babbling of rapid-fire Vietnamese, starting with a sputtering "*Khong! Khong! Khong!*"

"What the fuck?" Bam-bam said, frowning. "Is the son of a bitch admitting he's Cong?"

"I don't think so," Baxter said. " 'Khong' is 'no.' I think he's just pleading for us not to blow him away. How about it, son? " He pressed the PPK's muzzle a little harder against the man's skull. "*Co la nguoi VC, phai khong?*"

He didn't really speak the language, not well, at any rate. His accent, he knew, was horrific, and he always had trouble with Vietnamese tonals, but he'd memorized certain key phrases well enough to make himself understood. "You are VC, aren't you?" was one he'd used plenty of times before, during prisoner interrogations.

"*Khong! Khong!*" the driver said, shaking his head wildly and trying to pull back from the pistol. "*Toi khong VC!* Not VC!" He continued backing away until the driver's side door suddenly opened behind him, spilling him into the street. Luciano lunged across the back of the driver's seat, trying to catch him, but the man was up and running in an instant, shrieking at the top of his lungs.

"Well, that tears it," Jenkins said, slipping his sidearm back out of sight. "We just lost our driver."

"Yeah, that was some sort of setup, I think," Luciano said. "What you wanna bet, Lieutenant? Somebody back at Nha Be fingered us for the VC?"

Baxter shook his head. "I doubt it. I think he was just giving us a runaround."

"Speaking of runarounds," Bam-bam said, "I think we're about to get one."

A pair of South Vietnamese MPs were approaching the cab, and their grim expressions suggested that they meant business. They wore khaki uniforms, with the spotless white helmets, scarves, and gloves that had given them their nickname among American servicemen in Saigon: "White Mice." The natty look was augmented by their dark sunglasses.

"You men!" one of the two shouted, pointing with his nightstick. "Out of car!"

"This is called 'keeping a low profile,'" Luciano said, returning his knife to the sheath strapped to his lower leg. SEALs were constantly drilled on the necessity of staying out of the public eye, a necessity in intelligence work. "How you wanna handle this, Lieutenant?"

"Well, I'm damned if we're going to spend our liberty in jail." Holstering his pistol again, he climbed out of the car and faced the furious advancing White Mice.

"You steal taxi!" the lead Mouse said. "Turn around!

Hands on car!'' He was reaching for his sidearm.

Carefully, not wanting to startle the man, Baxter produced his wallet, drawing it from his hip pocket with thumb and forefingers as the MPs watched suspiciously. Flipping it open, he pulled out a small folder which held a card printed on rice paper.

MILITARY ASSISTANCE COMMAND VIETNAM
STUDIES AND OBSERVATION GROUP
APO SAN FRANCISCO 96037

Beneath the heading were blanks for Baxter's name, grade, blood type, and service number, as well as a space for his thumbprint. Underneath that, the card got—as Baxter liked to say—spooky.

SPECIAL IDENTIFICATION AND PASS
The person who is identified by this document is acting under the direct orders of the President of the United States!
Do not detain or question him!
He is authorized to wear civilian clothing, carry unusual personal weapons, transport and possess prohibited items including U.S. currency, pass into restricted areas and requisition equipment of all types including weapons and vehicles.
If he is killed or injured, do not remove this document from him. Alert your commanding officer immediately.

The card was popularly known among those who carried it as the "get-out-of-jail-free card." It also carried a darker and more ominous nickname, the "Death Warrant," for it was widely believed, and with some reason, that anyone carrying the card who was captured by VC or NVA forces would immediately be put to death. Its official name was the MACV Form 4569, and personnel to whom it was issued were warned never to let it fall into enemy hands; it was written on lightweight stock and never laminated specifically so that it could be eaten if necessary. People issued the thing were supposed to turn it in or destroy it after the current tour of duty was up, though Baxter had known men who'd managed to keep them as souvenirs.

Not all SEALs had the card. Baxter had one because he'd spent some time recently coordinating missions with Det Bravo—which had no connection with Bravo Platoon, of course, but which worked with a number of Provincial Reconnaissance Units, the mercenary PRUs. He'd been issued the card at the beginning of his tour, against the possibility that he would need it for some black operation with the PRU SEAL detachment.

The sight of that card stopped the two MPs dead in their tracks. The leader of the two reached out to take it, but Baxter shook his head and pulled it back out of reach. "I think the driver of this vehicle was VC," he said in a firm and no-nonsense tone of voice. He pointed. "He went that way. If you want to make yourselves useful, catch him!"

The MPs blinked, then pulled a hurried consultation with each other. The light had long since turned green, and the traffic was snarling around and behind them beyond all comprehension, until at last the leader hurried off into the crowd after the suspected VC, while his partner stood there by the cab, looking confused.

Baxter still wasn't convinced that the cabbie had been VC, but he wasn't worried about a possible miscarriage of justice. The man was long gone, vanished into the crowd.

Of course, there was the possibility that they would figure out who the man was if they traced the ownership of the vehicle. Hell, even if the driver had been planning on rolling the four SEALs, Baxter didn't like the idea of having him interrogated by the White Mice. There were plenty of unpleasant stories floating around about American interrogations of VC suspects, though outside of roughing them up from time to time or giving them a bad scare to loosen them up a bit, Baxter had never participated in any actual mistreatment of enemy prisoners. The ARVNs, though, and the South Vietnamese military police, were notorious for their brutal interrogations of suspects.

Baxter had been thinking a lot this day about the female prisoner his squad had brought in the day before. He'd turned her over to Captain Cole, who would pass her up the line to other U.S. military intelligence types, probably at MACV headquarters out at Son Tanh Nhut. But after that? They couldn't just toss her in jail, and they damn sure couldn't let her go. Unless she turned Hoi Chanh and showed promise of providing solid operational intel, she'd be turned over to the local authorities, and Baxter didn't like that. It made him feel . . . soiled.

He found himself almost desperately hoping that she would Hoi Chanh.

"I think we'd better go," he told the remaining MP.

"No, no!" the man said, shaking his head. "You stay."

"Shit." He looked at his watch. They were already late for their meeting with the rest of Bravo Platoon at the Victoria, and Baxter didn't feel like spending the afternoon at ARVN district MP headquarters. Smiling at the remaining Mouse, he climbed into the vehicle's front seat. Bam-bam had already slid over to the driver's side and was gunning the engine. "*Chao!*" he said brightly to the surprised MP. "*Cam on rhat nieu!*"

Thank you very much . . . which sounded strangely like "come on right now" to American ears.

"You wait!" the MP cried. "You wait!"

The light was red again, but with a smile and a wave, Bam-bam hit the accelerator and plowed ahead through the intersection, making the traffic snarl even more complicated than it had been already. As horns blared and drivers shrieked curses, Bam-bam took a hard left and dove down a narrow side street, putting some distance between them and any possible pursuit.

"Yes, men," Luciano intoned in a deep, lecturer's voice, "as SEALs you must learn the art of keeping a low profile. Your survival may well depend on it."

"Which way now?" Jenkins asked.

"*That* way," Baxter decided, pointing to another left turn at an intersection ahead. "Away from the river and back to the west. Got to be."

"Shit, Lieutenant," Bam-bam said. "I trust you fine in the Rung Sat, but I'm not sure you know what you're doing up here in the big city."

Baxter's guess proved to be a good one, though; he'd always had a good sense of direction, and he found it operated just as well in Saigon's crowded streets as it did on an op in the Rung Sat jungle. Traveling southeast, they found the buildings gradually growing less shabby, the avenues wider, and more likely to be lined with trees and pastel-painted buildings that looked European rather than Asian.

Saigon, as always, was a swirling mass of people, color, and pungent smells, a bizarre and alien mixture, to Baxter's eye, of East and West. Many of the people, especially as they moved closer to the center of the city's vast and chaotic sprawl, were in Western dress, though everywhere more traditional Oriental garb was common. Here and there, the bright yellow-and-saffron robes of a Buddhist monk stood out, or the colorful *ao* of a young Vietnamese woman. In the streets, pedestrians mingled cheerfully and with an utter disregard for safety, good manners, or common sense with hordes of vehicles—private autos, buses, jitneys, military jeeps, and two-and-a-half-ton trucks, motorbikes, bicycles, and the odd-looking, three-wheeled cyclos so characteristic of this ancient city.

The buildings sported facades of every color, and styles of architecture ranging from modes common in Southeast Asia to the more utilitarian forms of the West and even to the gingerbread and ornate stateliness of nineteenth-century Europe. Saigon clearly showed its origins as a French colonial city, Baxter thought. Many of the buildings looked as though they'd been transplanted from some city in France; indeed, Saigon's nickname had long been "the Paris of the Orient."

It seemed to Baxter, however, that the people in the streets had a more reserved, a more somber air than he remembered from his previous tour. In early '66, especially, when he'd arrived in-country for the first time, there'd actually been very little to remind the casual visitor that this was a nation at war. Now, though, the people seemed to be burdened by something unseen, a fear, a heaviness, or a war-weariness, perhaps, that had invaded even this bright and cosmopolitan city. Part of it, of course, was the fact that the buildings were showing the effects of wear. Whole blocks along the way they'd come had been devastated, and many of the buildings showed bullet holes and worse. Until a few weeks ago, Saigon's buildings had been as untouched by the war as the people seemed to have been.

Now though, all of that had changed.

Away from the rougher dock and riverside area, soldiers stood everywhere, guarding street corners, watching the crowds from the vantage points of balconies or sandbag emplacements on the rooftops, moving along the streets in small patrols. Most of the civilians kept moving; few stopped in the streets or walkways simply to talk, and more than one caught Baxter's eyes as the cab drove past, meeting his gaze with expressions that seemed carefully and deliberately blank.

The difference, of course, was *Tet*.

Chapter 6

Saturday, 24 February 1968

Saigon, Republic of Vietnam
1808 hours

For months, now, the brass and the politicians had been declaring that the war in Vietnam was all but over, that the end was in sight, that the "light was visible at the end of the tunnel." Then, on the last two days of January 1968, the Viet Cong and NVA regulars had launched a massive and devastating attack on cities, bases, and villages throughout the length and breadth of the Republic of Vietnam, coinciding with the new year holiday of Tet.

Fighting continued in some places, especially up at Khe San, where Marines had been under siege since January 21, a move that was now widely perceived as a diversion staged by the NVA. Still, the worst of the Tet fighting elsewhere throughout South Vietnam had been over within a few days. The VC had come out of hiding en masse, seized dozens of key villages, towns, and strategic points—including all of Saigon's Cholon district to the west. The fighting had been savage and brutal; for the first time in this horrible little war, American helicopter gunships had fired into buildings right here in Saigon, and bodies had been strewn about the streets, sometimes in piles.

But Saigon had never been in any real danger of being captured, and those places actually overrun had been secured after a few hours of intense fighting. Elsewhere in the country, American and ARVN troops had dug out the enemy and destroyed them with ruthless success.

And it *had* been a success. Every battle so far had ended with a decisive victory for government forces . . . and a high VC body count that was going to take the enemy a hell of a long time to recover from.

The avenue the SEALs were following expanded as they moved into a ritzier section of town than the riverfront area the vanished cabbie had been taking them through. Soon, they found themselves in known territory, on Thong Nhat Boulevard. Up ahead, easily seen for miles in this flat terrain, the brand-new American Embassy rose like a fortress behind the tall, stone wall surrounding it, six stories tall, a distinctive and monolithic landmark visible throughout this part of Saigon. The place *was* a fortress, Baxter reflected, with the chancery encased in a concrete shield that actually looked like a stylishly modern and decorative facade created from open cinder blocks, a kind of stone meshwork designed to protect its offices and interior spaces from rockets and grenades. At each corner of the compound, squat, round pillboxes stood guard, their firing slits covered over with wire mesh that served as antigrenade screens.

The cleanup of the embassy grounds, Baxter noted, was still going on. During the Tet Offensive, in the early-morning hours of 31 January, the embassy had been one of dozens of key targets throughout the city given special attention by VC infiltrators. Viet Cong guerrillas had seemingly materialized out of nowhere, appearing throughout Saigon, racing through the predawn streets of the city according to a carefully prepared and rehearsed plan. Nineteen VC had launched a suicide attack against the embassy compound, blasting a hole through the west wall and fighting their way onto the embassy grounds. Two Marine guards had been killed in the action, and the rest of the guard detachment had been driven back into the chancery itself. The Communist attack had faltered when the commandos' leaders had been killed just inside the wall; the remaining VC had kept the U.S. staff pinned down inside the chancery for hours until reinforcements could arrive. Eventually, all nineteen guerrillas had been killed or captured, and the embassy grounds were secured . . . but only just barely.

As Bam-bam drove them past and Baxter studied the embassy grounds, though, he couldn't help wondering what effect the incident had had on people back home. Everyone knew that the embassy battle had been widely reported. Some people he'd talked to, new arrivals from the States, had told him that Tet was being treated as a defeat back home, but he didn't believe it. Damn it, Tet had been a *win*, and a big one. . . .

Still on Thong Nhat Boulevard and leaving the embassy behind, they drove directly toward the Presidential Palace, a resplendent, modern building completed only two years before, now looming up ahead of them at the end of the boulevard. Dozens of ARVN soldiers patrolled the streets outside the tall, wrought-iron gates. A left turn before they reached those gates, however, put them onto Pasteur Street, heading out of the government district and back downtown. Before long, they'd pulled up outside the Victoria Hotel.

"So what'll we do with the cab?" Jenkins asked.

"Fuck it," Luciano replied. "Give it to the parking valet for a tip."

"We'll park it here on the street," Baxter decided. "Let's see how long it stays there."

"We could put in an anonymous call to the company," Bam-bam said. "Have 'em come get it."

"Maybe so."

Baxter, somewhat to his surprise, was worried about the

taxi's driver. If the guy was VC, he deserved whatever was coming to him, and then some, but if he'd just been an addled civilian, even a petty thief . . . damn, he didn't want the guy falling into the clutches of the White Mice, or even of the ordinary civil police. Those bastards could be vicious; hell, they were as likely to torture the guy to death trying to get an admission out of him that he was VC as anything else, and Baxter found that he didn't want that on his conscience.

The realization had opened a curious hole in Baxter's soul, one that he didn't particularly want to peer into but that held a kind of morbid fascination for him nonetheless, like a bloody accident on the highway that forced you to slow down and gawk whether you wanted to or not.

Baxter had killed plenty of men in this war. Hell, he was a SEAL, and SEALs were paid to kill. That had never made it any easier, though. Throughout training, he'd been conditioned to kill, conditioned as thoroughly as any of Pavlov's dogs. Combat practice in BUD/S, for example, often involved firing live ammo at cardboard pop-up, knock-down targets. There was a definite reward, a *thrill* associated with successfully "acquiring targets," as the military euphemism went. Punishment for failure was the laughter and ribbing from the others in his training unit, and the scathingly caustic comments of his instructors.

At the same time, everyone seemed committed to the idea of dehumanizing the enemy as far as possible. They were always "VC" or "NVA," Victor Charlie, or, more frequently still, "gooks" or "slopes" or "dinks" or even—if a bit incongruously in this war—"Japs." Somehow, the name-calling made it easier to see the enemy as a *thing*, a target . . . and not as another human being who probably wanted nothing more than to stay alive.

The four SEALs left the cab at the curb and sauntered across to the hotel's main entrance. From the outside, the Victoria wasn't much to look at. The massive gray-white walls were concrete, poured between enormous wooden forms that had left their impressions in the surface when they were removed. The place had a seedy, somewhat depressed air . . . and a number of pockmarks in the walls that were almost certainly bullet holes.

The Victoria Hotel—and specifically the bar up in the penthouse suite opening onto the rooftop swimming pool—had become one of the principal hangouts for SEALs on liberty in Saigon. It wasn't that they'd commandeered the place, exactly, but it did seem as though the men of other services—Marines, Army, Air Force, and even Navy personnel who didn't happen to be frogmen—found themselves . . . uncomfortable there. Only a handful of intruders had ever actually been chucked into the slimy green waters of the pool, which Baxter believed had not been cleaned in more years than he cared to think about.

This time, though, there were some nonfrog guests present, but these men had all been invited. They were the pilots, copilots, and door gunners who'd been on those two Seawolf helos during the op the day before.

SEALs *always* took care of their own, even if they didn't happen to be SCUBA-qualified.

With them was a platoon of SEALs, the other three men from First Squad, plus the six enlisted men from Second Squad, all gathered under the benevolent eye of Bravo Platoon's 2IC, Lieutenant j.g. Dorsey, and a single Vietnamese lieutenant. All were noisily occupying the high ground of a couple of pulled-together tables near the doors overlooking the pool, hoisting some cold beers while a pair of Vietnamese girls in tiny pink bikinis bumped and ground away on a small stage to the rock music in the background.

"Christ, Lieutenant!" Spencer cried as the four wayward SEALs approached the table. "What the hell happened to you guys?"

"Took a wrong turn," Baxter replied, nodding and grinning to the others. "Glad you guys didn't keep the party waiting on our account."

"Hell, I think we've already gone through all the good beer," Doc Randolph said, studying his glass with a critical eye.

"That's right," Dorsey added. "We've worked our way through the imports all the way down to the panther piss. The only thing worse in this joint is the local brew."

"We saved that for you guys, Lieutenant," Pettigrew said.

"Well, fuck you very much," Luciano said as they sat

down. He cocked his head, studying the lone man seated at
the table who was neither an American SEAL nor a member
of a Seawolf air crew. In fact, he was Vietnamese, and wearing the gray and black tiger-stripe camo favored by members
of the ARVN special forces. "And who might you be, sir?"

"Lucky," Baxter said, "all of you. This is my opposite
number with the PRUs I've been working with off and on
over in Det Bravo."

"Lieutenant Nguyen Van Thanh," the man said. He
smiled, a toothy grin somehow reminiscent of a shark. He
was short and very dark, with a thin face and strong-looking
hands. "*Lien Doc Nguoi Nhia.*"

"Well, that's different, then!" Lucky said, immediately
relaxing. "SEALs is SEALs, I guess."

Nguyen Thanh—he'd given the name its Vietnamese pronunciation, of course, which made it sound more like
"Nwyen"—was a member of the LDNN, the "soldiers who
fight under the sea," the South Vietnamese equivalent of the
SEALs. American SEALs with Det Echo had established the
LDNN program in the first place and helped them train in a
program every bit as brutal as BUD/S training back in the
States. So far as Baxter could tell, the only difference between the training regimens for U.S. SEALs and the LDNN
was the fact that the latter conducted a large part of their
training in *real* combat . . . one of the advantages, if you
could call it that, to a training program in a country at war.

Baxter had made a point of inviting the LDNN lieutenant
to this get-together. Bravo Platoon was going to be working
closely with Thanh's platoon pretty soon, and it would be a
good idea for the members of the two groups to start getting
to know one another as individuals.

"Shit," Bam-bam said, eyeing the Vietnamese. "Is *everybody* over here named 'Nguyen'?" His pronunciation of
the name was clumsy and harsh.

The others laughed. Chavez was the squad's newbie, a
replacement for Bill Tangretti. He'd only been in-country for
about two weeks now, and he still was having trouble catching on to some aspects of Vietnamese life and culture.

" 'Nguyen' is a pretty common family name," Thanh explained." A lot like your 'Smith.' "

"Right," Luciano said. "Except that over here, something like fifty percent of the families are named 'Smith.' "

"Must make for one hell of a family reunion," Pettigrew said, and the others laughed, including Thanh.

"Your family name," Chavez said, blinking. "Oh, wait. That's like Chinese? Where the last name comes first?"

"More or less," Thanh said.

"Bam-bam," Baxter said. "If you want to get along with these folks, get to know their customs. Get to know *them*. In Vietnam, the family name comes first, then a middle name, then the personal name. Your first name is Barry. Barry B. Chavez?"

"Yeah?"

"Middle initial B. What's that stand for?"

Chavez hesitated, looking uncomfortable. "Bernardo," he said at last.

"Barry Bernardo?" Jenkins asked, blinking.

"Shit, man," Chavez said. "Why do you think I prefer 'Bam-bam'?"

As the others chuckled, Baxter nodded. "Okay, in Vietnam, your name would be Chavez Bernardo Barry. Only everybody would call you 'Mr. Barry,' not 'Mr. Chavez.' "

"*Mister* Barry!" Pettigrew said, laughing.

"Nobody calls him 'Mr. Chavez' now," Jenkins added. "Right, Bernardo?"

"The Vietnam word for 'mister,' " Baxter continued, "if you want to show a man respect, is '*ong*.' So this is *Ong* Thanh. Get it?"

"I guess so." Then Chavez blinked, realizing that he was being prompted. "Uh, yes, sir. *Ong* Thanh, I didn't mean any offense with that crack about your name."

"None taken, Mr. Barry."

"Okay, okay," Baxter said, holding up his hands as the others howled with laughter. "We're here tonight to do some serious celebrating, and to thank these fine Seawolf gentlemen for hauling our asses out of the jungle yesterday down in the Rung Sat."

The SEALs cheered the Navy pilots and door gunners. "Hey!" Randolph yelled, flagging down a miniskirted waitress. "Let's get some more beer over here!"

"So why were you late, Lieutenant?" Spencer asked. "We were about ready to send Mr. Thanh here out as a one-man search party."

"That's right," Randolph agreed. "We told him, 'Hey, man, it's your city. You ought to know where they'd get lost!' "

"I'm still not sure what happened," Baxter said. Briefly, he sketched in their afternoon's adventure. "And that's the whole story," he concluded. "Anyone want a taxi? Low mileage. Great tires. It's parked right outside."

"Shit, Lieutenant," one of the Seawolf gunners said. "The guy must've been VC. You should've wasted him right there."

"Hell, the guy could've been Nguyen Ngoc Loan's brother, for all I know," Baxter said.

"Ong Loan's brother could *be* VC," Thanh said, with only a slight quirk of the mouth to show he was joking. "Maybe that's why he hates them so much." Nguyen Ngoc Loan was Saigon's chief of police. He'd won considerable notoriety throughout the world a few weeks before when he'd executed a VC prisoner with a point-blank head shot in the streets of Saigon. Photos of the execution had made page one on newspapers all over the world, while a short film of the incident had played on evening news programs throughout the U.S. and Europe.

"Hey, I'd watch that kind of talk, Mr. Thanh," Doc Randolph said. "We knew an LDNN once who said the wrong things and disappeared. His name was Nguyen, too." Nguyen Manh Quon had been an LDNN liaison officer with Team One during his '66 deployment. The man had been an excellent officer and a splendid intelligence source. Apparently, though, he'd also made some political enemies within the Saigon high command, and eventually he'd been denounced as a Communist.

"No relation," Thanh said, deadpan. "We have so many Nguyens in this country that even I can't keep up."

"Anyway, that was a long time ago," Luciano said. "Hey! Did you guys ever hear about the first time the lieutenant came to this hotel?"

"No!" Bam-bam said, grinning. "Something juicy, I hope?"

"Fuck you, Lucky," Baxter said, but he was grinning, too.

"We were with the L-T. That was, what? Your first tour in the Nam, right?"

"Hell, it was my first *day* in the Nam," Baxter agreed. "I was a cherry, all right."

"Yeah, and he meets this B-girl, right here in this bar, and she's all over him, rubbing her titties on him, you know, that kind of thing. Hey, you never told us, Lieutenant. Did you have a good time that night?"

"I had a good time." He scratched his head. "Damned if I remember much of it, though."

"And when he wakes up, all of his clothes are gone, all of his money. He ends wandering around the hotel wearing a sheet until he could secure a new uniform."

"Aw, shit, Lieutenant," Bam-bam said. "What'd you do?"

"What could I do?" Baxter replied. "The hotel had never heard of this girl. I figure she must've worked different hotels and bars, finding a patsy and rolling him."

"VC, you think?" Injun Joe Talbot, one of the Second Squad people, wanted to know.

"Not every gook in town is VC," Luciano said. "Just every *other* gook." He stopped himself and glanced at Thanh. "Uh, beggin' your pardon, sir."

"It's okay," the man said. " 'Gook' is a frame of mind. Me, I'm a SEAL."

Baxter shook his head. "There aren't that many VC around, especially in the cities."

Dorsey grinned. "Just seems that way when you get in a firefight with them."

"You got that right," Baxter replied. "Most of them are just looking out for Number One. But you guys ought to take that to heart, and look after Number One yourselves."

"You know," Luciano said, "I heard that there are VC whores, out to get U.S. servicemen. They slip broken glass up inside their boxes, see, and—"

"Aw, jeez, Lucky, that's sick," Spencer said. "You're one seriously twisted individual, you know that?"

"Hey, it's just what I heard."

"You've been in the Navy how long, son?" Baxter said, shaking his head. "And you still haven't learned to separate the sea stories from the straight skinny?"

The easy banter between enlisted men and their commanding officer was characteristic of the SEALs. The frogmen—whether SEALs or the UDT the unit had been drawn from—had always been more relaxed about the formalities due to commissioned officers than were other branches of the service.

"So, Mr. Thanh," Chief Spencer said, turning in his chair to face the Vietnamese lieutenant. "What's your assessment of the war? Did we win Tet?"

"That is affirmative, Chief," the LDNN lieutenant said. "A big win. Number one."

"Fuckin' A!" Luciano cried, and the other SEALs at the table raised their beers in salute.

The Communist Tet Offensive, in the end, had been a resounding defeat for the VC forces. General William Westmoreland himself had announced a figure of thirty-seven thousand VC and NVA regulars killed, and Baxter had seen numbers at the U.S. Naval Headquarters in Saigon that suggested the actual body count might exceed fifty thousand . . . this as opposed to some two thousand Americans and eleven thousand ARVN troops killed in the widespread and desperate fighting. It was widely acknowledged among Americas in Nam that if the Communists had scored a big win at either Khe San or with Tet, and especially if they'd been able to take the U.S. embassy, the propaganda value alone might have been worth the cost of the military defeat.

But they'd scored no successes, not one. For weeks now, ARVN forces had been celebrating what they considered to be their biggest victory yet.

"You know," Lieutenant Simmons, one of the Seawolf pilots, said. "Scuttlebutt has it that all the commies really wanted to prove was that they were still in the fight, that they weren't beaten yet."

"Oh, I'll grant them that, Lieutenant," Baxter said. "But from where I sit, it looks like the VC and NVA just bet everything they had on a single toss of the dice . . . and lost it all, big-time.''

"Affirmative," Thanh said. "Charlie's power has been broken, once and for all."

"What do you want to bet that the war's won and over by this time next year?" Dorsey said. "Home by Christmas! How's that?"

"Shit," GM2 Ken Lasky said. "Here it is February already, and I haven't even started my Christmas shopping."

"You think we're that close, Lieutenant?" Pettigrew asked.

"I'm not sure," Baxter said slowly. He was thinking of the Vietnamese civilians he'd seen earlier, the heaviness in their bearings as they walked through that war-torn section of the city. "We've hurt the VC damned bad. I guess it all depends on how much willpower there is with the leadership in Hanoi."

"We've broken the VC for good," ET1 Randy Thompson said.

"Right on, man!" Luciano said. "We've got this war won!" He held his glass out above the table. "*Sat Cong!*" *Kill Communists!* It was a popular toast.

"*Sat Cong!*" the others cried, clinking their glasses together and sloshing foam on the table top.

"*Su than trang!*" Thanh added. "Victory!"

And then the party began in earnest.

Chapter 7

Tuesday, February 27, 1968

Ocean Beach, San Francisco

It was one of those rough, wild days that Pat Halstead loved, more typical of the northern coast than of San Francisco. The waves were running high, and the sky was overcast. As she strode along the wide, low beach, she could see evidence of yesterday's storm, including a high-water mark that was a good three feet inland of last week's high-tide line. The waves had resculpted the beach, creating new dunes and leveling old ones. Walking along a beach after a storm always reminded her of the immense power of nature; it made her and her problems seem insignificant.

She stood with her eyes closed on top of a newly created dune, letting the wind whip her blond hair around her face, listening to the crash of the waves, soaking in the sharp sea smell. Somewhere out there, an insignificant gray mass in the midst of a vast and unfriendly ocean, was the U.S.S. *Edson*, Greg's ship. She wondered, as she had many times before, what it would be like to experience a storm like yesterday's from the deck of a Navy destroyer. It frustrated her that she didn't even know what a destroyer looked like. Greg had given her a lot of information on the ship when he first went aboard—she knew that the *Edson* was over four hundred feet long and weighed several thousand tons—but that didn't give her any kind of feel for how big it was, really.

Several benches, seaweed wrapped around the legs, were lined up along the edge of the beach. Pat strode over to one of them, brushed some of the sand off it, and sat down, drawing her lined raincoat close around her. It was chilly today, low forties, probably, but that hadn't been enough to keep her indoors. Growing up in Jenner, she had always loved taking long walks in any kind of weather, and she'd kept up the practice in college, much to the amusement of some of her classmates, who couldn't see the appeal of being alone for more than fifteen minutes at a time. Usually Pat liked to surround herself with people—she thrived on the interplay of different ideas and approaches to life—but there were times, her think times, she called them, when she craved solitude. It was funny, in a way. She'd always thought of her brother as something of a loner, uncomfortable in a crowd. Greg had always viewed her as a social gadabout, a people person who couldn't be happy unless she was in the midst of a gaggle of giggling girls. She chuckled. They'd been finding out through their letters that they were a lot more alike than either of them had thought.

She pulled Greg's latest letter out from an inside pocket of her raincoat. His first few letters, back when he was in boot camp in San Diego, had been terse and a little bitter, but after a while she'd managed to convince him that her feelings about the war didn't interfere with her caring for him, and he'd opened up quite a bit. In fact, they'd become closer in the past year than they'd ever been before he joined the Navy. By the time he'd been transferred to Treasure Island, out in the bay, for advanced electronics school, he'd actually been eager to see her. They'd walked this beach together a lot on his weekends off, arguing about everything from the war to philosophy to communism to the sexual revolution to early-American history.

The one thing they'd never talked about . . . was Marci.

Pat still saw Marci occasionally, but they were no longer friends. That afternoon in the snack bar last year, when Greg had announced that he was joining the Navy, Marci had been stunned . . . and bewildered. Pat had stayed with her all afternoon, trying to help her friend. She'd felt sure that Marci hadn't meant half of what she'd said to Greg, that she'd just been angry at being left out of his decision, that she'd been worried about where that decision might lead him.

But by the end of the afternoon Pat realized that Marci

had meant every vicious word she had spoken. Worse than that, she'd expected Pat to share her feelings, not only about the war, but about Greg. She'd actually said that if Pat didn't join her in condemning Greg's actions, then she was just as much of a fascist and warmonger as he was. Pat could still remember the chill that had come over her at that moment, the horror she'd felt at the vindictiveness she'd seen in Marci's eyes.

That had been the beginning of a change in Pat, as she realized that more and more of her friends in the movement were unable to make distinctions that seemed obvious to her. For Pat there was a big difference between the bureaucrats who were getting the United States deeper and deeper into a war that was none of their business, and the ordinary soldiers and sailors who actually prosecuted that war, between the policy makers and those who carried out that policy. But whenever she tried to suggest that idea to her friends, she found herself being argued into a corner. She couldn't pinpoint the flaw in her opponents' logic, but she was sure there was one.

She slit the envelope with a practiced forefinger and carefully unfolded the letter inside. Lately she'd gotten in the habit of never reading Greg's letters in her apartment, at least not when her roommates were there. While Beth and Janie weren't as rabid as Marci, they still found it difficult to understand how Pat could remain on good terms with her brother. Meanwhile Pat was wondering how long she could continue to remain on good terms with them. Family loyalty seemed a foreign concept to them. Her lab partner in organic chemistry was getting to be a good friend. Maybe she should try to room with Wendy next year. If she didn't end up moving in with Andy.

It was a fat letter. Greg usually wrote to her in bits and snatches over the course of maybe a week or two, and then packed the letter off in a hurry whenever they were in port or whenever a mail-and-supply ship came alongside. She glanced quickly over the datelines scattered throughout the letter, noting that he had started the letter right after leaving Subic Bay in the Philippines and that his last entry was about a week and a half after the first. From the dates she knew he must have heard about the Tet Offensive; she wondered what he felt about the horrors she'd been watching daily on the evening news.

He started out the letter, as he usually did, with a quotation, this one from Thomas Paine. She wasn't the history fanatic that Greg was—science was more her thing—but she did recognize that name. Paine's *Common Sense* had had a major influence on the American Revolution.

> *"Tyranny, like hell, is not easily conquered; yet we have this consolation with us, that the harder the conflict, the more glorious the triumph. [. . .] it would be strange indeed, if so celestial an article as FREEDOM should not be highly rated."*

Pat's mouth quirked in a smile. She could tell the direction today's discussion was going in—communism was tyranny, and it was America's duty to stop communism from taking over the rest of Southeast Asia. But where the argument fell down was in comparing Asian so-called democracies with American ones. What was right for the United States might not be right for South Vietnam. Anyway, why should *we* fight *South Vietnam's* war? She grinned as she planned her rebuttal. Greg wrote:

> *Happy New Year. It is now the Year of the Monkey in Vietnam, and it's looking like the war may be over before I can even get into SEAL training. Chief Clayton says that I should be able to take the qualifying exam as soon as we get back to Diego.*

Damn. So he still had this awful idea of being one of those Naval commandos she'd read about in *Time*. They sounded worse than anything the Army'd come up with—dirty, nasty, professional killers. Yet Greg was enthralled with the notion of becoming a Navy frogman. She'd been excited by Dad's stories, too, when she was a kid, but these new SEALs were a far cry from the UDT of World War II. Dad had told her they didn't even carry weapons, other than a diving knife; these new commandos apparently carried not only rifles, but

shotguns and machine guns and all kinds of things. She
wished Greg would give up the crazy idea and join the Hospital Corps, like their father had. It would be easier to explain
a brother who was a medic than one who was a commando,
though for some of her friends, being a medic was just as
bad as being an ordinary soldier. Worse, they said, because
medics patched people up so they could go kill again. She
continued reading.

*What we hear from Vietnam is that Tet was a tremen-
dous victory. They threw everything they could at us,
and we trounced them. My guess is that the war is
going to start winding down now, and I'll never get a
shot at it.*

Why was he so eager to get into the war? What was that
line from Paine? She flipped back to the beginning of the
letter. ". . . the harder the conflict, the more glorious the tri-
umph." That was it. Pat shook her head. She was proud of
her father and grandfather for serving their country, and she
was proud of Greg, even though she disagreed with him violently about this war. But she didn't understand, *couldn't*
understand, this fixation some men had with the glory of war.
There was nothing glorious about the scenes she'd seen on
TV, that Saigon policeman, for example, blowing the head
off a suspected VC. *Suspected* VC! They didn't even know!
So Greg thought they were winning. She wasn't sure
whether to hope he was right or not. What she wanted was
for the Americans to get out and let the Vietnamese deal
with their own problems, but she was afraid that the do-
nothings in Washington had pushed the country into a position they couldn't back down from. Or wouldn't. Damn
their bone-headed political pride. They were just as incom-
prehensible as soldiers fighting for glory. If only women
were running things, the world would be a much better place.
There were some women in politics now, not many, but a
few; but the problem was the only women that could make
it in that cutthroat world were the ones that acted like men!
Women like Marci.

Pat shuddered to think what Marci might be like in, say, ten years. She was graduating this year and headed for Chicago Law. If she opted for politics, Pat had no doubt she could go as far as she wanted to. What kind of senator would Marci make? Pat was suddenly struck with the realization that she would probably be no less ruthless, no less power mad, no more responsive to the will of the people than the hawks in Washington right now. She would have her own personal agenda, and to hell with anyone who tried to get in her way.

Pat wrenched herself back to Greg's letter. He definitely seemed to be enjoying the electronics work. Apparently the first class in charge of training him took his job seriously. Rather than just sticking Greg with the scutwork, he was actually teaching him everything he knew, which after six years at the job was quite a lot.

Bartlett grudgingly admitted yesterday that I wasn't shaping up too badly. Coming from him, that's high praise. He even suggested I might want to grease for officer someday. I wasn't sure at first whether that was a compliment or not! Most petty officers and chiefs don't seem to have a high regard for officers. But Bartlett explained that mustangs were different. That's what they call someone who comes up through the ranks. Unlike normal officers, especially ring-knockers—that's the ones that graduate from Annapolis—mustangs know what it's like to work for a living.

I'm not sure how I feel about the idea. The Navy has lots of programs to help you finish college, which I'd have to do, of course, before going to OCS—Officer Candidate School. So that would be a plus. But the problem is still what it was when I left State—what the hell would I do with a degree once I got one? Bartlett's answer was simple—three years' active duty and six years in the reserve—but not very helpful. Right now what I'm trying to do is figure out if I want to make the Navy a career. Electronics is a blast, and I could really see myself opening up a little shop in Jenner. So

*do I want that, or do I want to go career? I really
don't know.*

Greg as an officer, now that was an interesting thought.
Lieutenant Halstead. No, wait, that wasn't the lowest rank.
What was it? Ensign, that was it. Ensign Halstead. Hmm,
that sounded pretty good. As she had been discovering over
the past year, Greg definitely enjoyed being a part of something bigger than himself. The Navy was like a huge extended family; everywhere you went, you had a buddy. Pat
grinned, imagining what her roommates would say to the
idea of her brother going career. She was definitely going to
have to talk to Wendy about next year.

She glanced at her watch and saw that it was already
2:30. She'd better move if she was going to get any work
done this afternoon before meeting Andy for dinner. As she
put Greg's letter away and started walking back toward campus, she wondered about Andy. He wasn't a hawk, certainly,
but neither was he vocal in his opposition to the war. At
times it seemed as though he was an outsider looking in,
observing these strange life-forms and their curious ways. He
rarely passed judgment on anyone . . . but then he rarely be-
stowed praise either. It was as though he approached everything as the object of a psychological study and was
determined to be completely objective.

He was one of a handful of people she knew on campus
who didn't automatically condemn her brother for being
"part of the military-industrial complex." She wondered if
he would remain objective at the news that Greg was thinking about making the Navy his career. At first his impartial
attitude had appealed to her. It felt like he was being more
fair than her other friends, less prejudiced. But lately she'd
found herself almost wishing he would take a stand on something . . . *anything.* Pat herself was not judgmental—she
didn't condemn those who disagreed with her—but the people she found it hardest to understand were the ones who
didn't seem to have an opinion at all, who were just apathetic. Andy wasn't exactly apathetic, but he was so . . . removed, remote. Damn it, there were times she just wanted
to shake him.

San Francisco State University

"What *is* this stuff?" Pat made a face as she tasted the evening's Mystery Meat in the university's cafeteria.

"Hmm. I'd say minced animal protein, mingled with sufficient vegetable paste to thoroughly disguise the original attributes of the product in question, along with a certain quantity of processed grain to provide the illusion of nutrition," Andy said with a deadpan expression.

Pat grinned. "Mmm, sounds yummy!"

Andy looked at her and raised one eyebrow.

"You know, you look just like Spock on *Star Trek* when you do that."

"Alas, you do not say I *sound* just like Spock. Now there's a man to emulate. Total unemotional logic." He faked a plaintive sigh.

"Total logic isn't very sexy," Pat said.

"Then I'm glad my imitation of Spock is only eyebrow-deep. So who's your pick? Bones?"

"Mmm-hmm. Or Scotty. Chekov's cute, too."

"What?" he exclaimed in mock horror. "Not Captain Kirk?"

"No way! He's too full of himself."

She really loved Andy when he joked like this. He was so serious most of the time; when he let his funny side show through, he sparkled. Most people never saw that side of him. At times like this she thought seriously about his suggestion that she move in with him.

"So what do you think Walter's going to say tonight?" Pat asked. Walter Cronkite was just back from a trip to Vietnam, and he was doing a half-hour news special that night. She had always followed the news avidly, switching off between Cronkite on CBS and his rivals on NBC, Chet Huntley and David Brinkley.

Andy took a long swig of Coke before responding. "I guess that depends on what he found over there."

"That's a pretty weasely answer."

He raised both eyebrows this time. "Not at all. It's just that I can't get inside Walter Cronkite's head and figure out what he's going to say."

She decided to press him. "Well, what do *you* think the situation is over there? Who won?"

"You're speaking of the Tet Offensive."

"Of course."

"Not necessarily 'of course.' You could have meant the war as a whole."

"Stop being so nitpicky." His quibbling could be so irritating at times. Pat was reminded of why she hadn't agreed to move in with him.

"All right. I'll turn it around on you. What do you think he's going to say?"

"That we're winning? That we'll be getting out soon?"

Andy cocked his head sideways and pushed his lips out thoughtfully. "The tone of your voice leads me to believe that that's what you hope he'll say. And you hoped I would agree with your assessment."

"Damn it, Andy! I don't expect you to agree with me on everything!"

He grinned suddenly, transforming his rather homely face. "Good. Because I don't intend to."

Grudgingly, she smiled in return. "I really love you, you know. But you make me so darned mad at times."

"That's good. Anger can be healthy. What was it Taylor Caldwell said?—'Anger is a cleansing agent.' "

She was actually chuckling now. "Why? *Why* did I have to fall in love with a psych major?"

"The same reason I fell in love with a biology major. We're perfect for each other."

The words sounded great, but for some reason they made her uneasy. She didn't feel perfect, and she didn't really want to be thought perfect. She guessed what she wanted was just to be loved even though she wasn't perfect.

Later that evening they went back to her second-floor apartment on Acevedo Avenue to watch the Cronkite special. Beth was already there, along with Joe, but Janie and Mike hadn't gotten there yet.

"Go stake our claim to the sofa, Andy," Pat said as she took off her coat and hung it up in the closet. "I'll rustle up the grub."

"Hey, Pat, not to worry," Joe said from the kitchen. "There's room for three on the sofa."

"Three, Joe? And how are you doing in that remedial arithmetic course? There's going to be six of us tonight."

"No problem. Us guys'll sit on the sofa, and you lovely ladies will sit on our laps."

"Joe, I congratulate you. That sounds like a magnificent solution to our current topological dilemma," Andy said. "I don't see a problem with it, Pat. Do you?"

"Look, do you want a beer or don't you?" Pat tried to sound exasperated, but it didn't quite work.

"As ever, she knows the way to my heart." Andy grinned. "They rule us, Joe. We're helpless in their clutches."

"Helpless, my ass," Beth yelled as she walked in from the bedroom. "The only time you guys are helpless is when there's work to be done."

Pat got a six-pack out of the refrigerator and brought it out, along with a couple of bags of chips. Just then Janie showed up with Mike in tow.

"Didn't think you guys were going to make it," Beth said. "It's almost time."

Andy had already turned the TV on and changed the channel to CBS.

"Hey, cool it, Beth. We still got five minutes," Mike said. "And turn that thing down, will ya? We don't need to listen to that garbage."

"Pat was asking an interesting question at dinner," Andy said after he adjusted the volume. "What do you think Walter's going to say?"

"Yeah, good idea. Let's take a poll," Joe said. "What really happened in Tet—win, lose, or draw?"

"Well, I think it's a lousy idea," Janie said. "Betting on people's lives. If we kill more of theirs than they kill of ours, then we win, right?"

"I would think it would have more to do with the extent to which each side's objectives were met," Andy said, popping the top of a can of beer and expertly tossing the pull tab into a nearby flowerpot.

"Andy!" Pat exclaimed. She plucked the pull tab out of the pot and placed it in the wastebasket.

"So what would you say those objectives were, in the case of Tet?" Joe asked.

"Shut up, you guys. It's on." Mike moved over to the TV and turned the volume back up just as the words REPORT FROM VIETNAM BY WALTER CRONKITE filled the screen, then faded to a view of a distinguished-looking man with bushy eyebrows and a receding hairline.

"God, he's so sexy," Janie said from her perch on Mike's lap in the brown armchair.

"Walter? You've got to be kidding," Beth said, grabbing a handful of chips. "He's too old."

"Oh, but that marvelous voice of his!"

"Give me David Brinkley any day."

"Hey, guys, some of us would like to listen, okay?"

"Okay, okay!"

For the next half hour, they watched as different people Cronkite had interviewed in Vietnam gave their differing opinions on the war. The scenes of the rubble in the war-torn streets of Saigon were no longer a shock, after all the television coverage of the past month, but they were disturbing nonetheless. Pat's mouth grew dry as she thought about what might happen if Greg got his wish and became a SEAL.

After the last commercial, Cronkite appeared behind his desk in New York.

"This is it, guys," Joe said. "Now he'll tell us—"

"Shut UP!"

"Who won and who lost in the great Tet Offensive against the cities?" Cronkite paused for a moment, and then that deep baritone voice resumed, "I'm not sure. The Viet Cong did not win by a knockout, but neither did we. The referees of history may make it a draw. Another standoff may be coming in the big battle expected south of the Demilitarized Zone. Khe Sanh could well fall with a terrible loss of American lives, prestige, and morale, and this is a tragedy of our stubbornness there—"

"Stubbornness, yeah. He got that right," said Mike.

"Shut up."

"—but the bastion is no longer a key to the rest of the

northern regions, and it is doubtful that the American forces can be defeated across the breadth of the DMZ with any substantial loss of ground. Another standoff. On the political front, past performance gives no confidence that the Vietnamese government can cope with its problems, now compounded by the attack on the cities. It may not fall, it may hold on, but probably won't show the dynamic qualities demanded of this young nation. Another standoff.''

Pat tried to hold on to all his words, but failed. He kept repeating the phrase, ''another standoff.'' A quick glance around her showed the others just as intensely focused on the words of this respected journalist.

''. . . It seems now more certain than ever,'' he continued, ''that the bloody experience of Vietnam is to end in a stalemate. This summer's almost certain standoff will either end in real give-and-take negotiations or terrible escalation; and for every means we have to escalate, the enemy can match us, and that applies to invasion of the North, the use of nuclear weapons, or the mere commitment of one hundred or two hundred or three hundred thousand more American troops to the battle. And with each escalation, the world comes close to the brink of cosmic disaster.''

Pat was stunned. Cronkite had been a hawk since the beginning. If *he* thought they couldn't win . . .

''To say that we are closer to victory today is to believe, in the face of the evidence, the optimists who have been wrong in the past. To suggest we are on the edge of defeat is to yield to unreasonable pessimism. To say that we are mired in stalemate seems the only realistic, yet unsatisfactory, conclusion.

''On the off chance that military and political analysts are right, in the next months we must test the enemy's intentions in case this is indeed his last big gasp before negotiations. But it is increasingly clear to this reporter that the only rational way out then will be to negotiate, not as victors but as an honorable people who lived up to their pledge to defend democracy, and did the best they could.''

He looked up then and stared straight at the camera . . . straight at Pat. ''This is Walter Cronkite. Good night.''

Andy reached out and turned the TV off.

"Man oh man," Mike said. "Who'd have thought to hear old Walter the Hawk talk like that!"

"Did you catch that 'we must test the enemy's intentions' bit?" Beth asked. "It's going to be escalation, damn it!"

"No, wait!" Janie put in. "He said . . . what was it? . . . the only rational thing would be to negotiate, right?"

Joe snorted. "Since when have the bastards in Washington been *rational*?"

Pat said nothing. Greg had said they were winning. Walter said they were mired in stalemate. It didn't really matter who was right. What mattered was who the man in the White House thought was right . . . and what he would do about it. If he believed Walter, the war could be over in a year, in six months. And Greg would be safe.

But if not . . .

She suddenly wished everybody would leave . . . well, at least the guys. She needed to be alone to write to Greg.

Chapter 8

Tuesday, 19 March 1968

U.S.S. *Edson*, DD 946
In transit, Pearl Harbor to San Diego
1445 hours

"C'mon, Halstead. Hold the fuckin' light."

"The damn ship's rolling, Chief."

"I don't give a fuck about your troubles, kid. Hold the fuckin' light!"

Greg shifted his position a little, allowing him to brace his arm against a conduit to hold the lamp steady. The narrow, cramped space reminded him of the Jeffries Tube on *Star*

Trek, the angled shaft that gave the fictional starship's engineers access to her electronic guts. Of course, this Jeffries Tube wasn't nearly as comfortable, it was a hell of a lot more cluttered with primitive, twentieth-century cables, conduits, and wiring bundles . . . and it was *dark*. The fact that the *Edson* was wallowing along in a heavy sea didn't make things one bit easier.

"Okay," Clayton said, stabbing a greasy forefinger into an impenetrable forest of cables. "See this fucker here?"

ET1 Bartlett would ordinarily be the one to run Greg through this drill, but this time Chief Clayton had taken over for him. Many of the chiefs Greg had run across during his first year in the Navy didn't seem to do much actual work—Bartlett said they didn't like to get their hands dirty—but Chief Clayton was definitely an exception.

"Yeah, Chief." He wasn't sure what he was seeing. One simple fact had been painfully evident ever since he'd left school at Treasure Island. The stuff they taught you ashore, in those old but *spacious* military classrooms, couldn't begin to teach you about what working on the electronic equipment aboard a ship at sea was really like.

Edson was a tiny sliver of a world, a gray steel splinter 420 feet long and just forty-five feet across at the widest point in her beam. She'd been launched on the first day of 1958, at the Bath Iron Works above the mouth of the Kennebec River in Maine. Her nearly ten-to-one ratio in length overall to beam gave her a greyhound's speed of better than thirty-two knots. It also gave her one hell of a roll in a following sea, a wrenching, wallowing, corkscrewing motion that was much more disturbing than the usual up-and-down as she sliced through the waves. Greg was trying hard not to think about that corkscrew motion . . . but he had to think about it, to *anticipate* it, to keep the handheld work light steady, illuminating the tangled forest of wires and cables that Chief Clayton was working on.

Working with the chief always made him uneasy. At least Bartlett taught him something, but Chief Clayton usually acted like he was incapable of learning anything. No, that wasn't quite right. It was more like it wasn't *worthwhile* trying to teach the newbie anything. Probably because Greg had made it abundantly clear early on that he was aiming to get off this bucket just as quickly as possible, and into the SEAL program.

The SEALs. Sometimes the thought was all that kept him going. He enjoyed the electronics work . . . when he was allowed to do anything interesting, that is—in other words, when Bartlett was teaching him. When Chief Clayton took him in hand, he usually ended up just doing mindless makework and answering the chief's interminable questions. And he was looking forward to getting rated—getting to put ET in front of his name, not being just a trainee anymore; he should make third class when they got back to port. But then what? Another three years of tuning magnetrons and grounding out capacitors? The prospect didn't thrill him.

He was beginning to realize that he had the same problem in the Navy that he'd had in college—it just wasn't challenging enough. Most of the sailors that he'd talked to seemed content just to do what had to be done to get by. *Put in your four and get out,* was the usual way of expressing it, a kind of acknowledgment that a guy could put up with anything for four years, and then get on with his life. Even the lifers like Bartlett and Clayton had established niches for themselves where they knew exactly what was expected of them; they weren't learning anything new.

Greg wanted something more than that. He wanted to push himself to the limit, to see just how much he was capable of. He'd established a physical-training regimen for himself, a difficult thing to do aboard ship, but he knew he'd have to be in good shape to make it through SEAL training. He ran in place, did push-ups and sit-ups, always pushing himself to do a little more than he'd done the day before. His routine drew a good bit of good-natured ribbing from the other sailors, who felt that any exertion beyond the minimum required was crazy. When they found out why he was doing it, they started calling him Frogman . . . or less complimentary names like Froggie and Tadpole.

The *Edson* rolled and twisted, and Greg was unpleasantly reminded of the greasy scrambled eggs he'd had for breakfast. He swallowed hard.

He was becoming uncomfortably aware of something else.

It *stank* in here . . . a mingling of oil, grease, and the chief's breath and body odors that was rapidly becoming almost unendurable in this confined space.

He twisted in place, trying to get more comfortable, lost his balance, and leaned heavily against Clayton's side.

"I love you too, sweetie," the man growled. "But this don't mean we're gonna take long, lingerin', soapy showers together in the head. C'mon, dipshit. Hold the fuckin' light steady!"

He blinked at Clayton's casual vulgarity. Greg still wasn't used to the near-constant flow of profanity and ear-ringing invective.

"Okay, Chief. How's this?"

Clayton grunted something uncommunicative. *Damn* it was hot in this compartment. The tight-packed electronics gear in the EW suite gave off an oven's worth of heat, and the small ventilator fans and air shafts simply couldn't keep up with it. The wiring—or maybe it was just the rubber and plastic insulation—gave off a sour, familiar smell as it got hot. Greg swallowed hard against his rising gorge and tried to concentrate on what Clayton was saying.

"So anyways, as I was sayin'," the chief continued, picking up with his interrupted narrative. "I was a first-class ET on the *C. Turner Joy*. She was sister ship to this bucket. DD 951. A few months younger. Anyway, there wasn't no doubt at all that the dinks launched an attack on the *Maddox*. They came in with three torpedo boats, launched their torps, and missed. The *Maddox* blew one of the fuckers clear out of the water."

"Well, why the hell did they try it, Chief? I mean, three torpedo boats against a destroyer. . . ."

"Ah, shit. Who knows? It worked in World War II, when our PT boats went after Jap destroyers in the Pacific. The *Maddox* was about ten miles offshore at the time. The gooks might've felt threatened or somethin'. In fact, the scuttlebutt at the time had it that there was some sort of secret op goin' on, a raid on the North Vietnam coast by South Vietnam frogmen. The word was that the North Vietnamese were pissed, and they thought the frogmen were coming off the *Maddox*."

"Were they?" Greg felt a small thrill of excitement that helped dispel his queasiness. He knew that the South Vietnamese frogmen, the LDNN, were trained by U.S. Navy SEALs. The SEALs must have been close by that night.

"Hell, no. My guess is that *Maddox* was eavesdropping on the op, though. Listening to the dink radio transmissions, recording radar sweeps, checking on their reaction times, that kind of deep-spooky EW shit.

"Now, there's no doubt about it that the dinks attacked the *Maddox* that first afternoon. But where it gets kind of murky is what happened next. Y'see, the *Turner Joy* got ordered to join the *Maddox*, an' the two of us went in close again the next night, further south along the coast. There we were, runnin' in toward North Vietnam, just kinda darin' the dinks to come out and play. There was one hell of a squall blowin', lots worse than this 'un. She was blowin' a strong gale, an' no mistake. How bad a storm is that, Halstead?"

Greg hated these sudden, on-the-job inquisitions. It made him feel like he was still back in grade school, getting called on by the teacher. "Uh . . . Beaufort nine, Chief. Forty-one-to forty-seven-knot winds. Rolling seas, and visibility is cut down by spray."

"Fuckin' right. So anyway, the wind was howlin' an' the old *TJ* was bobbin' around like a cork. All of a sudden, we got the word that there was twenty-two fuckin' sonar contacts, comin' in from every point on the compass. They had the seventy-six-point-two mike-mikes bangin' away like a horny sailor on his first shore liberty in six months.

"Now, sonar claimed they had the contacts, an' radar claimed they picked up somethin', too, but nobody was able to confirm. It was a shitty night out, and the lookouts never saw anything, though the fire-control directors claimed they sunk three of the dinks. Christ on a crutch! They could've been lookin' at anything. Or nothing at-fuckin'-all."

"So what was it? A malfunction?"

"Sonar was picking up wave noise, probably. Radar could've been getting surface scatter. The point is that people was startin' to lose their heads. If anybody'd stopped and *thought* about what was goin' on. I mean, how fuckin' likely was it that those dink speedboats would try launching torps in a Beaufort-nine sea? Huh?''

For Greg, it was an interesting look at history in the making. Hell, he usually thought of history as stuff that had happened a long time ago, World War II and before, say, and the Gulf of Tonkin incident had taken place in early August of 1964, just over three and a half years ago. He was historian enough, though, to recognize that the front-page news of today was the historical footnote of a century hence. What fascinated him was the way an apparent series of accidental encounters, misidentifications, and poor judgment had led to Johnson's now-infamous Gulf of Tonkin Resolutions.

It hadn't *really* been a fraud, not entirely; the NVs had definitely attacked the *Maddox* on the afternoon of 2 August, though their reasons for doing so were a bit unclear . . . South Vietnamese LDNNs or not.

But Johnson had wanted more than one attack, in order to put America in a strong moral position. The events of the evening of 3 August had given him that position, letting him order retaliatory strikes against coastal targets near Haiphong from the carriers *Ticonderoga* and *Constellation*. It had let him demonstrate that he was not soft on communism—this in an election year—and it had let him win the authority he needed from Congress to widen the scope of America's involvement in Vietnam.

Was it possible, Greg the historian wondered, that other wars fought for glorious causes and with patriotic fervor had also started as blundering missteps, failed communications, and incompetence?

For several minutes now, Greg had managed to hold his rebellious stomach at bay by concentrating on Clayton's monologue, on holding the light, on the ironies of history. Now, though, the ship gave a particularly gut-wrenching roll, one that made his stomach feel like it was crawling up the inside of his throat. ''Uh . . . Chief.'' He clamped his mouth shut, swallowing his gorge. Nausea clawed at his gut and throat, the egg-stinking remnants of breakfast burning hot at the back of his mouth.

''Aw, shit, Frogface,'' Clayton said, disgusted. ''You're *not* gonna puke on me.''

The heat and closeness of the electronics access, the stink, the roll and pitch of the ship all conspired together to launch another assault on Greg's throat. "Chief . . . I'd better . . . get some . . . air."

"Shit. Go. *Go!* Get the fuck outa here."

"Th-thanks, Chief."

Slithering back out of the work space, fleeing the close warmth of the electronics suite, Greg bolted for the nearest passageway leading out, cranking open a watertight door and stepping into a blast of cold, wet air on the ship's starboard side, just aft of the bridge. A lookout on the flying bridge, bundled against the cold and wearing a bright orange life jacket and battle helmet, lowered his binoculars and glanced at him curiously.

Greg didn't vomit . . . not quite. Clinging to the life rail with white-knuckled determination, he gulped down lungful after lungful of cold air salty with sea spray. It was dark and overcast outside, with blue-black clouds scudding across the sky, and a heaving, dark sea streaked with lines of foam running in the direction of the wind. He was well above the water at this level, the ship's O-4 deck, but he was soaking wet in moments from the flying spray.

Another few days and they would be back at San Diego. That was good. That was *very* good. His first tour of sea duty had been interesting enough, taking him from San Diego to Pearl Harbor to Guam to Sasebo to Subic to Pearl again and now back home. The rolling of the ship had been strange at first, but he'd gotten used to it within a few days—"gotten his sea legs," as the old hands called it. But there'd been nothing along the way like this sickening, sour roll as the heavy seas came up on the *Edson*'s fantail. The worst of it was, there was no way to escape, no place to go to get away from the monotonous rise and fall and twist of the destroyer.

Maybe, he thought, *I should get back inside before Clayton gigs me for going AWOL.*

At the thought of returning to the cramped, hot confines of the electronics suite, however, his tortured stomach nearly rebelled once more. At the moment, there was nothing, *nothing* he wouldn't give for the solidity and unyielding firmness of solid ground.

Seasick. He was ashamed. Sailors weren't supposed to get *seasick*, for God's sake!

"Hey, Frogman, whatcha hanging over the rail like that for? Doing push-ups again?"

Greg turned and saw Bartlett grinning at him.

"Whoa, you look green-faced enough to be a SEAL already. Don't tell me this little, itty-bitty blow's turning your stomach, Halstead!"

"Knock it off, Bartlett. I feel like . . . like . . ." He stopped, trying to think of some way to describe the queasy churning in his insides.

"Like shit. That's what you feel like. I know, believe me," Bartlett said, leaning against the rail next to him.

"You know? What . . . ?"

"Yeah, sure, my first tour?" The first class shrugged. "Must've puked my guts out, oh, five or six times. We really had some weather that time. Got used to it, though. Eventually."

"Well, I don't think I'll ever get used to it. Maybe if I was on a carrier . . ."

"Aw, what would you want with one of those floating cities? Those damn things are so big you'd barely know you were aboard a ship. Where's the fun in being a sailor if you can't even tell you're at sea?"

"Yeah, well, that would suit me just fine, thank you very much." Greg managed to pull himself upright. "So. You call this an itty-bitty blow, huh? Man, I hate to be out in a real storm, then."

"Well, Met says this thing'll blow over by tonight, and we should have clear sailing all the rest of the way to Diego. Maybe then you'll get your chance to be a frog . . . man."

"Ribbit, ribbit," Greg said, and managed a weak smile. "I've got to pass the qualifier first."

"No problem, Frogman. As much PT as you do, you're in great shape. You're sure to pass, flyin' colors. C'mon, you can't let us twidgets down, now, can you?"

It was one of those ubiquitous nicknames that seemed to be spontaneously generated in the Navy, like snipes for engineers. Aboard ship all electronics technicians were twidgets.

"Hey, Bartlett, you got any idea where that came from? The name twidgets, I mean?"

He shrugged. "Hell, I don't know. My guess is it's because we're always twiddling knobs on electronic gadgets."

Greg laughed. "Sounds good, at any rate. Well, I'll do my best for the glory of the twidgets." He was beginning to feel better, though he wasn't sure if it was because his stomach was settling or just because talking with Bartlett was helping take his mind off it.

"So what's the news from the home front, Halstead," Bartlett asked. "Heard anything from that sister of yours lately?"

"Yeah." Greg frowned. "She keeps worrying about me."

Bartlett grinned. "What . . . she's afraid you'll get seasick?"

Greg mock-punched him and continued. "Naw, it's about me being a SEAL. First she got all freaked-out by Walter Cronkite talking about Vietnam being a stalemate and saying that if we don't negotiate it'll be major escalation, and then the *New York Times* came out with the story that Westmoreland is asking for 206,000 more troops, which seems to confirm the escalation theory. She's afraid that if I get into the SEALs, that by the time I'm through training the war'll be hotter 'n ever and I'll get sent over there."

"So is she afraid of you going into combat, maybe getting fragged . . . or is it just because it's Vietnam?"

Greg looked up and thought for a moment. He'd told Bartlett that Pat was against the war. "You know, I'm not really sure. She never was quite as deep into the antiwar stuff as Mar—I mean, as deep as some people I knew back in college, but she did go to marches and rallies and stuff. But lately she seems to have been, I don't know, kind of moving away from some of that. I know she's scared for me personally. What I don't know is, well, how she would feel about me really being a part of the war."

"Yeah, like would she be ashamed to admit she had a brother in the evil military, that kind of thing."

"Yeah." Greg thought back to his last conversation with Marci, almost a year ago. It didn't hurt to think of her anymore, at least not much. "There was someone in college.

she told Pat that since the Navy was part of the military-industrial complex, that someone in the Navy was just as . . . as guilty, I guess, as someone in the Army.''

"But Pat didn't buy it, did she?''

"I . . . I wasn't really paying much attention to her at the time. I guess she didn't. Her first letters back when I was in boot camp were pretty harsh, but she was kind of giving me the benefit of the doubt. Mar—'' He interrupted himself, the name sticking in his throat. "That other person never wanted to see me again.''

Bartlett nodded knowingly. "Ah. Your girl, huh?''

Greg didn't say anything, but he didn't deny it either.

"You gotta be careful with women, Halstead. Now I don't have a problem, my wife's a Navy brat like me, but you get someone who doesn't understand . . .'' He shook his head. "It can be a real bitch.''

"So what you doing married, Bartlett? I thought the rule was if the Navy wanted you to have a wife, they'd've issued you one with your seabag.''

Bartlett grinned. "Some rules are just made to be broken, Frogman.''

"Yeah, well, getting married's one thing I don't have to worry about right now. Not much chance to meet many girls aboard this bucket.''

"Ha! Y'got that right!''

"And from what I've heard I won't have a lot of free time during SEAL training. It'll be a long time before I'm looking for someone to hitch up with.''

"Don't be too sure of that, Frogger. I met Becky when I was back Stateside four years ago. Saw a lot of her for about a month, and then I was shipped out again. Six months and a heap of letters later I was back in port and we got married.''

"Where'd you meet her?''

"In the San Diego Library.''

"In the library! What the hell were *you* doing in a library, Bartlett?'' Greg pretended astonishment. Bartlett was probably the most literate sailor he knew. He often had a book with him during off-duty hours.

"A few of us do know how to read, Halstead.''

Greg turned and looked out to sea. His stomach was behaving pretty well for the moment. "Well, anyway right now my problem is not getting a girl, it's keeping my sister happy."

"Your problem may disappear come November. You heard the latest election news?"

"What? You mean McCarthy? I guess that's a hopeful sign for the peaceniks."

In a surprising showing, dark horse candidate Gene McCarthy had come within an ace of beating President Johnson in the New Hampshire primary. For Johnson to have come that close to losing a primary was definitely bad news so far as public support for his war effort was concerned.

"Yeah, not only that. I just picked this up yesterday. Bobby Kennedy's in the race now."

"Kennedy! I thought he said he wouldn't run against Johnson. Didn't want to split up the party, or something."

"Well, I guess he figured with what McCarthy did up in New Hampshire, the party's pretty well split already, so he might as well get a piece of the action."

"Well, I'll be damned."

"So tell that sister of yours that by the time you're ready to go, there may not be a war for you to go to. That should calm her down a bit." He pushed off from the railing and headed for the door Greg had come out of. "And if there still is a war by then, well, you'll have had that much more time to show her the error of her ways." With a grin he pushed through the door and was gone.

Greg walked along the starboard side railing for a bit, taking in deep breaths of the cold sea air. His stomach was pretty much back to normal, and he figured it was about time to get back inside. It had been good talking to Bartlett, though he hadn't yet decided what he wanted to say to Pat in his next letter. He was more determined than ever now to go to BUD/S and become a SEAL, but he didn't want to worry her, at least not more than he had to. Maybe next time he had leave, he could go back home and talk to Dad about it. His father would have had to deal with anxious family back home when he was stationed in the Pacific. Maybe he'd have some advice on how to handle Pat.

His next hurdle then was passing the qualifying exam and

getting into BUD/S. He'd been planning to apply for SEAL training ever since boot camp, but during this tour of sea duty, his desire had become increasingly urgent. He knew now he definitely wasn't cut out for life aboard ship. SEALs, he knew, had to go about in small boats, but he doubted that any assault craft could pitch and roll quite like this damned tin can. Hell, from what he'd heard, most of their ops in Vietnam were on rivers. Rivers he could handle. He'd been on the Russian River often enough, back in Jenner. Yeah, working on a river would be *great*.

Better yet, SEALs might sneak ashore from boats, but they wouldn't do it in a fucking *gale* . . . and they could always look forward to reaching the beach and moving about on solid ground once more.

God he wanted to be a SEAL. . . .

Chapter 9

Saturday, 23 March 1968

**National Naval Medical Center
Bethesda, Maryland
1315 hours**

"Come on, Doc," SN Bill Tangretti said. "I'm fine! I'm ready to go! How about a ticket out of this place?"

The doctor, a young lieutenant with the name Hoskins printed in white, engraved letters on the black plastic name tag pinned to his lab coat, looked up from the chart he was reading. "Son, do you have any idea how badly you were chewed up over there?"

Tangretti rubbed his stomach through his blue hospital robe. He was seated on his bed in Ward C. Elsewhere, nurses and hospital corpsmen made their rounds among the twenty or so other patients on the ward. Most, like him, were evacuees from Vietnam, though as far as he knew he was the only SEAL there. The rest, for the most part, were Marines evacked in from Danang, Hue, and Khe San.

"I have a pretty good idea, sir," he said. HM3 Raul Camacho had talked to him about his condition and even let him see his own chart once.

"I doubt that," Dr. Hoskins said. "I doubt that very much. You're lucky to be alive, and I'm damned if I'm going to let you go get yourself torn up again the moment we've got you pasted back together." He looked at the chart again. "SEAL, huh?"

"That's right."

"Something like UDT?"

"Something like that, sir."

"What the hell is a sailor doing getting shot at ashore? Corpsmen, I know, get shot at with the FMF all the time, but they're with the Marines. This SEAL thing is something new."

"We've been around since '62, sir. You haven't heard much about us because most of what we do is classified."

"Bunch of damned fool idiocy. You been a SEAL long?"

"A year now."

"Seen much action?"

"Yes, sir."

In point of fact, Tangretti hadn't seen that much action as a SEAL. Assigned to Bravo Platoon of SEAL Team One, he'd arrived in Vietnam in December of '67 and seen his first firefight two days before Christmas. One month and several firefights later, he'd been on patrol in the Rung Sat and managed to trigger a damned VC booby trap.

It was funny, really. He didn't remember actually being hurt. At the time, he'd felt something hit his back, but he'd brushed off Doc Randolph, grabbed his weapon, and kept going, convinced he was fine. It turned out later that a piece of shrapnel had gone right through his guts, punching through his small intestines and nicking a hepatic vein in the process. He'd damn near bled to death internally before Doc noticed him getting woozy and checked him over more carefully. He remembered nothing at all about the emergency surgery in Nha Be . . . or the medevac flight back to Bethesda Naval Hospital. He'd woken up a few days later and found himself back Stateside.

He'd been lucky, though most of the luck could be attributed to the skill of the medical personnel who'd picked him up and passed him along, from Doc Randolph on the ground in the Rung Sat all the way back to NNMC in the States.

The U.S. military forces in Vietnam had the most efficient medical triage and evacuation system ever known in any war. If a Navy hospital corpsman or Army medic could reach a wounded man and get him aboard a medevac helicopter within a few minutes of his being hit—and this was usually the case—his chances of survival were better than ninety percent. From a rear-area hospital, then, the more serious casualties were flown out of the combat zone; a wounded man could be at Clark Field in the Philippines less than two hours after leaving Nam, at Yokosuka, Japan, in six, or all the way back to the World, at a military hospital in the United States, in less than twenty-four hours.

Tangretti had survived, though he'd needed several rounds of abdominal surgery and numerous units of blood, and his intestines were a couple of feet shorter now than they'd been before. But except for a certain amount of soreness in his belly muscles when he stood or walked, he was ready to go. Sore? He'd felt a lot worse during Hell Week.

The doctor checked his eyes and ears, then had him lie down on the hospital bed and open his robe and pajamas. Carefully, Hoskins palpated his belly.

"Any pain?"

"Not a bit, sir!" He thumped his own stomach a couple of times above one of the surgery scars, ignoring the pain. "See?"

"Hmm. Nice try, son, but I've patched up some of you gung-ho types before. You're going to need at least six months more of light duty before you even think about re-joining your unit. And I'll tell it to you straight . . . there's a good chance that you won't be able to go back to being a SEAL."

That was bullshit, Tangretti thought, but he wasn't about

to say it to the doctor's face. Instead, he decided to try a different approach, one he'd been working on for over a week now.

"You know, sir, I don't plan to go back to the Teams immediately."

"No?"

"I never did get my rating. You know, like gunner's mate?"

"Your A-school. Certainly." The doctor nodded.

"And I'm going to have to get one pretty soon now. Basically, I have a year from the time I become a SEAL to qualify."

"What'd you have in mind?"

"Actually, I was thinking about the Hospital Corps."

Hoskins's eyebrows jerked higher on his forehead. "A corpsman? You?"

"Yes, sir."

"Why?"

Tangretti pulled his robe closed and sat up once more. Damn, he *was* sore down there, but he refused to show it. "My grades in high school were pretty good," he said. "And I always liked biology, that kind of stuff. And, well, I've been talking to some of the guys here on the ward. The corpsmen here. I kind of like what I've been hearing, you know?"

"They're good people." Hoskins began writing on the chart. "So what would you do once you become a corpsman, Tangretti? Go FMF?" Corpsmen in the Fleet Marine Force served with the Marines, who, unlike the Army, had no medics of their own.

"No, sir, I'm a SEAL. SEALs draw from Navy corpsmen, too."

He was thinking about Doc Randolph, the Team One SEAL who'd saved his ass in the Rung Sat. Until recently, the Teams had used FMF corpsmen, just like the Marines, but a few docs had gone through the entire BUD/S course, and from now on it was likely that most Team corpsmen would be SEALs.

"Well, at least you wouldn't have to pack a gun anymore," Hoskins said. "That'd be against the Geneva Convention, right?"

Tangretti carefully said nothing at that. In Bravo Platoon, Doc had always been armed, usually with an M-16. In fact, going out on patrol or an ambush, there'd been no way, just looking at Doc, to tell that he was any different from the other thirteen SEALs in the platoon. He carried an extra medical kit or two, and that was all.

"You applied yet?"

"I've sent in the paperwork, sir."

"Good. Good. I'll tell you what, son," Hoskins continued. "I'll put in a word for you with my commanding officer. That's Captain Hamilton. He's big on continuing education, and he knows people back at Great Lakes. Maybe we can get a recommendation put together for you."

"I'd appreciate that, sir."

"We'll see what we can do for you. Meanwhile, you stay in bed and give those wounds a chance to heal up. You hear me?"

"Yes, sir!"

A moment after Hoskins had left, HM3 Camacho walked over to Tangretti's bed. He was a small, dark Latino kid who'd had night duty a couple of weeks earlier, when Tangretti was just starting to take an interest in the world again. They'd started by trading sea stories—and Camacho was fascinated by Tangretti's stories of life in Vietnam.

"So, how'd it go?" Camacho asked.

"Okay, I think," Tangretti said. "I told him about my wanting to go to Corps School, and he said he'd put a word in for me."

"Hey, that's great!"

Tangretti chuckled. "He also said I wouldn't have to carry a gun if I went back to Nam."

"Ha! I know this HM1 up on Tower Three who went FMF," Camacho said. "He was with the 3rd Marines, and he said that he always went out armed with a sawed-off shotgun. When an ambush went down, blam! Blam! He started seeing how many trees he could cut down, man. Blasting away in every direction."

"He ever hit anything?"

"He never said. I doubt it. He's waiting for lab school now, so I guess he'll be drawing blood in other ways, now."

"How about you, Camacho? You ever think about going with the fleet?"

"Nah. I don't look good in green, man. I'm happy juggling bedpans and passing out meds. Put in my four and then I'm out. Hell, I joined the Navy so I wouldn't get drafted and sent to Vietnam, y'know?"

"Beats running off to Canada, I guess."

"You got that right. Uh, oh. Here comes the boss bitch, and she's definitely got a stick up her ass. I'd better look like I'm busy."

Lieutenant Commander Brewster, the ward's head nurse, stalked past a moment later, crisp and immaculate in her white uniform, her shoes click-clacking across the linoleum floor. She took no notice of Tangretti.

He was a little surprised by Camacho's admission. The corpsman had been so interested in his stories about Vietnam during their bull sessions that Tangretti had figured he was eager to go. Well . . . Tangretti had been there, and he knew that anyone eager to go to Nam was certifiable.

At least . . . unless they had a *reason* to go back.

For Bill Tangretti, there'd never been any question about what he would do. His father had been UDT in World War II, stayed with the Teams throughout the long years of the Cold War, and been a SEAL Team plank owner, one of the people who'd started the SEALs back in 1962 when John F. Kennedy himself had called for a new Navy special operations unit along the lines of the Army Special Forces. Like his half brother, TM2 Hank Richardson, Tangretti had enlisted in the Navy with a special request for BUD/S and the SEALs, knowing at the time that sooner or later they would be going to Southeast Asia. That, after all, was where the war was, and a SEAL's business was war.

Both of them had made it, too. Hank was still in Vietnam, as far as Tangretti knew, serving with Team Two on the Bassac River on the Delta. When Tet had gone down, he'd been way up the Bassac near the Cambodian border, where he'd gotten into a nasty fight with VC and NVA forces in a city called Chau Doc. SEALs didn't usually find themselves fighting house to house, but Team Two had taken it in stride, teaming up with Special Forces and Nung mercenaries to root the enemy out of the city block by block, rescuing some American nurses, and generally kicking ass and taking names.

Bill had never wanted to be anything else but UDT and then—when they came along—a member of the SEAL Teams, for as far back as he could remember. The moment he'd finally realized that he'd actually made it through Hell Week—after a shower, a hot meal, and twelve hours' sleep—had been the proudest in his life . . . and he'd been even prouder a few months later when he was assigned to Bravo Platoon, Team One, an honest-to-God SEAL at last. Even so, he was not typical SEAL material. He'd never been much of an athlete, never gone out for sports in high school or played games more strenuous than touch football with the neighbor kids. Short and a bit on the thin side, he was wiry rather than strong, and his instructors in BUD/S had leaned on him hard, certain that he wasn't going to make the cut.

He'd fooled them all. He'd fooled himself, since he'd not been sure himself that he was going to make it. His lifeline throughout BUD/S had been the knowledge that he *had* to make it, because if he didn't, he didn't have anywhere else to go.

"Hello there, Bill."

He started, sitting up so suddenly he felt the sudden pull in his belly like fire. "Mom! Hi!"

Veronica Tangretti stood beside his bed, her purse clasped tightly in both hands before her. "Visiting hours aren't supposed to be for another fifteen minutes, but they let me come on in anyway," she said. "I think they're getting used to seeing me hanging around the nurses' station."

"It's good to see you."

She leaned forward and kissed him. "They say you're lots better," she said, a little too brightly, Tangretti thought. "They say you'll be able to come home soon."

Did she sound hopeful? Or scared? Or possibly a little of both? Tangretti wasn't sure, but he knew that his mother was dreading the thought of him going back to the war.

The past few months had been especially rough on his

mother, he knew. She had not one, but *three* men in the Teams—him, Hank, and their dad, Steve Tangretti. She'd already lost one husband in another war; Hank's father had also been UDT, a member of the Navy Combat Demolition Units that had stormed *Festung Europa* on D-Day. He'd died on Omaha Beach. After the war, Veronica had married her husband's best friend—Steve Tangretti.

As far as Bill knew—though he was aware that parents often tried to hide things from their kids—theirs had been a happy marriage, if a somewhat unsettled one. Steve's career in the UDT had sent the family all over the globe, sometimes to some pretty wild places. He could remember a certain tension in the air, though, just after the SEAL Teams had been created in '62. Steve had been suddenly called away for several weeks at just about the time of the Cuban missile crisis. And after that, he'd been among the first of the SEALs deployed to South Vietnam to work with the locals in building up their own military capabilities.

For the past six years, Steve Tangretti had been gone more than he'd been at home, and both Bill and Hank had enlisted in the Navy, applied for BUD/S and, in turn, been deployed to Vietnam as well.

The strain was telling on Veronica. Hank had come through Tet all right, though Bill had heard that another SEAL in his platoon had been killed at Chau Doc. Bill had been wounded just before Tet. Dad had been wounded during Tet, and after a short stay at the Naval Hospital in Oceanside, California, he'd somehow managed to wangle a transfer to Bethesda.

So he could be with his son, though he would never admit that to Bill.

"So. Is Dad coming in today?" The elder Tangretti had been discharged from the hospital a week ago and was currently on leave. He'd been staying at home, back in Norfolk. Bill had taken that as a good sign; there'd been times, lately, when Steve had stayed on base rather than going home.

Not a healthy sign.

"Steve—Your dad said he'd be in a little later," she said. "He drove up with me, but he had some people to see here."

She shook her head. "You know him. Always the wheeler-dealer. Making *connections*."

Bill nodded. "That's the Seabee in him."

Before the creation of the Underwater Demolition teams in World War II, Steve Tangretti had been in the Navy Construction Battalion, the Seabees, a unit notorious both for its "Can do" motto and for the inventiveness of its personnel in performing the impossible and in manipulating the system. The elder Tangretti had a rep as a cumshaw king, someone who could find anything, however unlikely, from a distributor cap to a destroyer, no matter where in the world he happened to be. He'd been in the Navy now for . . . what? Twenty-seven, twenty-eight years, maybe. When you were in that long, you made connections, you knew people, and they owed you favors.

"He's put in his request for orders." His mother was carefully not looking at him. Bill had the impression she was trying not to cry. She looked like she'd been crying recently. "His *dream* sheet, he calls it."

"Where's he want to go?"

She shook her head. "Back . . . to that place. Damn him, he's *requesting* it. Sometimes I could just *shoot* him!"

Vietnam. It figured. "He's too senior to be put in a DA platoon, Mom." Direct Action platoons were usually led by lieutenants, but his father had too much time in grade and—*face it, Dad*—he was getting too old to wade around in the mud with kids half his age, setting ambushes and playing John Wayne games. "They'll probably stick him in Puzzle Palace East, or a staff command."

Puzzle Palace East was the popular name for the Military Assistance Command–Vietnam headquarters, an immense facility located between Saigon and the capital's Tan Son Nhut airport.

"Is that supposed to make me feel good? The enemy attacked the airport, you know, during Tet."

"Yeah, but they didn't get anywhere. And from what I've been hearing, they smashed themselves up so bad at Tet that they're going to have real problems continuing the war. I really wouldn't worry about it."

Somehow, the words seemed so inadequate.

"He was with Det Echo," Veronica said, a little bitterly, "when he was wounded. He'll probably be going right back into that. Working with those . . . those *people*."

Meaning, Bill thought, the Vietnamese. Det Echo had been working a lot both with the Vietnamese LDNNs and with the PRUs, the Provincial Reconnaissance Units. The idea was to set up small-scale Vietnamese SEALs and intelligence-gathering units, to get away from the monster-unit, bomb-'em-back-to-the-Stone-Age mentality that seemed to have mired both the Army and the Air Force. But he knew his mother didn't like the idea of Steve—or her sons—off by themselves in the bush, with no one to rely on but locals who might well turn out to be the enemy.

"He'll be okay, Mom," he said, feeling helpless. He never knew how to deal with her. "Really. When he got hit, that was when he was trying to warn somebody that Tet was going down. He got caught in the attack. It had nothing to do with his duties with the PRUs."

She sighed. "Bill, if there's excitement to be found, your father will find it. He's that kind of guy." She bit her lip, hesitated, and almost said something else . . . before reconsidering. "Anyway, we're not here to talk about him. How are you doing? Really?"

"I'm doing great. And you're right. They're talking about releasing me soon."

"Have you given any thought about . . . after that?"

She wants to know if I'm going to go back to the Nam, he thought. For a moment, he weighed the choice, wondering what to tell her. She would be relieved if he told her about his decision to try for Corps School . . . and the relief might make it that much harder when she learned that he was going to try to get back with his old platoon just as soon as he'd secured his rating. Corps School was four months long, and according to Camacho, he'd be assigned to pay-your-dues duty after that—probably with six months working on a hospital ward, like this one. There might also be a delay before he could be assigned to a class in Corps School.

Well, that gave him anywhere from four months to a year of grace, before he had to deal with that question.

"Actually," he said slowly, "I'm thinking of striking for

hospital corpsman. I've got to choose a rate, you know, and, well, the doctors here aren't going to let me go back to the SEALs, at least not right away.''

His mother's eyes widened. "The Hospital Corps!" He could almost see her thoughts chasing one another. He wouldn't be going back to the Teams. He might get sent out to the FMF, which would mean serving as a combat medic with the Marines . . . and getting shot at. Maybe he would give up being a SEAL and settle for duty in a hospital Stateside, or aboard a ship that likely would never see combat.

"That's . . . wonderful, Bill," she said, and he knew she wasn't sure yet whether it was wonderful or not. "So, you might end up down at Norfolk Naval Hospital, close enough to come home on weekends if you want."

"Well, maybe."

"Or would you want to go back to the SEALs?"

The question was out, point-blank.

"I don't really know, Mom," he lied. "I guess it'll be the same old story. 'Convenience of the government.' They want me someplace, that's where they'll send me."

"It's always that way," she said, a little bitterly.

The conversation veered to safer topics, after that. Half an hour later, Lieutenant Steve Tangretti entered the ward, leaning on a cane. "Hey, sailor!" he boomed. "How's the belly?"

Bill pulled himself up in the bed, extending his hand. "Great, Dad. Hey, it's good to see you!"

They clasped hands, and Steve clapped his son on the shoulder. "*Damn* it's good to see you sitting up like that!"

Steve Tangretti was an imposing six-one, with a squat, bluff, hard-as-nails attitude that reminded Bill of some old Navy chiefs that he'd known. His father was wearing his blue jacket, of course, and the ribbons covering his left breast gave him an oddly lopsided look. Bronze Star, with the added stars meaning he'd won the award more than once. Purple Heart. Navy Commendation Ribbon. Presidential Unit Citation. Hell, the three-wide rack of colored ribbons ran halfway down his chest to his belt.

In fact, he looked more like a chief than a lieutenant; he often joked about being the oldest lieutenant in the U.S.

Navy, and that probably wasn't far from the truth. He was a mustang, having started out as an enlisted man in World War II, and winning his commission in the late fifties.

"Bill was just telling me that he's thinking of becoming a corpsman."

His dad nodded approvingly. "Good rate. And the Teams can sure use 'em, that's for sure. You were telling me once you had a good doc in your platoon, weren't you?"

"John Randolph," Bill said. "Yeah." He looked at his mother, a little nervously. "You know, Dad, it's still not a sure bet that I'll even be able to go back to the Teams. The doctor just told me—"

"Shit, what do those quacks know?" his father said with a snort.

"Steve!" Veronica cried.

"Well, I mean it! Talk to some of the guys who've been there." He gestured at the other beds in the ward. "Talk to some of these boys in here. You'd be astonished at what the human spirit can accomplish that these doctor-types can't begin to appreciate!"

"I think I have some small idea about what the human spirit can accomplish," Veronica said, barely suppressing her anger. "And also what it can endure. But by God, there's a limit!"

"Jesus, Ron," Steve said, looking away. "Let's not go through this again."

"Yes, we're going to go through this again. We'll go through this again until you get it through that thick frogman skull of yours that—"

"The kid can do anything he damn well wants to, Ron, without having us push him around."

"That's exactly right, Steve! He can do anything, be anything . . . and he doesn't have to be one of your damned SEALs!"

"Uh, Mom?" Bill said. "Dad? We really don't need to discuss this here, do we?" It was embarrassing enough, sometimes, having his parents visit him on the ward, without having them starting a fight over him.

"He's right, Ron," Steve said. "Let's drop anchor on this right now."

"Sure," she said. Her eyes were red. She looked away. "Look . . . I'm going to go to the head and freshen up. You two . . . go ahead and talk." She patted Bill's arm. "Bill, I'm glad you're so much better. I'll see you again after a while, okay?"

"Sure, Mom. And . . ."

"Yes?"

"I don't know. Just, don't worry, okay? I'm going to be okay."

"I know. I'm . . ." She shook her head. "I know. Bye, now."

She turned and walked off the ward, back ramrod straight.

"She worries about us," Steve said. "I guess that's part of being a Navy wife and mother, huh?"

"Dad, about me going back to the Nam . . ."

He held up his hand. "Listen, son. Don't volunteer for a second tour because of anything you think I might feel about it, okay? You're my son, I'm damned proud of you, and whatever you decide to do is A-okay with me, right?"

"Sure. But, well, I guess I'm really kind of confused."

"Getting wounded'll do that. You know, Bill, your mother is scared that you're going to go back over there, maybe get your ass shot off again. And I can't blame her. If you want to know the truth, I don't want you to go back either."

Bill's eyes widened. "You don't?"

"Hell, she's scared because she's got a husband and two sons who might get killed. But you and me, we've been there, with unfriendly little brown brothers trying to make us dead." He sighed. "Bill, you put in your time over there. You joined up when other kids were running off to Canada or scrambling for college deferments. You volunteered for the toughest damned training in the Navy, hell, in the whole armed forces, and you toughed it out. You got your orders to the Nam and you went. You did your duty and maybe saved the life of one of your buddies over there. For my money, no one, *no one* could possibly ask any more of you."

" 'And when he gets to heaven, to Saint Peter he will tell,' " Bill quoted. " 'Another Marine reporting, sir, I've done my time in Hell.' "

"Where'd you pick that up?"

Bill shrugged. "One of the Marines on the ward, here. Seems appropriate for anyone who's been in Vietnam, though."

"Roger that. You've done your time, and I, for one, would be damned happy to see you land a nice, soft, safe billet Stateside, somewhere. Here at Bethesda, maybe, or some nice, tropical paradise where the natives aren't always shooting at you."

"I hear Roosevelt Roads, Puerto Rico, is nice."

"That's the ticket."

"There's just one thing."

"What's that?"

"The Teams, Dad. I can't let them down."

"You didn't. You came through when it mattered. You've got a Bronze Star and a Purple Heart that say so."

"I was there one month. A little over. Then *I* tripped the booby trap, remember, and almost got me and Lucky killed both. I feel like, I don't know. Like I left the guys holding the bag for me, you know?"

"Sure. That's part of being in the Teams. Always has been, with the UDT long before the SEALs were even a gleam in JFK's eye. I think it's the training that brings men together. BUD/S . . . and the buddy system they're always stressing. It gets you so you'd go to the moon for your buddies if you had to . . . or follow your skipper into Hell."

"Maybe. But it means that, well, I can't say I'm eager about going back to the Nam. I keep trying to, you know, to picture what it would be like . . . and all I can imagine now is that I'm going to be so damned scared of booby traps when I get in-country again that I, well, I might not be able to do my job. At the same time, how can I look Lucky or the L-T or Doc or any of the rest of them in the face again if I don't go back and pull my weight?"

Steve Tangretti sat in the chair for a long moment, arms folded, thinking. At last, he stood up. "I don't have any easy answers, son. And I sure as hell don't want to be the one to say something to make you go back. I'd be happier if you didn't."

"You could wrangle things, you know. I mean, I don't want you to, you understand, but you *could.* . . ."

"Yeah, and then I'd have to live with myself afterward. Cumshaw and old-boy networks are all fine and good, but I'm not going to screw up your life for you that way. I think you know that."

"I do, Dad. And I appreciate that."

"Everywhere you went in the Navy afterward, people would be saying, 'Hey, there's the guy whose daddy fixed things for him so he didn't have to go into combat.' Hell, it would be the kiss of death to your career. I won't do it." He hesitated. "As much as I might *want* to."

Bill shook his head. "And I wouldn't want you to."

"So far as being afraid of booby traps, well, all I can say is that, over there, the war can get damned personal. Especially for SEALs. It's not like it is for the flyboys, tootling along at forty thousand feet with a hot cup of coffee, push the button, and bombs away. It's you against some guy named Nguyen or Minh or Thanh, and you're trying to kill or disable him, and he's trying to kill or disable you, right?"

"Yeah. . . ."

"When Charlie Nguyen sets a booby trap, it doesn't have to kill you to disable you, does it? It could just blow your foot off. Or . . ." Steve leaned forward, tapping his finger against the side of his head. "Or it could just fuck you up here. In your head, where it *really* counts. That'll disable a man just as thoroughly as a chunk of shrapnel through the belly, and that's all Mr. Charlie really wants, isn't it?"

"You're saying it's all a mind game?"

"That's all war ever is, son. A mind game. Our politicians try to pressure their politicians, fucking with their heads, and theirs with ours. When the war starts, then, it's our soldiers against their soldiers, fucking with their heads. And them with ours. I guess all I'm trying to say is, you don't *have* to be a casualty."

"I don't know if I can help it."

"That's part of what SEAL training's all about, Bill. The knowledge that you can stand anything, because you've already been through it before. Think of the booby traps that way. You can stand it, because you've been through it before."

"Yeah. Yeah, I guess you're right."

"Just remember, Bill. You don't have to go back to Nam. And your mother and, well, and me, we'd both be a lot happier if you didn't. But you've got to do what you think is right." He grinned. "Hell, I gave up trying to tell you what to do a long time ago! You're big enough to make your own decisions."

"Well, I've got some time, you know. If I get accepted for Corps School, it could be six months or a year before I even see the Teams again."

"That's no time at all, son," Steve said. "Believe me, it's no time at all. Blink twice . . ." He snapped his fingers. "And you're there."

For a long time that afternoon, after his parents left, Bill Tangretti lay on his bed and thought about Vietnam.

He wondered what his buddies in Bravo Platoon were doing now. . . .

Chapter 10

Sunday, 21 April, 1968

Bravo Platoon Headquarters, SEAL Team One
Nha Be, Republic of Vietnam
0940 hours

"Come in, Lucky," Lieutenant Baxter said. "Grab yourself some chair. There's lifer's blood in the pot over there, if you want it."

As Luciano poured himself a mug full of the vile, black brew, Lieutenant Baxter shoved the papers on the gray metal desk in front of him to one side with an exasperated sigh. The paperwork, it seemed, never stopped.

"Keeping your head above water, L-T?" Luciano asked

as he slumped into the offered chair, coffee in hand.

"Shit, Lucky. They should've had us wading around in paperwork back at BUD/S, instead of mud. It'd have been more realistic."

"Oh, I don't know. We have our share of mud out here, too. Of course, it's not as *hostile* as the paperwork. A man can die from paper cuts out here."

"Paper cuts. Shit. Drowning's more like it. Or maybe writer's cramp. These REMF assholes want us to account for every round, every patrol, every gallon of gas for the PBRs. Pretty soon we'll be asked to write a full report on step, comma, every one taken, comma, BUPERS authorized, period."

"Shit, Lieutenant. You've got the wrong attitude. If the bureaucrats don't know what you're doing out here, how the hell can they tax it?"

"There's a scary thought."

"So you wanted to see me, sir?"

Baxter nodded. "Afraid so. What's your feelings about the Vietnamese, Lucky?"

"The gooks, sir? Their gooks or our gooks?"

"Ours."

Luciano shrugged. "That's kind of a broad question, Lieutenant. Marvin ARVN isn't worth the powder and detcord to blow him up. But some of the others are okay."

"The LDNNs."

"Sure. I like Lieutenant Thanh. He's okay—" Luciano stopped, biting off the end of the sentence.

"You were going to say 'Okay for a gook.' "

"Something like that."

"Could you work with them?"

"The LDNNs? Or the VNs? Shit, Lieutenant. You've heard the saying about the South Vietnamese flag, haven't you? The VNs are just like their flag. Half-red, half-yellow."

"Is that entirely fair? There are some good, brave men among them. And a lot of the others, well, I think the thing to remember is that they didn't ask for this war. For centuries they've been ruled by various foreign powers. The French. The Japanese. Now a lot of them see us as the new colonialist rulers. Most would rather that the rest of us, Americans and

North Vietnamese and Chinese and Russians and everyone the hell else, would just leave them alone. And some of the LDNNs are pretty damned good people." He grinned. "Even by SEAL standards."

"Those that hung around, yeah."

"What do you mean?"

"Well, the word is that some of our boys were over here right after the SEALs got started up, training the first batch of VN SEALs. On graduation day, half of 'em vanished, went right over the hill. They went north and set up Hanoi's version of a frogman program."

"Shit, Lucky. It wasn't quite that bad."

"That's the way I heard it." Luciano's eyes narrowed. "Hey, Lieutenant. What gives? You're not chewing me out for my bad attitude about the gooks, are you?"

"No. No, I'm not. But I am telling you to cut out that 'gook' shit. And I'm asking you to volunteer for something."

"Never volunteer for anything. Isn't that the Navy creed?"

"You volunteered for the SEALs."

He shrugged. "Hell, seemed like the thing to do at the time."

"Tell me what you think about the PRUs?"

Luciano made a face. "Aw, shit, Lieutenant. You wouldn't!"

"Believe it. I would."

"I'm a SEAL, L-T, not a goddamned *advisor*." He made the word sound like profanity.

"You finished with that shit?"

"Yes, sir."

"Very well. I regret to inform you, Lucky, that this war cannot always be managed to suit your convenience."

"Ain't that the fuckin' truth!"

"So." Baxter tipped his chair back. "You want a short-version briefing? Learn the straight skinny on why we're shagging your ass to the indigs?"

"Shoot."

"Okay. Here it is. Bravo Platoon is being redeployed as of the twenty-fifth of this month. Things have been getting quiet in the Rung Sat lately. Charlie's beaten there, and he knows it. The boss wants us to take the war to greener pastures.''

"The boss" was Captain Walter Klass, recently designated commodore of NAVSPECWARGRU-VN, the head honcho in charge of all Naval Special Warfare operations in Vietnam.

"Bravo Platoon is going to be operating down in the Delta for a time," Baxter continued. "Can Tho, on the Bassac River. We'll be taking part in Operation Game Warden, in which we'll be working in support both of Team Two and of several PRUs that have been operating in the area, along with our riverine forces. At the same time, I've been directed to provide one experienced man to work with the PRU in Vinh Binh Province."

"You've already been doing a lot of that PRU shit, haven't you, Lieutenant?"

"I haven't been in the field with any of the teams," Baxter replied. "But I've been working part-time, you might say, with some of the people up at NAVSPECWARGRU-VN. And I've been run through a quick course on PRU administration, with the idea that I can further train other people I think would be an asset."

Standing, Baxter went to the wall of his office, where a pull-down map of the southern half of South Vietnam hung from one curving, sheet-metal wall. "The Mekong Delta is distinct from the Rung Sat," he said, "though most of the REMFs back in Saigon don't know the difference." He'd been over the basic geography of the Mekong Delta more times than he cared to remember, while delivering briefings to Naval and Army officers at NAVSPECWARGRU-VN headquarters. He reached up with one forefinger and pointed out green, yellow, and blue areas of the map. "Okay, here's Saigon, the Sai Gon River, the Soi Rap, and the Rung Sat Special Zone up here. Down here, you have the so-called 'nine mouths of the Mekong.' The real Mekong Delta. The locals call the Mekong *Song Cuu Long*, the River of the Nine Dragons. That's supposed to refer to the nine mouths of the Mekong." He gave a lopsided grin. "Actually, there's only eight mouths, but eight is an unlucky number for the Vietnamese, so they squint their eyes and pretend there's one more. From northeast to southwest, and keeping things simple, the rivers are the My Tho, the Ham Luong, the Co Chien, and the Hau Giang, each with a big enough island at the end of it to turn one river mouth into two. The Hau Giang is usually known by its French name, the Bassac.

"Vinh Binh Province is this part here, between the Bassac and the Co Chien, and from this line between Vinh Long and Can Tho down to the sea. About twice the size of the Rung Sat, maybe twelve hundred square miles, and nearly all of it rice paddies."

"Open and flat," Luciano said. "Shit. No place to hide your ass."

"There's rivers and there's canals and there's mud," Baxter replied. "Nothing in the rule books say we have to stay in the jungle. In fact, anybody who went through BUD/S mud at Coronado's going to feel right at home."

"Roger that."

"The Mekong Delta is Vietnam's breadbasket," Baxter said. "Or, maybe 'rice basket' is more appropriate. The land is incredibly rich. Charlie has to control it if he's going to have a chance of winning this war."

"I thought the reports all said we had Charlie beat, sir."

"We've had him on the ropes since Tet, that's for sure. There've been reports from various intelligence sources, mostly captured VC or Hoi Chanhs, that the Viet Cong's NVA sponsors are starting to turn a lot of them loose, telling them to grow their own food, and raid American and ARVN dumps for weapons and ammo. That makes the Delta region more important to Charlie than ever. If he can control the Delta, he'll be able to feed himself . . . not to mention demonstrating to the civilian population that the Saigon government and the Americans can't protect their own food-producing regions. Our job is to deny this region to Charlie. "

Baxter tugged on the map and let it roll back up into its tube with a crack. Returning to his desk, he dropped into his chair.

"I know how you feel about the Provincial Reconnaissance Units, Lucky. Lots of the others feel the same way.

But there's a growing feeling within the American brass that we're not going to be able to fight this war for Saigon indefinitely. With our victory at Tet—and I'll remind you that the win was due as much to the success of the ARVN forces as to ours—Washington is beginning to get the idea that maybe Saigon will be able to prosecute the war to a successful conclusion on their own.''

Luciano grinned. "You believe that, sir?"

"It doesn't much matter what I believe," Baxter replied. "You know, there're a lot of people back in the World who think this war is wrong, who think we shouldn't be here. Sometimes I wonder if they're not right. It's kind of hard to imagine what our country's strategic interest might be in a hellhole like this.

"But right now, my orders are to set up platoon operations in Vinh Binh Province, to deny rice to rebel forces, and to develop the capacity of loyal indigenous forces to defend themselves and to undertake operations on their own against the enemy. And I intend to follow those orders."

"Yes, *sir*."

"As I said, Lucky, this is a volunteer operation. If you don't want a piece of it, nothing will—"

"Shit, L-T. I didn't say I didn't want a piece."

"Then you're in?"

"Hell, yeah, I'm in. Just one question."

"Shoot."

"Why me? Why *ask* me, I mean?" He shrugged. "Hell, you're the one with the experience with the friggin' PRUs."

"I'm not going," Baxter replied, "because I have a platoon to run, in case you haven't noticed.

"I asked you first because this is your third tour. You're one of the few men in Bravo with three tours' worth of experience with the people, and the country. You speak enough Vietnamese to get by."

"*Cam on, Ong,*" Luciano said. He made the expression, "Thank you, sir," sound sharply ironic. "But I didn't think learning the lingo would get me stuck off by myself in a rice paddy. Makes me feel like the bad boy at school, getting sent to stand in the corner."

"It won't be like we're abandoning you, Lucky. You'll

report to me periodically, as well as to Naval Intelligence directly, and you'll be working for . . ." He stopped to check the name on one of the papers in front of him. "Lieutenant Waters. A SEAL. He'll be running the advisors' group that you're being assigned to. Also, you'll be able to call on MACV for whatever air assets you need, both for transport, and for gunships. And if you need a platoon of SEALs, all you have to do is shout."

"That's nice to know."

"You'll have several liaison officers to deal with," Baxter continued. "Good people, most of 'em."

"These liaison officers. Christians in Action?" The tag was a popular SEAL nickname for the CIA.

"A number of the PRUs started out under Agency control," Baxter agreed. "The spooks are still running quite a few of them, mostly up north, on the Cambodian border. Our liaisons in the PRUs, for the most part, will be LDNN. Part of turning the show over to the indigs. The Agency's not happy about losing so many of its *assets*." He mouthed the word as though it had an unpleasant taste. "But, well, into every life some rain must fall."

"How about the PRU cadres, sir? I've heard . . . well, let's say, unflattering things about them."

Baxter chuckled. "That's putting it mildly, son. They are mercenaries, start to finish, and a tougher bunch of black-hearted bastards you'll never encounter . . . unless they're SEALs. Some of them are Nungs or Montagnards, who don't fit in with the Vietnamese culture to begin with. Some are Chinese bandits . . . Kuomintang left over from 1947. Some of them might be ARVN deserters."

"Deserters?"

"The ones who don't mind fighting, but who don't like ARVN pay or discipline. Most of them were South Vietnamese criminals who were given a choice—join the PRU or rot in a Saigon jail."

Luciano made a face. "Just fucking *wonderful!*"

"Well, hey!" Baxter spread his hands. "Isn't it nice to work with dedicated people with a genuine cause?"

"A cause, right. Money?"

"Yup. And that's an A-number-one problem, too."

"In what way?"

Baxter folded his arms across his chest, and shook his head. "God, you would never believe it. How long, do you think, have we been out here trying to pound home the idea with the brass that we need intel? That we need *prisoners* who can provide us with intel . . . to let us follow the VC infrastructure up the tree to higher and higher branches."

"Hell, I don't know. As long as I've been here."

"Affirmative. Our Christian friends set up the PRUs originally by establishing bounties for prisoners, for captured weapons, for enemy KIAs. Turns out that Saigon's bounty for a KIA is higher than for a prisoner."

"You're shitting me!"

"Nope. I speak the gospel truth. It's one of the points I've been fighting to change lately, in my dealings with NAV-SPECWARGRU-VN and the brass, but so far, no go. When you're out there with your people, Lucky, I want you to stress the importance of taking prisoners. We need intel. If we don't know what Charlie is planning, we're stuck. Believe me, Hanoi can grow new bad guys a hell of a lot faster than we can kill them off. If we have prisoners, we can get more prisoners . . . and more after that. Pretty soon, we'll nail the big fry, as well as find their caches of weapons, ammo, rice, and everything else they need to maintain a viable position down here. Do you read me?"

"Loud and clear, Lieutenant."

"One thing more."

"Yeah?"

"Some of the people in the PRU are likely to be VC."

"I'd already gotten that idea."

"Most of the PRUs are probably riddled with Communist informers, at the least. Some are probably just there for the money."

"How do you mean?"

"Sort of like taking a night job, you know? Being a guerrilla really isn't that good a career move. Lousy pay. Not much in the way of benefits. A really shitty life and major medical plan. Especially with the VC supply net hurting, lots of 'em are joining organizations like the PRU to augment their income."

"Good God. I never thought of that."

"Stands to reason, doesn't it?" Outside, a helicopter clattered noisily above the Nha Be camp. "Actually, it's kind of good insurance. They're not going to set up an ambush on their own unit, not if there's a chance that they're going to be caught by their own brothers and cousins and such."

"Yeah, well, the day I call muster for a patrol and half of my people don't show, that's when I'll ask the Seventh Fleet and Team One to come in and back me up."

"Needless to say, Lucky, it's going to take a firm hand to keep these people in line. The ex-prisoners, especially, aren't going to be a particularly tractable lot. They've been turning the PRUs over largely to SEALs or to the Green Berets, because nobody else knows how to handle them."

"Army Special Forces, huh?"

"That's right. Of course, they've been working with the likes of the Montagnards and the Nung up in the mountains near the Cambodian and Laotian borders for a long time. Since '64 at least. Tough customers, and most of them work as mercenaries in our pay."

"If the Green Beanies can do it, how tough can it be?"

"Shit, Lucky. That's your damned SEAL arrogance talking."

He laughed. "Got me. The Green Berets are good. Even the ones who don't talk like John Wayne."

"Well, the Green Berets can handle the PRUs, even the real cutthroats like the Nung, because they're tough enough and fair enough to win the respect of some pretty hard, bad-ass customers. You'll have to do the same."

"Hey, this is me you're talkin' to, L-T. The street kid from Southside Chicago."

"That's exactly why I think you're the one to handle this, Lucky. Spence has a hell of a lot of experience, and he's tough, but, frankly, I'd rather lose an arm than a good chief petty officer. Doc has experience and a fair amount of Vietnamese, but I don't think he's got the, I don't know. The mental hardness to walk up to one of his own men and blow the fucker's brains out to make a point to the others. Know what I mean?"

"Oh, he might do it," Lucky said. "If he had to. Then

he'd be so screwed up in the head afterward that he wouldn't be worth shit.''

"Affirmative. I think I'd have to say the same about most of the other old hands. Pet. PJ. And the new guys, Bam-bam and the others, they shouldn't have to face this kind of thing, first tour. Not yet." He folded his hands carefully on the desk top, leaning forward and studying Lucky with a hard, close appraisal. "So how about you? Could you shoot one of your own men?"

Luciano shrugged. "Hey, it's a hypothetical, right? But if I had to, sure. No sweat."

It's never that easy, son, Baxter thought. But he didn't reply. Instead, he pulled out a government form and picked up a pen. "So, you'll take this one on for me?"

"Sure, sure. I always got a kick out of the spooky stuff anyway." Luciano cocked his head to one side, a mischievous twinkle growing in his eye. "Actually, I'll tell you the truth, Mr. Baxter, this could be kind of neat."

"How do you mean, Lucky?"

"Well, hey. You've heard the barracks bull sessions, I'm sure. What does every SEAL coming over here want more than anything else? A chance to be an operator, a swinging dick. Able to come and go, do his own thing without getting hassled." He brightened. "Hey! You think I'll get issued one of those get-out-of-jail-free cards?"

"I imagine you will. And damn near anything else you need to 'operate,' too."

"Oh, that's sweet. On my own, huh?"

"Within certain limits, yes. I'll tell you, son. Competition for these slots is pretty fierce back in the States, 'cause there just aren't enough to go around. You're right, most SEALs would kill for a chance to run their own PRU. And here it's being fucking handed to you."

"Well, shit. 'Lucky's' my name, I guess."

"Let's clear up the paperwork, then. I think the way to do this is put you on TAD to the CORDS office in Vinh Long. We'll have you transfer there when the rest of the platoon goes to Can Tho."

"How long will this be for?"

"Not long. A month. You'll still be scheduled to rotate back with us in June."

"Aw, shit, Lieutenant. That's hardly long enough to make it worth unpacking my seabag."

Baxter smiled. "If you like the assignment, I'm sure we can work something out. MACV is looking for guys who can operate on their own. Independent duty. But you'll have to produce."

"Body counts?"

"*Information.* I can't stress this enough, Lucky. We need intelligence. We need prisoners. You're going to have to get your PRU to start bringing in a few that are still kicking if we're going to get anywhere."

"Got it. You'll be a man short, though."

"We'll cope. We're probably going to be getting away from the old, strict squad-and-squad deployment anyway. One officer and six men gets too damned predictable. I've been told to start experimenting with smaller units for some ops, especially snatches. And they want more active patrolling with the VNs, whether PRUs, ARVN, or some of the special forces, like the LDNN. For raids and bigger operations, the brass is looking for larger-scale deployments. We may even be joining up with Team Two for a little shooting and looting, now and again."

"Larger ops?" Lucky shook his head. "Shit. Don't know if I like the sound of that, L-T."

"Yeah? Why not, Lucky?"

"More people means more things to get screwed up. More possible security leaks. More thumb-fingered idiots getting their dicks caught in their desk drawers. Old Murphy shows up big-time when you've got a whole regiment working on something. If it's just you and a few buddies, you can pull it down, right?"

"I suppose I agree, after a fashion. On the other hand, the direction of this war is certainly heading toward bigger and better. With VC targets drying up in the Rung Sat, we're having to look farther afield, and we're going to be moving into areas where the enemy isn't a damned sampan with three papa-sans in it. It'll be a whole, friggin' VC battalion. Seven or fourteen SEALs can't handle that kind of firepower."

"I think the trouble, L-T, is having to rely on all those other guys to pull off their part of the op, you know? I mean, if it's you and Doc and Bam-bam and Pet and the others, well, shit. I know you guys know your jobs. You know I know mine. I trust the Seawolf guys, and the PBR crews. They know their shit. But ask me if I trust some Army cannon jockey to lay a round on the enemy and not on top of me. Ask me if I trust some two-year draftee who's stoned out of his head on pot or hashish to cover my ass in a firefight. Or some gook who could be VC cadre, for all I know."

"I hear you, Lucky. It's a fucked-up war. Write your congressman. Anything else to get off your chest?"

"Nah. I'll still be able to operate out there? Not get hassled by what I have to wear or what kind of heat I'm packing or how long my hair is?"

"Do what works for you. That's all I can say. I'm not going to hold inspection on you." He smiled. "Like you say, you'll be a real swinging dick."

"Yeah, and if General Westmoreland shows up unexpected-like one day, that's his lookout. Okay, Lieutenant. I'm your boy."

"Thanks, Lucky. I knew I could count on you."

"Yeah, well, if you want to hear my war stories when I get back, you're buying the drinks."

Baxter grinned. "Done. Looking forward to it."

Later, though, Baxter sat in his chair, staring at the door to the Nha Be SEAL platoon headquarters.

It is an axiom of warfare that military commanders must be prepared to lose men serving under their orders. High-ranking officers commanding many hundreds or thousands of men—too many men to know more than a handful personally—are often forced to think in terms of combat losses totaling some percentage of their total force. He recalled reading a history of the NCDUs at Normandy, forerunners of the modern SEALs, that stated bluntly and without elaboration that the D-Day planners had expected to lose over sixty percent of the NCDU personnel scheduled to hit the beaches ahead of the first waves of infantry. Dealing with numbers in that way, Baxter thought, numbers that represented men's lives, had always seemed obscene.

Whatever the practice or experience of other branches of the military, the SEALs had, throughout the six short years of their existence, been a tight and close-knit unit, in part because of their small numbers, in part because of the intensity and the brutality of their training. SEALs had died in Vietnam; their deaths hurt, like the death of a brother. If a SEAL died, it wasn't because of the odds or the estimated casualty percentages written up on some ops planning sheet. It was because someone had screwed up, and for that reason, SEAL officers tended to take the death or maiming of the men under their command far more personally than was healthy.

Perhaps, he thought, warfare tended to evolve into large and impersonal affairs because it hurt less that way.

Starting 25 April, Lucky Luciano would no longer be under Baxter's command, but Baxter found himself already worrying about the kid, the way he might worry about a strayed younger brother. He hadn't let himself say anything about it—he scarcely could make himself even think about it now—but he didn't trust the PRUs any more than Luciano did, and by heaven they'd better not give him a reason to go over to Vinh Long and knock heads together.

SEALs always look after their own, whatever the circumstances . . . and whatever the opposition.

Chapter 11

Thursday, 25 April 1968

PRU District HQ
Vinh Long, Republic of Vietnam
1030 hours

"So, you're our new PRU advisor?"

"Yes, sir," Luciano said, dropping his seabag by the door. Three men watched him as he looked around the office, a neat, comfortable room of painted cinder blocks, equipped with several desks and the usual assortment of maps, charts, and posted schedules. An air conditioner in one wall filled the room with air that, after the ninety-degree heat outside, was icy. "Reporting for duty."

"I'm Lieutenant j.g. Waters," the slender man behind the desk said. He was wearing khakis, and he couldn't have been more than twenty-four or so. "And this is Mr. Johnson, and Mr. Wilson."

Luciano carefully removed his poncho, shook it off by the door, and hung it on a hook mounted on the wall. It was raining hard outside, though Vietnam's real rainy season wouldn't start until June. He nodded to the other men, seated in folding wooden chairs beside the desk.

"I know Lieutenant Wilson," he said. "How ya doin', sir?"

"Been doing any water skiing lately?" Wilson said.

Luciano chuckled. "Actually, I haven't been able to get away much, sir."

Lieutenant Charles Wilson had come aboard as Det Delta's second CO in 1966, during Lucky's first tour in Nam. He'd arrived at the SEAL compound at Nha Be to find Lucky and several other Team One SEALs using a PBR—Patrol Boat, River—for recreational purposes. His abilities at sweet-talking, cajoling, and bluffing the high-ranking brass so that his SEALs could operate were legendary.

Johnson wore sunglasses and a casual, nondescript air. Wilson was tall, lean, and weathered. Both men wore civilian clothes.

"Mr. Johnson is a plumber," Waters explained, after a moment's hesitation. "You'll be working with him quite a bit, I imagine."

Luciano pursed his lips, then grinned. "Found any leaks, Mr. Johnson?"

"If I did," the man said, deadpan, "I wouldn't tell you."

"And if he told you," Wilson added, "he'd have to kill you. Grab a chair. Coffee mess is over there. Help yourself."

After Luciano was settled in a chair with a full charge of coffee in a borrowed mug, he gave the three men with him in the room a more careful appraisal. Lieutenant j.g. Fred Waters, he knew, would be his immediate boss, in effect the CO of a platoon of sixteen SEALs and, presumably, other military personnel as well, only instead of working together in one place as a platoon, each of those sixteen SEALs would be scattered at various AOs all around the Mekong Delta, each running his own PRU of anywhere from twenty to a hundred Vietnamese.

In theory, it was a way to really stretch SEAL training and experience, "maximizing total special operations training assets," as one classic piece of bureaucratic weasel-speak had phrased it. The Army Special Forces had been running PRU operations for some time, as well as the SEALs, and with considerable success. Baxter thought well of the program and had talked with Luciano about it at some length back at Nha Be.

Lucky wasn't quite sure yet what he thought of the program, but the chance to be an *operator*, a free-swinging dick, was just too damned good to pass up. Like he'd told Lieutenant Baxter, he definitely wanted a piece of this.

From what Luciano had heard, Waters was a good man, if a bit sticky about the paperwork. He would be Lucky's

main go-between with other Navy forces in the area, both
the riverine patrols of PBRs that moved up and down this
part of the Mekong, and the Seawolf helicopter assets based
in the region. For that reason alone Lucky was glad he'd
drawn another SEAL for his CO, and not someone with
Army Special Forces or the CIA. SEALs knew how SEALs
liked to operate . . . and wouldn't argue technique.

Johnson, of course, was his intelligence contact, or one of
them, but there was no way to evaluate him yet. Hell, he
didn't even know if the guy was CIA, DIA, or with Navy
Intelligence, and in fact, it didn't really matter. The
"plumber" joke was an old one and probably meant he was
one of the Christians in Action. Too often, in Luciano's experience, CIA field operatives came off playing a Mutt-and-
Jeff comedy routine, getting in each other's way, stabbing
one another in the back, muddying the waters, and generally
making class-A nuisances of themselves. Baxter had warned
Luciano that the only way to evaluate Agency personnel was
to test the intel they provided. Some was useless, hopelessly
dated, or just flat wrong, the product of guesswork by some
office-bound REMF or a rewrite of good intel by an office-
bound committee of desk-operators somewhere that had their
own political or career agendas to follow.

When the intel was right, however, it would be priceless.
The best intel sources would be Army Special Forces, other
native PRUs or Hoi Chanhs, or even other SEALs. Lucky,
after his crash course in PRU administration with Baxter over
the past few days, had already established an informal rating
system in his own mind for grading intel. Best was from
other SEALs or SEAL-run PRUs, which came straight to him
without first going up and down the intel ladder to district
headquarters or all the way back to Saigon. Worst came
down the ladder from Saigon or, worse still, from Washington. Intelligence sourced through Saigon was usually out-of-
date and had almost certainly been seen by VC agents, which
reduced its usefulness quite a bit. Intel coming from Washington . . . well, Lucky had seen some of that guesswork before while working with the Direct Action platoon. He didn't
know what they were smoking back there, but frequently he

wondered if they were looking at the same war . . . or even the same *planet* that he was.

All other sources, in Lucky's mind, fell somewhere between those extremes in usefulness and likely accuracy.

"How do you feel about working with us, Luciano?" Wilson asked.

"I'm looking forward to it, sir," he replied, truthfully enough. "I expect it'll take some getting used to."

Wilson laughed. "Roger that. I gather you haven't been through the training run in Saigon for this."

"No, sir, but my skipper with Bravo Platoon was, and he trained me. I think I've been pretty well filled in on what I'm supposed to do."

"Good." Wilson leaned back in his chair, his long legs stretched out, one ankle across the other. "I've been reading your files, son. You've been on quite a few snatches."

"A good many, sir."

"Hmm. Well, we've got something new getting under way," Wilson said. He glanced at Johnson. "This information, I don't think I need to add, is classified. You will not discuss it with anyone outside this room."

"Of course."

"I don't know if you're aware of this," Johnson said, "but you SEALs have started something out here. Starting back, oh, in '66 or so, the various DA platoons began developing their own native sources of intel."

Luciano glanced at Wilson and grinned. "SEALs have always been pretty hot on securing their own intel, sir."

"Well, the Direct Action platoons were the first to establish and use locally recruited and maintained intelligence nets on anything like a consistent basis," Johnson explained. "Especially in the Rung Sat Special Zone, where you've been operating. What has interested some of us is the success you've had establishing chains of intel through your snatch operations. You capture a prisoner, and he tells you where some more VC are going to be. You capture them, and they tell you where their leaders are. You capture *them* and get the dope on even more leaders, higher up the ladder."

"Not to mention," Waters said, "the locations of arms caches, rice stores, documents."

"The PRUs have been working with much the same idea for some time," Wilson said. "Unfortunately, there's still a, shall we say, a reluctance on the part of some of the local forces to bring 'em back alive. Especially among the mercenaries."

Luciano turned his gaze on Johnson. "That would be easy enough to fix, wouldn't it? I gather the bounty for KIAs is higher than the bounty on prisoners."

The corner of Johnson's mouth twitched. "I've, ah, heard that argument," he said. "Suffice it to say, it's not that simple."

"It rarely is." Luciano grinned. "But isn't this a chance to prove that capitalism works to the locals? Hell, that's why we're here, isn't it?"

"The bounty system," Johnson explained, "includes bounties on captured weapons. The locals got the idea a long time ago that it's easier to take the guy's weapon by killing the poor son of a bitch than convincing him to hand it over. We'd have to pay astronomical bounties to make it worth their while to take a prisoner."

"Screw that," Luciano said. "You guys set the bounties. Make the KIA bounties lower."

"Which could cost us our support base with our PRU assets," Johnson said. "That's always the risk you take when working with mercenaries."

"You should know," Lucky said. "You started the thing over here."

"We are beginning a new program," Wilson said. "Highly secret. And, we think, highly effective. It will use, in large part, our merc assets, as well as the SEAL platoons in-country, Special Forces, and various other operators. Your PRU is going to be one of our test cases, to demonstrate that what the SEALs learned on a small scale can be bumped up to big scale. You'll have all kinds of support at the top for this. The bad news, though, is that we're going to have to demonstrate a measure of success first. If we can bring back good, hard intel through PRU ops, we'll have more money to work with. You'll have more money to work with, in the field. You'll be able to pay your troops whatever you want."

"But we have to prove it first."

"Affirmative," Wilson said. "There have been . . . ah . . . difficulties with some of the mercenary units. Especially the CIDGs." He pronounced the acronym for Civilian Irregular Defense Groups "sid-gees."

Johnson took a deep breath. "There have been some real problems with the CIDGs. Defections. Even cases where they've turned on American forces stationed with them. The PRUs have a better record, for the most part, but my superiors aren't sure that this new program is going to work the way we want it to."

Lucky chuckled. "I can imagine."

The PRUs, for the most part, were tough, well motivated, and willing to take the war to the enemy, ready and willing to "prowl and growl," as the SEALs liked to put it. The CIDGs were more like armed civilian militias . . . and not very well armed at that, since their primary weapon was the World War II–era M1 carbine. It simply made no sense to send a half-trained gaggle of civilians armed with carbines up against AK-47s wielded by battle-hardened men who both knew how to use them and had the will to do so.

"So," Lucky went on. "What's this new program of yours, anyway?"

"I remind you again that this is top secret," Johnson said. He picked a manila folder up off Waters's desk and handed it to Luciano. "It's called Project Phoenix," he continued, as Lucky skimmed through the documents in the folder. "It should allow us to combine the best of both worlds, the SEALs' and Special Forces' interest in securing good sources of intel, and the PRUs', shall we say, *enthusiasm* for direct action."

"For killing people," Lucky said, smiling. "Sure."

Johnson looked uncomfortable. "We don't like expressing things in quite that blunt a fashion. We do not want people outside the program to get the idea that these are assassination squads. Especially the press. We're having a bad enough problem with media coverage of Vietnam now on the way the government is handling the war, especially since Cronkite did a number on us last month."

"Project Phoenix," Wilson said, "was first floated last year. The MACV brass sees it as one element of what they like to call the 'pacification' program. It's damned obvious by now that we can't win this war as a stand-up, conventional fight. Big guns against guerrillas usually ends up with the wrong people getting killed. If we know who to target, exactly, and go after them, we might be able to wreck the VCI.''

"VCI?" Luciano asked.

"Viet Cong Infrastructure," Wilson said. "REMF-talk for the VC political leaders, the guys who organize things and keep them running. Nail *them*, and we could see the rebel resistance to the Saigon government just wither and fall apart.''

"MACV and the Agency," Johnson added, "have been working a project called ICEX since late last year. It stands for Intelligence Coordination and Exploitation. It's really nothing more than what you SEALs have been doing for some time now. We're in the process of unifying all of the agencies that have been responsible for intel gathering in the past, putting them under one roof, so to speak. CIA. South Vietnamese CIA. Military Intelligence. National Police. By this summer, we plan to have the whole apparatus working under South Vietnamese government leadership.''

Lucky snorted.

"You have something to say about that?"

"Uh, no, sir." Lucky said. "Go on. This sounds fascinating.''

"At the same time we consolidate our intelligence sources," Johnson continued, "we will be acting on it in a consistent and organized manner. Phoenix is tasked with identifying senior members of the VCI and either capturing them for interrogation, or eliminating them.''

"We should stress," Wilson said, with a glance at Johnson, "that the word from the top is that Phoenix is not to be an assassination program, and it's not to become a tool for the South Vietnamese government, a way for President Thieu to eliminate political opponents.''

"*Perish* the thought," Lucky said.

"Though the emphasis will be on the Vietnamese running this program," Wilson explained, "it is vital that the American advisors keep hold of the reins, at least for now. We need our people to ride herd on the less-disciplined members of the PRUs. And on the VNs in Saigon who might try to use the program for their own ends.''

And that, Luciano thought wryly, was going to be like keeping baby snakes in a wire cage with a one-inch mesh. The Saigon government was corrupt. Hell, parts of the American intelligence community were corrupt, too, if half of what he'd heard was true. The VC were good, *very* good, at penetrating all levels of the South Vietnamese government, from the leadership councils of the hamlets and rural communities clear up to the halls of Presidential Palace.

Damn it, every time an idea worked out fine on a small scale in this damned country, some bureaucrat or general or politician decided to scale it up to a major operation involving thousands of people and millions of dollars and it just, plain, fucking never worked.

Still, he would have his chance at being an independent operator with this, and he would have the chance to make his small part of the thing work. It was worth a shot, anyway.

"I'll give it my best," Luciano told them. "I can't promise to keep President Thieu in line, but I sure as hell will run my PRU and make 'em produce."

"You haven't told him about the man he's replacing," Waters pointed out. He was leaning back in his chair, chin braced in one hand, fingers splayed across his cheek as he listened. Luciano had the impression that Waters wasn't totally enthusiastic about Phoenix. He'd not said much during this briefing, though he'd been listening carefully. "Or the, um, circumstances."

"Spec Sergeant George Hirsch," Johnson said. "Army Special Forces. Medevacked to Subic two weeks ago."

Lucky felt a cold breath at his back, raising the hairs on his neck. He shook the feeling off. "Go on."

"He took a round during an ambush he was working with the PRU," Wilson said. "In the *back*."

"Ah." Meaning they couldn't prove that his own men had shot him, but they damn sure had their suspicions. "What kind of leader was he?"

"By the book," Wilson said. "Tough, no-nonsense sort."

"A lot like you," Waters added, "judging by your record."

"I'll tell you the truth, sir. I'm not that much of a by-the-booker."

"Well, maybe a relaxed attitude about that sort of thing is what's needed here," Johnson suggested. "Hirsch might have been a little too rigid with men who don't respond to that kind of attitude."

"Shit," Wilson said. "What we're trying to do here hasn't been done before. How the hell can a guy follow the book when the fucking thing hasn't even been written yet?"

"He's got a point," Waters said.

"So, Luciano," Wilson said. "Knowing about Hirsch, you having any second thoughts about this assignment?"

"No, sir," Luciano replied. "I'll just . . . watch my back."

"Maybe you'd like to meet your new command," Wilson said. "They're in the camp right outside this base. Mr. Waters? Perhaps you'd care to give Luciano the grand tour."

"Aye, aye, sir." He stood up. "I don't *think* we'll need to go in armed and wearing flak vests. . . ."

Lucky jerked his thumb at his seabag. "Maybe I should find my BOQ, first," he said. "And, ah, check in with the base CO? I was told I'd better not omit the fine social points."

Wilson and Waters exchanged a shuttered glance. "That would be Major Sharpe," Wilson said. "Maybe you'd better get on up there, at that."

"Yeah," Waters added. "Frankly, if you're gonna need body armor, Sharpe's office is the place to do it."

"Good luck, Luciano," Wilson said, chuckling. "You're going to need it!"

Chapter 12

Thursday, 25 April 1968

3rd Battalion HQ
Vinh Long, Republic of Vietnam
1100 hours

"Torpedoman Second Class Luciano, reporting, sir."

Major Sharpe ignored him, continuing to write on the yellow legal pad on his desk for several long moments, the pen making a faint scratching noise that sounded unusually loud against the silence.

Luciano remained at attention, standing back rigid a few feet in front of the desk. He'd left his wet poncho outside, of course, and was wearing damp greens. Since he was uncovered, his floppy hat tucked into his belt just to the right of the buckle, he did not salute. He was aware, though, that Army saluting regulations were different from the Navy's, and he wondered if this bastard was waiting for him to snap off a salute.

He decided not to give him the satisfaction.

Luciano did wonder, though, what that smell was. It was strong, sweet, and cloying. He was also aware that the air in here was downright chilly, colder even than the PRU HQ building across the military compound from the Army building. Luciano had been living and working in Vietnam's ninety-degree heat for so long, that an office like this one, air-conditioned to seventy or below, was uncomfortably cold and dry.

At last, Sharpe placed the pen on the tablet, leaned back, and looked up.

"So," he said. "You're a SEAL."

Lucky could tell from the tone of voice that this was not going to be a pleasant meeting. "Yes, sir."

"Can you tell me what the hell the Navy is doing this far away from the ocean?"

The standard rejoinder to that question was that a Navy SEAL carried all the water he needed in his canteens, but Lucky wasn't wearing his combat gear at the moment. Instead, he glanced down at his wet uniform, then cocked his head, grinned, and nodded upward toward the Quonset hut's tin roof, where the rainfall kept up a wet, staccato drumming. "Seems to me, sir, there's a fair amount of water out there right now."

"Can the comedy, sailor! I am not amused." Sharpe stood up, scooted the chair back with a sharp squeak on the tile floor, and walked around his desk, closing on Lucky until his nose was six inches from the side of the SEAL's face. Lucky held himself at stiff attention, his eyes riveted on a featureless bit of concrete block wall past Sharpe's shoulder alongside of a glass-framed photograph of President Johnson.

Lucky could feel Sharpe's eyes flicking up and down his frame, taking in the tropics-weathered uniform, the tears and splattered mud, the length of his hair, all with disapproving scorn.

"I'm going to say something now," Sharpe said quietly, his voice dangerous. "And I'm just going to say it once. I've heard all about you SEALs, and I don't like you. I don't like you one little bit."

"Well, I'm very sorry to hear that, sir," Lucky said. He could feel something coiling up tight in his gut, but he was careful not to let any emotion show in his face. He had the impression that Sharpe was waiting for an excuse, *any* excuse, to strike.

"You SEALs are *assassins*." He worked the word out as though it were particularly foul and bad-tasting. "You kill people."

"Sir, that is what they pay me to do."

"Bullshit, mister. You kill people because you *like* to, and I find that disgusting."

Lucky had finally identified the source of the unusual,

cloying smell. It was Sharpe's aftershave, much stronger now, when experienced close-up. *Christ, this guy had better not go out on live ops,* Lucky thought. *Charlie'll smell the stink coming a mile away.*

Turning away abruptly, Sharpe walked back to his chair and slumped into it. He seemed a little unsteady on his feet, Lucky thought . . . and then it struck him. Sharpe was drunk . . . or very close to it. Luciano could smell the alcohol now, just beneath the heavier, sweeter whiff of aftershave.

"I've been to the SEAL base up at Binh Thuy," Sharpe continued. "You have any friends up there?"

If they were SEALs, they were friends, but Lucky thought it best not to say anything about that. "No, sir."

"Ever been there?"

"No, sir."

"A bunch of brawling, ill-disciplined jackasses that ought to be locked up in Leavenworth for the rest of their lives. *Cowboys,* mister. Loners who have no concept of what it means to work with the military, as a part of the designated chain of command, as a part of a larger plan. They have a sign up in their rec hall. It says, PEOPLE WHO KILL FOR MONEY ARE MERCENARIES. PEOPLE WHO KILL FOR FUN ARE SADISTS. PEOPLE WHO KILL FOR MONEY AND FUN ARE SEALs."

"I've heard about that sign, sir."

"It's obscene. *SEALs* are obscene, the whole idea of them. Well, I'm gonna tell you something, SEAL. Vinh Long is under the jurisdiction of 3rd Battalion, 47th Infantry, United States Army. In other words, it is under *my* jurisdiction. Do you understand that?"

"Sir, yes, sir!"

"Your orders read that you are supposed to be in charge of that pack of bandits camped outside my town."

"If you mean the Ving Long PRU, yes, sir."

" 'PRU.' " If anything, the way he pronounced the letters sounded darker and more disapproving than had the word "assassins" a moment before. "Bandits, cutthroats, deserters, jailbait, and VC. If they give me half an excuse, they're history, mister. You read me?"

"Loud and clear, sir."

"Last week some of those hooligans busted up one of the bars in town. They seem to feel they can get away with shit like that. They put two of my boys in a field hospital."

"Maybe they were just feeling their oats, sir."

"There is no excuse for that kind of behavior, mister! No excuse whatsoever!"

"If the men damaged civilian property, sir, they are in clear violation of both military and civil law. Were the men responsible arrested?"

"No. No one knows who did it, or they're afraid to point them out. Frankly, I think the whole lot of them are just plain rotten apples, and I will not have them coming into my town and making trouble. I will not have you making trouble in my town either. This is to put you on notice. Vinh Long is off-limits to you, mister, and to that ratpack you're commanding."

"Very well," Lucky said coldly.

"Perhaps I should warn you of something else, mister," Sharpe said. "Your predecessor, Captain Hirsch—"

"I heard all about him, sir."

"You hear he was fragged?"

"I heard he got shot in the back. Sir."

Sharpe's face creased in a scowl. "I don't think I like what you're insinuating."

"I'm not insinuating anything, sir. He was Special Forces. They're good. I wouldn't question his bravery."

"He got capped on a 'bush by those bandits he was commanding. You better watch yourself with your dinks, mister, or the same'll happen to you."

"Yes, sir."

"And just for your information, Special Forces doesn't cut it with me either. The whole concept of e-lite fighting units is bullshit, whether they're Army Special Forces or Navy SEALs. All those programs do is skim good people from the pool of available officers and men. That, and provide a refuge for John Wayne–macho six-shooter types who think they can win the war single-handed."

"If you say so, sir."

"I *do* say so. Modern warfare is not the province of gunslingers or amateurs. We will win in Vietnam when we force

Charlie into the open in conventional warfare. When we meet his weakness with our strength. And when we take and hold the towns and villages he currently uses as his bases of operation and eliminate his sources of supply.''

Lucky kept his face impassive. ''Maybe the brass should consider trench warfare. Sir.''

''Are you trying to be funny?''

''No, sir.''

''I am not stupid, mister. I know you're standing there laughing at me, you with your damned, smug e-lite superiority. Well, the laugh's gonna be on the other foot now, isn't it?''

Luciano blinked, bemused by the oddly mixed metaphor. ''I'm not sure I follow what you mean, sir.''

''You special-warfare Johnnies all think that this is some new kind of game. Go after the enemy's leaders. Hit the 'VCI.' Play tag with him in the jungle, setting ambushes and getting ambushed back. Well, you people play all the games you want to.'' Reaching up, he tapped his brass infantry badge. ''It's the *infantry* that fights this nation's wars. The infantry that takes the ground and pays for it in blood. The infantry that kicks ass.''

Luciano allowed himself to relax slightly out of his cadet-rigid posture, turning his head to look hard into Sharpe's eyes. For a moment, the two men stood there, eyes locked. Luciano gave a small, cold smile.

Sharpe blinked. ''You're at attention, mister!''

''Permission to speak freely. *Sir.*''

''Go ahead.'' The tone was a challenge.

''I'd have to say you have one hell of a lot to learn about leading men, sir. I was always taught that you led by inspiring them, not by knocking them and not by threatening them.''

''You cocky little son of a bitch. I'll see to it you're thrown out of my district, thrown clear out of this country!''

''You just go ahead and do that, sir. But maybe you should know that the aftershave trick doesn't really work that well.''

Sharpe's eyes narrowed. ''What do you mean?''

''Covering up the drinking. You really shouldn't be doing that on duty, you know. It's bad for your men's morale. Dulls the brain. Though, I'll admit, it does save the graves and registration people some trouble if you're already pickled while they try stuffing you in that bag. Sir.''

"Get the hell out of my office." The voice was a low, rumbling growl of warning. "Get out of my *sight*."

"Aye, aye, sir," Lucky said, deliberately using the Navy/Marine response to an order.

"How'd it go?" Waters had remained outside the office for Lucky's interview.

"Oh, not too bad," Lucky told him, retrieving his poncho from its hook and giving the Army clerk seated at the desk outside Sharpe's door a broad wink. The man stared back in bafflement. "He told me how he liked to run things, and I showed him how I ran things, and that's about all there is to say about it. C'mon. Let's go meet the troops."

The PRU camp was a collection of shacks and Quonset huts located well outside the edge of the town, as though forced into exile there. As they entered the compound gate, Luciano saw with some dismay that the place was little better than a pigsty. *Literally* a pigsty. Several Vietnamese pigs were running around loose within the compound, rooting about in a pile of garbage lying next to one of the sheet-tin and cinder-block hovels that had been designated as a barracks. The ground was a thick gruel of mud.

"They don't live here all the time," Waters said, almost apologetically, as they picked their way across a parade ground toward a line of barracks. "Most of them live in town, or at other villages in the area. They're supposed to show up here for drills, inspections, muster, that sort of thing. Somehow, it never quite worked trying to impress some kind of military order on them."

"Well, I kind of know how they feel," Luciano said, thoughtful. "I never much liked marching in boot camp myself."

About a dozen men were lounging outside the barracks. Two were eating rice with their fingers from small bowls. The others simply sat there, watching warily. The uniform of the day apparently was a ragged assortment of civilian clothes, tiger-stripe cammies, and army greens. Some were barefoot, most had their shirts unbuttoned, and those who wore hats favored ball caps or flop-brimmed boonies. Several, Lucky saw, wore knives of various makes and descriptions; two of the men bore nasty, ragged scars on their faces that might have been from combat . . . or could have just been old knife wounds.

As the two SEALs approached the group, Lucky could feel their eyes on him, measuring, appraising. Several more VNs appeared from inside the building.

"Good morning, men," Lucky began.

He was met with blank looks. Two men spoke hurriedly together in rapid-fire Vietnamese, heads close, laughing.

"Good morning, men," Lucky repeated, deepening and raising his voice.

"*Chung toi khong tieng anh,*" one of the men said. We don't speak English.

Great. Just fucking great.

Lucky could feel the mutiny behind those watchful dark eyes.

"Their pay was stopped," Waters said at his side in a low voice, "until Hirsch's death could be reviewed. I think . . . they're a bit resentful."

"Gee. Really?"

Lucky thought that over. He doubted that there'd been anything as coherent as a conspiracy in Hirsch's death, at least, no conspiracy more formal than a couple of disgruntled troops deciding to blow the guy away in an ambush. He had some latitude in dealing with the PRU, he knew; he also knew these people resented being punished en masse for what one or two of them had done . . . just as he knew that it would be impossible to find out which one or two had killed Hirsch. They would never surrender one of their own to the Americans, so playing detective and tracking down the killers would be an exercise in complete futility.

Better to try to pick up here and now, where Hirsch had left off, and see what could be salvaged.

A shape appeared inside the barracks door. Several of the Vietnamese sitting on the step rose and hastily moved aside. A man stepped out, a big man wearing fatigue pants, paratrooper boots, and a sleeveless, mud-stained red T-shirt.

Lucky had never met a Vietnamese like this. Most VNs

he'd known were shorter than he was, coming up to his chin, or maybe a bit higher. This man overtopped him by a good six inches, and he was bulked up and hard like a professional wrestler. He didn't look Vietnamese; at a guess, Lucky might have pegged him as Chinese. The man was egg-bald, with a long, black mustache framing his mouth like parentheses. A gold-loop earring in his right ear and a savage, lightning-jagged scar that just missed his right eye gave him a piratical air.

"So," the monster rumbled, the word coming up from somewhere deep inside that hard-muscled gut. "We got us another sailor boy, eh?" He spit a black gob of something into the mud, then spoke rapidly in flat-toned Vietnamese. Several of the others laughed, and Lucky wasn't sure whether the guy had just repeated his entrance line in Vietnamese, or insulted Lucky's mother.

"I'm Petty Officer Luciano," he said slowly. "SEAL Team One. You can call me by my nickname, though. *May man.*"

"You are not lucky today," the giant said. "Unless you here to tell us you pay. Then, maybe, you be lucky."

It seemed pretty clear that Man Mountain here was the leader of this PRU, whatever his rank or official standing might be. It was also clear that this was a test . . . and if he wanted to garner any respect at all with this crew, Lucky knew, he would have to pass it here and now.

"What have you done lately to earn that pay?" Lucky demanded.

The giant took three steps forward, planting himself in front of Luciano. One massive arm suddenly snapped out, the fingers closing on Lucky's throat. "I could start by killing me a SEAL," the giant rumbled with a malevolent grin. "I hear they good to eat. . . ."

Lucky saw money changing hands in the crowd . . . and wondered if that meant someone was actually betting for him.

Good bet, if they were. He stood his ground as the fingers tightened on his throat, reaching up with both hands, his right grabbing the man's wrist, his left touching a point at his elbow. BUD/S had included extensive hand-to-hand training, both in the Korean martial art form called *Hwrang-do* and in a general collection of dirty tricks and moves. His left knuckle touched a nerve; his right hand bent the wrist in a direction that the joint did not normally permit. Man Mountain's eyes went wide as the pain jangled up his arm and his shoulder went numb. Lucky took a step back, sliding past the outstretched arm, dipping until his right hand, closing now into a fist, almost touched the mud.

"*Xin loi*," he said, grinning. "Excuse me . . ."

Then Lucky's fist was rocketing up and around, catching the Chinese mercenary under the jut of his chin, the blow jarring Lucky clear to his shoulder as it lifted the giant off the ground, spun him halfway around, and laid him out, face-down, in the mud.

The crowd, chattering in Vietnamese a moment before, fell silent as death. Lucky went over to the supine form, reached down, and rolled him over onto his back. He checked first to make sure the giant could breathe, then shoved two fingers up under the angle of his jaw, checking the pulse.

Good. Man Mountain was alive; Lucky wasn't sure what he would have done if the man had been in cardiac arrest.

Or how he would have faced the paperwork that would have followed the man's death.

Straightening again, he swept his gaze across the watching VNs. Every eye was on him, some wide and afraid, some carefully shuttered and neutral. Lucky selected one of the big, scarred men in the forefront of the watching crowd. "Anh!" he said, stabbing his forefinger at the man's chest. "You!"

The man blinked, startled.

"*Ten anh la gi?*" Lucky demanded. What is your name?

"*Ten toi la Pham Nhu Truong,*" the man replied.

"Pham Nhu Truong," Lucky repeated. He was rapidly straining the limits of his command of Vietnamese. He decided to gamble. "*Ong co noi tieng anh khong?*"

"I . . . I speak," the man admitted with a stammer. "I speak English, yes."

"*Ong* Truong," Lucky said carefully, as if weighing the name, and tasting it. He pointed at the unconscious man. "When he wakes up, tell him his pay has been docked one day. I do not pay soldiers for lying in the mud. *Ong co hieu khong?*"

"I understand, sir. Yes. I tell."

"Do that." He looked at the other watching PRU mercenaries. "As for the rest of you, how much you get paid depends on how much you look and act like warriors. I was told that the PRUs were hot fucking shit, but all I've seen so far is a bunch of barefoot rice-paddy farmers lying around in the mud and the garbage. I'm losing fucking face just being *seen* with you assholes!" Planting hands on hips, standing with his feet at a shoulder's width apart, he eyed the men again, shaking his head. "Maybe all we have here are rice-paddy farmers. Maybe we don't have any warriors here at all!"

"We warrior!" one man, braver than the rest, called. "You pay dong, we fight!"

"So! One of you is a warrior!" Luciano nodded. "How many others? Sat Cong!" He raised one clenched fist. "Sat Cong! Kill Cong!"

Half a dozen fists raised. The response was scattered and weak-voiced. "Sat Cong. . . ."

"Shit! Let me hear it! *Sat Cong!*"

"*Sat Cong!*"

"*Sat Cong!* "

"*Sat Cong!*" The last repetition was loud enough to echo from the cinder-block walls of the barracks on the far side of the field at Luciano's back.

"Better," he said, approvingly. "Here's a new one. *Bat Cong!*"

The VNs stared at him, startled.

"You heard me! *Bat Cong!*" He shouted the phrase. "*Capture* Cong!"

"We . . . kill Cong . . ." one of the mercenaries began.

"You will goddamn kill VC when I fucking say to kill VC," Luciano said. "And, by God, when I say capture VC, you will fucking capture VC. *Hien?* You've gotta fuckin' well *bat Cong* if you're gonna *sat Cong!*"

There were several murmurs from the group, but he saw some nods, and . . . better . . . the shuttered expressions were gone. He thought he could see at least some measure of approval there.

"*Bat Cong!*" He shouted again.

This time there was a response, one almost delivered in unison. "*Bat Cong!*"

"*Bat Cong!*"

"*Bat Cong!*"

"*Sat Cong!*"

"*Sat Cong!*

"*Bat Cong! Sat Cong!*"

"*Bat Cong! Sat Cong!*"

The shouts became a litany . . . an incantation, a kind of magic ritual drawing the chanting men into a tighter and tighter circle, their fists stabbing upward into the sky with each punctuated syllable.

And Lucky knew that he had himself an army.

Chapter 13

Sunday, 12 May 1968

PRU 33
Over Vinh Binh Province
Republic of South Vietnam
0710 hours

Lucky Luciano sat on the deck of the UH-1B, flying above the flat checkerboard of rice paddies and squared-off blocks of forest that made up this part of Vinh Binh Province. Crowded aboard with six other men in full combat gear, he had his back to the pilot and copilot forward. The view out the open side door of the Slick was . . . spectacular, to say the least.

It was early morning—first light—a "morning glory" op, as some officer with a misplaced poet's soul had christened it, with beams of sunlight slanting in from the east and touching the landscape with gold. Much of the land below was shrouded in patches of snow-white mist, ragged-looking cotton balls that clung near to the ground. This entire region was pancake-flat, but occasional peaks rose a few hundred feet above the plains, and those seemed to attract the morning mist, like magnets. The land here showed the hand of man more than of nature, though for a change that hand had created beauty instead of devastation. The endless checkerboard of rice paddies formed an eerily geometric effect, with neatly ordered squares and rectangles interconnected by narrow canals and divided and delineated by raised, earthen dikes. Some of the dikes were wide and high enough to support something like a road. The water in the various paddies lay at different levels, making the checkerboard three-dimensional. The paddies reflected the sky but added colors of their own—greens, browns, and golds.

Though Lucky rarely thought about such things one way or another, the landscape below was, he now realized, dazzlingly beautiful. The air was crystalline, the sky achingly blue, the sundance on the motionless gold-and-green waters of the paddies an intense and flashing silver. The stink of the jungle, of the war, of death itself, was masked far below by an alien landscape that looked more like a painting than anything real. It occurred to Lucky that the land below had been sculpted into this surreal work of art over the course of many centuries, as generation after generation of local farmers had carefully tended the paddies.

Further to the southeast, closer to the coast of the South China Sea and along the banks of the major rivers running through this land, the hand of man had been more abrupt, more brutal. Huge areas of the landscape had been dusted with Agent Orange and other defoliants, transforming the once-lush paradise into a black and barren horror of twisted, dead tree trunks and stinking mud. Lucky had seen whole regions transformed into something that looked more like the surface of the moon than anything on Earth, with hundreds of scattered, sometimes overlapping craters, each transformed into a circular, blue lake, with every tree scrubbed away or stripped of foliage by the bombing strikes and napalm.

Here, though, the war seemed very far away. It was almost possible to imagine that the country below was at peace.

At least, the war seemed distant until he raised his gaze from the ground. The helicopters clattering across the landscape, arrayed in formation to left and right of Luciano's Slick, comprised an aerial armada, a total of eight UH-1 transports with an escort of four AH-1 HueyCobras. Aboard those helos were fifty-three men of the Vinh Long PRU.

Fifty-three VNs and one SEAL.

Luciano looked across the deck of the Huey at the Vietnamese soldiers on the Slick with him. One of them, Lieutenant Vo Tien Vang, watched him impassively from beneath a helmet just a little too big for his head.

Vang was Luciano's opposite number with the VNs, a member of the LDNN who'd begun working with the PRUs several years before. The top of his head scarcely reached to Luciano's chin, but he was stocky and powerfully muscled. Vang's eyes were as hard and as black as anthracite.

Technically, Vang was in command of the unit, though exact lines of command could be a little fuzzy in the freewheeling PRUs. Technically, Luciano was there as an advisor, but for all intents and purposes, what the American said was supposed to be law. So far, though, Vang had been less than cooperative with Lucky, saying little and keeping his thoughts—if he had any—uncommunicatively to himself. Luciano wondered if a character who looked as tough as Vang was going to take orders from anyone. Lucky had grown up on the south side of Chicago, and he'd seen that flinty stare before, in the eyes of a member of a rival street gang measuring him before a rumble.

On Vang's right was Pham Nhu Truong, looking grim as he clutched his M1 carbine, and to his right, with a Garand, was Hoa Li Xiang—a singsong mouthful pronounced Wah Lee Chang—the Man Mountain Lucky had decked at Long Vinh. Hoa, the SEAL had learned, was Kuomintang. His parents had fought the Communists and the Japanese under Chiang; as a teenager, he'd fled Canton when Mao's forces had won in 1947 and come here, part of the Southeast Asia–wide diaspora of anti-Communist Chinese. He'd been fighting Communists on his own since before Dien Bien Phu and joined the PRU so he could keep on fighting them.

All three men, Vang, Truong, and Xiang, spoke acceptable English, which was a relief, because Lucky's Vietnamese, despite the Lieutenant's assessment, was strictly of the "you go there, you do that" variety. It was a wonder he'd made himself understood that morning in front of the PRU barracks.

The important thing, though, was that he'd grabbed their attention and their respect . . . at least for the time being. The trick now would be to hold on to the respect he had, to build on it, in order to shape these people into an effective fighting and intel-gathering force.

At the moment, the one man Lucky wasn't sure of was Lieutenant Vang. The Vietnamese SEAL was a cocky little bastard who, judging from the reports Lucky had been reading lately, had some problems working smoothly with others. He wasn't afraid of a fight; in three years he'd picked up both the Vietnamese Cross of Gallantry and the Legion of Merit. He'd also refused orders on four occasions, been involved in diverting supplies from U.S. bases to the black market, and gotten into a fistfight with an ARVN major, which explained why he'd been put with the PRU. Neither he nor Lucky was sure whether that assignment had been punishment or a masterful appraisal of where he would fit best in the military machine; the problem was that as the PRU's senior officer he'd had room to operate. Then Hirsch had come in and taken over . . . and now Lucky was there.

Worse, Lucky had made him lose considerable face by forcing the men to clean up their compound—which they'd done in short order once they knew that their paychecks were attached to their performance and their attitude as soldiers. Lucky had said nothing to Vang about the matter one way or the other, but he could feel the man's simmering resentment.

He wondered if Vang had been on that patrol when Hirsch had been wounded.

As for the rest of the PRU, Lucky was still evaluating

them. He'd sent some of them out, a few at a time, on routine patrols and snatch raids. They'd brought back a prisoner, too, suggesting that the PRU could, in fact, learn to capture VC as well as kill them. *Bat Cong!*

For the most part, they seemed proficient enough. Certainly, they were more eager to come to grips with the enemy than Marvin ARVN generally was, given that getting paid depended on their performance in the field. There were a total of five LDNNs in the unit, including Vang, and Luciano was frankly glad to have them.

The rest of the troops in the PRU had had combat experience, but he still wasn't sure how much. Most were former ARVN soldiers; the best of those were former ARVN rangers, marines, and LLDB—the South Vietnamese equivalent of Army Special Forces—men who, for whatever reason, had left the regular armed forces and taken up with the PRU as mercenaries. While working with them over the past couple of weeks at their camp outside of Vinh Long, he'd easily spotted the men who knew how to handle their weapons, who routinely stripped and cleaned them without having to be told, who took care of their other equipment, seeing that it was properly cleaned and stowed after an exercise in the bush. These were men who'd been there, and who knew that going into combat and coming back out again depended on how well they treated their gear, especially their weapons.

Still, past or present membership in the Army of the Republic of Vietnam was not exactly a sterling recommendation, so far as Luciano was concerned. He'd heard all too many stories about Marvin ARVN lately, about mutinies and refusals to attack or aggressively close with the enemy. In one story he'd heard—and he was pretty sure it was true—an ARVN two-star general had refused to attack as part of a joint U.S.–ARVN operation and claimed his troops would not take part. The mission had been scrubbed as a result. According to scuttlebutt, that general had later been given a third star.

Which left the Americans feeling a bit futile, sometimes. General Westmoreland's request for more American troops two months before was still treated as something of a gallows-humor joke; why were Americans being drafted to fight in a war that the locals themselves refused to fight?

It would have been good, Luciano thought wryly, if he'd been able to work with these people a bit longer before going on live ops. After two weeks of training, formations, and several short-range reconnaissance and ambush missions with them, he still didn't know how far he could trust them . . . or the reports he'd read on their training and experience.

Even among those members of this PRU who'd had plenty of military experience, it was obvious that experience varied widely. Some of the ex-ARVN people were almost certainly deserters, though that wasn't a detail listed in their dossiers. There was also at least an even chance that some might be VC who'd infiltrated the group; that, as much as anything else, was what made Luciano nervous about working with them. Any one of these fifty-three men could be an enemy, and he had no way of evaluating any of them short of taking them into the field and turning them loose.

Always before when he'd worked with suspect indigs— Hoi Chanhs or VNs on loan from the LDNN or LLDB, there'd been the comfort of knowing that there were six or seven SEALs and only one potential traitor. Now, the numbers were reversed, and then some. If someone in PRU 33 wanted to take him out, there'd be no way of knowing which direction the bullet would come from.

As he'd told Waters, Johnson, and Wilson, he would have to watch his own back during this tour; he wished some of his buddies from Bravo Platoon could have accompanied him on this one, though.

His one small piece of satisfaction was knowing that these were men who, though they might not be eager for combat, at least were volunteers of a sort. True, many had simply been given the choice between prison and a combat PRU, but at least the confirmed cowards had all long since gone over the hill.

Today, though, they might well be up against something a bit stiffer than what they'd been used to. The op this morning wasn't anything complicated or fancy, but it *was* big, involving the entire fifty-three-man PRU. A report had come through the night before that a hamlet in Vinh Binh Province, a place called Giang Lon on the Co Chien River three miles northwest of the town of Phu Vinh, had been overrun by a force of VC operating in the area. The place had been garrisoned by a handful of ARVN troops; the survivors had reported that Charlie had come in early last evening, shooting government soldiers, murdering the village's chief, and demanding large supplies of rice.

It was an uncharacteristically bold move for Charlie, Luciano thought, but he remembered what Easy Baxter had told him about local VC units being cut loose by their NVA allies. If the Mekong was indeed the rice basket of Vietnam, villages like Giang Lon would be taking on a far greater importance now as sources of supplies—especially of rice—for the VC cadres. It sounded like this group had decided it was easier to raid Giang Lon for food than to grow it themselves.

That, or this bunch of VC was especially hard-up and growing desperate.

The usual modus operandi for the Viet Cong in a situation like this was to move into a target hamlet in the evening, take what was needed, and be gone by daylight. The chances were good that Charlie had hit the place last night and was now long gone, but it was vital for the Saigon government to make some show of protecting its own villages and hamlets. A large part of the VC campaign was to demonstrate where the real power in the country lay; a government that could not protect its own people was a government that could not survive for very much longer.

The PRU had been designated as a reaction force and ordered out by the regional commander at Phu Vinh. Apparently, the local ARVN garrisons were too shaken by the previous night's attack to be useful. Someone had decided that this was where the mercenaries would earn their pay, so the PRU was being sent in.

With Lucky Luciano at their head.

Waters had provided the air assets, a flight of Army Hueys and HueyCobras out of Can Tho. It made Lucky feel like the proverbial cavalry to the rescue, riding these clattering, metallic steeds through the sky to come to the rescue of the people at Giang Lon.

The helicopter's copilot turned in his seat and clapped

Lucky on the shoulder. "We've got the ville in sight!" he shouted, making himself heard above the thunder of the rotors. "Four miles!"

Turning and craning his neck, Luciano could just make out the village up ahead, a forlorn-looking cluster of hooches, thatched huts, and larger buildings nestled in beneath a line of trees. In front of the treeline were rice paddies, including one big, square paddy fenced in on three sides by dikes and situated directly adjacent to the south edge of the town. Lucky pointed at the open space. "Drop us off there," he shouted. "Doesn't look like anything else nearer the ville."

"Affirmative!" the copilot called back.

The pilot, on the right, was talking into his radio's mike, one hand touching the side of his helmet as he listened to something coming over his radio. Reaching back between the seats, he tapped Lucky on the shoulder, pointed at him, then pointed to his own ear. *Someone wants to talk to you.*

Nodding, Luciano picked up the radio headset, pulled off his boonie hat, and pulled the earphones down over his head.

"This is Lucky Strike," he said into the mouthpiece, raising his voice just enough so that he could hear himself over the rotor noise. "Go ahead!"

"Lucky Strike, this is Lightning One. We're over the target and have negative contact, repeat, negative contact."

Lightning was the code name for the flight of Army HueyCobras flying cover for the transports. Two of the Cobras would be circling above the village of Giang Lon now, checking it out, while the other two hung back and provided support if it was needed.

"Lightning, Lucky Strike," Luciano said. "How's the target look?"

"Looks deserted, Lucky Strike. Nothing moving down there at all but some pigs. No Indians, no villagers. Nothing."

Even the villagers gone? Possibly they'd all fled when the VC moved in.

"Okay, Lightning: Keep me posted. We're going in."

"Ah, that's a roger. Good luck, Navy."

"Thanks, Army. We appreciate you flying shotgun."

"Lightning, out."

Removing the headset, Luciano pulled his boonie hat back on. He felt oddly out of uniform . . . oddly because he was actually *in* uniform for the first time in many, many ops. Instead of his usual blue jeans, tiger-stripe fatigue blouse, combat vest, bandanna, and green and black face paint, he was wearing Army greens, a floppy green bush hat, and no more face paint than the daub or two that the VNs aboard the helo were wearing at the moment.

This was one time when he didn't care to stand out in a crowd. It was bad enough that some of his own men could be VC . . . and him with the bounty on his head that every SEAL carried automatically as a matter of course. If there *were* bad guys waiting in Giang Lon, the one man in the PRU with a green face and a uniform that looked like something thrown together in an Army-Navy surplus store would draw fire as surely as if he wore a big, red-and-white bull's-eye pinned to his shirt, front and back. The PRUs themselves were a mismatched bunch, some wearing ARVN uniforms, right down to their too-large piss-pot helmets, while others—the more experienced hands, Lucky thought—were more casually and comfortably dressed in various types of green or camo-stripe fatigues, bush hats, and load-bearing vests.

The unit was fairly well armed for a PRU. Ever since Tet, the Americans had been shipping M-16 assault rifles to the ARVN armed forces, replacing their World War II–era M1 Garands and carbines as quickly as possible. While line units were supposed to have first crack at the new weaponry, some of the PRUs had been getting the M-16s as well, particularly those that had good political connections, or that rated high with MACV-SOG and the CIA.

Or possibly, the PRUs with the best access to South Vietnam's black market were the ones getting the modern weapons.

Lucky wasn't sure which was the case here. About a quarter of the men carried M-16s, however, and he wasn't going to question how they'd come by them. The Vietnamese tended to be smaller even than Lucky, and considerably less muscular. The Garand was a big weapon, forty-four inches long and weighing ten pounds loaded, and was clumsy in the hands of most Vietnamese. The M-16, at eight pounds and only thirty-nine inches length overall, was a big improvement.

Of those men not yet issued with M-16s, most still carried Garands or M1 carbines. Several men had M79 bloop guns, four carried AK-47s that Lucky hoped had been taken from VC dead rather than having been brought along from their last duty station, and one had an M3 submachine gun—like the Garand, a relic from the Second World War.

Logistics for the unit, he was rapidly learning, were a nightmare, though once again the skill of the PRU's designated supply officers suggested black-market connections, and Lucky wasn't going to question anything that worked. So few things worked in the South Vietnamese bureaucracy these days, it was a genuine pleasure to encounter a system that actually managed to provide ammunition—7.62 x 63mm for the Garands, 5.56 x 45mm for the M-16s, 7.62 x 33mm for the M1 carbines, 7.62 x 39mm for the AKs, and all the rest—and on something approaching a regular schedule.

Lucky would have been astonished if he hadn't known that the PRU's supply officer was probably trading favors to get the deliveries. Hell, SEALs worked that way half the time themselves. No, he *definitely* wasn't going to question the system closely.

"Lock and load!" Luciano yelled, pulling a full-loaded, thirty-round magazine from his combat vest and snapping it home in his M-16, then chambering a single 40mm HE grenade in the M203 slung beneath the 16's barrel. Some fine-print regulation somewhere suggested that it was not a good idea to carry loaded weapons aboard a helicopter, with the idea that an accidental weapon discharge in flight could ruin your whole day. SEALs routinely ignored the rule, as did plenty of others in all services, but Luciano could understand the Army pilots wishing to enforce it with the VNs. Accidents seemed to happen around some of these people more often than was necessary to satisfy the strict observance of the laws of chance.

"Everybody check your buddy!" he called out, and, as Vang translated the order for the others, the six PRUs began checking one another, looking for gear adrift, for loose harnesses, for undone snaps. Luciano checked his own equipment a second time. His new Browning Hi-power on his hip, fourteen rounds loaded and ready to go. Parkerized SEAL knife in its upside-down scabbard on his combat vest. M-16/ M203, locked and loaded.

More important than any weapon, though, was the TR-PP-11B transceiver attached to his vest alongside the knife. The portable FM radio only had a range of about eight kilometers over flat terrain or along a clear line of sight, but even with its nicad battery it weighed just five pounds.

In fact, tactical doctrine for special forces personnel serving as advisors stated that they should carry light weapons only, such as the M1 carbine, in order to avoid getting bogged down in fire support in an action. Instead, their radio link to air assets or other units was far more valuable than any weapon they could have humped themselves.

Still, Lucky didn't want to give up his 16/203 combo; the weapon had served him well in a good many firefights, and he'd developed a near-superstitious attachment to it. Besides, the thumper's extra firepower never hurt in a tight situation, or when the Seawolves were delayed.

The helo slipped lower, edging toward the village as rotor wash set up a furiously thrashing, wet spray on the surface of the paddy below. "How's this?" the pilot yelled back to him.

"Good! Set 'er down! Set 'er down!"

With a stomach-twisting lurch, the Slick dropped from the sky, skimming in just above the wind-beaten water before going nose up, drifting lower and slightly to the side, hovering a few feet above the surface of the paddy. Holding his weapon high, Luciano stepped out onto the UH-1's starboard skid, then jumped the rest of the way, landing in knee-deep water with a splash.

He ducked his head and started moving clear of the helo, praying all the while that the VNs would follow him. He sensed rather than heard a splash at his back, followed by another . . . and then several more. *So far,* he thought, *so good. . . .*

Chapter 14

Sunday, 12 May 1968

PRU 33
South of Giang Lon
0724 hours

Elsewhere, strung out across the rice paddy, the other seven UH-1B transports were descending like great, clattering dragonflies, hovering just over the water long enough for the seven men aboard to jump off . . . then dipping their noses and angling away, banking to stay well clear of the village as the gunships circled warily overhead. Sometimes, if the VC were going to ambush a unit, they would set up a crossfire that would catch one or more of the helicopters as they moved in, but nothing was stirring in or near the village.

Luciano's helicopter was already dwindling into the distance; the four gunships circled ceaselessly overhead, but otherwise, the PRU force was alone. Lucky kept moving, his feet slogging through the thick mud of the paddy.

He detested this kind of warfare, large numbers of men maneuvering in the open. It felt unnatural, compared to the sort of sneak-and-peek swamp and jungle warfare he'd been trained for. Moving in the open this way, he felt as vulnerable and as exposed as a naked man at a formal dance, as visible as a big, fat cockroach scuttling across an empty dinner plate. The treeline was about two hundred meters ahead; a lesser treeline was to the west, perhaps one hundred meters to the left. If the VC were in there, there was no question whatsoever of sneaking up on them. The bastards would have heard the Slicks coming ten miles away, would have watched and counted every man coming off those helos, would know to the man how many men were in the force, how they were armed, and even how well they were organized.

Lucky had the feeling that somewhere up there among those trees, some VC or NVA commander was watching him through Russian-made binoculars, evaluating, measuring . . . and coming to a decision. *Run? Or ambush? . . .*

Vang was to his right and a few steps behind. "I suggest you deploy some of your men toward that part of the treeline to the left," Lucky told him, pointing. "And some more to the right. When they're in position and have checked out the cover there, you can send a patrol in to check out the town, backed up by three forces that have the place in a crossfire."

"Charlie is long gone," Vang replied. "We're not here to play games. The PRU will advance to the village and secure it."

"Negative!" Luciano said, shaking his head. "You don't know what the hell is waiting for you in—"

"I remind you, Mr. Luciano," Vang said coldly. "You are *only* an advisor. You are not in command here."

Luciano went cold. After an initial white-hot flash of anger, he could feel his blood freeze. The bastard was going to play it that way, was he?

"You're damned right I'm an advisor," he said. "And I *advise* you to do the fuck what you're told! We don't know that Charlie has abandoned the village!"

But the PRU was already moving ahead, a straggling gaggle of troops in less-than-military formation, some spread out too far from the main body to offer decent support, others clustered so closely together that a single mortar round would cut them down like wheat. He looked at Hoa, who stood near Vang, uncertain. The Chinese locked eyes with Lucky a moment, then shrugged dramatically. *What can we do?*

"Shit!" Luciano tightened his hands on his M-16. This was definitely a fucked-up way to fight a war. . . .

He heard the thump of the mortar, the shriek of the incoming shell. "Cover!" he shouted, lunging forward into the foul water. A geyser of mud and water erupted from the paddy eighty meters to his left, a thundering cascade that slapped him with its concussion, then filled the air with a dirty, windblown spray. As his head came back up above the water, a second mortar round whistled in, striking with a bone-numbing thump-*whoosh*, closer this time, and to the right.

"Move!" he shouted, waving his arm to give the command emphasis. "Move! *Di! Di!*"

Vang was a few yards away, his head and back just above the water, blinking at Lucky with a dazed bewilderment.

"Damn it, man," Lucky shouted. "*Di di* your ass out of there!" Looking around, he spotted three more VNs crouched in the water nearby. Pointed at them, he yelled, "You! You! You! Come with me!"

It was hard to see at this distance, but it appeared that the thatch walls of several of the hooches in and among the trees up ahead had literally been torn open or dropped away, like hatch covers on gunports, revealing hidden weapons emplacements. He could hear the harsh chatter of machine guns, Russian-made RPDs from the sound they made, mingling with the flatter crack of AK-47s and SKS carbines. Spouts of water flicked from the surface of the paddy a few yards away, stitching a line across the water, and Lucky heard the flat crack and chirp of rounds passing just overhead. The men of the PRU might as well have been smack in the center of a gigantic bull's-eye; the only thing that had saved them from being mowed down by the first volleys from those hidden automatic weapons was the fact that the helicopter drop-off had left them scattered all over the map. The enemy gunners, confronted with so many helpless targets, were having trouble deciding just where to concentrate their fire.

Still, they weren't doing badly. Two men were down so far, one shrieking wildly with a blood-churning wail of helpless, savaged agony.

Crouching in the water, Lucky reached for his primary weapon.

"Lightning! Lightning!" he called over the radio. "This is Lucky Strike! We're taking fire from the buildings and from the treelines. Do you copy? Over!"

"Lucky Strike, Lightning One-one. We're on it. Lightning Flight, this is One-one. Let's carve us a piece."

"Make mine well-done," another voice replied. Two of

the HueyCobras peeled off from the formation and angled in toward the village. Lucky saw puffs of smoke appearing behind the two-by-two mounted M60 machine guns, leaving chains across the sky as they strafed the VC positions. A white contrail stabbed up from the center of the village, arcing over as it zeroed in on the lead Cobra.

"Missile in the air!" one of the helo pilots yelled over the FM channel. "Missile in the air!"

"Break left, One-one!"

"Abort the run! We've got SAMs down here. . . ."

Not surface-to-air missiles, Luciano thought, but an RPG, which at ranges of under three hundred meters could be just as bad.

The Cobra banked sharply left, and the grenade, riding its own contrail, arrowed past the machine, narrowly missing. Seconds later, the grenade's explosion sounded a wet thump somewhere behind the PRU's position.

Machine guns continued to chatter from the village. Smoke spilled from the HueyCobra's engine mount, and the machine began to fall.

"Break off!" another helo pilot yelled. "Break off and abort! It's too damn hot down there!"

"Aw, shit! Jerry's going down!"

Lucky twisted around, staring up at the sky. The Cobra attack had been stopped cold by the RPG's threat, and by the hail of machine-gun fire snapping up from among the trees and village buildings. Even if the Cobras could press the attack, the transports were long gone, and he knew better than to expect them to come back into an LZ this hot for extraction and dust-off.

Luciano's training and combat experience were kicking in, though. When you walk into an ambush, there are several ways of reacting, depending on the exact tactical situation, but the idea is always to do the unexpected . . . and most important, to avoid getting pinned down in the middle of the enemy's kill zone. The usual argument held that a team taken under ambush would suffer fewer casualties if it rushed the enemy gun positions immediately, rather than hunkering down and becoming paralyzed. In an ambush, the attacker automatically held the initiative. The target's only real chance was to reach out and wrest the initiative back from him . . . in blood, fire, and steel if necessary.

More mortar rounds shrilled in, bursting with savage thumps in and around Luciano's scattered command, as RPD machine guns continued to rake the huddled PRU. The RPG fired again, and this time the heavy, spindle-shaped round hissed into the center of the paddy, detonating with a crash and a geyser of water that flung several men aside, shrieking. One thing was damned sure; if they stayed put, those mortars and machine guns would pick them off in no time. They would have to act now, or plan on taking up residence in this paddy as high-grade fertilizer.

Raising his M-16/M203 combo to his shoulder, Lucky slipped his finger into the grenade launcher's trigger housing just forward of the 16's magazine, took a guess at range and elevation, and squeezed. The weapon's butt kicked against his shoulder; the 40mm grenade thumped from the muzzle, traveling so slowly that Lucky could actually see it as a tiny, black speck for an instant as it reached the upper arc of its trajectory. A moment later, it descended, striking the water just short of the earth dike to the left, where the flanking fire was coming from. The explosion raised a column of mud and water. Quickly, he broke open the 203's breech, fumbled a second 40mm round from his load vest, and dropped it in. Snapping the weapon shut, he took aim again, lowering the muzzle slightly this time . . . fire! The weapon thumped again, and this time the grenade struck squarely on the top of the dike, exploding with a flash and a bang and a shower of dirt and gravel and at least one body flung to the side like a blast-shredded rag doll.

"Come on!" he yelled. "Come on! You squat here you're gonna get killed! Move! Move! *Di di!*"

He began wading forward, angling across the rice paddy toward the earth embankment on the right. Tactically, that made the most sense; if they tried retreating back out of that paddy, the PRU's cohesion was likely to disintegrate into blind panic, and he would lose half the force, or more. Besides, he didn't trust the embankment to the PRU's rear, to the southwest. The fact that Charlie had stayed in Giang Lon instead of pulling out during the night was damned ominous, and the fact that they'd had a missile ready was more ominous still. It suggested a carefully staged and prepared trap . . . and no self-respecting trapper would leave a line of retreat that obvious. In his gut, Lucky felt that the dike to the rear was either heavily mined and booby-trapped, or it concealed some other nasty surprise . . . like another company or two of VC armed with automatic weapons.

The best move, then, was to fight out of the ambush, to drive the VC back off the dike on the right because a head-on assault against the village would take them straight into a murderous crossfire. Lucky splashed ahead through the paddy, reloading his 203 as he moved. A muzzle flash flickered from the top of the dike; he triggered another round, sending up a geyser of mud, water, and gravel when the 40mm grenade detonated at the edge of the roadway.

"Come on!" he shouted. "Come on, damn it!"

A Viet Cong broke from cover and ran along the dike, half-visible on the heavy mist of white smoke clinging just above the paddy. Lucky fired a short burst from the M-16, and saw the figure stumble and fall. "Move! *Di di mau!*"

As he waded closer to the dike, a pair of VC appeared at the top, one with an SKS carbine, the other with an M3 grease gun. Luciano squeezed the trigger on his M-16 lightly, tapping off a three-round burst that caught the subgunner high in the chest and popped him backward off the dike, pivoting an instant later and sending a second burst into the guy with the carbine.

Pausing at the edge of the paddy, Lucky turned and looked behind him. Perhaps a dozen members of the PRU had followed him across the water from the center of the paddy, Hoa in the lead. The rest were still out in the middle of that huge, wet square, huddled together in small groups, hunkered down in the mud. Mortar bursts continued to fall among them, as the position was steadily raked by machine-gun fire. Two Cobras circled in the distance, and Lucky felt a burning helplessness. If he could just get some support, there. . . .

"Lightning, this is Lucky Strike," he called over the radio. "Lightning, Lucky Strike! Do you read me? Over!"

"Lucky Strike, this is Lightning One-three. We copy."

"Lightning, we are taking heavy fire, repeat, heavy fire.

I've got men down. Can you move in and take some of the heat off us? Over!''

"Ah, Lucky Strike, Lightning. That's a negative at this time, over.''

"Lightning, Lucky Strike. Damn it, my men are getting cut to pieces. We need you to suppress the fire from the village. Over!''

"Lucky Strike, I've been ordered to hold back and loiter, pending the arrival of air assets from Binh Thuy. You should have some relief in about twenty mikes, over.''

Twenty minutes! An eternity in an ambush kill zone. They would all be dead by that time.

"Lightning, if you don't get your ass down here and give us some fire support, I'm going to fucking shoot you down myself!''

"Ah, Lucky Strike, Lucky Strike. Your last transmission garbled. You are breaking up.'' There was a static-filled pause. *I'll break you up*, he thought, a little wildly.

"Lucky Strike, this is Lightning. Just hold tight down there. The Thunderchiefs will be in here in twenty mikes and goddamn level the place.''

"Lightning, Lucky Strike. Request you put some ordnance on the village. Over!''

There was no answer, and Lucky wondered if the guy had turned his radio off or was simply ignoring him.

Okay. No joy there. If the PRU was going to get out of this, they would have to do it themselves. Keeping low, Lucky scrambled up the side of the dike, which rose only about four feet above the level of the water. At the top was a long, arrow-straight dirt road running north and south the length of the dike, just about wide enough for the passage of an oxcart. Two VC bodies lay there; another floated face-down in the paddy on the other side. A stray round snicked past overhead, but he ignored it.

When he looked back at the PRU's location, he felt a jolt of realization when he saw what a difference just four feet of elevation made on this flat terrain. The paddy made a perfect killing ground. From this vantage point, Lucky could see five or six still forms floating in the water out there. That number again, and more likely more, would have been wounded by now; the VC fire was almost laughably inaccurate, but its sheer volume would quickly make up for the deficiencies of the gunners. If the rest of the PRU didn't move, they were finished.

Turning to look north again, to the right, he could see movement toward the village, a column of black-pajamaed figures moving through the paddy east of the dike, crouched to keep the dike between themselves and the PRU. Lying flat on his stomach, Lucky took careful aim and squeezed off a long burst from his 16. The figures scattered, taking cover in the muddy water of the paddy; Lucky couldn't tell if he'd hit any of them or not.

At least, that would keep them cautious for a while.

"Hoa!" he shouted.

The Chinese mercenary crawled up the muddy bank, fiercely gripping his Garand. "Yes, *May man*!"

"Set up with these men here on both sides of this dike! Hold it." He pointed to the spot where he'd seen VC. "I think Charlie's trying to send some more flankers down this way. I scared them off, but they'll probably regroup and try again. If he sends anyone else down this road, knock him off. You understand?"

"Yes, *May man*! Hold this dike! Kill Charlie!"

"I'm going back and get the others."

Hoa looked back toward the center of the paddy, his mud-smeared face clouded by doubt. "Let me go."

"Negative," Lucky told him. He pointed at the eleven PRU troops still crouched sat the foot of the dike. None were firing; all looked terrified. "I need you to hold these men here, to help them get their shit together." He was damned if he was going to lead a charge to take this dike, then give it back to the enemy. Hoa, he thought, had the guts and the stubbornness to hold the ground long enough to pull the rest of the PRU out of the trap.

"Affirmative, sir!" He began shouting at the others in Vietnamese. The men looked at one another, then at Hoa and Lucky, lying on top of the dike. Maybe they saw something in their eyes; reluctantly, they began crawling out of the water.

"Okay, Hoa," Lucky said. "Hold this dike! It's our god-damn ticket out of this cluster-fuck!"

Sliding back into the water, he began wading back into the middle of the rice paddy.

A fresh, deep-throated chatter of automatic weapons fire opened up . . . from somewhere directly ahead of Lucky, on the far side of the paddy. Ducking, he saw the muzzle flashes on the dike forming the west wall of the enclosure. Shit! Three or four bad guys at least had worked their way down the west embankment and were trying to flank the PRU from that side. If they kept at it like this, they would have the PRU surrounded.

Luciano thought he understood what the VC were after, now. Often, in ops like this one, they would try to down one or more American helicopters, if for no other reason than that it might make other U.S. helo pilots a little more cautious, a little less willing to press an attack or snuggle into an LZ in an unsecured area.

This time, though, the enemy had set the trap for the PRU. If they could bag a chopper or two, well and good . . . but their real target was the Provincial Reconnaissance Unit. They'd suckered the PRU in by capturing Giang Lon, anticipated where the Slicks would drop them off, and waited until all of the troops had been delivered. Now they would make the LZ so hot that it would be impossible for the helos to extract the force, and the VC would work their way around the paddy until the PRU was completely surrounded. Possibly, the VC would take prisoners, making the ambush a mini–Dien Bien Phu that would shake the confidence of every other mercenary VN unit in South Vietnam. More likely, they would slaughter the unit to a man. That would *really* shake things up . . . and probably force a reevaluation of the whole notion of using hired mercenaries to take the pressure off Marvin ARVN.

It was a pretty long reach for his 203, clear across the length of the paddy, just about at the edge of the weapon's 350-meter-range envelope. Carefully aiming just above the heads of the crouching PRU men in the center of the field, depressing the muzzle of his weapon as far as he dared, he squeezed the trigger and sent a 40mm grenade hurtling toward the far side.

The grenade struck the paddy beyond the PRU, but well short of the dike. The machine gun fire kept coming. The enemy gunners were making a mistake common for forces firing automatic weapons at a target below them; they were aiming too high, chewing up the water between Lucky and the PRU.

He kept moving.

Some of the members of the PRU were firing back, he was glad to see, but most of them appeared paralyzed. The numbers weren't looking good. Twelve of the fifty-three were at the east dike, and it looked now like eight or ten were dead or incapacitated by their wounds. That left thirty-one still in the middle of the paddy and able to fight, and he doubted if more than ten or twelve of that number were bothering to return fire. It was a problem that had plagued armies since Homer's day and long before that. In any army, a certain percentage of men, through training, experience, or mental makeup, would fight, while the rest would take cover and wait for things to blow over. The irony was that they almost certainly outnumbered the VC attacking them; certainly, they greatly outnumbered any one group of VC maneuvering on their flanks.

But they appeared completely unable to take command of the situation themselves. As he watched, three of them, wavering under the steady bombardment, suddenly broke and began running toward the south. Gunfire snapped up spouts of water at their heels; one threw his arms skyward, tumbled forward, and was still. The other two dove for cover, vanishing under the water.

Lucky was sprinting now, running toward the center of the PRU position. He saw Vang nearby, hunkered down so far that only his head and part of his back showed above the water.

"Vang!" he yelled. "Get these people moving! Now!"

Vang's eyes turned to meet his. At first, Luciano saw a blank emptiness there, a total lack of recognition. Then, emotion flooded the man's eyes, fear mixed with lethal hatred.

This is the guy who capped Hirsch, Lucky thought with grim certainty.

"Get your ass in gear, mister," Luciano snapped. "Unless you want to die right here in the fucking mud!"

He braced himself, ready to open fire if the man made a threatening move. For an agonizing second, the two stared into one another's faces.

Vang broke first, looking away, biting his lip.

Pham Nhu Truong was crouched in the water a few yards away. Vang suddenly lurched to his feet, splashed over to Truong, and grabbed the man's shoulder, sputtering singsong Vietnamese too quickly for Luciano to catch much more than *"Di di mau!"*

Truong rose unsteadily to his feet, his carbine clutched in hands that showed white knuckles through the mud. Vang grabbed another man, shoving him to his feet. One by one, then in twos, then in larger groups, the PRU began to move. Shouting orders above the roar of detonating mortar rounds, Lucky got them moving east. He kept himself behind Vang, Truong, and some of the others in the lead . . . just in case. "That way!" he shouted. They began advancing toward the captured dike.

Except that it wasn't captured anymore. He could see Hoa and the others scattering back across the paddy now, running as fast as they could to rejoin the PRU. *Shit!*

Now what? Now that he had them moving, he wasn't about to let them come to a halt. He might never be able to get them moving again. He had no idea what had panicked Hoa and his people; Lucky's first impulse was to charge the same spot on the dike again, but it was possible that the VC had reacted to his capture of the place by moving a large force in that direction. If so, Lucky thought, it might actually be smarter to rush the enemy's center . . . the village of Giang Lon itself.

"Vang!" he shouted. He cut loose with a burst from his 16, aimed in the air, to get the man's attention. "Vang! That way!"

Vang looked back over his shoulder and saw Lucky pointing at the village. Lucky held his breath, wondering if the man would go for it.

He did! Vang turned and began moving northeast, toward the angle between the village in the trees and the dike on the east side of the paddy. The others followed, wading ahead, leaning forward as though they were trying to make way against a fierce, sleet-laden wind.

In fact, enemy gunfire had fallen off in the last few moments. It took Lucky several seconds to realize that the Cobras were back, thuttering low above the village, and that most of the enemy troops must be shooting at them. A dense, black cloud roiled skyward above the village.

The gunships were back! Lucky felt a thrill of excitement. They were going to pull this thing off after all!

The gunships swung wide over the village, machine guns rattling. Two by two, unguided rockets hissed clear of their port and starboard hardpoint pods, exploding among the trees and buildings. More blasts followed, including a big one as stored ammo or explosives detonated in a secondary explosion.

The return fire from the ground grew hotter, and both helos began pulling back. An RPG hissed after them, falling short in the paddy and exploding with a wet thump.

Hoa splashed up alongside, his normally impassive face betraying a terrible anguish. "I try!" he shouted above the roar of gunfire and helicopters. "I try to hold. But VC there . . . and there . . . and there." He pointed, indicating the paddies on the far side of the eastern dike. "Three hundred meter. Many VC, *May man*! Many guns! They come!"

"It's okay," Lucky told him. "Gather your people! We're gonna take that village!"

The helo attack had broken the enemy's concentration. Now was the time to rush them. The entire PRU was in motion now, angling across the paddy, not headed directly toward the town but not moving away from it either. When they cleared the center of the kill zone, the mortar fire began slacking off as the enemy gunners lost the range. Machine-gun and autoweapon fire picked up, however, growing disturbingly more accurate as the PRU closed the range.

Five feet ahead, Truong suddenly shuddered, his carbine flying up into the air. He spun in place and collapsed, a ragged, black-and-red hole punched through his face where his nose had been an instant before.

Lucky kept moving. Something hit him in the left shoulder, a hard punch . . . but there was no pain and he continued walking, assuming that he'd just been brushed by a spent round. Twenty paces farther, and he could feel his arm growing numb. He looked down and saw the dark, purple-red stain spreading across the top of his fatigue shirt.

"*May man*, you hit!" Hoa said, concerned. "You sit, rest. . . ."

"Negative!" Lucky snapped back. "We're gonna take that fucking town! Move! Move, all of you, damn it! Get the lead out!" He started to run, slogging through water and mud on legs that were beginning to ache with the unrelenting effort.

Amazingly, the others were running, too, almost forty men strung out in a long, ragged crescent, racing across the paddy, kicking up a spray of water in their wake. He was shouting at the top of his lungs . . . and he heard the others shouting as well. He'd moved out ahead of Vang and the rest, heedless of the danger. All he could focus on was the line of higher ground just meters ahead now, topped by trees and dense foliage, the cluster of hooches and nipa-palm-thatched huts . . . and the wildly erratic stutter and flicker of VC muzzle flashes.

A line of geysering spouts flicked up where a string of bullets lashed the water. Three rounds slammed into Lucky's stomach and chest, hammering him backward. Vietnamese soldiers raced past him to left and right, charging the enemy guns; Hoa, however, reached Lucky in a few seconds, holding him above water, cradling his head.

Lucky died staring up into the expatriate Kuomintang's tear-streaked face.

Chapter 15

Bravo Platoon HQ
SEAL Base, Can Tho
0935 hours

"Lucky?" Baxter felt as though a stiff punch to his gut had just driven the wind out of him. "Lucky . . . dead?"

The small, green-painted office they'd assigned him at Can Tho suddenly seemed claustrophobically small, stiflingly close. The mug of hot, black Navy coffee he'd just poured for himself steamed silently on his desk.

No. Not Lucky. . . .

Lieutenant j.g. Fred Waters nodded. "I thought I'd grab a chopper and come on over myself to let you know myself, Lieutenant. Instead of having it, well . . . go the official route."

"I appreciate that." Baxter leaned back, hands over his face. Damn it . . . not *Lucky*. Not on his third tour. Not with less than a month to go before Bravo rotated back to the World. Not . . .

"Shit." He dropped his hands, looking across the desk at Waters. "What happened?"

Waters shook his head. "Damn. It should have been routine. Nothing special, you know?"

"No combat op is routine."

"Well, yeah. But you know how some ops look hairy going in, and others you know are probably going to come up as dry holes. This one felt dry. He was leading his PRU in a reaction strike against a VC unit that took a town in his

170

district. Hell, all we were really doing was sending his PRU in to make sure Charlie was gone, show the flag, that kind of thing. Turned out to be a trap. Not for the helos, for a change. Charlie was targeting the PRU. The Japs waited until they were on the ground and moving toward the town, out in the open. Then they hit 'em. Came from all sides, trying to surround them.

"Lucky called in repeated air strikes, despite taking heavy fire. At one point, he, well, he threatened to shoot down a gunship that wasn't giving his unit close support."

"Oh, Christ. Lucky . . ."

"The choppers came in. Laid down enough fire that he could get some room to work with. He personally led two charges against enemy positions, engaging the enemy at close range with automatic rifle and grenade fire. According to what the PRU guys tell me, he single-handedly won that battle, got his unit moving just when it looked like they were going to be completely surrounded and overrun. The PRU rallied and fought their way out of the trap by overrunning the village."

"What was the final score?"

"Seventeen VC KIA, definite, though we think a lot more were killed than that."

"They carry off their bodies when they can."

"Yeah. There were blood trails. Lots of 'em. The PRU took seven KIA, and fifteen wounded. God, Lieutenant, Lucky came through that thing looking like goddamn Captain America or something."

"He's a SEAL."

Waters shrugged. "I got all the depositions down, of course. Intelligence estimates that there were a couple of VC companies in that village. Call it a hundred, maybe a hundred twenty bad guys. Lieutenant Vang, the LDNN officer with the PRU, gave the credit for the win to Lucky. So I'm putting him in for a CMH."

Baxter blinked. "Shit," he said, the disgust evident in his voice. "You know that'll get shot down!"

"Damn it, Lieutenant," Waters replied. "He deserves it. Two charges against defended positions, single-handed? That's blue-button stuff."

"Oh, I agree. A hundred percent." Baxter sighed. "But he won't get it, Fred."

"How come?"

"First off, all of your reports are from VNs . . . and the helo pilots he was threatening to shoot down. Right?"

"Yeah, but—"

"No buts. MACV isn't going to pay any attention to reports filed by gooks. You know it, and I know it."

"Shit, Lieutenant! That ain't right!"

"As for the helo pilots, they weren't on the ground, didn't see the action with their own eyes, up close. Besides, there's the officer factor."

"Officer factor? What the hell's that?"

Baxter hesitated, before reaching out and picking up his half-full mug of coffee. "The Congressional Medal of Honor is the highest award this nation can bestow on its fighting men." He took a bitter sip.

"Sure. 'For conspicuous gallantry in action above and beyond the call of—' "

"Yeah, yeah. I hear you." He set the mug down again and leaned back in his chair, studying the other man. "Let me tell you a story, son. A true one. Back in World War II, we didn't have the SEALs yet, of course, but we had the UDT, God bless 'em. They made a habit of swimming ashore on unfriendly islands, often in daylight, in clear view of and under fire from Japanese troops. They were supposed to restrict their activities to the water, of course. Technically, the high-tide mark was the limit of their AO. Lots of time, though, they ignored that limit.

"Anyway, to make a long story short, a lot of these UDT guys were getting put in for medals for what they did. Hell, they were crawling ashore to plant explosives on enemy beach obstacles, digging up mines, measuring the depth of water over coral reefs . . . and all while taking rifle, machine-gun, and mortar fire from the enemy. Gutsy stuff."

"Sure. I read about all that." He cracked a cold smile. "They also started pulling that 'Welcome, Marines' shit, leaving signs on the beaches they reconned for the Marines to find."

"Yeah. So the word comes down from the top. Anybody

who swims ashore on an enemy-occupied island is going to get a medal. Here's the kicker. Every officer who pulls this goddamned stunt off gets the Silver Star. Every enlisted man who does it gets the Bronze Star.''

''Shit! I never heard that!''

''Straight skinny. God's truth.''

Waters folded his arms. ''So what makes an officer better than an enlisted guy? The fact that he's got a better education?''

Baxter rubbed the side of his jaw. Waters, he knew, had gotten his commission through the back door, through an ROTC program at college and an appointment to OCS. His parents were working-class; his father had been a sergeant in the Marines in World War II, not the usual background for Naval officers. He tended to have an egalitarian point of view, one that was shared by most SEAL officers.

But then, SEAL officers took great pride in the fact that they went through the same training as enlisted personnel, and even more in the fact that they had to earn the respect due them by their men, not have it handed to them on a gold-striped epaulet.

''How long have you been in the Navy, Waters?'' The question was rhetorical. He knew the answer.

''Uh, two years. Almost.''

''Surely that's long enough for you to know what a blue-blooded establishment our Naval officer corps is, then. The Navy places *great* stress on the nobility and the bravery of the so-called officer and gentleman. And it rewards him accordingly.''

Waters looked stubborn. ''That's bullshit.''

''I don't know. Maybe it is. Or maybe Washington figures that the enlisted guy isn't as brave as an officer because he's just in there following orders. Maybe it's because the officer is supposed to be smarter and has a better idea of what he's running up against. But I think that's a big part of the reason that the Teams have never been that interested in medals. They *know* it's a lot of bullshit. It's never the medal, Waters. It's the *man*.''

''So what does all this have to do with the CMH?''

''Sorry. I get pissed and it makes me ramble. The word

has come down, Mr. Waters, that *when* a SEAL wins the Congressional Medal of Honor, that SEAL *will* be an officer.''

"Fuck me!"

"Got news for you, Fred. The Navy already has."

"No, I mean . . . you're not serious about this, are you?"

"I'm perfectly serious. You know, I got to talking with a guy on NAVSPECWARGRU-VN staff, up in Saigon a couple weeks back. He was telling me about an incident, in March, I think, over in Team Two. A SEAL chief named Finnegan took on a whole mob of VC in a running gunfight and hauled his patrol leader's ass out of Dodge while doing it. Like you say, blue-button stuff.

"They put him in for the CMH. But Finnegan's not an officer. He may get the Navy Cross instead."

"REMFs."

"Amen."

"Aw, *shit!*"

"What?"

Waters slapped his forehead with his hand. "I just realized. There's a third strike against him."

"What's that?"

"The write-up for the medal would have been routed up the ladder through Sharpe's office. Major Sharpe . . . you know him?"

"I know him." Baxter had been in and out of Vinh Long several times while working with the local PRUs, and when he'd been setting up the paperwork for Lucky's transfer. He'd met Sharpe on each occasion and had usually been forced to listen to the man's single-minded diatribes against special warfare ops in general and SEALs in particular. He sighed. "The man doesn't care much for SEALs, does he?"

"Hell, I think he's the one that arranged for the Vinh Long PRU to go into Giang Lon."

"You're not saying he knew it was a trap."

"No. But he might have suspected something was wrong from the debriefings of the VN troops who bugged out of there. Or maybe he just figured it was a shit detail worthy of SEALs and VN mercs."

"I feel like I have a score to settle with that man."

"Don't bother," Waters said. "The man's a thoroughgoing bastard, and over here that generally is a guarantee of promotion and God's blessing." Waters leaned back in his chair, nearly tipping it. "He's only over here to get the combat-in-Vietnam signoff in his record. Guaranteed promotion to light colonel, you know. And full bird after that."

"I know the type," Baxter said. "And you're right. If our friend Sharpe has anything to say about it, Lucky'll be doing good if he gets a posthumous pat on the head. *Maybe*."

"Shit. And all because he did what he did on his own. With a bunch of VNs." Waters shook his head. "You know, Lieutenant. Maybe that's the real measure of a guy's courage. He did what he had to, and no one was there to see him do it. No one except the VNs whose lives he saved."

"I also know Lucky," Baxter said quietly. "He didn't do it for the medal. He did it because he thought he had to. Because it was his duty. Because he was a *SEAL*."

Waters held his mug aloft. "Hooyah." It was the SEAL battle cry, taught to every trainee in BUD/S, an inversion of "yahoo" . . . and a half-bantering mimicry of the Marines' "oohrah."

Quietly spoken instead of screamed, it became a toast. A *salute*.

To a fallen comrade.

Baxter lifted his own cup. "Hooyah, Lucky."

He sat, arms folded on his desk, and stared at the door for a long time after Waters had left.

He felt as though he'd failed.

The hardest part about leading small military units was always the knowledge that what you did or said or ordered could result in the deaths or maimings of your people, men who were looking to you to say or do or order the right thing and bring them through in one piece. SEAL commanders, he thought, felt it worse than others. A Marine colonel *knew* that some percentage of his regiment wasn't going to come through, but then, he knew them as names on a roster and vague and somehow indistinguishable faces on a parade ground inspection.

But a SEAL lieutenant expected to bring his men, *all* of his men, back alive.

He'd asked Lucky to volunteer for the PRU assignment. *Damn. Scratch that,* he thought. *That's a bad way to be thinking, right now. You had to send someone, and Lucky was the best.*

Why did it have to be Lucky?

Briefly, he jotted some notes down on his desktop log. He would need to check with personnel and see if Lucky had left any family back in the States. He didn't think so, but he had to check. If there was anyone, he probably should write them a letter. That was one of the chores he hated the most. He would also have to send someone up to Vinh Long to pick up Lucky's effects. Scratch that. He'd go himself, maybe this afternoon.

First, though, he had to finish the requisition for the helicopters for the combined op the next day, and he had to get it done this morning, with a deadline of high noon. He felt like a cold bastard, throwing himself immediately back into his bureaucratic make-work as though any of it were worth a damn, but he knew that it was the routine that would get him through the hardest part of the grieving. He'd lost friends before in the war. He would lose them again. The comforting tedium and idiocy of the paperwork, though, would always be with him.

Sometimes, Baxter thought, the paperwork seemed an insurmountable obstacle, with the bureaucrats worse enemies than Charlie. Requests for helicopter support, for instance . . . the request form for that seemed to go on forever, and it had to be submitted by 1200 hours the day before the op was scheduled to go down. He began ticking off the points, filling in the blanks.

Number and type of helicopters required: five UH-1B transports—two to carry the SEALs and the LDNNs, and three for the POWs they hoped to liberate—plus five gunships to fly cover. The helo commands were nervous after the cluster-fuck at Giang Lon. That many helos probably meant a C&C chopper as well, with an airborne controller.

Reporting to: Lieutenant Edward Baxter . . . and including his phone number at the Can Tho SEAL HQ, his radio call sign, "Hammer," and his assigned frequency.

The time period covered by the request: Two hours . . .

though that, frankly, was a guess. Two hours would serve if the op turned into a straight in-and-out, with no unforeseen glitches.

And when the hell did an op ever run *that* smoothly?

Gunship cover provided by: Army. Unfortunately. *Damned* unfortunately. There'd been a lot of friction lately between the Army and Navy over helo assets. Personally, Baxter would have preferred Navy Seawolves, but he'd already been informed that the local Seawolf detachment would be flying with a Team Two op further north this day. Using the Army helos might help smooth over some of the rough bumps left by the problems at Giang Lon. He hoped so. It didn't help to have Navy personnel threatening to shoot down Army helicopters.

Not that he blamed Lucky. Navy SEALs got very touchy about chopper pilots who refused to get in close enough to get the job done . . . or who even refused to enter a hot LZ. Most SEALs thought the Seawolves were the only helicopter pilots who knew how to do it right . . . a heavily biased opinion that tended to get reinforced each time some Army pilot gave the SEALs on the ground a hard time.

Command control: This was another touchy one. He would have preferred to maintain operational control himself, but that would mean he would have to stay in a helicopter where he could oversee the entire operation from the air. He wasn't about to relinquish command on the ground, however, so the air element would be under the control of a helicopter C&C element . . . probably a colonel or a light colonel embarked aboard a Loach.

Control headquarters: That would be Can Tho.

Staged from: Again, Can Tho, though the Army might be bringing in some of its birds from Binh Thuy.

Ops briefing: Easy enough. Tomorrow morning, 0930 hours . . . assuming everything went smoothly through channels and all of the helo pilots got the word to show up for the briefing in the right place at the right time. Again . . . what were the odds of that happening in anything resembling an orderly and proficient military manner?

Control frequency and call sign: Call sign for this op would be Sky Strike. The radio frequency depended on the type of radio being used, both among the helicopters and by the assault force on the ground. In this case, 14.5 megacycles.

Size of unit to be lifted: Four SEALs, nine LDNNs, and all of their gear, plus one Hoi Chanh guide. That was going in. On the way back, there might be some prisoners. Damn . . . how do you answer some of these questions?

Center of mass of operation: This was where the war-college boys had fun, playing with ideas popular at the time at West Point and Annapolis. Battles were regarded as living, moving organisms with a center of mass . . . which could be designated by a six-digit coordinate taken from a standard ops map. In this case, center of mass was located on an island near the mouth of the Bassac River, in a heavily forested area southeast of Can Tho near Tam Binh.

And, finally, other: This was where Baxter was allowed to get a bit creative, since he was expected to list everything that might be of importance in the mission and how the helicopter assets might be expected to deal with it. Would the insertion be made by daylight or after dark? Would there be a predark recon of the LZ . . . a vital point in a situation like this, where the enemy might well have booby-trapped likely open clearings in hopes of bagging a helicopter or three. Would the helos be expected to wait in the area, or RTB back to Can Tho or Binh Thuy? Would extraction be on call, or at a designated time and place? Were there backup LZs in case the primary landing zone was hot, and had those been reconned? Were there special ID protocols in force? Was a dress rehearsal required?

Most of the individual questions were answered easily enough. Sky Strike was being kept as simple as possible, if for no other reason than that the maneuvering of so many helos made it complex, and Baxter didn't want the thing growing so complicated that it bogged down under its own mass. Still, there were so many of them.

The work, however, steadied Baxter and helped him hold Lucky's death at arm's length for a while. Later, maybe at the bar in Can Tho that the SEALs had appropriated for their own use, there would be time to remember the guy.

But not *now*.

Chapter 16

Quoc Te Bar, Can Tho
1740 hours

Baxter paused on Hai Ba Trung Street, staring up at the garishly painted facade of the Quoc Te Bar and wondering if this were a good idea. Can Tho was fairly large, as cities in Vietnam went, the capital of Can Tho Province and the political and economic center for the entire Mekong Delta. Across the street from the cluttered facade of bars, hotels, and shops, the Bassac River ran sluggishly past the city, reflecting the distant green shoreline in its gold-brown waters. Hai Ba Trung Street ran parallel to the river, a cluttered and brightly colored marketplace that extended out onto the water on stilted piers and myriad sampans and small boats.

The streets of Can Tho weren't as bustling or as crowded as Saigon's, of course. The city was primarily agricultural, with rice-husking mills just outside the city boundaries to the southwest providing the principal industry for the area. Still, lots of people on the street wore Western dress, marginally outnumbering both those in more traditional peasant's garb and the Vietnamese soldiers in uniform passing back and forth along the sidewalk. They ignored the American for the most part, but the crowd hastened his resolve to square his shoulders and push on inside.

The bar was dimly lit, crowded, and noisy . . . a typical Vietnamese bar, in fact, though considerably less classy and flashy than the joints that crowded one another for space in Saigon. As he walked in, a pretty Vietnamese girl closed on him with the instincts of a heat-seeking missile. "Hello, Lieutenant," she said in thickly accented English. "You like buy me Saigon Tea?"

"This isn't Saigon," he said with a smile. The smile vanished. "What the hell makes you think I'm a lieutenant?"

"You *look* like lieutenant," she said, smiling sweetly. "I *know*. . . ."

"Hmm. Well, in any case, I'm not in the market for companionship, miss. I'm just meeting some friends."

"Okay. You like good time, you call Patti, A-okay? I bring friends for your friends, too."

"Some other time, maybe."

She smiled at him, a dazzling show of teeth, then licked her lips. "Numbah-one blow job," she told him. "Numbah-one fuck. You bet."

Baxter had been in Vietnam long enough to be used to such blunt and casual propositions, but it was still unsettling to hear them from the lips of a girl who would have been in high school back home. It wasn't enough to remind himself that this was a different culture than his; this was a different culture that had been twisted and broken until it resembled neither the original, nor the Western culture it was trying to copy.

God, what have we done to this place, he thought. Sometimes, in his more depressed moments, he wondered if America would have to answer for what they were doing to this people.

The girl caught sight of a pair of American soldiers—obvious with their crew-cut hair despite their civvies—coming in the door and sauntered off to meet them. Baxter stood just inside the entrance for a moment longer, letting his eyes grow accustomed to the light. Hard behind his concern for what was happening to the Vietnamese people came the worry about whether any of the B-girls or hookers they had working the place were relatives of VC . . . or VC agents themselves. It had sure as hell been known to happen.

He remembered Lucky's wild story about VC whores booby-trapping their privates. *Poor Lucky. . . .*

One of the Americans brushed past him with the Vietnamese girl hanging on his arm. "Watch it, fella," Baxter murmured. "Some of them bite."

"Yeah, I'm countin' on it," the man replied, leering. "I like 'em wild, y'know?"

A lot of Americans were in the Quoc Te already, filtering in as they got off work at one of the various nearby bases or installations. It seemed a little strange, Baxter thought, to run the war on a nine-to-five schedule, especially for SEALs who did most of their operating at night.

Still, most military life in Vietnam, at least the life of personnel who weren't out in the sticks, was almost identical to that Stateside, with more or less regular hours, and plenty of opportunities for entertainment as soon as they got off work. Watering and whoring holes like the Quoc Te sprouted up in every town and outside the gates of every military installation in the country, he thought, with the speed and stubborn persistence of mushrooms shooting up after a rain. Even base camps and firebases out in the boonies tended to attract civilians making their livelihoods off of the rich Americans, usually through liquor, sex-for-sale, drugs, the black market, or some combination of the four. Places that might be bone-dry-dead came alive as soon as the Americans started "getting off work."

A wave from across the room caught his attention, and he began threading his way across the crowded floor, past the bar, to a table at the far side. The rest of Bravo Platoon was there, gathered around a couple of pushed-together tables.

"Hey, Easy," Spencer said. He rarely called Baxter by his nickname, and never while on duty . . . but this was different. "Drag up a stool."

"Where you been, Lieutenant?" Pettigrew asked. "I was by your office this afternoon to let you know we were getting together tonight. They said you were out at Vinh Long."

"Yeah, I ran out there to pick up Lucky's gear," Baxter replied. "I got your message when I got back. Came right over as soon as I read it."

"We were just gettin' started, Easy," Dorsey said, pouring himself a generous shot from the whiskey bottle already on the table.

"Yeah," Bam-bam said. "Glad you could make it, Lieutenant."

"Here," Injun Joe Talbot said, handing him a glass. "You'd better get in the proper uniform of the day."

"That's regulation civvies *with* glass . . . or bottle, your option," Pettigrew said.

"And here's ol' Doc's prescription to go with it, Easy," Doc Randolph added, passing a bottle of scotch. There was no label on the bottle, and, knowing Doc, it was at least possible that the "scotch" was in fact medicinal ethanol colored with a few drops of tincture of iodine—an old Hospital Corps trick—but right now he didn't care where it came from, so long as it was alcoholic.

"To Lucky," Baxter said, raising his glass. "Hooyah!"

"Hoo*yah!*" the others chorused, not in a shout, but quietly, with an intensity that felt almost akin to reverence. SEALs didn't often go in for religion, though there were some exceptions to the rule. Luciano had been Catholic, though as far as Baxter knew he'd never attended Mass while stationed in Nam. The ceremony in the bar, however, had some of the emotional trappings of a church service.

He downed the glass of liquor, savoring the cold fire in throat and gullet. It wasn't colored ethanol, at least. It *was* scotch, though Baxter sincerely doubted that it had ever been within ten thousand miles of Scotland. The ethanol might have been smoother than this stuff, and he normally didn't drink it neat . . . but right now he just didn't give a damn. He poured himself another shot and listened to the conversation unfolding around him through the faint buzz brought on by the whiskey.

Oddly, the talk at the table rarely touched on Lucky, or even mentioned him. An empty chair had been left at the table's head, and it was as though Luciano were a silent member of the party, watching, listening in, being a part of the banter, but not participating out loud. If he was a little quiet this evening, Baxter thought, then so, too, were the rest of them. Lucky's death had shaken the platoon, coming as it had just four months after Bill Tangretti got tagged by a booby trap.

The skyrocketing statistics on SEALs killed and wounded in Nam were on everybody's mind.

Baxter knew the stats on Navy Special Warfare people killed in Vietnam only too well. Until recently, SEAL casualties had been relatively light. In three years, from 1965 through the end of 1967, seven Navy SEALs had been killed in Vietnam—five in firefights in the Rung Sat, one from drowning, and one dead in a mortar attack up in Da Nang. Except for the guy in Da Nang, a Navy commander working directly for SOG who'd been the very first SEAL fatality in the Vietnam War, all of the casualties had been from Team One.

In the past five months, eight more SEALs had died—one from drowning, one by so-called "friendly fire," and the rest from enemy small-arms fire, ambushes, or booby traps. Three of those had been from Team Two; the rest had been Team One.

A large part of that jump in casualties, of course, was due to the increase in the number of SEALs operating in Nam, but even now there weren't more than about two hundred SEALs in-country at any one time. It was hard to find a SEAL nowadays who hadn't had at least one tour in Nam, and everyone, it seemed, had either known a good friend or known a friend of a friend who'd been killed.

The SEAL community was close, and so many deaths within the community tended to make them closer.

"So anyway," Doc said, picking up the thread of an earlier story. "You all remember Nguyen Ngoc Loan? We were talking about him that night at the Victoria in Saigon."

"Sure," Bam-bam said. "Saigon's chief of police. The guy that blew that VC's brains out on the street during Tet."

"You know," Dorsey said, "the press has been having a field day with that back in the States. I got a clipping from my wife the other day, with that photo in it, the one where Loan is holding his pistol to the guy's head, just as he's pulling the trigger. She keeps asking me what I'm doing over here."

"Blowing VCs' brains out," Pettigrew said. "What the fuck else would you be doing here?"

"Well," Doc went on, "the word is that the guy he wasted

had just murdered a police major, then done his entire family with a knife. The major was a good friend of Loan's, and there wasn't any question about the guy's guilt. He was caught at the scene, with a bloody knife.''

"So maybe he had his reasons for capping the guy, huh?" Bam-bam said.

"Hey, it was a summary court and execution," Dorsey said. "The city was a war zone at the time, as I recall."

"Fuckin' A," Pettigrew said. "Hey, they can shoot you back in the States if you're caught looting a store in a riot, right?"

"If the place is under martial law," Spencer pointed out.

"Where'd you hear this about the police chief?" Baxter asked Doc.

"You know Nguyen Van Thanh."

"The LDNN liaison guy? Sure."

"Turns out it's a small country. Maybe half the people here are named Nguyen, but in this case, it happens to be the *same* Nguyen. They're cousins ... which means a little more over here than it does back in the World. He got a little drunk the other day and was telling me about it."

"Shit, Doc," Bam-bam said. "I remember us talking with Mr. Thanh about it. He said something about Loan's brother being VC. He was joking, I think, but sometimes it's hard to tell. If he was a cousin, Loan's brother would be his ... wait a minute. I think I'm getting the family relationship stuff tangled up."

"He *was* joking," Baxter agreed. "Even though, for a lot of these people, it's no joking matter. You never know who the enemy really is over here."

"That was Ong Thanh's point," Doc said. "Only about us. You see, he can't figure out whose side the American newspapers and TV news reporters are on."

"I haven't figured that out myself," Charles Gittano, one of the Second Squad people, said. "I keep getting letters from my wife about how all the movie stars back home are coming out against the war, kids marching and demonstrating."

"Man, it ain't exactly like World War II, is it?" Spencer asked. "With the whole country behind you. These days, you walk into downtown 'Frisco in uniform, and you're liable to get spit on. Or start a riot.''

"Well, Ong Thanh understands the idea that we have freedom of the press," Doc said. "He just has this screwy idea that reporting in our news media ought to be fair and balanced and impartial, right? He wants to know how come the papers and magazines that ran that photo of his cousin didn't print the whole story. About how that guy *wasn't* a suspect, like they always say. He was a bloody-handed murderer, caught in the act.''

"Fuckin' reporters," Spencer said quietly. "They wouldn't know the truth if it bit them.''

"Point is," Dorsey continued, "the Saigon chief of police has become downright notorious because of that photo. There's talk back in the States about war crimes and shit like that. And the guy was perfectly in his rights doing what he did. It ain't fair.''

"It ain't a fair world," Talbot said. "Or a fair war.''

"I'll give you fair," Baxter said. "Don't know if you heard, but the j.g. who was running Lucky's PRU told me this morning that he'd put Lucky in for the blue button. I think you all know how much chance he has of getting it, but I thought you guys would like to know.''

"Shit, man," Doc said, shaking his head. "I wouldn't want the Congressional Medal of Horror draped around *my* neck.''

"Fuckin' A," Pettigrew agreed.

SEALs held mixed attitudes toward the CMH, but most, in Baxter's experience, at least, shunned it . . . the way they shunned men who claimed they wanted it. Some men would do crazy things in combat to win the coveted award, and crazy things could get people killed in a firefight. Most combat vets with any sense at all didn't want to be too close to a glory hound or a hot dog.

"Uh-oh," Baxter said. He nodded toward the front of the bar. "I think we've got trouble.''

"Who's that, Easy?''

"His name's Sharpe," Baxter said. "Army major. I don't think any of you have had the pleasure.''

"We're going to," Spencer said. "He's coming this way."

Sharpe had obviously spotted Baxter and was zeroing in on their table, making his way across the room in an unsteady, less-than-straight line. What was it, Baxter wondered about himself, that made him stand out so well in a crowd? First that hooker had spotted him as an officer, and now Sharpe appeared to have followed him all the way from Vinh Long. He was wearing slacks and a sport shirt and was obviously very drunk.

"So!" the Army major declared in a loud and faintly slurred voice as he reached the table. "So! It's Lieutenant Ed big-macho SEAL Baxter, is it not? An' with all his friends! What we got? Some more loudmouthed SEALs here, maybe? Huh?"

"Major Sharpe," Baxter said, rising. "I think maybe you'd better lower your voice a bit. We don't want to attract any attention here, do we?"

SEALs preferred anonymity, if for no other reason than that the VC had put prices on all of their heads. Sharpe's performance was likely to attract attention, all right. The wrong sort of attention.

"What's matter wi' you?" Sharpe demanded, his voice louder. "You SEALs shy're somethin'?"

"I think we'd better get the major out of here," Baxter said, rising.

"A-ffirmative," Spencer replied.

"I heard you came by t' get that little shit's gear," Sharpe said. "The other SEAL. Whasisname? Thought he was a badass SEAL, but y'know what happened t' him. Gooks shot his ass, an' it might've been his own people who did it."

Baxter slipped his left arm under Sharpe's right, supporting him. "Come on, Major. Time for you to—

"Hell no! Get your freakin' hands off me, filthy SEAL! Won't take tha' kinda shit from you. Won't take it from anyone. . . ."

Bam-bam advanced, black anger darkening his face. Pettigrew had his fists curled into tight, hard balls and looked like he was about to launch himself across the table. Some of the others looked like they were ready to pound Sharpe into small, bloody scraps.

Deftly, Baxter pivoted around Sharpe, stepping between the major and Bam-bam's advance. "Sorry," he said, though he didn't feel sorry at all. As his left hand braced the man upright, his right shot up, short, fast, and hard, the heel of his hand impacting beneath Sharpe's chin with a teeth-rattling crack.

Sharpe's eyes, already glassy, glazed over completely as he sagged backward. Spencer was up, grabbing the man's left arm and helping to support him long enough to ease him down into a waiting chair.

"What the hell are we going to do with him now, Easy?" Spencer asked, glancing left and right. No one in the bar appeared to have taken notice of the short, sharp action. Still, Baxter was worried that someone had heard the word SEALs and might even now be talking to VC agents outside. Damn . . . talk about keeping your low profiles. . . .

"You heeled?"

"Yup," Spencer said, reaching around to touch the small of his back. The others nodded as well. SEALs rarely went anywhere in Vietnam without at least one holdout weapon concealed somewhere.

At the moment, Baxter was carrying Lucky's sidearm, which he'd picked up at the barracks earlier. The CIA-issue Browning Hi-power was in its holster clipped to his belt, concealed beneath the long tail of his sport shirt. He'd not wanted to ship it back with the other stuff and had planned to check it back into the armory at Can Tho. Now, however, he was damned glad he was carrying it. If they had attracted the wrong sort of attention, it might come in damned useful.

"Okay," Baxter said. "We're drunk. We're walking our buddy home. Bam-bam, you take point. Talbot, you're drag. No weapons in sight. Just take it casual . . . and don't bunch the hell up once we're in the street. Right? Let's go."

"Yeah, but where are we going to take him?" Spencer wanted to know. "Drop him off with the MPs?"

"Might serve him right," Pettigrew said.

"No," Baxter said, suddenly inspired. "No, I don't think he'd learn from that at all. Hang tight a sec. I got an idea."

Baxter looked around the bar until he spotted Patti. Holding up a twenty-dollar bill, he used it to wave her over. "You change mind, Lieutenant?" she asked.

"Not for me," he said. Leaning closer, he whispered for a moment in Patti's ear. She giggled, ducked her head, then snatched the twenty from Baxter's hand. "Okay, Lieutenant!" she said. "You and your friends help?"

"Lead the way."

Baxter and Spencer frog-marched the unconscious Major Sharpe through a back door to the bar, down a grimy and cockroach-scuttling hall, then up some ancient and rickety stairs. Inside a windowless room that stank of urine, booze, and sex, they left Sharpe sprawled faceup across a stinking, bare mattress on the floor. "Have fun, honey," Baxter told Patti as they squeezed past her in the hall.

"You like me make him feel real good?"

"Not really," Baxter said. A new idea struck him. "You have a rubber band?"

Her eyes widened. "Rubber? . . ."

"No. Rubber band." He looked about, spotted an open door nearby with an office desk inside. Ducking through the door, he emerged a moment later, holding a rubber band. "Here." Handing it to her, he whispered a moment more.

She looked shocked. "You no like him?"

"No. I don't like him." He handed her another twenty. "Now don't injure him permanently. But I want you to leave him *hurting*. You understand?"

She giggled. "I understand, lieutenant. You one mean son of a bitch!"

Baxter and a grinning Spencer rejoined the others a few moments later. "What the fuck, Easy?" Doc said. "You actually paid to have that bastard's ashes hauled?"

"Not exactly."

"Just what do you mean, 'not exactly'?"

"I told her to give him the same treatment I got my first night in this land of enchantment," Baxter said. "She's going to take every stitch of clothing he has and leave him there. He'll wake up when the management calls the MPs sometime tonight to come get the naked guy out of the back room. Oh, and we left him with a little extra present, from Lucky's buddies.''

"He found her a rubber band," Spencer said.

"A rubber band?" Bam-bam said. He looked puzzled.

"Some of these girls are real good at stimulating a guy all the way to the point of cutting loose, then just holding him there. Sometimes they'll use a rubber band to kind of tie him off, know what I mean? Keep him hovering there at the edge until she's ready to let him go. Only, well, I told Patti to set him up, and leave him.''

"Oh, shit!" Talbot said, his eyes wide. "Talk about blue balls!''

"Black-and-blue, actually. He won't remember the stimulation part, but when he wakes up he's going to find himself, um, kind of distended and swollen, with a rubber band tight around the base of his cock that's going to be a real bastard to get off. It kind of gets buried down inside the skin you know?''

"*Ow!*" Pettigrew said. Some of the others looked pained.

"And when you add in how much he's obviously been drinking lately," Doc added, "the pressure's gonna be kind of excruciating.''

"Exactly," Baxter said. "He'll be sore as hell for a month. Not to mention having to explain to a medical officer what happened.''

"Is he gonna come looking for you, you think?" Talbot asked.

"In his condition, I don't think he'll connect us with what happened. If he does, all he knows is I popped him one ... and let him try pressing charges when I point out that he was babbling classified information while publicly intoxicated.''

"He won't connect it, huh?" Spencer said. "Pity. It'd be nice to leave that bastard something to remember us by.''

"Aw, don't be vindictive, Chief," Bam-bam said. "I think I feel sorry for the poor bastard.''

"After what he said about Lucky?" Dorsey said. "No way!''

"Easy," Doc said, grinning, "I didn't know you had it in you.''

"Yeah, Lieutenant," Pettigrew said. "I didn't know you were such an expert on, um, the erotic arts. Does your girl back home know about this?"

"Yeah," Dorsey said. "Where do you learn stuff like that, Easy?"

"Hey. All part of being a SEAL."

Spencer laughed. "I'm just glad the guy's on our side. C'mon, guys. Let's blow this joint."

"Right," Bam-bam said. "Before Sharpe does."

They decided to hit all of the bars in Can Tho, in Lucky's honor.

Chapter 17

Tuesday, 14 May 1968

Helo Assault Force Hammer
20 kilometers northwest of Can Coc Island
0935 hours

Intelligence. That was what it was all coming down to.

Baxter sat in the Huey transport, watching the placid, rice-paddy-checked landscape drift past half a mile below. He was more convinced than ever, now, that the SEALs' primary contribution to the war would be securing timely and accurate intelligence.

Yesterday, he'd read the voluminous report summarizing a series of actions carried out recently by SEAL Two. Late in April, Two's 10th Platoon had been guided by a Hoi Chanh to a meeting of high-level VCI near My Tho. As the SEALs held the villagers at gunpoint, the Hoi Chanh had pointed out six Viet Cong, who'd been turned over to the Vietnamese National Police for questioning. Information se-

cured from those six during interrogation had led to the immediate arrest of over one hundred more VCI, plus the
capture of hundreds of pounds of documents. It turned out
that the VC had infiltrated every government agency, base,
and military unit in the My Tho region, including a number
of supposedly "secure" American units. The arrests that followed that revelation had broken the Viet Cong's intelligence
net throughout the district and blinded them—temporarily,
at least—to allied operations in the area.

If he ever ended up as a SEAL instructor again—he'd
already spent one nine-month stretch a few years back training would-be SEALs at BUD/S, Coronado, and hoped to be
posted there again—he was going to stress the need for
SEAL platoons to establish their own intel sources. That lesson had been going the rounds of all the units stationed in
Vietnam, winning additional confirmation with each successful ambush, raid, or snatch made possible through the
use of information supplied by Hoi Chanhs, villagers, and
prisoners.

Good intel—at least, Baxter *hoped* it was good intel—had
made Sky Strike possible.

Several days earlier, a woman had come to the National
Police headquarters in Can Tho with a report that her husband, an ARVN soldier captured during the Tet Offensive,
was being held in a VC prison camp. Her story, insofar as
it could be tested, had checked out . . . then been further cor-
roborated by information received from a Hoi Chanh who'd
defected from a VC battalion operating near the mouth of
the Bassac River, at Can Coc Island.

Sky Strike had been assembled by a Task Planning Group
at NAVSPECWARGRU-VN. Prisoners of war held by the
enemy—both Americans and ARVNs—were increasingly on
everyone's mind lately, ever since President Johnson's surprise announcement in March that he would seek to negotiate
a peace with Hanoi. During the Korean War, the North Korean Communists had used captured Americans and ROKs
as bargaining counters throughout the long peace talks at
Panmunjom, and everyone assumed that the North Vietnamese Communists would do the same. The fewer prisoners the
VC and NVA were holding, the better the allies' position

when it was time to sit down at the negotiating table.

Baxter cast a long and appraising look at the Vietnamese riding in the Huey with him. His name was Ngan An Ninh, and he'd been provided to Bravo by the Hoi Chanh center in Can Tho.

How far could the defector be trusted?

That was always the question with Hoi Chanhs, of course. Most SEALs assumed as a matter of course that a certain percentage of the Viet Cong who took advantage of the Chieu Hoi program were agents deliberately sent in to penetrate and subvert the allied intelligence networks, to at the very least provide false information to confuse the overall intelligence picture.

So how did you tell the good guys from the bad?

The answer, of course, was that you didn't. You crosschecked every piece of information you could, using at least two different sources and more if you could manage it. When you took a Hoi Chanh with you to finger the tax collector or the local VCI, you made it clear to him that he would be the first to get blown away if he was leading you into a trap. And you worked out a plan of operations that covered your ass six ways from Sunday, just in case.

There were no other options. The SEALs had learned long ago that they needed to develop local intel sources if they were going to have any chance at all of operating in this country. Vietnam was a small country, with North and South together a bit larger than the state of New Mexico. But when the terrain was mostly jungle, swamp, forest-covered mountain, and rice paddy, finding something as small as a particular guerrilla base camp, or an arms cache, or a tax collector, or even an entire NVA battalion became a far more difficult proposition than locating the proverbial needle in the haystack. You had to rely on local sources because the Americans couldn't be everywhere at once. You had to believe that a certain percentage of the local population hated the Communists and was willing to chance retribution in order to be rid of them.

Ninh, Baxter thought, was the genuine article. According to the National Police who'd interrogated him, he'd been a rice farmer born and raised in the village of Nui Sap. In his whole life he'd never gone more than twenty kilometers from his home . . . until the Cong came to his village one day and told him he'd been drafted. He had no political convictions one way or the other, had never fired a weapon save in rare training sessions, and more than anything else in the world want only to return to his wife and family in Nui Sap. One night, while he'd been on sentry duty on the shores of Can Coc Island in the lower reaches of the Bassac River, he'd seen his chance to get away. Stealing a sampan—he wasn't much of a swimmer—he'd slipped across the river during the night to Mac Bat and turned himself in to an ARVN garrison there, waving a safe-conduct pass that had been dropped over Can Coc a few days before in a cloud of leaflets.

His story of a jungle prison camp on Can Coc dovetailed well with the story told by the wife of a captured ARVN soldier. Reportedly, she'd found out where the man was being held through relatives, who either included some VC or were on gossiping terms with them. Were the VC clever enough to plant both sources, the farmer turned defector and the grieving wife? Anything was possible, of course. The VC were short on technology and equipment, often, but they were anything but stupid. Sometimes the best weapon they had was a skillful use of intelligence—whether lifted from supposedly secure bases by deeply planted agents, or turned against the government as disinformation.

Still, Baxter had worked with a lot of Vietnamese sources, including Hoi Chanhs, and to him Ninh's story, and the way he told it, felt honest. They'd brought him along this morning so that he could lead them straight to the enemy camp.

Normally, Baxter would have taken Ninh up in a single helo to look the target over first, giving the defector a chance to point out key targets or landmarks from the air . . . and possibly to get him to make a statement about topography or geography that would catch him in a lie. There was a rush on this op, however. The VC could easily decide to move their base of operations and their prisoners at any time, and they were likely to do so as soon as they realized that their security might have been compromised. The camp was probably already aware that Ninh was missing. What they didn't know was whether he'd deserted, been captured, or been killed, nor would they know whether he would be willing to work for the government against his former "comrades." Right now, the VC commanders of the Can Coc base would be weighing the difficulty of moving their encampment against the likelihood that they'd been compromised. No doubt, the VC were now trying to find out if Ninh had indeed defected and been interrogated by the National Police; how fast they got that information depended on how thoroughly the National Police headquarters in Can Tho had been penetrated by VC agents.

Despite all of that, if they moved quickly, the allied forces had a good chance of catching the base before it was dismantled. It took time for messages to make their way back and forth between Communist agents and the VC bases that needed the information. They had a chance to pull this off, and Baxter was determined to take it.

This was Ninh's first time up in an aircraft of any type. He'd been scared at first, but now he was exhilarated, bouncing back and forth in his seat and pointing things out to Lieutenant Nguyen Van Thanh, who was along as his interpreter.

Thanh caught Baxter's eye. "He says he's never been able to see so far before," the LDNN said, shouting to be heard above the roar of the rotors.

"Do you think he'll be able to recognize things from up here?" That was always a key problem in this sort of situation. Some people simply didn't have that twist of mental geometry necessary to relate visible points on the landscape to marks on a map . . . or to see the ground from the air and think of it as an enormous map. This was especially true of people who weren't widely traveled and had little experience with maps, like Ninh.

"He identified the Bassac River and May Island, below Can Tho," Thanh reported. "I think he's . . . what is it you say? The real thing."

"Let's hope so," Pettigrew said. He was the other SEAL in the Huey with Baxter, unrecognizable in thick green and black face paint and a floppy-brimmed boonie hat pulled down almost to his eyes. He was carrying an AK-47 for this op; Baxter had chosen his usual M-16.

"You worry too much, Pet," Baxter told him.

"Shit, Lieutenant. It's a dirty job, but somebody's got to do it."

Grinning, Baxter turned in his seat and looked down. The Bassac, broad and green-gold-brown in color, flowed southeast almost below the helo's skids. Ahead, a cluster of slender teardrop-shaped islands crowded one another at the mouth of the Bassac, turning one mouth into many. Beyond, sun glint touched the southern horizon and the South China Sea, turning it silver-gray.

Ahead, between the helicopter and the nearest of the islands, he saw a small flotilla making its way southeast down the broad and muddy Bassac, two LCMs—Landing Craft, Mechanized—plus a pair of Navy PBR gunboats riding shotgun. The LCMs, slow and chunky-looking craft that were relics of the Second World War, carried twenty or thirty PRU troops apiece, led by SEAL and LDNN advisors. They were a vital part of Sky Strike, which was one of the biggest joint SEAL-PRU operations to date. The PRUs had been drawn from the Vinh Long unit. *Lucky's people,* Baxter thought.

He looked off to the side, studying the other helicopters in the flight. There was a total of five Huey transports, counting the one he was on. Three were empty, while the other two carried a mixed force of Bravo Platoon SEALs and LDNNs. Spence and Bam-bam were on the other loaded aircraft, along with five more LDNNs.

To starboard was the Command and Control helicopter, an OH-6A "Loach," a distinctive machine with an egg-shaped body, slender boom, and sharply backswept tail and dorsal fins aft. Designed strictly for observation and C&C work, it was unarmed, but from what Baxter had seen of the birds so far, they were superbly maneuverable, much more so than the older, clumsier UH-1s.

The stars of the air show this morning, though, were the five AH-1 HueyCobras, the deadly Cobra gunships. These were brand-new birds, Baxter understood; the first Cobras had arrived in Vietnam on September 1, 1967, less than nine months ago. The machine scarcely looked like an aircraft, so narrow and upright a profile did it have when viewed from dead ahead. The fuselage was so slender in the beam that it looked as though the pilot and gunner wore it rather than flew it.

The firepower packed by one of those aircraft was staggering. Armament configurations varied with mission profile and requirements, but these carried an Emerson TAT-102A turret system beneath the nose, mounting a single 7.62mm Gatling machine gun with eight thousand rounds of ammo, plus four pods slung two-and-two from the stubby wings to port and starboard, firing a total of seventy-six 2.75-inch unguided rockets.

Baxter was well aware, however, that Lucky had had four Cobra gunships covering him the day he'd set down in a rice paddy with his PRU and begun moving toward the objective.

Damn. What had gone wrong with the helicopter support for the PRU mission at Giang Lon? There was friction between the Army and the Navy, yeah, but it sounded like things had been a bit extreme there. Hell, the Army and the Navy might have occasional turf and power wars, might fight over the odd appropriation at the Pentagon, but out here they were supposed to be on the same side.

The pilot leaned back and tapped him on the shoulder, then pointed ahead. Turning so he could brace himself between the pilot and copilot seats, Baxter peered ahead through the windscreen. "There's our objective," the pilot yelled. He pointed at a blur of dark green, squeezed in among similar blurs in the river up ahead.

"Okay," Baxter said. "Let's get down on the deck and make our swing-around."

The plan was fairly direct and simple. The two LCMs would disembark their PRU elements at a landing zone designated Red Beach, on the southeast shore of Can Coc Island. No one expected the PRUs to move with anything like stealth; likely, any VC on the island would see them coming and move to stop them.

The helicopters, meanwhile, would circle east, then swing in from the northeast to hit the island from the opposite side. The Hueys would drop off their passengers, then haul ass before Charlie decided to investigate. The Cobras would move in as though covering the LCM landings . . . and with luck, Charlie would never know that a small and deadly strike force had landed.

Baxter had submitted another plan earlier, one that he thought would have had a better chance of success. He'd suggested that the SEALs swim ashore at night from PBRs, take up positions on the island, and recon the objective well before the LCMs moved in, just so they would have a good idea of what was waiting for them on Can Coc. The idea had been rejected, however, on the grounds that the PRUs needed a more visible role in the op. Someone in Saigon, Baxter thought wryly, was afraid the small SEAL assault team would move in, capture the ville, rescue the POWs, and secure the entire island before the VNs even reached the beach.

Well . . . if it worked, why not? Unfortunately, this war was often as much about public relations and outward appearance as it was about the real business of war. SEAL ops had upset nice, tidy routines for deskbound gold braid more than once already, and Baxter had learned long ago that the best way to survive was to keep a low profile . . . both from your enemy, and from the people supposedly on your side.

After a fifteen-minute circle well to the northeast of the island, the Hueys came back, arrowing in at treetop level, then dipping lower to skim the surface of the Bassac. Baxter stayed crouched between the cockpit seats, trying to see everything at once. If they started taking fire from that mass of jungle up ahead, they would have to break off and reinsert elsewhere. Fortunately, it was a sizable island, and the VC weren't strong enough to cover every approach. By now, the LCMs would be approaching on the other side of the island, and most of the VC would be on their way to meet them.

Baxter hoped.

The lead Huey braked to a hover, lifting its nose and raising a white spray from its rotor wash. Drifting slowly now, it skittered in over a sandy beach just short of the treeline, hovering just long enough for the seven men—two SEALs, four LDNNs, and one Hoi Chanh—to jump out of the doors and drop to the ground.

Baxter hit first, splashing into a foot or so of water and

pounding up onto the beach as the Huey roared above him. Throwing himself flat, he brought his M-16 up, ready to open fire on anything that moved . . . that even *thought* in his direction. The vegetation lashed back and forth under the rotor wash, but there was no other sign of life. The Huey hovered a moment, then lifted, skimming across the trees; Baxter saw the starboard-door gunner give a brief wave, and then the aircraft was gone.

The second Huey touched down fifty meters upstream, and Baxter saw Spencer, Chavez, and the other VNs splashing ashore. In moments, the two teams had joined up and moved inland, hurrying to get clear of the shoreline just in case the helicopters had attracted unwanted attention.

Ten minutes later, Thanh touched Baxter's sleeve. "Ninh says that the base is about one hundred meters ahead," he said, pointing.

"Okay." He signaled the others. *Spread out. Keep down. Keep quiet.*

They made their way slowly through the forest, taking their time, studying each additional meter of ground before they crossed it. They were slowed up only once, when Ninh pointed out a trip wire, forcing Thanh and one of the other LDNNs to circle around. In the distance, off to the southwest, they could hear an occasional thump of gunfire. The LCMs had landed.

Finally, Baxter reached the edge of the forest, emerging on a slight rise covered with ferns and heavily shaded by the forest canopy overhead. He saw movement and froze, then turned, holding his clawed hand up in front of his face, the sign-warning meaning *enemy in sight.*

Turning back to face the objective, he began taking note of the layout. The village clearing was completely surrounded by dense forest. A dozen hooches were visible, and several smaller buildings as well. Cooking pots hung over open-air ovens or campfires. Fifteen men, all VC soldiers, were in sight, and they appeared to be excited about something. The nearest were only about thirty meters away, and Baxter could hear them calling to one another.

Carefully, silently, Thanh crawled up to take a position next to Baxter. "Okay," the Vietnamese SEAL said. "Ninh says that they know they're under attack. They've spotted some boats in the river, and he says they're getting ready to go hit them. They're also worried about the helicopters.''

''I would be, too.''

Thanh pointed out a row of huts. ''He says those are where they keep weapons, supplies, and ammunition. The prisoners are over there, in the middle of the clearing.''

Baxter looked in the direction Thanh was pointing. He hadn't recognized the things at first, not at this distance . . . but now that he studied them closely, he could see that there were a number of low, bamboo boxes or cages gathered in the middle of the village clearing. Camouflage netting had been stretched above them to disguise their shape and to hide them from overflying aircraft.

''Okay.'' Baxter gave a series of hand signs. *Spencer . . . take your people that way. Pet . . . you're with me.*

The op now could go down any of several ways. What Baxter was hoping would happen was for all or most of the VC in the camp to rush off to fight the PRUs coming ashore at Red Beach. These people were probably too well disciplined for all of them to rush off into the woods, but some of them would go, certainly, and the more, the better. The mission orders left it up to him as to when to launch his assault. He could wait until the PRU arrived if he wanted, and take advantage of their extra firepower.

He'd already decided, however, that he was going to make his move before the PRU got close. Having two large, heavily armed and very excited forces blundering around in the same patch of jungle was a guaranteed recipe for disaster. The most important aspect of the assault would be to get between the VC guards and the cages as quickly as possible, to keep the enemy from killing the prisoners.

One VC was moving toward the treeline where the SEALs and LDNNs were hiding. One of the LDNNs lying in the ferns nearby turned his head, looking at Baxter, who raised his hand in warning. *No! Not yet!*

The Viet Cong came closer. He was, Baxter saw now, a boy, a teenager, holding an SKS carbine casually in one hand, and he was walking directly toward the part of the treeline where the SEAL-LDNN force lay hidden.

A kid. Goddamn it, why did the VC have to recruit kids?

Baxter weighed his options. It might actually be possible to take the kid down silently, to knock him out and save him as a prisoner. Johnson and Captain Warner, the team's NILO at Can Tho, wanted some prisoners from this op.

Somebody, one of the LDNNs, moved suddenly, rising and swinging his weapon around to bear on the boy, who froze where he was, eyes widening. They'd been seen. Baxter squeezed the trigger on his M-16, sending a single quick, sharp burst into the kid's chest, sending him spinning around, arms flying up, carbine spinning away; then the rest of the hidden commandos were firing as well, sending a devastating, rolling volley of full automatic fire into the VC troops gathered in the village.

"Aim high!" Baxter snapped at the others. "And watch your targets!"

Chavez had his M60 in operation, its deeper, jackhammering war cry blending with the higher-pitched cracks of the M-16s, sending a stream of bright red tracers across the clearing, rising slightly, then plunging into the cluster of VC troops on the other side. The Viet Cong, caught suddenly between the sounds of an advancing enemy to the southwest, and the gunfire erupting from the solid wall of jungle to the northeast, seemed paralyzed by indecision. Two were down . . . then three. Abruptly, the rest lost all heart for a stand-up fight and fled.

One figure in black pajamas was running toward the bamboo cages, an AK-47 cradled in his arms. Baxter rose from cover to gain a better line of sight, taking aim and squeezing off a short burst. The man stumbled, took another few steps, then collapsed. The others, Baxter saw, were in full flight now, vanishing into the trees.

But they could be back any moment.

"Cease fire! Cease fire!" Baxter ordered. Moving forward, he emerged from the forest, the muzzle of his M-16 tracking back and forth as he watched for stay-behinds or hidden snipers.

"This way!" Thanh called. "Ninh says this way!"

"Hold it!" Baxter snapped, going to one knee. "Let's not get so excited!" Selecting three of the LDNN SEALs by pointing at them, he then pointed in different directions, ordering them to set up a perimeter defense. SEALs were always at a disadvantage once they left their natural habitats of jungle, swamp, or water and entered open ground . . . or the well-marked and highly visible clearing of a village. If they got too preoccupied with the rescue, they could find themselves attacked from cover in the same way as had the VC in the camp.

Next he sent Bam-bam and Pet to set up a defensive position between the cages and the southeast side of the clearing, positioning themselves so that they had a clear field of fire in case the VC tried a counterattack from that direction. Then he led the rest of the group to the bamboo pens in the middle of the clearing.

Baxter had heard about these things, seen write-ups about them in various reports, but had never seen one for himself. Called "tiger cages," they were open-mesh boxes made of bamboo and wire, a few feet square and standing no more than five feet high. There were eighteen of them standing in three rows of six, clustered close together and well concealed from the air by the camouflage netting and palm fronds strung overhead. Six of the cages were empty; the other twelve held pitiful, stooped and filthy scarecrows that at first glance seemed to deny their humanity. Several of them were naked, save for the filth they lay in. Most were clad only in ragged undershorts or the remnants of half-rotted uniform trousers. Three or four reached out through the bars toward him as he approached; most simply sat or crouched where they were, eyes glassed-over and nearly lifeless.

Baxter felt a thrill of excitement at having carried off this rescue . . . mingled almost at once by a small, answering inner sag of disappointment. None of the men watching him with hollow, half-dead eyes from those cages was American.

Shit! He cursed himself for the thought . . . but it was true that he'd been hoping to liberate American POWs here, and he was bitterly disappointed.

Angrily, he smashed open a lock with the butt of his M-16 and pulled the chain free. The man inside staggered out, blinking. "*Cam on,*" he croaked. "*Cam on rhat nieu. . . .*"

"That's okay," he said. He pointed to Thanh. "*Lai day. Lai day.*"

"*Cam on, Ong.*"

If these wretches had been soldiers once—even ARVN—they showed no sign of it now. They were broken, physically and emotionally, unable even to straighten up after being released from those torture pens.

At that moment, Baxter knew he was never going to allow himself to be captured by those VC bastards. He'd heard stories, certainly . . . scuttlebutt and rumors and tall stories about the tortures the enemy employed, tales told to frightened new recruits.

He'd never entirely believed them, though, until now. Oh, he'd seen evidence enough of Charlie's cruelty, usually to his own people. It was no tall story that traitors to the Communist cause were disemboweled alive. He'd seen the photographs that proved it.

But it was different, somehow, seeing these men emerge in the flesh from their cages like the walking dead, and realizing that this had been done by their own people.

"Move it!" he rasped to the others. "Check out those hooches! Move! Move!"

"Twelve POWs," Thanh said, approaching him a few minutes later. "I'm afraid none was American, however."

"I know."

"One of the rescued men says there were four Americans, but the VC took them out two days ago. He doesn't know where they took them." Possibly, the VC had moved the Americans as soon as Ninh had turned up missing. Or perhaps they routinely shuffled their more valuable prisoners around, just to be safe.

"How are your people, Lieutenant?"

"They will . . . recover. Several have been held in those cages since Tet, over three months. They are suffering from malnutrition and exposure. Most have been beaten and tortured as well."

"We checked all the hooches, Lieutenant," Spencer said. "Some documents . . . and a strongbox with a pile of money. Those sheds do indeed have some weapons and ammo. I saw a pile of homemade rockets in there, about 120 mike-mike.

Five cases of CHICOM ammo. A couple of U.S.-made 75 mike-mike recoilless rifles. Three mortars, 81 mike-mike, looks like. A couple of boxes of mortar ammo. Mines. Blasting caps. Claymores—''

"We'll destroy the stuff in place," Baxter decided. "It's not worth hauling with us, but we're not going to leave it here for *them*. See that documents and money are secured, though."

"Right. What do you want to do about the buildings?"

"Burn them," Baxter said. "Burn them all. And blast those cages, too. I don't want anything left behind they can use."

"You got it, boss."

As the LDNNs moved the rescued POWs out, herding them back into the forest, well clear of the danger area, the SEALs ran among the hooches, tossing Mark 14 flares in among the nipa palm thatching. In seconds, dense clouds of white smoke were roiling through the clearing and staining the sky above the village. Spencer moved down the line of tiger cages, tossing grenades among them. The explosions shredded the bamboo, scattering shards and splinters everywhere. Then the fires touched off the stored ammo, and a fireball rose into the morning sky.

As the flames mounted higher, Baxter pulled his radio free and began speaking into it. "Sky Strike, Sky Strike, this is Hammer. Do you copy?"

"Hammer, Sky Strike. We read you. Over."

"Sky Strike, Moonshine. I say again, Moonshine." The code word meant the primary objective had been accomplished. "We're ready to extract."

"Roger that, Hammer. Good work! Will meet you at Sierra Bravo Hotel."

"Roger, I copy. Sierra Bravo Hotel, confirmed. See you there. Hammer out."

Gunfire still snapped and crackled off among the trees to the southeast, as the PRU tangled with fleeing VC. The C&C chopper would be responsible for coordinating that part of the op, having them break off the action and fall back to the waiting LCMs.

"Primary extraction site," Baxter told the others. "Let's

move it, before Charlie comes back to investigate our hand-iwork.''

The primary extraction site was a clearing about two hun-dred meters through the forest to the north. With Spencer on point and Pet, Baxter, and Bam-bam bringing up the rear, walking backward some of the time to keep an eye on the forest behind them, the column made good time slipping through the woods.

Reaching the extraction site, Baxter had the other SEALs circle the area, checking for the enemy. When they signaled the all-clear, Baxter got on the radio again. ''We're at the extraction site,'' he said. ''Come and get us.''

''We're over the island now, Hammer. Let's see your ID.''

''Popping smoke,'' Baxter said. At his nod, Pettigrew tossed a canister out into the middle of the clearing. Violet smoke boiled from the end.

''Hammer, Sky Strike. I see purple smoke.''

''Confirm purple smoke, Sky Strike. Come on in.''

The Hueys made their approach, then. The forest clearing was too small for more than one helicopter at a time to set down. First on board were the freed POWs, seven on the first transport, five more on the second. A third Slick angled in, kicking up clouds of dust and a whirling blur of violet smoke as it settled in. Seven of the VNs scrambled aboard, and the Slick lurched into the sky as quickly as it had descended. As soon as it was clear, the last helo settled in. Bam-bam jumped aboard with a helping hand from one of the door gunners, then both turned and helped Spence and Pet. Baxter stayed on the ground until Ninh, Thanh, and an enlisted LDNN named Vo Huynh climbed aboard, then swung up himself. ''Go! Go!''

The UH-1 lifted. Something struck the aircraft's fuselage, a solid thump. Baxter looked around, checking out the open door, and saw several running figures pursuing them out of the woods. The door gunner was leaning against his harness, the muzzle of his M60 tracking the targets, then cutting loose with a thunderous roar that outshouted the Huey's rotor noise.

Then woods and clearing were dropping away beneath the Huey's skids. The door gunner pivoted, still firing, the spent brass from his weapon flashing and spinning as it popped from the weapon's breech. As they gained altitude, Baxter could see the village, marked by an ugly black pall of smoke and the vivid yellow lick of flames.

Then they were out over the Bassac River again, heading north.

Another thump sounded from the helo's fuselage, this one from somewhere below. "Shit!" the starboard door gunner yelled. "We're taking fire!" He pivoted his weapon sharply down and started firing back, the gun's hammer filling the helicopter's cabin.

Baxter looked out the door and could see the tracers floating up toward the Huey from the trees just beyond the riverbank. There were at least four weapons down there, hurling streams of lead into the sky. "He's right!" he yelled. "Get us the hell out of here!"

The helicopter banked sharply, trying to pull away from the fire zone. The tracers followed the machine, lacing the sky to either side with green sparks and flashes that looked as large as tennis balls to Baxter.

"We got problems, Lieutenant," the Huey pilot yelled back. He was pulling all the way up on the collective, cranking the throttle to full open, and still the turbine's whine was dwindling and the machine was starting to fall.

"Goose it, Boss!" the copilot screamed.

The pilot shook his head. "The bastard's fucked. Losin' oil pressure. . . ."

Smoke spilled from the engine cowling, up above the cabin, and the rotor downdraft sent it swirling through the aircraft. The rotors were slowing with a grinding sound like bearings cracking.

"Hang on tight, everybody!" the pilot yelled. "I can't hold her. We're going in! Watch the left side! I'm putting her over!"

The SEALs and Vietnamese in the back scrambled to grab hold of cargo straps, seat backs, anything they could. The Huey's deck slanted sharply, and Baxter found himself looking out the right-side door . . . straight down into the treetops less than thirty feet below. The pilot, he realized, was trying to put the helo over on its side, partly to stop the spinning rotors so they wouldn't slice up everyone aboard when they hit, and partly so that the engine mounted overhead wouldn't come smashing down and crush them all on impact.

God, we're going in, Baxter thought wildly. He clung to his seat a little tighter. It wasn't fair. He'd thought if he was going to die, it would be in a firefight, someplace. Not falling helplessly out of the sky.

But then, that was the SEALs, he thought. SEa, Air, and Land.

Trained to die anywhere.

Chapter 18

Tuesday, 14 May 1968

Helo Assault Force Hammer
15 kilometers northeast of Can Coc Island
1046 hours

Then the helicopter hit the top canopy of the forest, branches whip-snapping past the opening. The aircraft lurched suddenly, wrenching Baxter from his death grip on his seat and flinging him toward the opening in the side . . . which was now almost directly below him. He struck the side of the cargo compartment and grabbed a canvas strap, just as the Slick lurched back the other way and threw him against Huynh.

Crashing through a densely woven net of branches and foliage, the helicopter struck a webwork of branches, clung for an instant, then broke through, hit another branch, then struck the ground with a rib-rattling thud. Baxter was thrown violently against the deck as the helicopter lurched to a stop. The helicopter's engines howled protest as the rotors slashed through the treetops, then stopped with a shriek of tearing metal. The silence was startling in its intensity.

Fortunately, they'd not fallen far, and the crash had been reduced to a staged series of lesser impacts as they'd plowed down through the trees. The pilot's attempt to throw the aircraft on its side had worked, it seemed. The machine was a total wreck, but the passengers and crew were alive. Someone started screaming in the smoky half-light. "One of the doorgunners," Chavez said. "He's trapped! Spence! Pet! Gimme a hand!"

Smoke filled the Huey's after compartment. "Out!" Baxter snapped. "Everybody out!" The greatest danger of the moment was fire. Aviation gas was leaking from the aircraft's tanks. He could smell its sharp, acrid tang.

The starboard-side doorgunner was pinned under his machine-gun mounting, which had crumpled backward with the impact. Spencer, Pettigrew, and Chavez began pulling the man free; blood, dark and wet, glistened on his arm and chest.

With the aircraft lying almost all the way over on its starboard side, the port-side door was overhead. The VNs were already scrambling up the deck and hoisting themselves out. Thanh and Huynh had left their weapons behind. Baxter was about to say something, then decided against it. The first thing he was going to do once they were clear of the wreckage was call in an air strike against the downed Huey, to render it and all its contents useless to Charlie. And the SEALs carried firepower enough to protect the party while they were calling in another bird for pickup.

He started moving toward the front of the machine, where pilot and copilot were locked in a desperate, silent struggle. "Jimbo!" The copilot cried as Baxter approached. He was tugging helplessly at the pilot's seat harness. "Jimbo—he's out! He's trapped! Help me!"

Baxter drew his SEAL knife and sliced through the nylon harness, then helped the copilot drag the unconscious pilot out from between seat and instrument panel. The smoke was growing thicker, and both men coughed as they crawled through the tangled, topsy-turvy wreckage aft, hauling the pilot between them, picking their way along, using the cargo deck's disarrayed seats as hand- and footholds.

Spencer was there, and Chavez, lying on top of the helicopter's port side, reaching down into the cabin with extended arms to pull the three men up. Baxter and the copilot passed the injured man up, then scrambled up and out themselves.

"Let's *di di*, boss," Spencer said, as they slid down the Huey's belly and onto the forest floor. He picked up his Stoner and eyed the jungle suspiciously. "I think we must have overflown a pretty big VC encampment. The little bastards are gonna be all over this area faster than you could shake a stick at 'em."

"Roger that. C'mon. First, though, let's move these people over there, clear of the bird."

Thunder rolled overhead . . . the warm and blessedly comforting *whup-whup-whup* of helicopters circling at treetop altitude. The Huey had made a fair-sized hole in the canopy coming down; through the clear patch overhead, Baxter caught a glimpse of one of the Cobras as it overflew the site.

The downed party gathered at the base of a huge, moss-covered tree fifty meters from the wreck. There was a thin haze of smoke hanging above the downed machine, but Baxter was pretty sure that if it hadn't caught fire by now, it wasn't going to. Aside from cuts and bruises, all but the two badly wounded men seemed intact. The pilot had hit his head on something hard enough to split his helmet open and leave him unconscious; the door gunner's right arm was badly mangled, and he probably had some broken ribs as well where the 60's butt had smashed into his chest.

Baxter pulled out his radio, checked the battery leads, then switched it on, clicking it to the op's tactical frequency.

There was a lot of chatter on that channel. "Bird down! Bird down!" he heard over the speaker. "No smoke. Repeat, I see no smoke."

"Strike One-niner, do you see any survivors? Over."

"Ah, One-niner, that's a negative. But we're taking fire in area three-seven. Over."

"Break, break," Baxter called, cutting through the chatter.

"Sky Strike, this is Hammer. Do you copy? Over."

"Hammer, this is Sky Strike. Good to hear your voice! Are you okay?"

"Sky Strike, that is affirmative. We're down in one piece, with two wounded." He glanced back and forth, trying to penetrate the forest. This was definitely Indian country, and chances were the bad guys were listening in on this conversation. "Ah, listen. We're going to have to pull a fast fade down here. Recommend you bust the bird as soon as we're clear. Can you give us a direction to travel in?"

"Ah, that's a roger. Do you have the ops map?"

Baxter was already pulling the plastic-covered sheet from its waterproof pouch and unfolding it on his knee.

"Roger, Sky Strike. I've got it."

"Ah, recommend you make for point sierra-one-two, tango-niner-three. Over."

He found the indicated coordinates. They'd gone down roughly *here*, about ten to fifteen kilometers north of Can Coc Island. The nearest village of any size was Mac Bat, on the river between Can Coc and the crash site. The helicopter pilot was telling them to head west-southwest for about eight kilometers . . . to a region of broken forest and savanna-type grassland, extending all the way to the Bassac River just upstream from Can Coc Island.

That made sense. There was an ARVN garrison at Mac Bat, a little closer, but Charlie often kept a small force in or near such garrison points, just to keep an eye on things, and they would be watching for the downed party to try hiking to the nearest town. If the grounded party headed straight for the village, they were just asking to be picked up . . . or picked off.

"Roger that, Hammer. That's sierra-one-two, tango-niner-three. We'll call you once we get under way. At that time, come in and burn the bird. Over."

"Roger that, Hammer. Check in with us every hour, so we can correct your course as we need to."

"Affirmative, Sky Strike. This is Hammer, out."

The copilot was looking scared. "Look, Lieutenant!" he said. "There's a pretty good break in the trees where we went down right over there. If we sit tight, we could get someone in here with one of those harness rigs, you know? There's not enough room to land a helo, but they could hoist us out."

There were a number of extraction rigs available for that type of rescue. Baxter had used several of them himself during various training operations. But they didn't have time to pull eleven people up out of the jungle one by one, especially with two of them wounded, and anything like a SPIES rig that could haul more than one person would not be regular equipment aboard the helos of Sky Strike. There was no time to wait for special gear to be brought in, no time to do anything but get clear of the wreckage as swiftly as possible.

"That's a negative," Baxter told him. "You can bet that Charlie's coming along through the woods, hot on our trail. We hang around here for long, and we're dead meat."

"Aw, shit, Lieutenant!" the copilot said. "That's five miles! Maybe more, and through the jungle! We'll never make it!"

"A walk in the park, son," Baxter told him.

"We're gonna die, aren't we?" the copilot said.

Baxter considered a sharp reply, then stopped himself. "What's your name, son?"

"Jowoscieiski, sir. Second Lieutenant Jowoscieiski. But they all call me 'Woz.'"

"Okay, Woz. I'll tell you straight. We're in Indian country, true enough, but you got shot down with the very best there is. You stick with us, you do what you're told, and you'll come through just fine. My personal guarantee."

"Yes, sir . . ." He didn't sound convinced.

"The only thing that worries me is the possibility that one of your flyboys loses it. I'm going to need you to watch out for your people, Lieutenant. You understand?" In fact, there were three other Army helo crew members in the group, one of them wounded and now sedated, the other wounded and unconscious. The remaining door gunner was a tough-looking sergeant named Colt who'd said little so far and appeared to be both proficient and composed.

But being reminded of his duty seemed to steady Jowoscieiski. "Yes, sir. I . . . we won't let you down."

"I know you won't, Woz." He turned to the others. The

LDNNs and Ninh sat quietly, watching him. Spence, Pet, and Bam-Bam had vanished, checking the surrounding area silently for signs of the approaching VC.

His eyes picked out Ninh, and he wondered once again if the ex-VC was going to cause any trouble. No . . . he'd come through this well so far, providing information that had been right on with the single exception that there'd been more VC troops and more weapons on Can Coc than he'd told them originally. That, Baxter thought, was more likely due to his unfamiliarity with weapons or large numbers of people than anything else . . . or it meant that Can Coc had been reinforced after he'd deserted.

Ninh could have broken and run for the trees any number of times during the fight, Baxter thought . . . but that was probably not looking like a real good career choice right at the moment. If his former comrades caught him, he'd likely end up tied to a tree eating his own entrails, a decent incentive to stay close to his new allies and help them in every way he could.

"Lieutenant Thanh."

"Yes, sir." His use of *sir* indicated his tacit assumption that Baxter was in command here.

"Take Huynh, Ninh, and Sergeant Colt. Rig a couple of litters. There's some bamboo over there . . . and you can cut up some of your load-bearing vests to tie them together. Get what you need from the helicopter."

"Yes, sir."

It took no more than five minutes to rig a pair of litters for the two wounded men. While Thanh's people were busy, Spencer materialized out of the forest.

"What's the word, Spence?"

"Not good. We can hear 'em coming this way. Two, maybe three hundred meters." He pointed south. "That way. And they're moving damned fast and not worried about who hears them. They'll be here in ten minutes at best."

"Okay. Let's round everybody up and get moving."

"Lieutenant . . ."

"What?"

"We could leave a couple of men here. 'Bush the bastards when they arrive."

Unspoken was the assumption that the men left behind would be Spencer and one other SEAL volunteer.

"Negative, Spence," Baxter said. He jerked his thumb over his shoulder at the VNs and Army helo crew. "We need all hands to get this motley bunch to the LZ."

"But—"

"No buts, Chief. Now get your people and gear and let's move out."

"Aye, aye, Lieutenant."

Minutes later, the column of VNs, SEALs, and Army personnel was moving as rapidly through the forest as the uneven ground and thick vegetation would permit. This region was not true jungle; enough light was filtering down through the tree canopy to allow dense plant growth on the forest floor, and the foliage, together with the large number of fallen, half-rotted logs and twisted roots, made progress slow. Baxter put Pettigrew on point with a map and a compass, moving in the most direct possible route to the west-southwest. Baxter, Spencer, and Chavez stayed in the rear, hurrying the column along when necessary, and hanging just far enough back to make sure the pursuing VC weren't overtaking them unseen.

After they'd traveled a distance of a kilometer or so, Baxter stopped the other two. "I think we need a watchdog here," he told them. "We're leaving entirely too obvious a trail here." He pointed to the line of broken vegetation, muddy footprints, and scuffed-up patches of moss where the column had passed. "A blind man could follow this bunch."

"Sounds good," Spencer said. "Bam-bam? Cover us with your hog."

As Chavez set up his M60 to one side of the trail, Spencer pulled a claymore mine out of one of the black nylon pouches attached to his web gear and began concealing it among the ferns, using the peep sight in the top to aim the concave plate with the legend FRONT TOWARD ENEMY back down the trail in the direction from which they'd just come. Baxter, meanwhile, strung a length of transparent plastic fishing line across the trail, rigging it between two wide-spaced saplings and running the free end back to the claymore.

The M18A1 antipersonnel mine weighed just three and a

half pounds. One and a half pounds of C4 explosive fired seven hundred steel balls like the blast from a titanic shotgun. Normally, it was triggered electrically by a handheld firing device attached to a blasting cap inserted in the detonator well, but Spencer was rigging this one to fire when a hard tug yanked the pull pin from a fuze igniter.

"All set," Spencer said.

"Good." Baxter looked up the trail, studying the jungle beyond the kill zone. "You know, when this thing goes off, the ones still on their feet are going to be mad as hell." He pointed. "They're going to be nervous about following our trail, but they're going to want to catch us. My guess is, they'll cut to the right. Probably between those two big trees just this side of that log."

"Good bet, Lieutenant. Another claymore?"

"Let's do it. We should have time."

Nearly twenty minutes later, the SEALs caught up with the rear of the column as it stopped for a short rest.

"You run into anything back there?" Thanh asked as the SEALs slipped out of the forest.

"No. But we may have bought ourselves some time. C'mon. You people can sit on your asses once we're back home. Let's move it! *Di di mau!*"

Several of the VNs grumbled or groaned as Thanh and the SEALs urged them to their feet. "Let's go, let's go," Spencer said. "The only easy day was yesterday."

That old SEAL expression—a relic from BUD/S training that might well have gone back to the original Navy Combat Demolition Unit training in World War II—felt as reassuring to Baxter as a pair of comfortable old boots. He was about to say something about it to Spencer when a heavy boom sounded from the east, sending a shiver through the air and trees and causing a sudden outburst of birdsong and animal cries in the forest.

"That puts them about two hundred meters behind us, Lieutenant," Bam-bam said.

"Yup. It'll take 'em a while to figure out we're not waiting back there with an ambush," Baxter said. "Let's go!"

A few minutes later, as they proceeded again through the

woods, a second explosion sounded behind them, only partly muffled by the vegetation.

Thanh looked at Baxter, raising his eyebrow and giving an inquisitive grin. Baxter just shook his head and motioned with his hand. *Go! Go!*

It was just past 1200 hours when Baxter called a halt. Gunfire, sporadic and scattered, sounded in the distance, but Baxter wasn't worried. Quite the contrary, in fact. The random shots were most likely VC "reconning by fire," blazing away at the jungle periodically in hopes of eliciting return fire from their quarry. The shots were far away . . . at least half a kilometer, which told Baxter that they had time for a breather. The SEALs were holding up well, of course, as were the LDNN. The Army people, however, were staggering in the heat.

"Catch your breath, everybody. I'm checking in with the guys upstairs." Pulling out the radio, he opened the tactical channel. "Sky Strike, Sky Strike, this is Hammer. Do you copy, over?"

"Hammer, this is Hard Strike," a voice, different from the voice he'd talked to before, announced. "What is your position relative to the crash site, over?"

That's rather stupid, Baxter thought. *Or else he thinks I am.* "I'd rather not say on an open channel." He listened for a moment. He could still hear the drone of a helicopter; indeed, at least one aircraft had been circling in the area since they'd gone down, though they were keeping their distance in order to avoid pinpointing the people on the ground for the VC.

"Okay," Baxter said after a moment. "I hear a helo approaching my position. The tree cover's not too thick here. I will show you the hot end of a Mark 13. When you spot it, you'll be able to feed me compass directions to the nearest clearing without tipping off Charlie."

"Just keep your shirt on, Hammer," the voice replied. "We have to figure some things out up here."

Baxter's jaw tightened with a white rage. Who *was* this REMF bastard?

"Ah, listen, Hammer," Hard Strike added a moment later. "There's been a slight change in plans. We want you to return to the crash site and secure it. We have a heavy lifter on the way. We're going to hook the wreckage out to deny it to the enemy. Over."

Baxter's jaw dropped. It took him a moment to gather his thoughts. "Ah . . . Hard Strike, your last transmission garbled. Thought you said to return to the downed bird."

"That is affirmative, Hammer. Return to the bird and secure it for recovery."

"Hard Strike . . . *are you out of your fucking mind?*"

"Attention to orders, Hammer! I won't tolerate—"

"Who the fuck is this?"

"I am in command of this operation, and I am directing you to return to the crash site and—"

"Why the fuck didn't you burn that bird?"

"This," the voice said coldly, "is Colonel Arlen Wintergreen of the 45th Army Tactical Air Division, and I am giving you a direct order, Mister!"

"And I am disobeying that order." For a moment, Baxter wondered if the voice on the radio could be an English-speaking Vietnamese, trying to direct him into a trap. There'd been reports over the past few months of VC tricks like that . . . imitations of the colored flashing-light signals used to call in PBRs for a river pickup, or false radio signals using common identification codes and procedures. It was possible that this was the same sort of trick.

But he discarded the idea almost as quickly as it occurred to him. The Viet Cong had brains. They would never be so foolish as to try to trick the Americans with such an abysmally *stupid* idea.

"Hard Strike," Baxter said, speaking slowly, almost crooning the words. "Hard Strike, why the hell didn't you bust that bird when I told you to? That area's gotta be crawling with VC by now!"

"Are you refusing my direct order?"

"You bet your sweet ass I am." Hell, by now the VC would have the downed aircraft half-disassembled. "We have confirmed hostiles following us and I will not risk the lives of these people on a harebrained stunt like that. I strongly suggest that you launch an immediate rocket attack on that wreck. You might catch some of their engineers in the bargain, before they can set up one of their jungle workshops on the site."

A crashed helicopter would be an incredible treasure trove for the resourceful VC . . . and not just because some weapons and ammo had been left aboard. Nuts, bolts, washers, hundreds of yards of copper wiring, sheets of plastic and steel and aluminum, engine parts . . . God, even the tires and the seat cushions would be used. The VC were better scavengers than Navy Seabees and would utilize the wreck as thoroughly as the American Indians had used the buffalo, right down to the nylon webbing on the seat harnesses and the empty shell casings from the machine guns.

"Now I suggest," Baxter continued, "that you give us instructions on how to get out of here. If we have to walk the hell out of this jungle on our own, we will. And when we do, I will *personally* track you down and let you know exactly what you can do with your heavy lifter."

The heavy lifter Wintergreen was talking about was probably a CH-54 Tarhe, one of the big skyhook helicopters used to transport heavy loads in and out of the jungle. It was also unarmed and wouldn't stand a chance against the VC, who must be looting the crashed Slick at this very moment.

And there was no question about the SEALs going back in and clearing the Injuns out of Injun country, either. Four SEALs and a handful of VNs could inconvenience Charlie, but they had neither the firepower nor the ammo to take the offensive.

"Hammer, this is Hard Strike. You've just bought yourself a shitload of trouble, Mister. For your information, the entire area around Mac Bat has been cleared of all VC for weeks, now. If you just keep your head and stop panicking, everything—"

"Listen, asshole. This is getting us nowhere. Either make sense, or get the hell off the air and put someone on who does."

"Either you cooperate, or you can walk all the way to Mac Bat, and then I'll see your ass in a court-martial!"

"Break, break," another voice said, interrupting. "Ah, Hammer . . . not all of us up here are assholes. Us pilots, we want to thank you for looking after our people, for getting them out of there. Most of the gunships here are with you one hundred percent, *whatever* the assholes have to say about it!''

"What? What?" Colonel Wintergreen sputtered. "Who is this? Identify yourself!"

"Hammer, anything you need, you've got it. Just call for 'Sky Strike.' We'll get it."

"Thank you," Baxter said, "*whoever* you are."

"Who is this?" Wintergreen demanded. "What's your call sign?"

"What the hell is going on up there?" Spencer asked. He was standing next to Baxter, listening in on the by-play.

"Sounds to me like a small mutiny. Better show the hot-ass end of a Mark 13, before someone changes their mind."

"Aye, aye, sir!"

Baxter keyed the radio. "Sky Strike. Hammer."

"Hammer, Sky Strike. We're with you."

Baxter waited, listening. "I can hear one of your aircraft now, Sky Strike. It's pretty close. I'm going to pop the night end of a Mark 13. Have your people keep an eye out." He didn't want to use smoke, not yet. The chance of being spotted by Charlie was too great.

"Roger that, Hammer. I'll pass the word."

Baxter waited a moment more, peering up through the fronds of the nipa palms. There . . . one of the Cobra gunships was moving low across the forest canopy. Baxter tugged the igniter on the flare and held it aloft, the night end of the signaling device creating a dazzling red star above his hand.

"Okay, Hammer," Sky Strike called a moment later. "One of my boys has you in sight."

"That's real good to hear, Sky Strike. Have him give me a vector on a decent place for an extract. Over."

"Hammer, he says . . . bear one-nine-three from his position. You're about three kilometers from a blow-down of some sort. We'll pick you up there."

"Roger that, Sky Strike. We'll be waiting for you."

Baxter grinned at Spencer, relieved. He didn't much care what happened with Colonel Asshole. At the moment, he felt a camaraderie with those Army helo pilots akin to the brotherhood he knew with other SEALs.

Sometimes, though, it was a little hard determining who the enemy really was.

Chapter 19

Tuesday, 14 May 1968

15 kilometers northeast of Can Coc Island
1407 hours

It took nearly two more hours of toiling through the forest to reach the site, as the midday temperatures climbed higher and higher. Clouds of mosquitoes—"the national bird of Vietnam," as Spencer called them—descended on the party. They didn't seem to care much for the face paint of the SEALs, but they feasted on the others and added to the torture of the hike.

At last, though, they reached the clearing. There'd been no further argument from Hard Strike, and Baxter was beginning to think the son of a bitch had given up and gone home. He waited until Spencer, Pettigrew, and the two LDNNs has swept through the entire area, checking for hidden ambush.

The area was clear.

Helicopters circled in the near distance as Baxter stepped from the treeline. He didn't want to pop smoke for an ID. The chance that the VC would see it was too great. Instead, he got on the radio, calling the circling helicopters. "Sky Strike, Sky Strike, this is Hammer. Do you read me? Over."

"Hammer, Sky Strike. Go ahead."

"Sky Strike, we have the LZ secured. Come on in and pick up the package. Over."

"Copy, Hammer. The Slick is on the way."

"Thank you, Sky Strike. We'll be waiting. Hammer out."

"Lieutenant!" Pettigrew called, signaling frantically from the edge of the forest. "Quick!"

Baxter hurried back to the edge of the woods. "What?"

"We got problems, sir. About twelve of 'em, and they're coming this way fast. Spence just spotted them." He pointed. "That way. Eighty meters."

"Bam-bam?"

"He's with Spence."

"Okay. I want you to take charge here. Get these people on the helicopter when it comes in. If we're not back, get yourself aboard and get the hell out of here."

Pettigrew's face showed several emotions through the greasepaint. Then he shook his head. "I'll get them on board, sir. But you know I'm not gonna leave without you guys."

"Shit, Pet, don't you give me a hard time, too. Now go follow orders!"

Pettigrew gave a wry smile and touched two fingers to his forehead in a mock salute, then hurried off to consult with Lieutenant Thanh. Baxter shook his head as he checked his M-16, then began moving along the indicated line, looking for Spencer and Chavez. Commanding SEALs, he'd long ago decided, was the single greatest privilege afforded by commissioned service in the U.S. Navy. It could also be one bastard of a headache, considering what independent, self-motivated, antiauthoritarian free spirits some of these guys were. They worked together superbly, but only because they wanted to, because they took pride in their unit and in the execution of their mission. Getting them to follow orders, sometimes, was more a matter of winning voluntary cooperation than it was a question of leadership and military discipline.

He found the other two SEALs on their bellies, well concealed in the ferns and ground vegetation, The forest was fairly open beyond their position, in a low, swampy area perhaps fifty meters across given over to numerous small, slender trees but without much in the way of ground cover.

The VC appeared to have stopped at the edge of the thicker woods on the far side of the low ground and were looking at a map, talking quietly with one another on a relatively open patch of forest floor another fifty meters away. As Baxter silently dropped into place next to Spencer, the chief rolled to his side until his lips were nearly touching Baxter's ear. "We spotted them moving this way a few minutes ago. Then they stopped to talk things over. I think they're not quite sure where the LZ is."

Baxter nodded. If the VC had been monitoring the U.S. communications frequencies for the past few hours, they would know that the downed party was making for a clearing large enough to serve as a helo LZ, and might have guessed which one from the position of the circling helicopters. This was probably one of dozens of patrols they had out, looking for the fugitives. *The area around Mac Bat is secure. Yeah, right!*

The SEALs watched and waited. If the VC patrol was lost, it might head off in the wrong direction. At this point, it would be better to avoid contact. A firefight would attract every other VC patrol in the region that happened to be within earshot.

No such luck. One of the men pointed almost directly in the direction of the clearing and said something loud and decisive, though he was too distant for Baxter to catch the actual words. The others began queuing up and the group moved forward, entering the low area slowly, watching the forest around them with evident care. One had an RPG, another a Chinese-made Type 53 machine gun. Most of the rest carried AKs, which made them an unusually well-armed force.

The local bad guys in this district must have pulled out all the stops to round up the downed helo crew. Baxter's thoughts flashed briefly back to the tiger cages in the Can Coc prison camp, and he knew that he was never going to let these bastards take him alive.

"Hasty ambush," he whispered to the others. He pointed toward the left, at an open space ahead of the VC column. "Kill zone from there . . . to there. On my signal."

Carefully, he slipped back from his position next to Spencer, then worked his way over toward the left about twenty meters, and falling back toward the LZ. He found a place of concealment, looking almost straight down the length of the enemy column from beneath a large, fallen tree trunk. Spence and Bam-bam would have a flanking angle on the enemy column, if he stopped them right . . . about . . . *there!*

He squeezed the trigger on his M-16, sending a long burst raking down the VC column. The lead soldier flopped over backward as though he'd run into an invisible wall; the man behind him took three more steps, staggered, then slumped to the ground.

At almost the same instant, Bam-bam's M60 opened up from Baxter's right, jackhammering a stream of lead into the Viet Cong column's flank, sweeping from one end of the column to the other, while Spencer joined in with his Stoner. Two more Viet Cong went down, screaming, including the one with the rocket-propelled grenade launcher. The one with the Chinese machine gun opened up, firing blindly, until Bam-bam hosed his 60 across the enemy machine-gunner's position and knocked him down. Three VC, clad in black pajamas, dropped to the ground, firing wildly in every direction, while two in more varicolored peasant garb dropped their weapons and fled back the way they'd come.

Baxter's magazine ran dry. He pulled an M26 grenade from his combat vest, pulled the cotter pin, then let fly with a stiff-armed toss over the top of the log. Bullets slammed into the log, splashing chunks of wet bark and moss into the air. Then the grenade exploded . . . followed a heartbeat later by a second grenade blast as one of the other SEALs added a second package of high explosives to the fireworks.

The silence following the two ringing blasts was eerie. Two or three of the enemy, Baxter thought, had managed to get away, but the killing ground was covered by still, sprawled forms. After snicking a fresh magazine into his weapon, he carefully rose from his hiding place and advanced into the low-lying area. One of the VC was writhing in the mud in teeth-clenched silence, his arms folded over his belly. Baxter triggered a short burst from his M-16, and the movement stopped. Another of the forms gave a high-pitched whine, like a puppy, and tried to rise on hands and knees. Baxter fired again; the form gave a spasmodic shudder, then slumped motionless.

Baxter made a circling motion with his hand. Search the area. Carefully, he checked the two he'd just killed. The first was a teenage boy, his intestines spilling from his ripped-open belly; the second was a young woman.

Damn ... damn ... damn ...

Don't think about it. Don't think about any of it. Just do the job. ...

He rolled the woman onto her back. Her little-girl breasts were exposed, her black pajama blouse shredded by the grenade blasts. A savage hole in her side exposed white ribs and torn, bloody meat.

"Some papers, boss," Spencer called softly, holding up a waterproof pouch. "Damn, we're not going to get all of these weapons out, though."

It was standard operating procedure to retrieve enemy weapons after a successful ambush, to deny them to the VC. But Baxter could hear the thutter of approaching helicopters and knew they didn't have the time to grab everything. "Take the RPG and the machine gun," he said. "Leave the rest ... with a few surprises." He nodded in the direction in which several of the ambushed VC had fled. "We're going to have beaucoup company real quick, now."

While Bam-bam covered them, Spencer and Baxter left the "surprises." There was no time for anything elaborate. Spencer replaced several of the curved, thirty-round AK magazines with magazines he routinely carried for just such an opportunity. It was a favorite and particularly devilish SEAL trick, one performed by all of the platoons operating in Vietnam and fondly thought of as payback for all of the VC booby traps they'd encountered. One of the 7.62 rounds in each new mag had been disassembled, the cartridge emptied of powder and repacked with C4, and then the round was carefully reassembled and replaced in the magazine, several rounds down the feed line. The next VC to use that weapon would squeeze off a burst ... and when the jimmied round reached the firing chamber, the firing pin would come down and the C4 would detonate ... ruining Charlie's weapon and taking an eye or a few fingers or even part of his face as well.

Baxter didn't have any prepared magazines. He contented himself with pulling the pins on a couple of M26 grenades and leaving them underneath two of the bodies on the ground, the arming lever on each carefully held in place by the body's weight. The VC always tried to recover the bodies of their dead in order to confuse U.S. intelligence estimates on VC casualties. If they found these bodies, apparently undisturbed and with weapons still lying nearby, they would recover the weapons and start to drag the bodies off.

The SEALs might claim another few kills that way.

A Slick was hovering low over the LZ. Baxter signaled the others. "Time to get out of Dodge!" he called.

They reached the clearing just as the Huey gentled in. Pettigrew was standing in front of the aircraft, hands raised, guiding the machine down as he kept an eye on its tail rotor and the perilously nearby trees. Thanh gave a signal, and the VNs and Army helo crewmen hiding just inside the treeline sprinted toward the Huey, heads down to clear the slightly drooping rotor tips, carrying the wounded with them.

Baxter started toward the helo, signaling Pettigrew to get aboard. Spencer and Bam-bam were just behind him.

Gunfire crackled from the north side of the clearing, at Pettigrew's back, and the SEAL flinched, then toppled over to the side, collapsing in the tall grass. Machine-gun fire laced across the clearing, zeroing in on the Slick.

"Gimme the RPG!" Baxter yelled at Bam-bam, who was shouldering the ungainly weapon with one hand while he lugged the heavy M60 with the other. Chavez handed him the launcher.

Advanced SEAL training gave considerable emphasis to foreign weapons of all types, with special emphasis on those used by likely enemies. Laying his M-16 aside, Baxter checked that the grenade was properly seated and wired, knelt in the clearing with the tube across his shoulder, and aimed just above the muzzle flash across the clearing. "You're clear!" Spencer yelled, letting him know that no one was standing in the deadly back-blast zone directly behind him. He squeezed the weapon's trigger; an explosive charge tossed the spindle-shaped projectile clear of the muzzle, sending it dipping toward the ground before the rocket motor ignited, kicking the grenade hard, lifting it again, and sending it arcing toward the enemy gunner.

The explosion shredded leaves and vegetation and hurled it skyward in a mingled cloud of dust, debris, and smoke. Bam-bam and Spencer raced past Baxter, firing as they ran. The machine gun did not open up again, but other weapons were firing from the treeline. The Slick pilot was signaling frantically, and Baxter wondered if he was going to lift off again, to try to get clear of the hot LZ.

Ignoring the pilot's signals, Baxter dropped the launcher, retrieved his assault rifle, and ran as hard as he could toward Pettigrew's position. SEALs *never* left their own, dead or alive.

Pet was still alive. Reaching down with his left hand, Baxter scooped the wounded man half to his feet, all the while continuing to squeeze off short bursts one-handed with his right. Clumsily, he tried to move backward, but Pettigrew was too heavy and the ground too uneven. Bullets snicked and whimpered just above his head. He'd lost his boonie hat sometime in the past thirty minutes, and he was conscious of his hair flying around his forehead as he kept trying to move and fire.

He stumbled, falling heavily backward. Pettigrew groaned. "Shit, Lieutenant. Get the fuck out of here!"

"Negative, sailor. You think I'm letting you go AWOL, you're out of your fucking mind!" Rising, he slung his weapon and started dragging the wounded SEAL again, moving back toward the Slick. Nearby, Chavez was leaning into the butt of his 60, pouring streams of red tracers into the jungle.

"Bam-bam!" he yelled. "Spence! I got him! Get out of there!"

Both men rose and turned, scrambling madly back across the clearing, Bam-bam lugging the cumbersome M60, Spencer both his Stoner and the captured CHICOM machine gun. Muzzle flashes flickered against the shadows at the base of the treeline. From the sound of its rotors, the Slick was lifting off, and Baxter felt a mind-numbing blaze of white anger. The bastards were leaving them here!

Turning, he glared back over his shoulder at the Huey . . . and felt an almost palpable wave of relief. The chopper pilot had lifted the aircraft a few feet up off the ground and allowed the tail rotor to swing the machine around counterclockwise, giving the right-side door gunner a clear field of fire at the enemy-occupied treeline.

Thanh was there . . . and Ninh as well. Baxter passed his M-16 to Thanh, then managed to get under Pettigrew and hoist him into a fireman's carry, fully across his back and shoulders. Chavez and Spencer flanked him, backing toward the Huey now, continuing to fire at the treeline as the door gunner ripped loose with a long and thunderous volley that burned through the air just a few feet above their heads.

Explosions ripped through the treeline. As Baxter reached the helicopter, as the men already aboard grappled Pettigrew's body and hauled him into the aircraft, Baxter turned and looked up. A pair of HueyCobra gunships, their weird, narrow, insect faces glittering in the sun, dropped out of the sky, 32.75-inch rockets hissing two by two from the tubes to either side, arrowing across the clearing on white contrails, and slamming into the forest with savage flashes and claps of man-made thunder.

Someone grabbed Baxter's arm and dragged him upward. He managed to catch the Huey's skid with one black coral sneaker, and then Thanh, Huynh, and Ninh were gathering him in and dragging him aboard.

"*Go! Go! Go!*" Spencer was yelling at the pilot. He added his Stoner to the crashing full-auto melody being played by the door gunner. The ground dropped away before Baxter was all the way in. He clung to the deck as the others grappled with his combat harness and arms, heaving him up and into the aircraft once more. He could feel the aircraft's sluggishness; it was overloaded and having trouble grabbing altitude. The bird was so crowded that some of the VNs were standing on the landing skids, hanging on to their buddies or the deck. Somehow, though, the pilot nursed an extra bit of lift out of the straining rotors, dipped the machine's nose, and set it moving low above the treetops. The Bassac River glittered in the near distance.

Rolling onto his side, he looked back into the clearing, where Cobra gunships circled like angry hornets, blasting away at the jungle with rockets and machine-gun fire.

Chavez was kneeling by Pettigrew in the crowded compartment, tucking sterile gauze pads into a hole in the kid's back. When he looked up and met Baxter's eyes, though, he lifted one bloody hand and gave a thumb's-up. *He's going to make it.*

Thank the god of battles. Baxter wasn't quite sure he could have taken a second KIA among the SEALs of his platoon. He lay there for a long moment, trying to think something suitably dark and bloody about that son of a bitch colonel who'd given him so much grief, but found he didn't have the strength.

It was enough to have survived, to be *alive*, and to be homeward bound again.

Chapter 20

Saturday, 1 June 1968

Jenner, California
0945 hours

Electronics Technician Third Class Greg Halstead leaped off the last step of the Greyhound bus, tugged the jumper of his white uniform straight, and stretched. *Man, it's good to be home*, he thought as he pulled his white hat out of his waistband and placed it squarely on his head. This was his first leave since just after boot camp. He'd taken a number of seventy-twos while he was at Treasure Island, but he'd been ordered down to San Diego as soon as he'd finished school, and then he'd shipped out. Shortly after the *Edson* returned to port in late March, he'd taken the necessary tests to qualify for BUD/S and to his delight had passed quite easily. At least, the timed runs and the calisthenics had been easy. The swimming ... well, coming straight off of months of sea duty with no chance to swim, he was lucky he'd been able to make the time. He was planning to get in a lot more practice over the next two weeks.

But after hearing that he'd qualified for SEAL training, it'd been the usual hurry-up-and-wait, SOP for the Navy. He'd had to stick around in San Diego, still based on the *Edson*, waiting for the next training class to open up across the bay in Coronado. Now finally it was only a couple of weeks away. *Yahoo!*

The driver had opened up the cargo compartment and was pulling out the passengers' luggage. Greg grabbed his bag and headed off along the sidewalk. Jenner wasn't big enough to have a real bus terminal like San Francisco or San Diego did. Instead buses just stopped at the general store on Main Street, only a few blocks away from Halstead Drugs. After thirteen hours on a bus, he wished it was a longer walk. The weather was terrific, clear and sunny and not too hot. He was looking forward to a long hike soon, maybe this afternoon, maybe tomorrow. The folks would probably want to go to church in the morning, but maybe afterward. He planned on doing a lot of running, too, over the next two weeks, as well as swimming. From all he'd heard, SEAL training was brutal, and the better shape he was in going into the course, the easier it would be.

"Howdy, sailor!" a man passing him said with a wave.

"Hi, there," Greg called back and grinned. That was a nice change from San Francisco. There'd been a brief layover in 'Frisco, so he'd gotten off the bus to get a bite of breakfast. In just the fifteen minutes he'd spent in the terminal, he'd been glared at or studiously ignored by almost everyone he passed, been spit at several times, and heard himself called "baby-killer" or "pig." It seemed that just being in uniform was enough to identify him as a warmonger or worse. Maybe

Marci's attitude wasn't that uncommon, not in the big cities at least.

Here in Jenner, though, it was a different story. A lot of the people he'd met in the Navy had come from small towns, where there was still a sense of patriotism, where the idea of serving your country wasn't met with scorn. His mother had kept him posted on local events in her letters, telling him about her friends' sons who'd joined up. That man who'd greeted him could have had a son in the service, or a neighbor's son. He might even have served himself; there were a lot of veterans in this town. He noticed a bumper sticker on one of the cars parked along Main Street—AMERICA: LOVE IT OR LEAVE IT.

"Greg? Greg, is that you?" a woman's voice called.

He turned to see a couple coming out of a side street toward him, the woman peering at him through tiny glasses. She looked familiar, but he couldn't place her. "Ma'am?"

Her face lit up. "It *is*! Oh, isn't this marvelous! Look, Harry," she said to the man next to her. "It's Doc Halstead's boy, young Greg. *You* remember, the one Kathy was so sweet on?"

The name Kathy jogged his memory. "Good to see you again, Mrs. Whitman, Mr. Whitman," he said, shaking their hands. The Whitmans were good friends of his parents, and their daughter Kathy had developed a crush on him when she was nine and he was twelve. "How's Kathy doing these days?"

"Oh, fine, Greg, just fine. She just finished her first year at college. Up at State with your sister Pat. We'll have to get together sometime while you're home. Wouldn't that be nice, Harry?" Harry nodded and smiled. "Ellie told me you were coming home," she continued, "but I'd forgotten it was today. How long will you be staying?"

"I've got two weeks' leave, ma'am. Then it's back to San Diego."

"Oh, good. Then there's plenty of time. Tell Ellie I'll give her a call this afternoon and we'll work something out."

They chatted for a few minutes more—or rather she chatted, he and Mr. Whitman listened—and then he was able to break away and continue down Main Street. He grinned.

Mrs. Whitman was matchmaking again, no doubt about that. Well, he sure wasn't looking for a steady girl, but it wouldn't hurt to take Kathy out to a movie while he was home. She'd always been a nice kid, if a bit flighty. He'd have to ask Pat about her.

Several more people greeted him during the remaining block and a half walk, some of them people he knew, some of them just being friendly to a sailor. He was whistling by the time he pushed open the door to Halstead Drugs. Molly turned at the sound and shrieked, "He's here, Doc, he's here!" Greg barely had time to whisk his hat off before she enveloped him in a huge hug.

"Whoa there, Molly!" Greg said, laughing. "Take it easy! You're squeezing me to death."

"Mind if I cut in?"

"Dad!"

And David Halstead wrapped his arms around his son, then held him at arms' length and looked intently at him. "Greg, my boy," he said. "*Damn*, but it's good to see you."

"Good to see you, too, Dad." Greg was grinning from ear to ear. "It's great to be home."

David fingered the device on Greg's left arm, a bird with outstretched wings above two intersecting ovals above a wide V, picked out in Navy blue on the sleeve of his white jumper. "I remember when I got my crow. Proudest moment of my life. Jerry!" he called. "Rustle up your best banana split. There's a third class out here who's hungry."

"Right away, Doc!"

"Come on, Dad, it's the middle of the morning."

"Need to fatten you up. They're obviously not feeding you down there in San Diego." David lowered his voice. "Or else getting seasick on the *Edson* permanently depressed your appetite."

"Dad!"

"Sorry, son."

Greg never got to finish his banana split. Mrs. Whitman must have spread the word, because it seemed like everybody in town dropped by the pharmacy to see him. He'd take one bite and then he'd hear Molly say, "Why yes, Mrs. O'Connor. Greg's right back there at the fountain." So then he'd have to spend the next few minutes listening to Mrs. O'Connor gush all over him. Finally she'd leave and he'd take another bite and it would start all over again.

After about an hour of this, his banana split was soup.

"Jerry, I don't know," he said, shaking his head. "Your banana splits just don't seem to have any staying power."

"Hey, come on, Greg," Jerry protested with a grin. "It's not my fault you take forever to eat the thing!"

David chuckled. "Son, I think we'd better get you out of here. Jerry, why don't you drive our war hero home."

"Be glad to, sir." Jerry took his apron off and tossed it on the counter.

"Jeez, Dad. What do you suppose they'd do to me if I really was a hero?" Greg grimaced. "I don't think I want to know."

David looked thoughtful for a moment. "You know, Greg, you represent something very special to the people of this town. Do you remember Robbie Andrews?"

"Short, skinny kid, couple of years behind me? Wrote for the *Jenner High Journal*?"

"That's the one," David said, nodding. "Well, it seems he flunked out of college last year, fall semester. Ran up to Canada right after Christmas. His folks had one letter from him, saying that as long as they were supporting the war, they had no son. After that, nothing. Justin won't allow Robbie's name to be mentioned, and Margaret's been just sick with worry. The whole incident has left a . . . a sour taste in people's mouths."

"Yeah, I bet." Greg remembered Robbie as an earnest, clean-cut kid, a bit opinionated, but then most teenagers thought they knew everything. It jarred him to think of Robbie turning into a radical draft dodger.

"So when folks see the other side of the coin, when they see a young boy who still retains the values and ideals he was raised with, well, is it any wonder they make a fuss over you?"

"I . . . I guess not."

"I'm ready when you are, Greg," Jerry said.

David stood up. "Don't take too long, Jerry. I'll have some deliveries for you to make by the time you get back."

"Yes, sir. Come on, Greg. Babe's right out back."

Greg grinned. "You been taking good care of her, Jerry?"

"Sure have. Wash her every week and wax her once a month. And she runs great too. I got a buddy who's terrific with cars. He helps me keep her in tip-top shape."

By the time they turned onto Pleasant Avenue, Greg could see Pat waiting on the porch. As soon as she saw Babe, she turned and said something through the screen door, then started running out to the sidewalk. When Greg had unfolded his tall frame out of the VW bug, she squealed, "Greg!" and threw her arms around him. He picked her up and swung her around.

"Good to see you, sis," he said when he finally put her down. She made a face. He knew she hating being called "sis," but he loved to tease her.

Jerry swung Greg's bag onto the sidewalk. "I'd better run, Greg. See you later."

"So long, Jerry. Thanks for the lift."

Arm in arm, brother and sister walked into the house. "Mom's in the kitchen, preparing the biggest lunch you ever saw!" Pat said. "And wait till you see what she has planned for dinner!"

Greg groaned. "Everybody's trying to fatten me up. At this rate I'll be a blimp by the time I get to Coronado."

"Not with your metabolism, young man," Ellie Halstead said, wiping her hands on her apron as she came out of the kitchen. "You burn calories just sitting and thinking."

Greg put his hands on his hips and gave a wolf whistle. "I don't know how you do it, lady. You just get better-looking all the time."

"Well, of course she does," Grandpap said. "The Halstead men have always picked beautiful women."

"You two," Ellie said, laughing. "I don't know which of you is worse."

Pat hadn't exaggerated; the dining-room table was piled high. Fortunately everyone kept asking him questions, so he ended up talking too much to overeat. At the end of the meal Pat asked him to explain the device on his arm.

Pointing to the bird at the top, Greg said, "This is the crow. That means I'm a rated petty officer."

"Crow!" Pat exclaimed. "It looks more like an eagle."

Greg grinned. "Well, crow is what we call it. The V means I'm a third class. That's the same as a corporal in the Army or the Marines. Two Vs is a second class, and three Vs a first class."

"Sounds backwards to me. One V for third, and three for first."

"Well, that's the Navy for you. This thing in the middle like an atom with electrons going around it means I'm an electronics technician. So put it all together and you get an electronics technician third class or ET3. That's me." Greg pushed his chair back from the table and gave a satisfied sigh. "That was magnificent, Mom. I think I need a long, slow run after that meal. Want to join me, Pat?"

She laughed. "Well, I doubt I'd be able to keep up with you. I haven't done much running since high school."

"I'll go easy on you, kid. Get my real exercise later."

"Okay, you're on. I'll go get my sneakers."

Greg quickly changed out of his whites into jeans and a T-shirt, and the two of them headed out the door and started jogging. They stuck to the sidewalk for the first few minutes, but it wasn't long before they were in real country and jogging along a trail Greg remembered running in high school. Back when he'd joined the cross-country team, Pat had been in junior high. She'd idolized her big brother and had often gone running with him. They'd been very close back then but had drifted apart by the time Greg had gone to college. The past year they'd been able to recapture some of that closeness.

For a long time there was silence except the slapping of their shoes on the dirt path, the sound of their breathing, and the occasional chirp of a bird. Finally Pat pulled up, panting. "That's it, sailor boy. You've done me in."

"You're doing great, kid. We've done over a mile, easy. That's more than some of the recruits I trained with in boot camp could do, first time out. Let's keep walking though, okay? You'll cool out better, and besides this way we can talk."

"Give me a breather first, okay?" Pat leaned against a nearby tree.

"Sure. Take your time."

"What's SEAL training going to be like, Greg? Do you know?"

Greg shrugged. "Not the details. From what I've heard, it's like boot camp squared and cubed. Really intensive physical training designed to weed out the people who don't have the stamina to stick with the program. Lots of running, lots of swimming, lots of time in small boats. After that, a lot of specific training in demolitions, weapons systems, amphibious operations, parachuting . . ."

Pat's eyes grew wide. "Parachuting! Like out of airplanes?"

"Sure," he said with a grin. "Sea, Air, and Land. SEALs are a triple threat."

She pushed off from the tree and started walking. "You really want this, don't you, Greg?"

He looked at her sharply. "Yes, I do. Does that bother you?"

"Well . . . it makes me a bit uncomfortable."

There was an edge to his voice as he said, "So. You'd be ashamed to admit you had a brother who was a naval commando, is that it?"

"Of course not!" Anger flared in her eyes. "I couldn't be ashamed of you. But . . . but I do worry sometimes. If you do become a SEAL and get sent to Vietnam, that means that you might have to kill someone. Doesn't it."

"Yes. That's what I'd be trained to do."

"Do you think you could do it? If you were out there face-to-face with a Viet Cong, the enemy, another human being . . . do you think you could pull the trigger?"

Greg almost came back with a flip answer, something like "well, it's him or me," but then he stopped. The question was a serious one, and it was one that had been in the back of his mind ever since his dad had told him about the SEALs and he'd started thinking about becoming a naval commando. "I'm not sure, Pat. I would hope I'd be able to."

"But why? Why would you *want* to be able to kill another human being?"

He didn't say anything for a long enough time that she must have thought he wasn't going to answer. "Greg?"

"Oh, I heard you all right," he said slowly. "It's a tough question, Pat. I guess that . . . well, they're all related, these things you're asking. And what it all comes down to is I need a challenge, I need to have something to reach for. That's why I left college, really. It seemed like I was just marking time there, never striving for something beyond myself. No, that's not right. I wanted to strive for something *within* myself. SEAL training will be a tremendous challenge, not just physically, but mentally."

"You mean all the things you have to study?" Pat sounded puzzled.

"No, I'm not talking about an intellectual challenge, I'm talking about a mental challenge, a challenge of heart and mind and soul. Do I have what it takes to keep going when I'm dead tired or in pain or terrified? Can I conquer fear . . . or will it conquer me?"

Pat shook her head. "I don't think I can understand why you would want to place yourself in a position where you would be likely to be any of those things, dead tired or in pain or terrified. Look, I'm not saying you should run from them, but do you have to seek them out?"

"They're out there, Pat. If I don't find them, they'll find me. Maybe not for years, but they'll find me. I want to know I can face them when they do."

They walked along in silence then. There were a few clouds in the sky now, just enough to look pretty. "It's so beautiful here," Greg said. "I want to run out here every day. I need to do a lot of swimming, too. Do you know if they keep the high-school pool open during the summer?"

"Mmm-hmm. Jenner Recreation uses it for classes. I'm pretty sure they have open swim sessions, too. Mom might know the times."

"Good. I didn't do so well on my qualifying swim. I passed, but just barely. I really need to get my swimming muscles back in shape. I got a start on that down in San Diego, but I need to keep it up."

"Hey, why don't we take a day and go over to Goat Rock. Have a picnic, go swimming in the ocean."

"That'd be great, Pat."

"Oh, I've been meaning to ask you. Who're you going to vote for Tuesday?"

"Tuesday?"

"Greg, where have you been? The Democratic Primary!"

"Oh, right." He chuckled wryly. "You get sort of out of touch in the Navy sometimes."

"I'm voting for Bobby Kennedy. What about you?"

"Right, I remember hearing about him entering the race just after we left Pearl the last time. Well, I don't know. I'd go for Johnson if he were still in the running, but I'm not sure how I feel about Humphrey."

"Well, he's not running in California. It's basically between Kennedy and Gene McCarthy."

"Hmm. What little I've heard McCarthy say seems to be mostly attacks on Kennedy. At least Kennedy talks about the issues. Who do you think's going to win, Pat?"

"My money's on Bobby. He's got a lot of support in this state. I've been putting in some time at his San Francisco campaign headquarters."

Greg grinned. "I bet you're hoping that if Kennedy wins, he'll go on to win in November and get us out of Vietnam so fast I won't have to go."

"Well," Pat admitted, smiling. "I have to admit that would be a nice side benefit. Let's stay up together on Tuesday night and watch the returns, okay?"

Chapter 21

Tuesday, 4 June 1968

Jenner, California
1915 hours

"I know it's not looking good right now." Pat was sitting on the edge of the sofa in the living room, leaning forward toward the television set. The whole family had gathered there to listen to the election returns. "But I still think he can pull it off. And I'll bet he'll sweep the convention in August, too."

"My, that would certainly be an upset," Ellie said.

"Not as much as it would have been if this was Johnson's second term," David put in. "The fact that he declined to run was practically an admission that his program had failed. And Humphrey *can't* come up with a substantially new policy, not when he still has to be Johnson's vice president for the rest of the year."

"Anyway, Bobby's doing well in South Dakota, and that wasn't looking good earlier either," Pat added.

"I'm getting a beer." Greg stood up and headed for the kitchen. "Can I get anybody else anything?"

"A ginger ale would be wonderful, Greg," Ellie said, smiling. "Not too much ice."

"I'll take a beer, son." David was sitting between Ellie and Pat on the sofa, with his arm resting on his wife's shoulders.

Grandpap pushed himself up from his easy chair. "I've got a good book waiting for me upstairs. I reckon I'll get me a glass of water and head on up."

Pat got up to give him a kiss. "Good night, Grandpap."

Grandpap smiled and patted her arm. "You're a sweet child, Pat. Don't ever let anybody tell you anything different."

"Eh, she'll do," Greg said from the kitchen.

"I'll get you later!" Pat yelled.

There was a commercial on by the time Greg got back with the drinks and a big bowl of pretzels. He sat down in the green leather chair and took a long swig of his beer. "Man, that's good." Turning to Pat, he studied her face for a moment. "How're things going with you and Andy, kid?"

She frowned. That was a subject she'd been thinking a lot about lately, and not exactly enjoying the process. "Not so hot. He . . . he's just so detached from everything all of the time, like he doesn't really care about anything. But I *know* that's not true. It must just be that . . . that he doesn't want anybody to know that he cares."

"Hmm. Doesn't want to appear vulnerable?" Greg hazarded.

Pat looked up at him. "Could be. Yeah, that kind of fits. But you have to let down your walls if you're in love, you *have* to let yourself be vulnerable. Don't you think?"

"Oh, I don't know. I can imagine getting hurt enough that you might not be willing to face the prospect again." He looked away from her as he spoke.

Pat lowered her voice. "Did . . . is that what happened to you, Greg?"

He glanced over at her quickly and then turned away again. "I don't think so. I mean, you gotta put things like that behind you, know what I mean?"

In other words, don't talk about it! Okay, I get the message. "I really don't know what to do about Andy. I've been waiting to see if he would write me, see what his letters are like." She grinned. "You can tell a lot about a person by the letters he writes. Ask me how I know that."

"All right, I'll bite. How do you know that?" Greg grinned right back, knowing she meant him.

The commercials ended with a cut to a newsbreak. Angry young faces under waving signs and clenched fists filled the screen. STOP THE WAR, one sign read. Another, carried by a pretty girl in jeans and a bare midriff, said, MAKE LOVE, NOT WAR. A young man cheerfully waved a Viet Cong flag for the cameras' benefit.

"Ho! Ho! Ho Chi Minh!" the crowd chanted with a near-hypnotic monotony. "The NLF is going to win!"

The camera angle shifted, and Pat recognized some buildings in the background—it was Berkeley. Suddenly, with jolting force, she remembered Marci . . . and wondered if she was in that crowd somewhere.

"Traitors," David said bitterly. Then he glanced at Pat, as though wondering if she would react. She looked at Greg, who watched the chanting crowd, thin-lipped, expressionless.

The news announcer had been speaking for several moments, and Pat forced herself to listen to the words.

". . . another demonstration today at the Berkeley campus of the University of California. Organizers of the march claimed twenty thousand participants. San Francisco Mayor—"

"What are you thinking, Greg?" she asked.

He shrugged. "Hell of a way to support our boys over there," he said. "Sometimes feels like we're in a civil war, you know?"

"I was just thinking about Marci."

He looked at her for a long silent moment before saying, "Me, too."

The news break ended, and the family focused on the election coverage once more. When the announcer said that Kennedy had definitely won in South Dakota, Pat jumped up and shouted.

"He seems to be pulling up a bit here, too, Pat," David said.

"What did I tell you!" Pat looked smug for a moment, then relaxed and grinned. "It's not just the war, you know. Why I'm for him, I mean. It's everything. He really cares about people. McCarthy says all the right words, but you never feel that he really means it. Did you know that Bobby got a plane for Coretta King so she could fly down to Memphis to get Dr. King's body after he was killed? All the others showed up at the funeral because they had to; Bobby went because he cared!"

David chuckled wryly. "Except for Johnson. If anybody should have gone to Martin Luther King's funeral, it was our revered president, Lyndon Baines Johnson. But no, he sent his tame lapdog, Humphrey, instead."

"Is that a lack of respect for my commander in chief I hear in your voice, Dad?" Greg asked with a twinkle.

"The *office* of the president of the United States I revere and respect, son. There's nothing in the Constitution that says I have to like the man personally."

As the evening wore on and more votes came in, Kennedy's standing continued to rise. Pat was getting exuberant.

"He's going to do it, Greg!" Pat was almost bouncing in her seat. "All the networks are projecting him as the winner now."

"But look how many votes still aren't in," Greg countered. "If McCarthy got the rest of those, or even most of them, that could put him over the top, couldn't it?"

"Don't you know anything about statistics, brother of mine? The odds against the trend changing now are, well, astronomical."

"I'm glad you're so knowledgeable about such things, sister dear. You want another beer?"

"Not now. I'd float away." Pat settled back in the sofa, more relaxed now that her hero seemed to be ahead. "By the way, I told you, didn't I, that I'm not going to be rooming with Beth and Janie next year?"

"Yeah. What's her name, Wendy?"

"Mmm-hmm."

"What's she like?" Greg reached out for a handful of pretzels.

Pat paused for a moment, thoughtful. "She's tall. A lot taller than me, at any rate."

"That wouldn't take much, pip-squeak."

She stuck out her tongue at him. "She's got short red hair. She's very smart, very funny. I think you'd really like her."

"If she's so great, then what's she doing hanging around you?" Greg asked, teasing.

"Cute, Greg. Real cute. Anyway, one nice thing is, she's doesn't automatically assume that anyone in uniform is a pig or a fascist."

Greg grimaced. "Yeah, I got a few of those thrown at me on Saturday."

"Greg, no, that's terrible! What, not here?" Pat was horrified.

"Oh, no, up in 'Frisco. Why the hell can't people see others as individuals?"

"Herd instinct, Greg. There's a basic human need to categorize, to think in terms of 'us' and 'them.' That way you don't have to think."

2345 hours

Greg and Pat continued talking with the returns playing softly in the background. Their parents had gone upstairs hours before, and the conversation had touched on many things. Kennedy's victory. The war. The protests that were tearing the country apart. The future.

Greg reached for the volume knob. "We don't need to watch this anymore, do we? We know how it's going to turn out now."

"Oh, leave it on, Greg. They'll probably broadcast his victory speech," Pat said. "I'd really like to hear it."

Greg shrugged and joined Pat on the sofa, grabbing some more pretzels on the way down. "By the way, do you see anything of Kathy Whitman up at State?" he asked casually.

Pat's eyes twinkled. "Kathy Whitman, eh? Why do you ask?"

"Oh, no special reason. I just wondered, since they're coming over for dinner tomorrow." He had noticed Kathy at church on Sunday, sitting with her folks. She'd caught him looking at her and smiled. She'd really grown up in the past few years.

"I saw you two talking away a mile a minute last Sunday," she said accusingly.

"Just being polite with the daughter of friends of the family."

"Right." Pat smirked.

"Patricia."

"Ouch! All right, all right!" She sighed. "Actually, I suppose she's a pretty good kid. I've talked to her some. She seems a bit, I don't know, at loose ends, I guess. Of course, she's only a freshman, but she doesn't seem to have any idea of what she wants to major in or even why she's in college in the first place.''

Greg snorted. ''I've known some juniors who didn't know that.''

''Yes, but that was because you were looking for something more. With Kathy, it's more like . . . like she's just drifting.'' Pat shook her head. She reached out to put a hand on Greg's arm. ''Don't pay any attention to me, Greg. After all, I don't really know her all that well. I could be all wrong about her. If you want to ask her out, go ahead.''

''Who said I wanted to ask her out?''

''You can't pull a fast one on me, brother dear. I know you too well. Oh, here it is!''

The scene on the television screen shifted to the Ambassador Hotel in Los Angeles. It looked like a ballroom, with an elaborate glass chandelier hanging from the ceiling. An exuberant Bobby Kennedy walked onto the stage and the crowd erupted in applause, chanting, ''*We want Bobby! We want Bobby!*''

Greg only listened to the speech with half an ear. Kennedy started it off with the usual thank-everybody-for-all-their-hard-work, and when he said, ''I want to express my gratitude to my dog Freckles,'' Greg burst out with ''Freckles! What the hell—?''

''That's his cocker spaniel,'' Pat said. ''He takes him everywhere. He's really cute.''

Greg grinned. ''Who, the dog or Bobby?''

Pat swatted him on the arm. ''Be quiet, I want to listen.''

He could understand why Pat would be thrilled about Kennedy's victory since she'd actually campaigned for the guy, but he was more interested in watching Pat and thinking about what she'd said about Kathy . . . and about what she *hadn't* said about Marci. Kathy probably wasn't the right girl for him. On the other hand, he was only going to be here for another week and a half; they could probably have some fun in that time without either of them feeling like it had to lead to something. He'd expected too much from his relationship with Marci. He wouldn't make the same mistake again.

He got up and took the empty cans and the pretzel bowl out to the kitchen. Pat really was a great kid. He wished she could find somebody better for her than this Andy character, though. She cared so deeply about things, and not blindly either. She was an emotional creature, but if her emotions conflicted with her reason, she kept digging until she resolved the conflict. She needed someone who wasn't afraid of believing in something, who wasn't afraid to stand up for his belief. He discovered he was feeling protective of his little sister, and it was a strange feeling for him. She'd always seemed so self-contained; she didn't look like someone who needed protection.

"Oh, my *God!*"

Pat's horrified shriek brought him back to the living room in a hurry.

"What—what happened?"

Pat just pointed at the shaken-looking newsman on the screen.

"Once again, just moments ago as Senator Robert Kennedy was leaving the Ambassador Hotel here in Los Angeles, a gunman pushed through the crowd and shot him at close range. The assault took place in the kitchen pantry as Kennedy was moving from the Embassy Room where he had just delivered his victory speech to an ecstatic crowd of eighteen hundred followers to the Colonial Room where a news conference was scheduled. I believe two doctors are with the senator now. We have no word on his condition but will update you as details become available."

Greg felt a chill. He remembered very clearly the day President John F. Kennedy had been shot. It was a Friday, and he'd been in his senior English class when the announcement had come out over the loudspeaker. No one got much work done the rest of that day. And now JFK's brother . . . It just seemed incredible.

"First Dr. King . . . now Bobby. What's going *on* in this country?" Pat looked over at Greg with tears in her eyes. "I'd met them both, did you know that? I met Dr. King last year in New York. He was the gentlest man I'd ever met. And Bobby . . .'' She gulped and took a deep breath. "He came up to campaign headquarters in San Francisco once when I was there. He was . . . it was just electrifying when he came into the room. He actually shook my hand! And now . . .''

She collapsed in Greg's arms. He held her gently, keeping an eye on the screen. His eyes dropped briefly to a *Saturday Evening Post* on the coffee table. It was the latest issue, and it had a smiling Bobby Kennedy on the cover. First Martin Luther King two months ago, then Kennedy. Both outspoken opponents of the war in Vietnam. Then he remembered something one of his profs had said about John F. Kennedy. It was Dr. Aldritch's class. They'd been discussing assassinations throughout history, and he'd told them that he'd heard that Kennedy had been about to recall the advisors from Vietnam. Apparently he'd been scheduled to make the announcement on Monday, November 25.

But he'd been killed the previous Friday, LBJ had taken over in the White House, and the escalation had begun. Now Jack Kennedy's brother, who as president would almost certainly have pulled out of Vietnam as quickly as he could, had been shot. And Dr. King—not a politician, but a powerfully influential man who had also been opposed to the war—had been murdered, too.

"We've just had word," the reporter announced, "that the gunman who shot Senator Kennedy just fifteen minutes ago as he was heading for a news conference following his victory in tonight's presidential primary has been taken into custody by the Los Angeles Police Department. The senator is now being carried out on a stretcher to a waiting ambulance which will take him to Central Receiving Hospital. We still have no word on his condition at this time. The gunman has not yet been identified.''

Probably another lone nut, Greg thought. Like Lee Harvey Oswald or James Earl Ray. He glanced at the *Saturday Evening Post* again. Under Bobby's picture was a teaser for the main article—CORRUPTION IN VIETNAM. He wondered what next week's cover would look like.

Saturday, 15 June 1968

1430 hours

It was a dreary day, chilly, overcast, intermittent rain. Somehow it suited Greg's mood.

Only Pat was here to see him off—he'd said his good-byes to the rest of the family earlier. They were parked on Main Street in his mother's car, waiting for the Greyhound to arrive to take him south to Coronado and the start of his SEAL training. A piece of a song trickled through his head, one of those mournful ballad-type folk songs he'd heard a lot in college. "Five hundred miles, five hundred miles, five hundred miles, five hundred miles. Lord, I'm five hundred miles away from home." Only in his case it would be six hundred miles. For some reason it was more of a wrench to leave home this time than it had been when he'd left for boot camp.

"I don't know how often I'll be able to write you during training," he told Pat. "I've heard they keep you pretty busy in BUD/S."

She smiled weakly. She'd been looking drawn and tired the past week or so, ever since the night of the election. They'd followed the news closely the next few days, hoping, *praying*, that the news would be good. Kennedy had been transferred to Good Samaritan Hospital early on Wednesday morning and operated on there within hours of having been shot, and for a while Pat had really believed that he would recover. Then the following morning, they'd heard on the radio that Robert Francis Kennedy, junior senator from the state of New York, had died at 1:44 AM.

"You don't have to write as often as I do. Just write whenever you can."

"Hey, I might not even make it through the training. I could wash out the first week. Go running back to the fleet with my tail between my legs."

Pat looked stern. "Now none of that, Gregory Halstead. You'll make it. You'll do splendidly. I'm counting on it."

Greg wasn't sure how to respond to that. He didn't think

she was any happier about his becoming a naval commando than she'd been before. It was probably just that she didn't like the idea of him failing. He decided to change the subject.

"I hope things work out with you and Andy."

She made a face. "Somehow I'm inclined to doubt it. I've been doing a lot of thinking about him this past week. Part of what made Bobby Kennedy so great was his caring for people, especially those who never had the advantages you and I have grown up taking for granted. I can't see myself spending my life with someone who doesn't care deeply about other people, someone who doesn't want to help them in any way he can." She turned her face toward Greg. Her eyes were filled with a calm sadness. "I'm really not sure Andy has that kind of caring in him."

"I'm sorry, Pat."

"It's probably just as well," she said deliberately. "I don't particularly want to get serious about anybody right now. I've still got a year of college to go, and then I've got to figure out what I want to do next."

"Any ideas?"

"Not any that I'm happy with. I've always thought I was going to be a nurse like Mom, but now I'm not so sure. I might just come back here and work at the old family business until I have a better idea." She tossed her head, sending her blond hair flying. "What about you?"

"What about me?"

"Come on, Greg. You and Kathy! Do you have something good there?"

Greg shrugged and looked in the rearview mirror to check for the bus. No sign of it yet. "I don't know," he said finally. "We had fun going out. I think she . . . she seems to like me a lot. She asked me to write to her."

Pat grinned. "I bet she never got over that crush she had on you when you were kids. She's probably been pining away, waiting desperately for her white knight to return for her."

"Knock it off, you nut!" Greg punched his sister playfully.

"So are you going to write to her?"

"Guess I'll wait and see what her letters are like. Some

wise person once told me you can tell a lot about a person by their letters."

She stuck out her tongue at him. A low rumble behind them made her turn around. Greg checked the mirror. "That's it," he said.

They got out of the car, and Greg grabbed his seabag from the backseat as the bus creaked to a halt opposite the general store.

"You're a damn fine sister, you know that?" he told Pat.

"Well, you're not half-bad yourself, brother." She grinned. "Now you just go and be the best . . . damn SEAL you can be, you hear me?"

He saluted sharply. "Yes, *ma'am*," he said, deliberately putting a fearful quaver into his voice.

She sobered as she put her hand on his left arm, fingering the device on the sleeve of his uniform. "Take care of yourself, Greg," she said and hugged him.

"Time, mister," the bus driver said.

Greg hugged her hard and then released her. "You too, kiddo." Then he climbed aboard and found a seat on the right side so he could see her out the window. He waved as the bus started up. She was still waving when the bus rounded a curve and he lost sight of her.

He wondered why this departure seemed so different. Maybe it was the uncertainty, not knowing exactly what BUD/S was going to be like, not knowing for sure whether he could handle it. After all, his dad had been able to tell him what boot camp was like, and he'd gone knowing he wouldn't have any trouble, either with the physical training or with adjusting to Navy life. But this was different. The Navy didn't turn out SEALs to fill a quota; you had to meet SEAL standards or you didn't pass. He'd heard stories—he wasn't sure if it was just a rumor or whether it had actually happened—of one SEAL training class that hadn't graduated anybody. The entire class had washed out.

He took a deep breath and expelled it forcefully. Well, that wasn't going to happen to him. He knew it would take every ounce of determination he possessed, but by God Greg Halstead was going to become a *SEAL*!

Chapter 22

**Basic Underwater Demolition/SEAL Class 42
Coronado, California
0610 hours**

ET3 Greg Halstead stood at attention on the grinder, the broad, paved parade ground behind the BUD/S barracks at the Naval Amphibious Warfare Training Center, Coronado, California. Along with the fifty-eight other trainees of BUD/S Bravo Section Class 42, he wore OD utility trousers, white T-shirts, green-painted helmet liners, and the heavy black work shoes known throughout the Navy as "boondockers."

I made it! I made it! I made it!

The silent refrain ran through Greg's head like a litany. After months of wanting, the reality had descended on him with a startling suddenness. It was hard to believe that he was actually, *finally* here.

His final orders had arrived just a few weeks ago: *You are hereby required and directed to report to Basic Underwater Demolition/SEAL training, Class 42, U.S. Navy Amphibious Warfare Center, Coronado, California. . . .*

And now he was here, on Day One of his training as a U.S. Navy SEAL.

A group of officers and senior petty officers was standing to one side, apparently conferring with one another. Greg found that ominous. He knew what was coming . . . or he thought he did. Navy boot camp had been much the same— at a milder level, naturally—a course designed to toughen the trainees' bodies, break them down, then mold them into something new. Still, he'd heard plenty of stories. BUD/S training was supposed to be the toughest of its kind in the world, and he'd heard some pretty wild rumors about Hell Week.

One of the instructors broke away from the rest of the group and advanced with long, confident strides toward the formation. He looked as hard as though chiseled from basalt, and his skin was dark, Latino-swarthy. He wore a blue ball cap with the word INSTRUCTOR written in gold letters, dark aviator's sunglasses that gave him an ominous anonymity, and a dark blue windbreaker with the legend GOD above the jacket's breast pocket. A cigar jutted from his mouth, somehow coexisting with a wad of chewing tobacco tucked into his cheek.

"Well," he said, and he let the word hang there in the air for a moment. "Anyone here want to quit?"

There were a few nervous chuckles from the ranks.

"C'mon," he continued. "You can't *all* be here because you want to be *frogmen!*"

"Sir!" a voice called out from somewhere to Greg's right. "We're here because we want to be SEALs, *sir!*"

The instructor named God wheeled like a bird of prey intent upon its victim. "Sweet Lord, is *that* what you want, maggot?" He closed in on the man until his nose was inches from his victim's face. "To be a SEAL? I got news for you, swabbie. You ain't gonna make it!"

"*Sir*, yes I am, sir!"

"Don't you *dare* call me sir, you sorry excuse for fish bait!" the instructor screamed into the man's face. "I *work* for a living!"

"Sir—uh . . . yes!"

"My name is Ferraro and my rank as you can clearly see, those of you who can read, is God. You may call me *Instructor* or *Petty Officer Ferraro*, but you will not call me *sir*!"

He whirled on the trainee standing next to the first kid. "You're laughing at me, boy, aren't you?"

"No, Petty Officer Ferraro!"

"Hit the deck! Both of you! Take your position!"

Both trainees dropped to the extended push-up position.

"Gimme fifty!" He continued walking down the line as the hapless trainees pumped away. He walked down to the far end of the line, looking the trainees over, his expression carrying a mixture of disbelief and dismay. He shook his head, his long face sorrowful. "It is my duty," he told them, "to take you *volunteers* and make something of you. Specifically, I am to make you into genu-wine shockproof, waterproof, chrome-plated, antimagnetic, rootin', tootin', fast-shootin', fightin', fornicatin' frogmen, and I am here this morning to tell you that I am *not* going to be able to carry out that order. It's impossible!"

He paused a moment to let the words sink in. "You . . . *people* . . ." He put such a sneer into the word that Greg winced. "You people are so low that right now *whale* shit looks like shootin' stars to you! The United States Navy in its infinite wisdom has ordered me to turn you, you *people* into frogmen, but I cannot in good conscience turn such a motley collection of scumbags and maggot vomit as you into *anything* that would bring credit to the service and the Teams that I love! I have only one way out, one honorable course in my dilemma, and that is to make you quit." He whirled, one lean forefinger coming up to stab at one of the trainees like a dagger. "And that is exactly what I am going to do. I am going to protect my beloved Teams from the likes of you by *personally* seeing to it that you quit, give up, surrender, throw in the towel . . . that you realize that you are slime with no higher ambition in this man's Navy than to crawl back to the fleet and hope they take you in, that you fall down on your scabby knees and ask your God why, why, in the name of all that is holy, why you were ever even *born!*"

Ferraro resumed his pacing, the rich invective rolling from his lips with a polished and professional ease that was a marvel to behold. Greg was surprised that the man never used profanity and rarely even relied on obscenities to shock. Possibly, that was a means by which he kept himself separate from the trainees, on a different, a higher moral and physical plane. He was able to shock by the sheer, dynamic force of his personality.

The finger stabbed again. "Why are *you* here, maggot?"

"To learn to be a frogman, Petty Officer Ferraro!"

"A *frogman*?" He plucked the cigar from his mouth, turned his head, and sent a thin, brown stream of liquid squirting to the grinder. "Son, you've just made one *hell* of a mistake!"

Turning away abruptly, he jammed the cigar back in his mouth.

"You people are disgusting! You people are *not* frogmen. You are not frogman material. You are not trainees. You are not tadpoles. You are not even maggots, because that appellation is insulting to maggots everywhere. You are . . . *bananas!*"

The unexpected word made several in the ranks flinch, and someone—shockingly—giggled. Ferraro was on the unfortunate soul in an instant. "You! Banana! What's your name?"

"G-g-gunner's M-mate Third Prescott, si—I mean . . ."

"I don't care what you mean, Prescott. Do you think it's funny being a banana?"

"No, uh, Instructor Ferraro!"

"Do you know *why* I call you a banana?"

"No, Instructor!"

"Because you might think you're some rough, tough stuff . . . but inside, you're really soft and squishy. And come to think of it, you're all soft and squishy *outside*, too. Just exactly like a banana. And it is my job to toughen you up. *Bananas* will not graduate from this course. *Bananas* will not become members of my Team! Anyone who doesn't toughen up is out! Back to the fleet. You bananas understand me?" He paused. "I said, you bananas understand me?"

A straggle of voices answered.

"Yes, sir!"

"Yes, Petty Officer."

"Sir, yes, sir!"

Ferraro shook his head. "I can see we're gonna have a problem communicatin' here. I'll keep it simple. When you bananas want to answer me as a group, you will give the approved SEAL war cry. Hooyah! Lemme hear it!"

"Hooyah!"

"Pathetic! My eighty-seven-year-old maiden aunt could do it better!"

"*Hooyah!*"

"I can't hear you!"

"*Hooyah!*"

"Again!"

"*HOOYAH!*"

"I am shaking in my boots." He turned away, then, glancing at the officers watching the ceremony from the side of the grinder. One, taking his glance as a cue, broke away from the others and strode across the grinder to take his place in front of the formation. He wore olive green utilities, a blue instructor's ball cap, and the black, double bar of a lieutenant pinned to his collar. Ferraro saluted him and the salute was returned. "Class Forty-two, Bravo Section, ready for your inspection, sir!"

"I'll just address the men, Ferraro, if you please."

"Yes, sir!"

"Good morning, men," the officer said. "I am Lieutenant Ed Baxter, the senior training officer of this platoon. Welcome to BUD/S.

"I am not going to deliver any impressive or patriotic speeches this morning. I'm sure as hell not going to try to encourage you. Each of you men is a volunteer. Each of you has your own reasons for being here. None of that is important right now. What is important is your motivation for being here, and how deep it runs. All of you want to pass BUD/S training. Well, you'd better want it more than anything you've ever wanted in your lives if you're going to have a prayer of seeing it through to the end.

"And you'd better want something else, too. You'd better want to be part of a *team*, because that's the only way you're going to make it. We turn you men over to the tender mercies of instructors like Petty Officer First Class Ferraro here precisely to weed out the unfit, the weak, the lone wolf, the cowboy, the maladjusted . . . anyone who can't cut it physically or emotionally or who can't work with the team. You will be assigned to a boat crew, seven trainees to a boat, and you are going to learn to work together. You will be assigned a swim buddy, and you *will* learn to work together.

"You've heard the lecture before, I'm sure. I'm going to give it to you again, in the hope that just maybe it'll finally sink in. You all volunteered for this program. We have no draftees in the SEALs. You have to want to be a SEAL very, very badly. If you're here because you thought it would be fun, or because you want to be some sort of gung-ho hot-ass commando, or because you want to kill commies, or because you think you're really hot stuff and want to play with the big boys, I'm here to say that you'd better quit right now. The SEALs have no room for cowboys. No room for loners. No room for gunslingers. We need people who can work as part of a team. And we need people who don't just want to be the best. We need people who *are* the best!

"You are about to undertake the most demanding course of military training in the world. I can tell you now that out of 1,924 applicants, only 116 were left to make up Class Forty-two. I suppose you can feel pretty good about that, being the top six percent, and all of that.

"In fact, we had so many qualified volunteers for this class that we've had to split you up into two sections. Alpha Section is the responsibility of Chief Groton and his instructor team. You fifty-eight men, Bravo Section, will be the responsibility of Petty Officer Ferraro here.

"But I'll tell you right now that a lot of you men standing here this morning are *not* going to complete this course. You will quit, because you are not going to be able to handle the challenges we throw at you here.

"Why do we make it so tough? I'll tell you. This program traces its beginnings back to the Naval Combat Demolition Units of World War II. The NCDUs were Navy men trained to wade ashore ahead of the main landing force on D-Day, attach explosives to the German beach defenses at Normandy, and clear the way for the incoming landing craft. Men who were paralyzed by fear, terrified of explosions and machine-gun fire and all the rest, would be useless when it came to wiring explosives to those defenses. It was decided that the only way to prepare men for what they were going to encounter in Normandy was to subject them to something that came as close as possible to combat.

"Your training here is divided into three phases. Phase One is primarily physical, but it's also designed to weed out the men who aren't going to fit in. You will find that you are going to be wet a lot of the time. That you will be uncomfortable a lot of the time. That you won't be able to get enough sleep. That you will be under tremendous pressure. We are going to keep you wet and uncomfortable and sleepless and under pressure as much as we can so that when you are given a job to do and you have to do it while someone's shooting at you, you won't freeze up. And you won't let your teammates down.

"The good news is that BUD/S training is based on our belief that a human being is capable of ten times his normal exertion when he is properly motivated. And believe me, we are going to do our very best to motivate you!

"This course is not for everyone. And, unfortunately, we don't know any other way of finding out ahead of time who is going to succeed, and who is going to fail." Baxter pointed across the grinder. "Over there, you will see a post. On top of that post is a brass ship's bell. Anytime you are too cold or too hungry or too sleepy or too uncomfortable, or you hurt too much, or you think you can't stand the program another minute, all you have to do is walk over there, toss your helmet down at the foot of that post, and ring that bell three times. That's all. Simple. In five minutes you'll be enjoying a hot cup of coffee. In twenty minutes, I promise you, you'll be back at the barracks taking a nice, hot shower, thinking about how nice it's going to be to get a full, hot meal in your stomach and ten or twelve solid hours of uninterrupted sleep in a comfortable rack . . . and all of this unpleasantness will be just a fading, unhappy memory.

"For those of you tough enough—or *dumb* enough—to hold on and who manage to stick it out all the way through Phase One, you'll go on to the more technical aspects of being a SEAL or UDT man. Learning SCUBA, demolitions, and weapons training. For now, though, trust me. You'll have your hands full just surviving Petty Officer Ferraro!

"While you're here, for as long as you're here, there is only one general order. Do it! You will be given orders that at times will seem pretty senseless. You will be harassed. You will be bullied. You are expected to take it, to do what you're told, but you're also expected to *adapt*, to overcome the hardship, to win! To accomplish that, you are allowed to do anything, whatever it takes to survive, whatever it takes to overcome, whatever it takes to win against some damned heavy odds. Your enemies will be these gentlemen up here wearing the instructor caps, because they are going to be doing their dishonest best to break you and make you quit. If you want to succeed, you're going to have to beat them. You can lie, you can cheat, you can do whatever it takes to *win*. The only rule of engagement is, don't get caught! If you can learn to handle what these men dish out to you over the next few weeks, if you can beat the program, if you can beat *them*, then you'll know you have what it takes to beat the North Vietnamese, or the Russians, or the Chinese, or whoever you find yourself matched against in the future!"

He turned to the instructor. "Petty Officer Ferraro? Thank you. I hope I didn't just make your job harder."

Ferraro grinned. "Not a chance, sir. These pussy bananas are no match for *me*."

"Very well. They're all yours. Carry on!"

"Aye, aye, sir!"

They saluted one another, and as Baxter walked off the grinder, Ferraro looked over the trainees . . . and *smiled*, a thoroughly chilling sight. Greg was astonished at how that long, swarthy face resembled a grinning skull beneath the dark glasses.

Greg was honestly unsure, though, which had been more demoralizing . . . Ferraro's break-down-the-newbies routine or Baxter's simple speech. He'd been expecting something like Ferraro's ranting. It was part of the mind game that always faced trainees. He'd faced it in boot camp and endured a very mild version as an ET trainee. He'd heard that cadets at Annapolis went through the same thing.

But Baxter, with his matter-of-fact discussion of how things were, had just told them all that it would be extraordinarily easy to quit. Greg shifted his eyes, looking at the brass bell. Plenty of the men standing in ranks around him, he knew, would be ringing that damned bell before this class graduated.

But ET3 Halstead was *not* going to be one of them.

"So, bananas," Ferraro said. "Now you know the truth. I am your enemy. I am, in fact, your worst nightmare come to life. For the next few weeks, it will be my pleasure, and the pleasure of Petty Officers Kemper, Scholkowski, De La Palma, Grollier, and our assistants, to mold you bananas like wet clay. At the end, most of you will have had enough, come to your senses, and gone back to the fleet. Whatever is left, well, maybe . . . maybe we can make something out of you.

"But I doubt it! Awright, bananas! Enough gabbing! I've got better things to do than stand up here explaining the facts of life to a bunch of losers! Count off by twos!"

"One!"

"Two!"

"One!"

"Two!"

The cadence ran through the group, starting with the front rank right and ending with the last man in the rear.

"All you 'twos,' " Ferraro said. "Take a look at the 'one' on your right. All you 'ones,' have a gander at the 'two' on your left."

Greg, a "one," looked to his left. The man looking back at him was shorter than he was by a couple of inches, with sandy brown hair, green eyes, and a knowing, this-is-crap expression on his face. They knew nothing else about each other, save the obvious fact that both wanted to be SEALs.

For the moment, for Greg, at least, that was enough to mark the guy as okay.

"That homely godforsaken creature you're looking at," Ferraro said, "is your swim buddy. Get to know him, ba-nanas, because you two are going to be *very* close. Your life is his. His life is yours. For the next six weeks, or until one or both of you quit, you two are gonna breathe each other's air, eat each other's food, drink each other's spit, bathe in each other's mud, and get blamed when the other guy screws up. Get it through your heads, bananas. You're responsible for your buddy. Your buddy's responsible for you. Introduce yourselves. Be friendly. Because from here on out, you two are gonna be closer than lovers in the clinch."

Greg stuck out his hand. "ET3 Greg Halstead," he said, smiling.

"Casey," the other man offered. He had a strong handshake, but there was something about his eyes that suggested he was uncomfortable with this ritual, that he was happier doing things on his own. He confirmed it an instant later when he added, "Just don't slow me down, kid."

Greg's smile faded. The arrogant son of a bitch!

"Eyes front! Can the chatter!"

A silence descended over the formation. Ferraro looked at something on his clipboard, then did a sharp series of right-angle turns and strides that put him in front of the first man on the right of the front rank. He walked past three men before stopping in front of a tall, gangling youth with a friendly smile on his face.

"You, banana!" Ferraro snapped. "You eyeballin' me, boy?"

"No, Petty Officer Ferraro!"

"You're eyeballin' me, banana. Hit the deck! Hold that position!"

Leaving the man in extended push-up position, he continued down the line. Greg kept his eyes glazed over, focused on a bit of ocean that he could see between two of the barracks buildings across the grinder as Ferraro breezed past . . . and escaped notice. Ferraro caught several more in the inspection, though, trainees "eyeballin' " him, or smirking, or breathing too hard, anything, in short, that made them different. Greg remembered hearing of an old Japanese saying: "The nail that sticks up gets hammered down."

Eventually, the inspection tour was done, and Ferraro arrived once again at the front of the formation, thumbs tucked into the waistband of his trousers. "You bananas on the deck! Attention!"

He waited then, surveying them all with a death's-head grin, working at the cigar stub. "I don't see anything here that I like, bananas. You are all soft and mushy and unfit for useful work.

"And so, bananas, we're going to see what we can do to toughen you up. We're going to start with a little run, just across those dunes over there, and then you bananas are gonna hit the bay. You're all nice and dry now. Remember that feeling, because memories are all that you're gonna have to go on for the next six weeks. Now . . . left . . . *face*! Double time . . . *harch*! *Hit the bay, bananas!*"

They began running.

Hours later, Greg realized that they had run *everywhere* . . . that the haranguing they'd received on the grinder was the closest thing they had to a rest for that entire day. They'd started, as promised, by running across the dunes and down to the beach, running at full tilt out into the water. The water had felt good, and some of the men, forgetting themselves, had started skylarking, splashing one another and shouting to each other above the noise of the water.

That had not pleased PO1 Ferraro. He'd ordered them to form ranks . . . while standing in the water. They were on the bay side of the Coronado Peninsula, so the surf was not heavy, but there was enough of a swell to jostle the men about a bit as they stood there. Ferraro, after telling them some more about their physical and moral shortcomings, had signaled one of the junior instructors, who'd produced, of all things, a folding beach chair. Ferraro had lain back in the chair, pulled a paperback novel out of his hip pocket, and proceeded to read . . . while the men of Bravo Section, Class 42, stood in the water, in ranks, watching helplessly.

It seemed like a rest at first, but before too many minutes had passed, Greg started feeling cold. It started in his back and shoulders, where water kept surging across him, soaking his T-shirt, then exposing it to the breeze which was surprisingly brisk and chilly, it seemed, for June. Then the cold began spreading, settling in along his legs and arms, working its way into his groin, chilling his toes and fingers, and slowly, slowly turning his lips a deeper and deeper shade of purple-blue. In twenty minutes, his teeth were chattering . . . and so, too, were the teeth of every man within earshot. The entire section stood at attention, shivering violently, entering, he was now convinced, the early stages of hypothermia, while Ferraro read a paperback thriller on the beach.

"Anybody want to quit?" Ferraro called. When there was no answer, he stood up, signaled for one of his assistants to take away book and chair, then stood in front of the group, fists on his hips. "No one? Okay. Let's say we get warm.

Forrard . . . *harch!* Comp'ny . . . *halt!* Right . . . *face!* Double time . . . *har!*''

They started running.

Greg had never realized just how hard it was to run in sand. Worse, his boondockers and socks were soaked now with seawater, and his feet felt lead-heavy to begin with, but each step in the sand required a measure of strength to keep going and not to slip or stumble. He started to feel tired and winded after thirty minutes.

He was starting to hurt after forty.

After an hour, it was a little better. The circulation was going and he felt lots warmer, but he was having trouble even feeling his legs from the thighs down.

They ran half of the twelve miles clear down the peninsula toward Tijuana and the Mexican border. Then they turned around and ran back.

And that was just the beginning. . . .

Friday, 21 June 1968

Basic Underwater Demolition/SEAL Class 42
Coronado, California
1525 hours

Lieutenant j.g. Frank Richard Casey had never even seen the ocean until he'd joined the Navy. He was a cowboy, or so he liked to claim, from the wide-open spaces of eastern Montana.

He claimed also to be a member of that dying breed, an American patriot. An uncle had been in the Marines in World War II and won the Bronze Star on Okinawa; his father, also a Marine, had been lost during the long march back from the Chosin Reservoir. Frank had been a child of the Cold War; he still remembered the atomic air-raid drills they'd had in his kindergarten, and later, after his mother and stepfather moved to a suburb community of Billings, he'd played war with the neighborhood kids with plastic guns, fighting the godless commies.

As he'd grown older, though, the Soviet Union and communism had become darker and more serious menaces, a threat that seemed to live just beyond the cold, north wind of the Montanan winter. Worse, he'd begun questioning his father's death in North Korea—not the *fact* of his death, necessarily, but the apparent uselessness of it. As he'd learned the history of the Korean War and the way the American and UN forces had been hobbled by the politicians in that inglorious little "police action," he'd acquired a loathing both for the Communists and their obvious lust for world domination, and for the bureaucratic pus-guts and REMFs who oozed platitudes from the safety of their desks while American boys were getting killed for utterly pointless and idiotic fine points of a screwed-to-hell foreign policy.

With his stepfather's political connections, he'd been accepted into Annapolis, graduating in the Class of '65, an honest-to-God ring-knocker. After graduation, he'd volunteered for UDT/SEALs because they seemed to offer the best chance of coming to grips with an enemy that seemed always to remain faceless, unreachable, and as cold and remote as the icy mountains above the Chosin Reservoir.

They'd told him that Navy Special Warfare was a dead end, so far as his career in the Navy was concerned, that if he hoped to advance to the rank of captain or beyond, he'd be better off sticking with the *real* Navy.

Well, screw that.

The SEALs, Casey thought, were the ideal weapon against the Communist menace. From what he'd heard about the Teams, they did the job, and they did what had to be done to do it. He'd heard stories about Navy SEALs illegally sneaking into Cambodia and North Vietnam, and to hell with the politicians and the bleeding hearts and the antiwar traitors back home. *That* was what it took to win the war with an enemy who didn't care about the rules or about international boundaries to begin with. Decision, action, and the will to win!

And judging from Lieutenant Baxter's little welcome-aboard speech, that was all it would take to make him a SEAL.

Casey and the rest of the section sat in the sand, warily listening to Ferraro as the cocky little first class introduced them to a very important piece of frogman equipment.

"This," Ferraro announced, striding around the jet-black object that was unfolding itself on the sand before them, "is your basic IBS. That means Inflatable Boat, Small. It is a CO_2-inflatable rubber boat that can carry seven men and one thousand pounds of equipment. It is twelve feet long, with an overall beam of six feet, and has a weight, complete, of two hundred eighty-nine pounds. It can be dropped by parachute from an airplane, shoved out the side door of a helicopter thirty feet above the water, or with some minor modifications to its inflation valves, launched from the deck of a submerged submarine.

"You bananas have been assigned to what we have laughingly called boat crews. Each boat crew will be assigned one IBS. That IBS will be the supreme responsibility of that boat crew. You will carry it with you wherever you go. When you go to the chow hall, you will leave it outside with a guard, and you will see to it that the man on guard is relieved in time to eat. This is a highly technical and expensive piece of U.S. government property, currently valued at much higher than the cost of your worthless hides. At night, you will stow your IBS in the designated stowage locker after washing it down *thoroughly* stem to stern, top to bottom with fresh water. . . ."

Casey stole a glance at the other members of his boat crew, Crew Three. The fifty-eight-man training platoon had been divided that morning into eight boat crews, with seven men apiece except for Crews Five and Seven, which took in the leftover men.

He was still trying to get a feel for the others in his crew. His swim partner, Halstead, and one other guy, Pogue, both seemed steady enough, if a bit young, skinny, and wide-eyed innocent. Markham, Patterson, and Rodriguez were all pretty much cut from the same cloth, big, muscular types, the sort who probably went out for football in high school. Zelasnik was a short guy, shorter than Casey, but he had powerful arms and a barrel chest, the sort of small-but-tough powerhouse who ought to make out well as a frogman.

Casey still hadn't gotten close to any of the others and didn't yet know how close he wanted to be. They'd all been somewhat taken aback when they learned that he was an *officer* . . . and a ring-knocker at that. Naturally, though, he'd been made coxswain of Boat Crew Number Three, and he was working now to get to know his people better.

Of them all, Pete Zelasnik seemed the closest to a kindred spirit. He was a lanky, good-natured kid from Alabama, an engineman's mate second class who claimed to have but one overriding passion.

"Y'all just watch my smoke," he'd told them during a brief rest period a couple of days before. "I ain't one to brag, but I'm gonna come back from over there with the little blue button, just see if I don't!"

The little blue button. The Congressional Medal of Honor. Casey himself wasn't particularly interested in winning medals, not even that one, but Zelasnik claimed that his father, a U.S. Marine, had won the coveted ribbon in World War II, and he was not going to do any less.

Yeah. Casey could understand where Zelasnik was coming from. Who your father was, *what* he was, could drive a guy sometimes. The trick was to grab control yourself, to take your own life and run with it.

Frank Casey knew exactly what he was going to do with his life. He was a warrior, a *professional* warrior, and he was going to take the war to his country's enemies.

And maybe extract a bit of vengeance for his dad. . . .

Chapter 23

"Platoon . . . *halt!*"

The formation stopped in place, standing on the end of a long pier extending into South San Diego Bay from the Naval Amphibious Base at Coronado. Thunder rolled overhead as a Navy A6 Intruder howled in toward the North Island Naval Air Station.

Directly across the bay, two miles distant or less, was the U.S. Naval Station at Thirty-Fourth Street in San Diego. A number of Navy ships were tied up there, great, gray bulks shouldering one another like pigs at a feeding trough. Greg recognized a fleet oiler, a fleet transport, an ocean minesweeper, a couple of destroyers.

One of the DDs was the *Edson*.

"Take a good long look, bananas," Ferraro called out to the formation. "That's where you pussies belong, back in the fleet. We don't have any room for pussies and bananas in the Teams, and we're gonna run you right back where you belong!"

This was becoming a regular part of the routine. Every few days, the class would be run-marched to the end of the pier, where they would have a chance to look at the mammoth gray shapes across the bay and be told that they belonged back in the fleet. It no longer bothered Greg . . . though the first time or two had been pretty rough. By now, he'd decided that there was no question about it. He wanted to be a SEAL, not a regular enlisted guy aboard ship . . . and the fact that he'd been so seasick that one time out between Pearl and San Diego didn't really have that much to do with it. He wasn't going back to the fleet, no way.

Bravo Section was down to thirty-seven now. They wore shorts, white T-shirts, boondockers, and green helmet liners, along with the heavy and water-soaked kapok life jackets that had virtually become a part of their uniform.

This morning had been spent at the base pool, "drown-proofing" the trainees. Having your hands tied behind your back and your ankles tied together, then being tossed into water twenty feet deep could be scary at first, but by now the evolution was becoming routine, a kind of mental conditioning aimed at eliminating any fear of the water and at convincing future SEALs that the water was their ally, not an enemy.

It was Saturday, and Saturdays were relatively light duty. Though there were exceptions, the usual routine had the class working as usual in the morning, then free in the afternoon as well as all day Sunday. Unlike during boot camp, they could even catch a ferry across the bay into town, so long as they didn't miss their one-in-three fire and security watches at the barracks. Married men, whose wives were staying nearby in base housing, could even go home, if they wanted. The vast majority of BUD/S trainees, however, used the time more constructively . . . to polish their boondockers, wash their uniforms, and catch up on personal matters like letter-writing and sleep, if nothing else. There would be time enough for bar- and bed-hopping later, after they'd graduated.

In Greg's opinion, Boat Crew Number Three had come a long way since its formation during the first week of BUD/S. They worked well together, and Lieutenant Casey seemed to have an instinctive knack for pulling the men together and keeping them focused on the task at hand. He also had a wry disregard for the bullshit aspects of training. They'd learned to march with their IBS balanced atop their heads; Dixie, the shortest man in the boat crew, used a coffee can wedged between his helmet liner and the bottom of the boat, just so that he could carry his own share. So far, they'd had one dropout from their crew, Patterson. The others had gelled well together and had reached the point where they were beginning to think of themselves as old hands, whatever Ferraro might say or think. They'd adopted nicknames, the "handles" that real frogmen tended to sport, like the call-sign names of Navy aviators. Greg's, somewhat to his horror, had become "Twidge" or "Twidgie," drawn from his "twidget" days as an ET, with an underhanded reference to the stick-thin British fashion model Twiggy. The others, with the possible exception of Ralph "Pogie Bait" Pogue, had pretty cool handles that fit their frogman tough-guy personas—Carl "Mark One" Markham, Richard "Bandit" Rodriguez, and Pete "Dixie" Zelasnik.

Whatever their handles, though, all of them were good guys, good friends, good people to have at your back. As for Lieutenant Casey, he'd worried Greg for the first week or so, coming across first as a lone wolf, then as some kind of super commando with an intensity and a single-minded determination to excel that could be scary at times. After a few days, though, Greg had decided that Casey was simply so gung ho, as the Marines would say, so focused on what he wanted to do and be, that he generated that lone-cowboy image. Greg had found it a real challenge keeping up with his swim buddy but soon realized that meeting that challenge was helping him over the hump in SEAL training.

That was okay with Greg. Judging from some of the scuttlebutt he'd been hearing lately, their fifth week of training was going to be the biggest challenge yet.

But he was ready to meet it. *Hooyah!*

He smiled at the sight of the Navy ships across the bay.

"Okay, bananas. That's enough rest. We're gonna double-time it back to the barracks! About . . . *face!* Double time . . . *har!*"

Sunday, 14 July 1968

Golden Neptune Bar
San Diego, California
1735 hours

Ed Baxter had gotten into the habit of holding his planning conferences "ashore," meaning off-base, and usually in one of the handful of San Diego watering holes claimed by SEALs and UDT personnel stationed in the area. It was a part of his deliberate effort to separate himself as much as he could from some of what had happened in Nam. There were times, like last night, when he would dream. Usually it was stupid stuff, watching a VC slowly raise his AK, while Baxter stood frozen in place, trying to get his M-16 to fire and the damn thing was jammed. Sometimes, though, it was a lot worse. There was that one dream he kept having about shooting those kids on Can Coc Island that kept waking him up, sweating and retching. . . .

Meeting with members of his staff at one of their homes off-base or here in the Golden Neptune was better. Somehow, all of the bustle and chatter of people, the droning of the TV over the bar, the clink and tinkle of glassware combined to remind him that he wasn't *there* anymore, in *that* place.

He was seated at a table with GM1 Mike Ferraro, Chief Phil Groton, and Chief Joseph West. All four wore civilian clothing, though in downtown San Diego, anyone with their hard-muscled frames and crew-cut hairstyles had to be either Navy or Marine.

A miniskirted waitress served their drinks, gave Baxter a playful wink as she tucked their money into her bodice, then walked away with an exaggerated grind to her hips.

"I think that one has the hots for ya, Lieutenant," West said.

"I doubt that it's anything personal, Chief," he replied. The others laughed.

The group enjoyed a friendly camaraderie that easily transcended the barriers of rank—or race, for that matter. Joe

West was black, one of the very few black men to have made it into the SEAL program so far. One of the old hands at the Coronado BUD/S, he was primarily responsible for the logistics and supply end of the program, though he'd trained his share of frogmen as well.

Phil Groton was a big, slow-talking country boy from Memphis, Tennessee—the archetypal Southern redneck—except that he seemed completely unaware of the color of West's skin.

"So, Phil, Mike," Baxter said. "You two have anything special planned for next week?"

Ferraro smiled. "I'm gonna have 'em begging for mercy, sir. Hell Week's where we definitely do some major separation of the men from the boys."

"Roger that," Groton said, his cold grin echoing Ferraro's.

"Okay . . ." Baxter started to say something more, something light about "just don't wipe out the whole class," but he thought better of it. It was true that NAVSPECWARGRU Washington was pushing hard for more and more trained SEALs and UDT personnel, and there'd been plenty of talk about cutting back on the rigorous requirements. It only stood to reason: graduate ten percent of the class instead of five, and you have twice your usual number of frogmen coming out of BUD/S.

But the concept was a sore point with most BUD/S instructors and most SEALs, especially those who'd seen combat in Vietnam. The U.S. Marines had been going through something like the same problem when they'd been forced to begin accepting draftees in order to meet their manpower requirements. For a service that took fierce pride in being a volunteer organization, that had been a difficult choice, and one that was still controversial. The Marine Corps had survived attempt after attempt to eliminate it from the U.S. Armed Forces by proving that they were more than just soldiers who could wade ashore from boats. Being forced to accept draftees was a serious blow both to their pride and to their credibility as an elite combat unit.

How long could the SEALs endure as an elite naval commando unit if the REMFs insisted on watering down the curriculum to the point where *anybody* could join?

Better not even to bring the subject up.

"So," Chief West said, crooking one arm over the back of his chair. "You were telling us war stories. Whatever happened to Colonel Asshole, anyway?" They'd been discussing the unknown colonel who'd wanted Baxter and his team to go back and secure the crashed Huey.

"Knowing Lieutenant Baxter," Ferraro said, rubbing his hands together slowly, "it was something involving a midnight insertion and the brake cables on the guy's jeep."

"Shit," Groton said. "More likely a midnight insertion on the colonel's old lady."

"Actually," Baxter said with a small grin, "Mrs. Colonel Asshole was not a target of opportunity. And neither was the colonel, for that matter. I did some checking when we got back to base. Turned out this guy was in charge of the area where we got shot down and had been claiming to Saigon that he had the whole province pacified, from Vinh Long to the sea."

"What," West said. "He didn't want to look bad?"

"Seems he had a bad case of believing his own numbers. Since there couldn't be any active VC in the area, then nobody could have shot down our chopper. If no one shot down our chopper, the crash must have been due either to mechanical failure or pilot error. Since this guy was also in charge of maintenance at the air base where this bird came from, he had a very real incentive to be sure it wasn't mechanical failure. His only hope was to prove pilot error."

"If there were no VC in the area," Ferraro asked, "how come he wanted the SEALs to go secure the bird?"

"I don't know. Maybe he was afraid our people were going to tamper with the evidence. I do know that that helo had more holes in it than Swiss cheese. That pilot was damned lucky, or damned skillful, or damned both."

"So." Joe West grinned. "Did you track down Colonel Asshole and wax his tail?"

"Negative. When I got to his office, about twelve hours after getting back to Can Tho, I found out he was in Da Nang. After that, I think he was transferred back to the States."

"It would be interesting to learn," Ferraro said thought-fully, "whether he arranged for the transfer, or his superiors did. Uh-oh . . ."

"What?" Baxter turned. A young lieutenant j.g. in dress whites was walking toward the table.

"One of ours?" Phil Groton asked.

"One of mine," Ferraro growled.

"Easy, Mike," Baxter said. "Let's see what he wants."

It was Lieutenant j.g. Casey. "Excuse me Lieutenant, Petty Officers," he said. "I don't mean to intrude, but—"

"You already have, banana," Ferraro snapped. "What are you doing ashore?"

"Weekend liberty, of course," Casey said. He seemed un-usually self-assured for someone still in training.

"Who do you have spit-polishing your boondockers for you?" Baxter asked quietly. It seemed to be something of a tradition that officers in training programs would have en-listed personnel take care of such chores as polishing shoes or ironing clothes, which gave the officers extra time for picking up girls or other pursuits ashore.

"Actually, sir, I have several extra pairs of polished shoes in my locker. A trick I learned at Annapolis."

Ferraro started to say something, but Baxter silenced him with a look. "What's your question, son?"

"I know that Hell Week's coming up."

Ferraro started to rise from the table. "S'help me, if you're looking for special treatment, banana—"

"Not at all. The men in my boat crew are going to be subjected to some pretty brutal stress. I know that's all part of the program, part of the routine, but I'm wondering if there's anything I, as the senior officer, should know . . . ei-ther about the program itself, or about what I should watch for in my people."

"Son of a—" Ferraro began.

"Belay that, Mike." Baxter studied Casey for a moment. "Son, there's nothing we can or should tell you. You're go-ing to have to find your own solutions. That's also part of the routine."

"I see, sir. A second question?"

"Go on."

"My boat team is short a man now, since Patterson rang the bell."

"So?"

"Will the instructor staff be redistributing personnel among the boat crews again, to make them even?"

The attrition of the trainees had continued during the past weeks. Boat Crew Number One still had its original seven men. Number Three had started with seven and was now down to six.

The other crews were rather worse off, with four defections apiece so far from Two, Five, Six, Seven, and Eight, and three from Number Four. Since they mustered twenty-one men left between them, the instructors had combined the skeleton crews, so Boat Crews Two, Four, and Five were back to their original seven-man strength, while Numbers Six, Seven, and Eight had vanished.

Back to the fleet.

Number Three, however, was a man short since Patterson had left, which put them at a distinct disadvantage.

"I mean, sir," Casey continued, "it's not exactly fair."

"Tough titty," West said.

"Your boat crew's gonna keep going until the last man left is still carrying his IBS around on his head," Ferraro growled. "All two hundred and eighty-some pounds of it. And *I'm* gonna be inside, bouncing up and down on his head."

"If you're looking for fair, Mr. Casey," Baxter said evenly, "I'm afraid you're in for a disappointment. Life is not fair. The VC are not fair. Therefore, *we* are not fair."

"I see, sir." Casey seemed to digest this. He nodded. "Very well. Thank you for your time, and please excuse the interruption. May I buy you gentleman another round of whatever you're having?"

"You may not," Ferraro snapped. "If I were you, banana, I'd get my pink little tail back to the barracks and get some rack time." He gave his best death's-head grin. "Zero-five-hundred hours is gonna come awfully early tomorrow. And that's when your ass is gonna be *mine*!"

"Yes, I guess it is. Well, thank you, gentlemen." He turned and walked away, heading for the bar.

"Well, I'll be swizzled," Chief Groton said. "Was that young son of a bitch just running an intel op on us?"

Baxter chuckled. "I think it was a fishing expedition, Chief. He was looking for whatever he could get."

"I'll give him something," Ferraro said.

"What's Casey like?" Baxter asked him. "I've seen his jacket, of course, but haven't followed the actual day-to-day that much."

"Overachiever type," Ferraro replied. "Gung ho, and then some. Athletic. The physical stuff doesn't faze him much. Usually pretty smartly turned out at morning inspection. I have to hunt to find something to gig him for, every once in a while. He's good material, overall. He's a competitor, and it's hard to hold him back sometimes. The tough part is keeping him from getting too damned cocky."

"I know the type. Lone wolf? Cowboy?"

"Not too much, though I haven't seen all that much compassion for the troops. That's why I think that bit about looking out for his people was bullshit. He was looking for hints about Hell Week."

"Well, keep an eye on that one."

"I keep an eye on *all* of them. Sir. But I know what you mean. His type often reaches a point where they decide to try to beat the system."

"We do encourage them to try just that," Baxter reminded him. "We're not here to turn out puppets. We're looking for people who show some individual initiative."

Groton laughed. "Y'know, Lieutenant, it's been my experience that if the trainees who try to beat the system put even half as much effort into just solving the problem or running the course or whatever, they'd come through with flyin' colors."

"You may be right," Ferraro said. "But they're always trying. God help us, they're always trying."

"God help the VC," Baxter said, "when we turn this lot loose on them."

Chapter 24

Basic Underwater Demolition/SEAL Class 42
Coronado, California
0002 hours

Even though he'd been expecting something like this, the explosion of noise brought Greg Halstead out of his rack, heart pounding, eyes wide. Gunfire cracked and pounded just outside the barracks windows, as instructors slammed into the barracks, screaming wild and contradictory orders, hauling SEAL trainees bodily out of their racks, slamming the lids down on the shitcans.

"All right! All right! I want you squirrels out of your trees! *Hit the deck hit the deck hit the deck!*"

A fire alarm was braying somewhere. Thirty-four trainees stumbled from their racks, some wide-awake, some still blinking sleep from their eyes, all utterly bewildered by the pure and savage cacophony erupting around their ears. Greg squinted at the big electric clock on the barracks wall. Just past midnight? The bastards had promised an oh-five-hundred reveille!

"Fall in on the grinder! *Now! Now! Now!*"

"Uniform of the day is jockstrap and boondockers! Move it, people! Move it!"

"Yes, it's *morning*! I want to see nothing in this barracks but amphibious green *blurs*!"

As they stampeded out of the barracks, other instructors were waiting for them . . . with hoses and wake-up blasts of icy water. "Get wet, you pussies! You want to be frogmen,

271

you're gonna get wet! *Move! Move! Move!*'' Explosions were going off, sharp punctuations against the ongoing wail of sirens. One of the junior instructors held an M60, its stock against his thigh, its muzzle pointed into the night sky over Coronado, and he was firing burst after burst with one hand, feeding the ammo belt through with the other.

Seems like a hell of a waste of ammo, Greg thought. He wondered if spent rounds were coming down on Main Street across the bay in downtown San Diego.

Shivering, the trainees fell in outside on the grinder, some in shorts and T-shirts, others just in jockstraps and boon-dockers. Ferraro stalked down the front rank, somehow managing to look immaculate in his trademark blue ball cap and God windbreaker.

"Good morning, tadpoles! It is now zero-zero-twelve hours on Day One of Week Five of your training. In other words, it is Hell Week, gentlemen, and I'm here to welcome you all to Hell!

"Up until now, we've been going easy on you. Gentling you in. Breaking it to you . . . *easy*. But I'm here this morning to tell you, bananas. The only easy day was *yesterday*!"

Yeah, that was true enough. The instructors hadn't let up on Class 42 for the entire past month; if anything, each day had been harder, rougher, more brutal, more demanding both physically and mentally. Greg had been learning the truth about that ''only easy day'' adage.

He was cold. It had been a hot night when he'd hit the rack a few hours ago, but the shock of being roused suddenly in the middle of the night, the blasts of cold water, the chilly night air, all combined to make him start shivering. He tried to focus on Ferraro's spiel.

"You all know about Hell Week," Ferraro was saying. "It's something of a tradition for the Teams. It got started back in World War II, with the training program for the Navy Combat Demolition Units at Fort Pierce, Florida, as the best way they could think of to show the newbies what combat was really like. In twenty-five years, the U.S. Navy has not found a better way of doing that. You will be kept on the go for the next five days, during which time you will be allowed to have approximately four hours of sleep . . . if you're lucky . . . and if you can manage to sleep in the mud. But believe me. After the first day or two, you'll find that you can sleep anywhere!''

Ferraro's head snapped around, his eyes singling Greg out from the rest. ''You! Pussy Halstead! Are you . . . cold?''

''No, Petty Officer Ferraro!''

''You look cold to me. You all look cold. I think we need some warm-up stretches. *All* of you pussies! Hit the deck! Gimme fifty!''

Most of the trainees were so bleary-eyed they had trouble matching their down-and-up counts to those of the recruits around them. The instructors counted out the cadence in loud, friendly bellows. ''And *one* and *two* and *three* and *four* . . .''

And by the time the count reached fifty, Ferraro had decided that they weren't doing it correctly. ''Sweet Christ on a crutch! Can't you pussies get it right? You're supposed to do it *together*! Now! Gimme fifty more! And *one*! And *two* and *three* and *four* . . .''

Somewhere around his ninetieth push-up, Greg began to warm up.

Tuesday, 16 July 1968

1045 hours

''Wrong, tadpole!'' Ferraro barked through the bullhorn. The words rang and squealed above the surf's thunder. ''Bravo Section, one step to the rear . . . *hut!* Sing out!''

Shivering violently—the water temperature was in the sixties, but they'd been immersed long enough that they were beginning to chill—the class began singing . . . or shouting might have been a more accurate description. They had to make themselves heard above the roar of the Pacific surf.

''*When the war is over and the WACs and Waves are home,*'' they bellowed, more or less to the tune of the Georgia Tech football fight song. ''*We'll swim back to the USA and never more shall roam!*

''*All the local maidens will get the best of care, and we'll raise a bunch of squallin', bawlin' Demolitioneers!*''

For the past two hours, they'd been standing in formation, as Ferraro, equipped with beach chair, suntan oil, and bullhorn, had relaxed ashore. The trainees had had no sleep at all since Sunday midnight and were getting a bit groggy. Ferraro would lie in the chair and fire questions at specific trainees. If the targeted person got the question right, the entire class got to take one step forward, toward beach and warm sun. If he got an answer wrong, they took a step backward . . . and had to sing another chorus of ''The Song of the Demolitioneers.'' Some of the questions had been legitimate, if somewhat involved and picky . . . like describe how to carry out an underwater search, or list the sizes and locations of the towing and mooring D-rings on a standard IBS. Other questions, though, seemed totally random and nonsensical, such as the distance from the Earth to the Moon in meters . . . or the depth of the ocean at the Marianas Trench.

Frank Casey shivered and sang with the rest of them and wondered what that bastard Ferraro was going to hit them with next. Ferraro had been riding Casey extra hard for the past couple of days; a good quarter of the questions had been directed at him, and all of them impossible to answer . . . which meant that the rest of the class blamed *him* when they had to take a step backward and sing another verse.

Damn the man. They'd been through that damned song so many times, he'd lost count. Was he going to go another round?

''Out of the water! *Move! Move! Move!*''

Evidently not. Now what?

The trainees broke from formation, jogging through the low surf, across wet sand, and up toward the dunes. ''Hit the Pit, tadpoles! *Move! Move! Move!*''

Casey noted an interesting datum with some part of his tired brain. Ferraro wasn't calling them ''bananas'' nearly so much now, after over four weeks. Now they were ''tadpoles,'' though that didn't necessarily win them any additional respect. It was all bullshit, of course. Bullshit custom tailored to wear them down and make them quit.

''The Pit'' was a patch of low ground behind the sand dunes along the Coronado Strand, a vaguely crater-shaped depression centered around a pool of mud and decorated with a scattering of telephone poles.

The boat teams had been working pole drill since Week One, but the program had gone into high gear with Hell Week. Each team, chivvied along by the instructors, approached one of the creosote-soaked poles, lining up behind it, listening to the instructor's orders.

"By the numbers! *One!*"

The line of men bent over, cradling the log in their arms. "*Two!*"

Together—no longer clumsily, as had been the case during their first week—they hoisted the pole to waist level.

"Thu-*ree!*"

The pole was jerked up to shoulder level.

"*Four!*"

Backs heaved, arms strained, and the pole went all the way up, the line of trainees standing in a line unsteadily beneath its mass.

"Thu-ree!"

Back to shoulder height.

"Two!"

Back to the waist.

"*Thu-ree! Four! Thu-ree! Four!*"

Casey stood in line with his crew, straining against the weight of the pole. Ferraro, he saw, was making himself comfortable again, unfolding his beach chair on the top of the dune nearby, seating himself, then smiling as he continued to call out the cadence through his bullhorn.

"*Thu-ree! Two! Thu-ree! Four! Thu-ree! Two! Thu-ree! Four! . . .*"

The astonishing thing, so far as Casey was concerned, was that each day he found that he was able to do more. He'd been in pretty fair shape, he thought, coming into the BUD/S program. But now, after four and a half weeks of this nonsense, he was in better shape than he'd ever been in before.

It was the mind games that were getting to him . . . the crap delivered for crap's sake, the mind-fucks that left the trainees reeling when they fell into another of Ferraro's traps. *The bastard's not gonna get me!*

"Thu-ree! Two! Thu-ree! Four! Thu-ree! Two! Thu-ree! Four! . . . and thu-ree! Two! One!"

The log thumped to the ground.

"Okay, you pussies. That's obviously getting too easy for you. On your backs! We're gonna bench-press those things!

One with his team, Casey dropped to the mud. The cadence began again. . . .

Wednesday, 17 July 1968

2145 hours

"No! I tell you it's okay!" Markham said. "I talked to Sally. Everything's set!"

Greg shook his head. "Man, I really don't like the sound of this!"

"Hey, you heard 'em, back on the first day of this bullshit," Casey said. "The only rule here is don't get caught!' "

"Yeah, and they're going to catch us!"

"Aw, don't be a pussy, Twidge!" Rodriguez said. "What could possibly go wrong?"

Greg could think of quite a few things as he leaned into his paddle, but he was aware, too, that the other five members of his boat crew were determined to go through with this, and standing against them, even arguing about the issue with them, would be a kind of betrayal.

And that was a cardinal sin in the Teams.

They were in their IBS, paddling against the current in a roughly northerly heading. The Point Loma Lighthouse gave a clear, white flash every few seconds; so long as they steered just to the right of that light, they would hit San Diego Bay okay.

But a combination of nerves and the violent, up-and-down rippling of the twelve-foot rubber boat were conspiring to make Greg sick. *Oh, God,* he thought. *Please, not again!*

As coxswain, Casey sat in the stern, steering with his paddle and calling out the cadence. The other five leaned over the side and paddled as hard as they could against the off-shore current, which was running against them this evening.

They had a hell of a long way to go.

The exercise scheduled for this evening was a simple one. It had started after dinner with the class run-marching south along the Silver Strand Highway, to a point on the slender Coronado Peninsula some three miles south of the base, each boat crew carrying its IBS on their heads. Inside each boat rode one of the instructors, standing up with paddle in hand, doing everything he could, it seemed, to throw the trainees underneath the twelve-foot craft off-stride. The instructors jumped. They bounced from side to side. They exploded in fury if the boat crews stumbled enough to throw them down. They held mock races with one another, paddling furiously over the side as the trainees ran grimly on, even reaching underneath and hitting the "motor" with the paddle if the men weren't fast enough, seemed unresponsive to orders, or weren't performing the evolution with the proper aggressive spirit.

At the assigned point, the boat crews had hit the surf, entering the sea on the Pacific side of the strand, with orders to start paddling north-northwest, a race that would take them all the away around the Coronado Peninsula and into South San Diego Bay.

The Coronado Peninsula was a long, extremely narrow strip of land curving north-northwest from Imperial Beach, almost on the U.S.–Mexican border and extending to the flat, thumb-shaped swelling at the tip called North Island. To the west was the Pacific Ocean; to the east the single, phallus-shaped body of water artificially divided into North and South San Diego Bays. Another finger of land reached out from the coast and the city of San Diego proper, extending west between North San Diego Bay and Mission Bay to the north, then curving around sharply south to Point Loma, just opposite the North Island Naval Air Station.

For the night's exercise, the boat crews were to paddle up the Pacific coast of the strand connecting Imperial Beach and North Island, enter North San Diego Bay between Point Loma and North Island, follow the coast around to the east and south along North Island and down into South San Diego Bay, until at last they passed the Navy Amphibious Base and made it all the way to Silver Strand State Park beach, just across the narrow peninsula from their starting point. Total distance for the exercise, point to point, was about twenty miles.

Most of the SEAL trainees enjoyed exercises involving the Silver Strand beach, for throughout the summer it was a frequent hangout for young, attractive, bikini-clad girls who came there to soak up some rays and maybe catch a glimpse of the Navy commandos-in-training. This exercise, however, would be at night, and there wouldn't be any girls to ogle on the beach.

There wouldn't be any time to ogle them in any case. This was a race, a competition between the boat teams, and the last boat in was certain to garner some extra attention for itself.

They stroked together, slowly making headway against the current. Greg's stomach twisted again, threatening to betray him. He shook his head with disgust; he'd been so damned glad to get off the *Edson* and into BUD/S. He'd not expected to have to put up with seasickness here!

Greg tried concentrating on the paddling, on the movements of the others in the boat, on the patterns of light scattered across the horizon. He was not, he realized, thinking very clearly. Since he'd been blasted awake a few minutes past midnight Monday morning, he'd had perhaps an hour or an hour and a half of sleep, some of it while crouching in the water of San Diego Bay, some of it while lying in the mud of the Pit. For the first forty-eight hours, he'd actually felt pretty good, alert, clear-headed, even buoyant, but during the past twenty hours or so he'd been getting progressively slower, both in physical reactions and in thinking.

A shark fin sliced through the water to his right. "Christ! Shark! A big one!"

"Where?" Casey demanded.

"I don't see nothin'," Rodriguez said.

"Where'd you see it?" Pogue asked.

"Right there!" Greg pointed. "Right there. Two feet away."

"I didn't see anything," Casey said quietly. "And I've been watching all around the boat. I think you've got yourself some sleep-deprivation whim-whams, Twidge."

"Shit. . . ." It had been so real. He blinked, trying to clear his eyes. He was so tired. If he could just close his eyes for a bit . . .

"C'mon, guys, keep up the pace!" Casey snapped. "Get it together!"

For a long time, it seemed as though the lighthouse continued to recede in front of them, but at long, long last, they passed the buoys marking the entrance to North San Diego Bay, and the dazzling pulse of the Point Loma Light was slipping past to port and into the night behind them. Greg's arms were turning to dead, leaden weights.

"Hey, Greg!"

"What?"

"What do you mean, 'what'?" Casey asked. "What's wrong?"

"You called my name."

"No, I didn't. Listen, Halstead. Are you okay?"

"Y-yeah. Yeah, I'm fine." But he wasn't fine. He'd just seen the fish with Don Knotts's face swimming alongside the raft, and it had called his name. Now he *knew* he was hallucinating.

He just didn't want the others to find out.

Casey reached forward and clapped him on the shoulder. "Okay, Twidge," he said, and that hard and determined fire was glowing behind his pale blue eyes. "It's your call, for the whole crew. What's it gonna be?"

Greg had already decided. He couldn't go against the others, couldn't let them down. "I'll go with it," he said. "I'm in!"

"All right!" Rodriguez called back from his spot in the IBS's bow, and several of the men broke the stroking cadence to give one another high-fives or clap Greg on the back.

"Yeah, we won't get in trouble," Pogue said, grinning. "They told us to do whatever we *had* to do, right?"

"Yeah, just so long as we don't get caught!"

"It's getting caught that bothers me," Greg told the others. "Ferraro's not stupid. Other trainees must've thought of this dodge, too."

"None like this one," Dixie pointed out. "Man, none like this one!"

"They thought they had it covered with the checkpoint at North Island," Casey said. "But they're not expecting us to have an agent on the *inside*!"

They'd all heard scuttlebutt about what had happened to other crews presented with this exercise who'd tried to cheat by short-cutting across the Strand. It was a real temptation, of course, for the peninsula was only a few hundred yards across at the widest point, and in places it was nothing but the Silver Strand Highway and a bit of beachfront and sand dunes to either side. But the checkpoint up at North Island would catch any crew stupid enough to try the overland route.

What Casey had worked out, though, was pretty slick, Greg thought, and he couldn't really see how it could go wrong. Their "agent on the inside" was Sally Markham, Mark One's wife. Markham was one of the relatively few married SEAL trainees, a torpedoman's mate first class who'd been in the Navy for seven years and married for six. Though generally he was only able to see his wife on weekends, he'd been able to call her up that afternoon, as soon as the trainees had learned what the night's evolution was to be.

Everything was set. Nothing could go wrong.

Except that Greg still had the nagging feeling that, where Ferraro was concerned, something was *bound* to go wrong. . . .

2335 hours

"That's the last of them," Baxter said. He was standing at the checkpoint at the north tip of the North Island Naval Air Station, squinting into the eyepiece of a bulky, tripod-mounted Varo image-intensifying sight. Even at almost midnight on a starless, moonless night, the starlight optics gave him a day-bright image of the northern bay. He could see Boat One, struggling along dead last, perhaps two hundred meters behind Boat Three. "So far, so good."

"Yeah, but we might have some trouble, sir," Ferraro said

with a grin. "A buddy of mine in the duty office at the air station's front gate tells me there's a strange car parked on Orange Street, down by the water."

"Well, well, well," Baxter said, raising his eye from the nightscope. "They're getting creative, aren't they? What are you going to do about it?"

"I think," Ferraro said, the grin widening, "that I'd like to give them a bit more rope and see if they'll hang themselves from it."

"Sounds like a plan, Mike. Let's go."

Thursday, 18 July 1968

0014 hours

The frogmen-in-training crouched at the water's edge, carefully checking in all directions. The city lights from San Diego cast a dazzling glow across the water at their backs, but they'd slipped up to the beach in the shelter of a jetty, taking full advantage of the shadows beneath the ancient, weed-and-barnacle-encrusted timbers.

"There she is," Markham said. A station wagon was parked at the end of the street. To the right, the chain-link fence separating the naval air station from the community of Coronado rose from the shadows. The trainees moved toward the car.

"Carl!" A pretty blond woman opened the car door, then ran down the short length of street to the waterfront. "Carl, honey!"

Casey turned away as the two embraced. "Okay, frogmen," he said. "Let's stow the IBS. Snap it up, now!"

It took only a few minutes to partially deflate the IBS and stuff it and the paddles into the back of the station wagon. Pogue's idea that they secure it to the luggage rack on the roof had been hooted down when he'd suggested it earlier; anyone who saw a civilian car driving down the Strand Highway with a goddamn IBS tied to the roof would know what was going on. Once the IBS was secured, they crowded inside to ride in relative comfort to a spot they knew well at the state beach. Getting six men into the car was a tight squeeze, with Markham next to his wife and Pogue next to him, and the other four squeezed into the backseat. The bulky kapok life jackets had to come off to manage the fit; they rode in the back with the IBS. Any discomfort the trainees might have felt was immediately alleviated by the cooler full of well-iced beer.

Fifteen minutes later, the car pulled to a stop at a deserted stretch of the Silver Strand State Park beach.

"Man, how long we gonna wait?" Rodriguez wanted to know as they climbed out of the car.

"It would be kind of stupid to show up an hour ahead of everybody else, right?" Casey said. He took a swig of beer. "Oh, *man*, that's good!"

"We'd better not come in first," Greg said. "First crew in is going to call as much attention to itself as the last. We should be second or third."

"Agreed," Casey said. He checked his watch. "Right in the middle of the pack. We'll hide out here until the lead boat passes, then slip in behind them. Hey, who knows? If we pass 'em honestly, then . . ."

"So, what do you think, Lieutenant?" Markham wanted to know. He had one arm around his wife's shoulders. "Think Sally and I have some time for, well, a little reunion?"

"Carl!" She punched him in the side.

"Well, c'mon, Sal! I don't get to see you that much anymore!"

"Think you're up to it, Mark One?" Dixie asked.

"Hey, the basic Mark One frogman is always ready!"

"Fifteen minutes," Casey said, looking at his watch again. "No more."

"Would you gentlemen mind, ah, waiting on the other side of this dune?"

Greg chuckled. "Well, we *do* have to start reinflating the IBS," he said. "C'mon, guys!"

While Markham and his wife climbed over the grass-topped dune with a blanket, the other five stayed by the road, hauling the IBS out of the car, unrolling it, and taking turns with the hand pump reinflating it. They stayed low and behind the station wagon, just in case some of the instructors were out patrolling the strand, but there was no traffic. The crew had the highway to themselves.

At one point, Greg heard a moan from the far side of the dune, started to call Markham to see if everything was all right, then realized what the sound must be.

"Well, it *was* his girl that made this work," Rodriguez said, grinning. "Seems only fair that he gets a special reward."

"I'm still wondering about Ferraro," Greg said. He stood up, peering across the top of the dune toward San Diego. The water was lit brightly enough that they would be able to see the other boats going past—or a motor launch conned by one of the instructors.

"Don't worry about him," Casey said. "I saw him up at North Island when we passed. Him and Lieutenant Baxter were giving us the eye through some kind of telescope, probably a starlight scope. They were backlit by the landing lights at the air station."

"Doesn't mean they're still there." Greg looked up the highway. "In fact, if they drive down this road now, we're in a world of shit."

"Ah. They're probably already at the take-out point, waiting for the first boat. Just play it cool, Twidge." Casey knocked off the last of his beer.

"Sure, man," Rodriguez said. "Besides, we can see traffic comin' for a mile in either direction. Plenty of time to lie low."

The noises from the other side of the dune were getting louder, more insistent. "Go, Mark One!" Dixie said, grinning.

"Hey, Mark One!" Casey said, raising his voice. "Wrap it up, man! We gotta get moving!"

"I'm coming!"

The waiting trainees burst into laughter.

0038 hours

"Shit, I don't believe this," Ferraro said. He was lying sprawled atop a sand dune alongside Kemper and Lieutenant Baxter. "One of 'em's goin' for a little I 'n' I."

He handed the powerful nightscope over to Baxter, who carefully focused on the wayward band of SEAL trainees. From here, he could see both sides of the dune; to the left, between the station wagon and the sand dune, five trainees were slumped in the sand, smoking cigarettes and drinking beer. To the right, above the high-tide line, the sixth trainee was on his back with a pretty girl riding astride his hips. She was bucking up and down now, head back, hair flying, as he reached up and played with her breasts.

I & I. Intercourse and Intoxication, an old Navy play on the term R&R.

"Is that Markham?" Baxter asked.

"Sure is. And his wife. I think her name's Sally."

The night-vision starlight scope gave everything in view an eerie, silvery green glow, which if anything gave the scene an added erotic twist. Baxter turned away, disliking the role of a peeping Tom, and mildly angered that he was enjoying himself this way.

"Well, let's go pick 'em up."

"Shame to just barge in that way," Kemper said. He was nearby, watching through binoculars.

Ferraro reached into the front seat of the gray Navy truck they were driving and picked up a bullhorn and a handheld spotlight. "You know, Lieutenant. We could play this a little creatively and have some fun."

Baxter was interested. "What did you have in mind?"

0052 hours

Casey took another hard, long look across the top of the sand dune, studying the sparkling waters of the bay. "Man, where are those guys?" he asked. He was beginning to wonder if he'd miscalculated, if the other four IBS crews had already slipped south past this stretch of beach.

"I'm thinking maybe we should go on," Greg said.

"I'm thinking you're right. Psst! Markham!"

"Yeah, yeah," Markham said. He staggered a bit coming up the slope of the dune, his arm around his wife. "You guys ready?"

"We're ready," Dixie said. "Are you?"

"Yeah," Pogue said. "You're looking a bit run-down."

"All I want to do is sleep for about a month," Markham said, the words slurred.

"Yeah, who doesn't?" Rodriguez said.

"That's what you get for relaxing in the middle of Hell Week," Greg said. "Kind of a shock to the system, huh?" He thumped the IBS with his hand. "Pumped up and ready to swim, Mr. Casey."

"Okay. Mark One, say good-bye to Sally and let's get out of here."

Carefully, the trainees policed the area, making sure they had all of their paddles and life jackets. Sally gave Markham a last kiss and received handshakes and busses on her cheek from the rest. Then she was gone, the taillights of her station wagon dwindling down the road.

"Where the hell are the other guys?" Pogue wanted to know.

"I don't know," Casey said. "I'm beginning to think maybe they got stopped at another checkpoint. I've been watching. I had this planned so we'd be sure to see them against the lights on the bay. I don't see how we could've missed seeing them."

"Maybe," Greg said, "they just—"

"Attention!" a voice boomed across the dunes out of the darkness to the south, bullhorn amplified. An electronic squeal sounded, grating like nails on a blackboard. "Attention! This is the United States Immigration Service! Put your hands up!" There was a pause. "*Attencion! Este es el Servicio Immigracion de los Estados Unidos! Leva su manos!*"

"Shit!" Pogue cried. "The Border Patrol!"

"Run for it!" Casey snapped. The trainees, dragging the IBS between them, scrambled over the top of the dune.

"*Alto!*" the amplified voice barked. Full-auto gunfire thundered in the night. "*Alto ahora!*"

"*Shit! Shit! Shit!*" Dixie said. Gunfire barked again, kicking up geysers of sand, and the trainees sprawled onto the beach, hugging the wet ground. A dazzling light ignited in the darkness, the blue-white beam sweeping across the beach, touching them once, then centering on them.

"Hey! We're Americans!" Pogue yelled as loud as he could.

"Yeah," Rodriguez added. *"Somos Americanos!"*

"Come up off the beach with your hands up! This is your final warning!"

"That light's pretty far off," Casey said. "A hundred, hundred fifty meters at least. C'mon! We can make it to the water!"

"No, man!" Dixie said. "We should give ourselves up. They'll see who we are and turn us over to the base."

"Yeah," Greg said. "And then we're *all* out of the program! No way!"

"The water's right there!" Casey said, pointing at the low surf rolling in off the bay, just a few yards down the slope. "What do they always tell us? When you're in trouble, head for the water!"

"Hey, that's right," Markham said. "We can swim for it."

"We take the IBS and paddle for it," Casey said. "They won't see us on the water."

"Attention! Attention! You on the beach! Raise your hands and come toward the light!"

"You guys all with me on this?" Casey said, looking at the faces of his crew. "Twidge? Dixie?"

"I'm with you," Greg said. His face looked paste white.

"Yeah, right," Dixie said. "Let's do it."

"Okay! Let's go, before they get any closer!"

Crouching low, they dragged their IBS to the water and plunged in, then straightened up and ran as hard as they could, splashing ahead until the water reached their hips. Several more bursts of automatic fire followed them, but their unseen attackers seemed to be having trouble getting the range. The searchlight followed them, lost them, touched them again . . . then slipped past. They piled into the boat, grabbed their paddles, and started stroking, pulling hard straight for the center of the bay.

Casey paddled too, cursing under his breath. If he got his people shot by the goddamn *Border Patrol* . . .

Tijuana and the Mexican border were only another eight miles south; Casey had heard stories about one BUD/S class that had run a bit too close to the border and come under fire from some serious bad guys—smugglers of either illegal immigrants or drugs—who'd thought the trainees were government agents. Since that time, at least half of the weapons carried by trainees on maneuvers in that area were always loaded, just in case.

Man, the Immigration Service must *really* be touchy around here! They could all have been killed. . . .

He started stroking harder.

0136 hours

"Damn! I lost them," Ferraro said. He lowered his M-16. "You see 'em, sir?"

Baxter squinted into the eyepiece of the starlight scope, sweeping the bay. Part of the problem was that there was actually too much light reflected off the water from the city and the Navy base across the bay.

"Negative," Baxter said. "Not bad use of cover and concealment, I'd say. I'd have to . . . ah! Hold it. There they are. Good Lord! I never saw men paddle an IBS so fast! They must be halfway to San Diego already!"

Ferraro peered into the night. "Where?"

Baxter pointed, then passed him the starlight scope.

"Ah ha!" Ferraro said, acquiring the distant target. "You know, most tadpoles don't have that much energy halfway through Hell Week."

Kemper laughed. "That's right. I don't think we've been working these boys half hard enough!"

"What do you think, sir?" Ferraro asked. "Administrative discipline on this one?" He grinned his nastiest grin. "Or we bear down a bit harder to let them see the error of their ways?"

"Man," Baxter said. "Tough call. They disobeyed orders. Technically they went AWOL by leaving the assigned course. I should kick their butts clear out of the program, or at least rotate them back and make them start training all over again. But I have to admire their initiative."

"Aw, give 'em to us," Kemper said. "Please!"

"That's right," Ferraro said. "We'll even the score."

"Deal," Baxter said. "I don't want to lose them if there's another way."

"Oh, we still might lose 'em," Ferraro said. "Their asses are *mine* until we secure Hell Week in . . ." He looked at his watch. "Another forty hours or so. I'm afraid I can't promise that any of them will want to stay with the program!"

"Tell me something, Mike."

"Yeah?"

"What would you have done if they'd surrendered to the, ah, 'Border Patrol'?"

"Held the light in their eyes so they couldn't get a look at us. Make 'em get face down in the sand. Handcuff 'em, blindfold 'em, and take their clothes. Tell them in a muffled voice that we're gonna deport their asses back to Mexico and chuck 'em in the back of the truck. Ride around with them on bumpy, backcountry roads for a couple of hours, then turn 'em in to Amphib Base Security. And when they reported to me in the morning, I'd sign their papers and send them back to the fleet, no ifs, ands, or buts."

"No second chances?"

"Hell, Lieutenant. If they'd surrendered to us, I'd have *known* they weren't SEAL material! SEALs *never* surrender! This way, well, there's still a chance, a *small* chance, that they'll make it. . . ."

Chapter 25

Basic Underwater Demolition/SEAL Class 42
Coronado, California
1630 hours

The trainees, the twenty of them who were left, sat shoulder to shoulder in the mud pit. Greg had no idea what time it was. A dim, distant voice was telling him that he could take a look at the sun, at least to get an idea of whether it was morning or afternoon. Simple. If it was morning, the sun would be above Mission Bay and the urban sprawl of San Diego to the east. If it was afternoon, the sun would be over the Pacific, to the west. Simple.

Unfortunately, at the moment, Greg had no idea which way was east or west. He was sitting in the mud, completely covered over like his nineteen classmates, and the surrounding sand dunes prevented him from seeing the horizon in any direction. Besides, the sun was behind him right now, and it would have been too much effort to turn his head and look.

What day was this? He couldn't remember. He'd had something like two or maybe three hours of sleep since Hell Week had begun, and he was now operating in an almost dreamlike state where things he did, things that happened to him, seemed to be happening to someone else entirely. Greg Halstead was little more than a detached observer, watching his battered and exhausted body respond to orders like an automaton.

Hell Week had started off bad, harder than anything he'd imagined possible.

Things had gotten a lot harder since the IBS exercise in the bay on Wednesday night.

They know, he thought, remembering the escapade on the beach. *They've got to know.* And yet the uncertainty was part of the ongoing torture.

After making their getaway from the Border Patrol, they'd paddled south to the extraction point, to find Ferraro waiting for them. They were first to arrive, and with good reason.

The total route, from insertion point to extraction point, was twenty miles. They'd gotten out of the water at about mile twelve, then driven down the Strand Highway to mile eighteen—a trick that should have saved them six miles out of the twenty, as well as guaranteeing that they wouldn't come in last.

What they'd not known, however, was that the other boat crews had been intercepted at the Amphibious Base at about mile sixteen and told to paddle back the way they'd come, to extract at their insertion point. It was just the sort of dirty trick the instructors loved to play on the trainees, a way to turn a twenty-mile course into a thirty-two-mile route, a way to catch them just as they thought they thought they only had four miles to go.

But *somehow* Boat Three had missed the intercept.

Ferraro had expressed his concern in careful and loving tones, explaining that the Coast Guard had been alerted and was now searching the bay for them. It would have been *tragic* if an entire BUD/S boat crew was lost in an exercise!

He then ordered the tired Boat Three crew to get their IBS back in the water . . . and to head for the proper extraction site—less than one hundred meters away across the sand dunes and beach of the Silver Strand, but twenty long miles by sea. He also told them not to get picked up by the Coast Guard, because SEALs were expected to be masters of evasion in and on the water.

That return trip had been a nightmare that Greg knew he would never forget as long as he lived. They were all hallucinating at one point; Pogue kept carrying on a conversation with a mermaid that he insisted was swimming alongside, and Rodriguez was certain that the light from the Point Loma lighthouse was a UFO. Three times they ran ashore to avoid a passing Coast Guard cutter; once, Dixie had started to wander off on his own, muttering to himself, but Greg and Casey had gone after him and dragged him back. By the time they were past Point Loma and heading into the final six miles or so of their epic voyage, Markham was out cold—asleep or unconscious, there was no way to tell which—and the six rowers were down to five. For the last three miles, Ferraro and several other instructors paced them in a Boston Whaler. They pulled Markham out and took him ashore, then returned an hour later to follow the IBS closely, keeping them on course, bellowing insults at them, and suggesting that they might like to quit.

When they reached shore at last, it was dawn, and the rest of the section had been in for hours. Ferraro stood them in a line and berated them for coming in last, for missing the navigational point, for making a mistake that—had this been an actual wartime operation—would have cost them the mission and possibly their lives. While the rest of the class had breakfast, they had to wash down their IBS in fresh water, stow it properly, then double-time back to the Amphibious Base.

The rest of Thursday had been a nightmare. Even now, Greg could remember only disjointed pieces of it, endless push-ups, log drill, running the obstacle course again and again. Markham had returned to Boat Crew Three, which had then been designated the goon squad, the screwups who could do nothing right and were forced, therefore, to do everything two or three or even more times before Ferraro and the other instructors were satisfied. Every few hours, Ferraro would line them up, dirty, cold, wet, and exhausted, and as they stood there, swaying, scarcely able to stay on their feet, he would tell them again to quit, to walk the few short feet to the bell and give the requisite three rings.

"C'mon, guys!" he said, almost pleading. "Quit now, ring the bell, and we'll have you enjoying showers, hot coffee, and full meals before you know it!"

When none accepted, he'd made them do squat thrusts and interminable push-ups.

Markham had vanished sometime late Thursday. Greg didn't know if he'd quit or injured himself, and no one else seemed to know either. Somehow, Mark One's disappearance was more unnerving than would have been his simple declaration of "I quit."

Boat Crew Number Three was down to five, now. Bandit Rodriguez. Pogie Bait Pogue. Dixie Zelasnik. Twidge Halstead.

And, of course, Mr. Casey.

The lieutenant, Greg thought, had seemed unstoppable. He'd continued pushing ahead, no matter what happened, no matter what garbage the instructors dumped on his shoulders. He didn't apologize to the others for the escapade Wednesday night and, in retrospect, Greg decided that they'd all agreed to the thing, so they were all equally guilty. Now, though, Casey was clearly close to the breaking point, with that far-off look that Greg had heard described as the "thousand-yard stare" when it was applied to Marines who'd been in combat for a long, long time.

Greg wanted to be around to see it when the human dynamo finally ran down . . . but doubted that he was going to last that long himself.

Friday, the last day, they called "So Solly Day."

This was yet another tradition reaching back to the first training program of this type, the NCDU program at Fort Pierce, Florida, during World War II. On the final day of what had eventually come to be known as Hell Week, trainees had been forced to run difficult and complex obstacle courses, wade through mud, and race across sand dunes in mock landing exercises, as instructors had set off demolition charges of various sizes, just to keep things interesting.

An explosion thundered to Greg's left, tearing at him. He was hanging head down, hands and knees wrapped around a slender wire rope suspended six feet above yet another mud pit. Spray cascaded into the air, then fell, drenching him. The stink of gunpowder mingled with the more organic odor of the mud.

Why even go on? They fucking said it was impossible. . . .

The rope across the mud pit was yet another tradition. It was said that no one had ever made it all the way across. So far, every man to try in Bravo Section had gotten perhaps halfway before finally losing his grip and falling into the soupy mud below.

Greg clung to the line, reaching out, taking a fresh hold, hauling himself along. The rope was slick with mud, most of it deposited by the trainees who'd gotten this far before falling off. His hands were coated with the stuff, as was the rest of him. His kapok life jacket was so soggy now that wearing it was like wearing a vest made of lead. He was having trouble breathing, trouble even moving. Somehow, he hauled himself along another twelve inches.

"C'mon, tadpole!" Kemper bellowed. "What, you think this is a playground? If you can't play with the big boys, then get out! Quit! *Quit!*"

He was tempted. He was very tempted . . . but up ahead he saw Casey sitting in the mud, staring with glassy eyes up at him as more explosions went off to either side. If he quit, Boat Three would be down to four men, and that would make it harder than ever for them to pull through.

The whole section was down to what, now . . . twenty? Four boats with five men apiece? Something like that, though he'd lost count. Several times during the morning he'd been roused from what passed as sleep—in the midst of more calisthenics or holding a rest position with rigidly locked arms—by the sharp *ting-ting-ting* of another trainee giving up.

Another explosion thundered, and his ears rang. Exhaustion dragged at him, and despite a scrambling grab with his free hand, his fingers simply lost their hold and he dropped into the mud below with a sharp splat.

"Halstead! You banana! Go back around and do it again! *Move! Move! Move!*"

They made him cross the pit, hanging from the cable, three more times. Each time, he made it halfway, then fell in. Then it was double time over the dunes and, "*Hit the bay, you tadpoles! Get wet!*"

But Ferraro stopped the goon squad, ordering them to stand to apart from the others. Once the rest of the class was in formation, standing in the surf, the five men of the goon squad were forced to sit at the edge of the surf, legs pointed toward the sea and spread apart, their hands holding their

trouser cuffs open as the surf surged around them. Each wave
brought a cloud of grit and sand and broken seashells, which
was deposited in growing, gritty lumps around their thighs
and buttocks and over their genitals. Then, as the rest of the
class watched, the goon squad picked up their boat and began
running back and forth, up and down the beach, holding the
IBS, with Kemper aboard, over their heads. Within twenty
minutes, their privates were rubbed raw and they could
barely walk.

"Quit! Quit! Quit!" The instructors were chanting at them
as they stumbled into formation in the surf once more, re-
joining the others. The chant had an almost hypnotic quality
about it.

"I'm . . . I'm going to quit," Casey said. He was standing
next to Greg, the two men leaning against one another, holding one another up. The surf pounded about them, knocking
them about.

"Shit, Casey!" Greg said. "No way! We're in this together!"

"I don't think I can . . ."

"What time is it?" Rodriguez wanted to know. He was
standing to Greg's right, next to Pogue.

Greg blinked. Salt water was burning his eyes. He looked
up at the sun, which was westering toward the Pacific at their
backs. "I don't know. Late afternoon, sometime." The realization struck home. "Yeah. Listen, Casey! It's Friday!"

"Friday . . ." The word didn't seem to carry any meaning
for him.

"So Solly Day, man. Hell Week's almost over. You can't
quit *now*!"

"Man, I don't think I can go on! I gotta quit!"

"We ain't gonna let you," Rodriguez said. "Are we,
Greg?"

"That's right. We all stay together!"

"How many are left?" Dixie wanted to know. Greg shook
his head, uncertain. Once it had been twenty, but he thought
three or four more had dropped out in the past couple of
hours. What did that make it? Sixteen, maybe.

"Look . . . I gotta quit!" Casey said, his voice ragged,
close to tears. "Those bastards have been ragging us ever

since that stunt with the rubber boats, man. It's me they want. I was responsible.''

"Look," Greg said, with a sudden flash of insight that seemed brilliant in his muddled condition. "If you quit, we all quit. And then the whole thing'll have been for nothing! You can hold out another few hours! We all can! Right?''

"Right!" "Yeah." "Sure," the others agreed.

"Stop that talking in ranks!" Ferraro bellowed over his bullhorn. "I think you guys still got too much energy. Out of the water! Move! Move! Move! Hit the Pit! *Now!*''

"The Pit" was part of an extensive mudflat that once, his instructors had told them with some relish, had been a sewage field. The smell was hideous enough, though the men had grown so accustomed to it that it didn't bother them much anymore. The *taste*, however, was indescribably foul, and the instructors made certain that all of the trainees had ample opportunity to know that taste during the past several weeks. They'd crawled through the stuff, faces in the mud. They'd lain in the stuff, facedown, while Ferraro and the other instructors walked across their backs, occasionally stepping on their heads "by accident." The instructors seemed to have spent extra time and attention to the goon squad. After running races through the mud—crawling, inching along, pushing the creosote-soaked telephone poles in front of them—they'd been given a rest at last, sitting together in the mud, growing colder and colder, until the only way to stay warm was to huddle together . . . and shiver.

Someone suddenly staggered to his feet, lurched across the pit, splashing, and scrambled onto dry ground, a shambling figure covered head to toe in mud. He reached the bell, pulled off his helmet, tossed it down, and gave the three rings. He stood there then, scraping the mud from his face.

It was Pogue.

Shit . . .

As usual, the trainees were clad in trousers, T-shirts, water-logged boondockers, water-logged kapok vests, and a heavy and soggy layer of black, stinking mud. The mud had removed every trace of individuality each man might have thought he possessed. When he glanced at Casey, sitting next to him, Greg honestly couldn't tell if it was his swim buddy sitting there or not. He could make out certain features—bloodshot eyes that appeared and disappeared as the man blinked, a nose, a pair of lips bright blue where the mud was thinnest, trembling with the cold. Greg was pretty sure he recognized Casey now by his eyes, but it could have been *anybody* sitting there.

The class, Greg realized with a sudden, tired burst of insight, could not look like anything even remotely human . . . fifteen humped backs and bowed heads, all uniformly coated with slimy mud, a single, wallowing beast glistening as it trembled, breathed, and shifted in the wallow. Greg thought he heard machine-gun fire in the distance, then swore at himself, at his overactive imagination. The sound was the chattering of his own teeth. Damn. Here it was July in sunny southern California, and his teeth were chattering with the cold. It didn't make sense. Nothing made sense anymore.

Why, he wondered, was he putting up with this nonsense? The whole exercise, Hell Week, especially, but everything from day one had been continuous and unrelenting crap. He was stronger now, yes. The long runs, the endless swimming—much of it against the pounding California surf—had toughened him, made him stronger. The drownproofing exercises in the BUD/S pool, the exercises with the IBS and crawling past live explosions had all served to increase his self-confidence. He could see, could *feel* the improvement there.

But why the endless games, the mind-fucks that the instructors seemed to delight in playing? Somehow, Greg could not imagine getting to Vietnam and finding the VC using weapons like sand up the trousers . . . or the threat of standing for hours in the pounding surf, or even making them paddle around the island once more. The instructors were harassing them just for the hell of it, and Greg had had more than enough.

Ferraro, Kemper, and the other enlisted instructors had settled themselves down on their folding beach chairs and seemed content to lie back and soak up the sun. Possibly, Greg thought, this respite in the mud was intended as an opportunity for the class to grab another few minutes sleep.

It would be a hell of a shame if he missed such a golden opportunity. He closed his eyes. . . .

Somehow, though, he sensed a stir among the other trainees. Alert to the possibility that the instructors were trying to trick them again, he snapped his eyes open, his head up. There were more people up there on the sand dune. It took him a moment to register the fact that the new arrivals were women.

Beautiful women. His eyes locked onto one tall, leggy blonde in particular, who was draping herself across Kemper's lap, one arm around his neck. She was wearing extremely short shorts and an impossibly clean white blouse, and she was holding a six-pack of beer in her free hand.

Greg dropped his eyes, shaking his head. No. He was hallucinating again. *Damn, you see such weird things with sleep deprivation.* He remembered the talking fish. . . .

He could hear the girls laughing.

"Thought we'd take it easy today and maybe party a bit," Ferraro said. Reaching over, he accepted a can of beer from the blond woman, ripped off the pull tab, and took a long swig. "Too bad you tadpoles are too stupid to come up out of that hole, or you could join us!" He took another swig, a longer one. "Man, oh, man, that tastes *good!*"

"C'mon up and ring the bell," Kemper added. "We've got a cold one waitin' for ya!"

This, Greg thought, was downright inhuman. Shit . . . didn't they want any of them to make it through this insane torture? Didn't they want *any* of them to become SEALs?

The blonde suddenly stood up, stretching sinuously, her arms over her head. From the way her nipples pressed out against the white material, he knew she wasn't wearing a bra. After a moment, she reached down and began unfastening her shorts.

The eyes of every man in the pit were on her as she slowly drew down the zipper, tugged a bit at the waistband, gave a delightful little shimmy of her hips, and let the shorts slide down those long, glorious legs. Underneath, she was wearing the tiniest bikini bottom that Greg had ever seen. It was bright blue and the triangular scrap of cloth in the front only just covered her pubic mound. When she turned and bent over, he could see the way the material vanished between her taut, smooth buttocks.

Greg had not thought it possible for him to even have a sexual thought. Even in the earlier weeks of Phase One, he'd generally been too tired to do more than talk about women and sex, and then only on the weekends when the training pretty much stood down. Some of the men in the class, especially the officers, liked to boast that they'd gone across the bay to San Diego and made it with airline stews on the weekends, but Greg had always had his doubts. Damn it, sleep—*real* sleep—was too important to lose at this point.

But watching that girl with Kemper hit Greg now with a pounding and irresistible erotic hunger, a driving lust that left him shaking helplessly. His erection *hurt*.

He tried to look away. The other girls were with the other instructor petty officers, but none appeared to be putting on a show. They giggled and spoke in nervous whispers, as though they were embarrassed, and Greg realized then that this was a put-up job, another mind-fuck, a way of kicking the trainees in yet another unexpected and vulnerable spot just to see if they would twitch. The women must be wives or girlfriends of the instructors, he thought. Ferraro was the only one up there alone.

That figured. The bastard couldn't possibly have a wife. No woman would be able to stand him.

No, not quite alone. His chair was set up next to the pole on which the bell was mounted. He was running his hand up and down that pole now with one hand, sipping beer with the other. "Anyone want to quit?" he called out happily.

The blonde stood next to Kemper for a moment longer, watching the huddle of SEAL trainees, laughing . . . laughing at *them* as Kemper casually reached out and caressed her leg, running his hand up and down the outside of her thigh from hip to knee and back again, mimicking the way Ferraro was stroking that pole. Greg hated her, hated Kemper, hated Ferraro, hated the bell, hated the whole damned United States Navy more than he'd ever imagined was possible. The only thing keeping him in the Pit right now was sheer physical and mental exhaustion . . . that and the somewhat irrational fear that if he stood up, everybody would see his erection.

At the same time, he had sanity and reason enough remaining to recognize the fact that his psychological reactions were screwed up beyond all recognition. He still wasn't even certain that what he was seeing was real. This could be another hallucination, and he didn't want to humiliate himself in front of the others by acting as if it *was* real.

He tried to jar himself back to reality by imagining what would happen if he actually tried to go anywhere near the woman. Her, sleek and tanned and beautiful; him, covered head to toe in reeking black muck. Once, in ninth grade, back in Jenner, he'd tried to ask Alice Simmons, the prettiest girl in his English class, for a date, and he'd done it so clumsily that she'd laughed at him.

He could just imagine the blonde laughing at him as he stumbled up out of the mud. All of them would be laughing . . . because if he left this hole, it would only be to ring the bell and quit.

Come to think of it, the blonde looked an awfully lot like Alice.

Oh, God. Oh, *God*! She was starting to unbutton her blouse.

She did it slowly, even more slowly than her act with the shorts, the tip of her tongue sliding out and running across her lips as she unfastened the last button, held her blouse tightly closed for a moment with both hands, then quickly pulled her hands apart, exposing her breasts to the shivering SEAL trainees.

She wasn't wearing anything underneath the blouse. Her breasts were large and round and perfect and delightfully capped by sweet, brown, high-riding nipples.

Greg heard a low, almost subvocal groan running through the other trainees and knew only then that it wasn't a hallucination. He felt a sudden, sharp pulsing in his loins and an answering flood of red-hot shame. He thought he must be blushing furiously, though no one could possibly see through all of that mud.

He hadn't touched himself, hadn't even moved. This, he thought wryly, had to be the most acute case of premature ejaculation on record.

Dimly, he heard a clanging sound. Blinking through the

mud, he looked at Ferraro. Dixie Zelasnik, he saw, had somehow scrambled out of the pit, staggered up to the bell, and
given the requisite three rings.

No! Not Dixie, too!

Ferraro stood next to him, speaking to him softly. Zelasnik
shook his head, a sharp and brutal gesture; Ferraro patted his
shoulder despite the mud, and the trainee—the ex-trainee—
shambled off over the dune.

Fourteen.

The lust was gone now, vanished as suddenly as it had
arrived. He looked at the girl again ... and blinked. Her
blouse was buttoned and she was wearing her shorts once
again. Damn ... had it been a waking dream after all? Or
maybe not a *waking* dream; it was entirely possible that he'd
fallen asleep, right there in the mud.

Ferraro faced the class, fists on hips. "All right! All right!
Rest period's over, tadpoles. On your feet! Time to get wet!
Hit the bay!"

It was almost more than he could manage to stagger to his
feet with the others, then slog out of the mud and up the
dune. As he stumbled over the top, he passed within a few
feet of the blond woman, who was sitting now on the sand,
knees drawn up, her hair streaming past her face in the
breeze. "Good luck, sailor," she said.

Good luck ... sailor?

Had she spoken to him? Or had she been speaking to the
whole class, giving them a covert bit of encouragement? He
didn't know, didn't care. He didn't hate her anymore, and
that was good. Mostly, though, he was looking forward to
hitting the water again, to letting the salt water blast the
stench and filth from his body.

"You three!" Ferraro boomed through the bullhorn. "The
goon squad! As you were! Hit the deck! Assume the position!"

Rodriguez, Casey, and Greg dropped where they were,
holding themselves in the push-up position, arms locked, legs
straight, while the rest of the class splashed into the surf. He
was expecting more push-ups ... but Ferraro walked past
them, his beautifully spit-shined shoes gleaming in the afternoon light as he paced up and down the beach.

A minute passed. Then two. Then two more. The mud coating their bodies was impossibly heavy; worse, as the breeze blew in off the ocean, it was beginning to dry, turning sticky in some places, remaining heavy and liquid in others. Greg's back, neck, and groin were starting to itch madly; his thighs and buttocks, already sandblasted raw, then soaked in salt water, burned, hurt, and itched intolerably all at once, as though they'd been baked in the sun.

"You gentlemen want to quit yet?" Ferraro was standing just a few feet away. His voice was low, unheard by any save the three of them.

None of them answered.

"You're just bringing lot of unnecessary pain on yourselves, boys. All you have to do is quit. You're *not* SEAL material, you know."

Greg's heart was pounding now. His arms were hurting, a deep, spasming pain extending into his shoulders and back. He didn't think he could hold himself up much longer.

"Halstead," Ferraro said. "I understand from your application you really want to be a SEAL. You know, don't you, that no one ever promised you SEAL out of BUD/S. You could end up in UDT. Is that what you want? Blowing up obstacles, playing with high explosives? Maybe blowin' off your hand or your eye? I'm not going to sign you off as a SEAL, so that means you'll end up in demolition. Why not quit? Go back to the fleet? You're a twidget. You'll get a nice, soft billet playing with knobs and dials. That's better than this crap, isn't it?"

"I am not going back to the fleet," Greg said through clenched teeth. "I get seasick."

Ferraro snorted and made a wheezing, strangled noise that almost made Greg look up. He held his position though, as he realized that Ferraro had simply guffawed. "Oh, man, that's great. A seasick sailor! Okay. On your feet, you three. Hit the water!"

Greg tried to stand up, but his arms betrayed him. He collapsed on the sand, unable to move.

"C'mon, tadpole!" Ferraro said. "I said get wet!"

Greg tried to rise again, and failed. Ferraro started to close in, but then Casey and Rodriguez were there. "We've got him, Ferraro,'' Casey said. His voice was slurred and broken. He sounded as though he'd been drinking, and Greg wondered if he sounded as bad.

The two hoisted him up off the sand, and after a bad, rubbery moment, Greg managed to get his knees to lock. Half-supported by Casey and Rodriguez, he managed a stiff-legged lurch into the water. The surf blasted over his body, scouring off the filth. It was freezing. It felt wonderful.

Standing now in formation, the three survivors of Boat Crew Three stood arm in arm, swaying and staggering as each wave broke around them. It was true, Greg thought with a detached wonder. The ocean was the SEAL's best friend, the place to go whenever he was in trouble.

God he was cold. The shivering wouldn't stop, and his feet felt numb.

The rest of the class, he realized, wasn't in much better shape. Ferraro hadn't been riding them as hard, but to a man they were stooped, red-eyed, blue-lipped, pasty-faced, walking zombies, the dead risen from their graves. The instructors were in a huddle up on the beach. Lieutenant Baxter was there, too. Oh Christ, what now? What were they planning on springing on them now? . . .

Ferraro turned smartly to face the trainees, raising his bullhorn to his mouth. ''Bravo Section Class Forty-two,'' he said. ''Secure from Hell Week!''

Secure . . .

What?

What had he said?

Greg took a cautious look to left and right. The others seemed as stunned as he. Several men started moving toward the shore. Someone lifted a fist into the air and shouted a feeble ''Hooyah!''

''Hooyah!'' Others took up the cry. They'd made it. They'd made it! Greg turned to Casey and managed, somehow, to balance himself upright as he threw the man a very smart salute. Casey returned it, then grinned, reached out, and shook Greg's hand. Rodriguez draped his arms over both their shoulders. ''Oh, man, guys! We *made* it!''

''Together,'' Greg added.

''Team,'' Casey said.

Greg tried to walk out of the surf, but his legs failed him again. The three had to support one another, and even then several of their classmates had to come back into the surf and help the three of them stagger out onto the beach.

Greg tipped back his head, staring up at an impossibly blue sky.

"*Hooyah!*"

Chapter 26

Thursday, 12 September 1968

Sick Bay
Basic Underwater Demolition/SEAL Compound
Coronado, California
1430 hours

"Aw, man!" Greg said, shaking his head in pure, trembling frustration. "I make it all the way through Hell Week, and then *this* happens!"

The duty corpsman gave him a sympathetic grin. "Well, let's have a look," he said. "Hop up on the table and get the shoe off."

Greg did as he was told, grimacing as the corpsman applied pressure here, then there, gently moving his foot around.

"It's pretty swollen," the corpsman said. "How'd this happen, anyway?"

Hell Week might now be a fading dream. The trainees were no longer called "bananas," and, as a kind of outward sign of their inward transformation, the weekend after Hell Week they'd been issued new, olive drab T-shirts to replace their old white ones. Nonetheless, the calisthenics, the long runs, the longer swims had continued. They were learning how to use SCUBA rigs now in the deep pool on the base, and their obstacle-course runs were beginning to include more interesting evolutions, such as rappelling down the side of a fifty-foot tower. Hand-to-hand combat techniques were being explored now, including the liquid and lightning-fast moves of a Korean martial arts form called *Hwrang-do*.

That morning, Greg had been chosen as the crash dummy for a demonstration by their Hwrang-do instructor, Kim Sung Li. Greg had come at the instructor with a knife, as ordered; he still wasn't quite sure what had happened, but it involved a wristlock, an ankle-sweep, and a wildly gyrating landscape. One instant he'd been staring into Kim's bland, round face; the next he'd been lying flat on his back, staring up at the fleecy white clouds drifting above Coronado.

He'd known at the time that he'd hurt his right ankle when he hit. Instead of landing on the mat with a slap and a roll as he'd been taught, some stubborn, inner survival mechanism of his had taken over. He'd lashed out with arms and legs, trying to regain his footing before he landed like a huge, ungainly cat. The result had been a painfully throbbing ankle, which, of course, he'd ignored.

Unfortunately, immediately after the Hwrang-do class the trainees had been put in formation for a ten-mile run down the Silver Strand Highway. Greg had pushed on for as long as he could, lacing up his boondockers tight and grimly ignoring the sparks and bolts of pain that kept lancing up his leg. Four miles into the run, his maltreated ankle had simply given out, and he'd ended up facedown in the sand. Ferraro had used a radio to call for a jeep, which had run him back to the Amphibious Base sick bay.

"So," the corpsman said when he explained what had happened. "You're into Phase Two, huh?"

"Yeah. Got through Hell Week, and I thought I had it made. Ow!"

"That hurt?"

"Nah. Not really."

"Right."

"Look, Doc. I don't know if you can understand this, but

I really can't have this lay me up. I need to stay with my class."

"Oh, I understand, all right."

Something about the way the guy said that made Greg take a closer look at him. He was hard, lean, and muscular, though his face looked open and mild. He looked pretty young; he'd been wearing whites with the single stripe and the Hospital Corps caduceus of an HM3 on the left sleeve of his short-sleeved shirt when Greg had come in, though he'd donned a lab coat when the examination had begun. He seemed like a nice guy at first glance; with a second glance, he looked like a tightly coiled spring, hard, dangerous, and ready to let fly. There was a *look* about him.

"Can I ask you something, Doc?"

"Shoot."

"Are you a SEAL?"

The mild eyes flickered up, registering surprise. "Sure am. Class 40." He held out his hand. "Bill Tangretti."

"Greg Halstead. They call me 'Twidge.' "

"Hey, Twidge." His handshake was hard and warm.

"What are you doing *here*?"

"Who better to look after BUD/S trainees who get themselves dinged up than another SEAL?"

"Well, yeah. But I thought—"

"That I'd be over in Nam?" He grinned as he went to a small freezer unit nearby and extracted a plastic bag. From the way it cracked and crackled as he worked it between his hands, it was full of crushed ice. "I was, end of last year. But I didn't stay long."

"Yeah? What happened?"

"First cardinal sin of combat. I was stupid. Here. Hold this on your ankle."

The chill of the ice made him flinch. As he held the bag around his ankle, Tangretti started tying it in place.

"You got shot?"

"Booby trap. It laid me up for a while. Then I went to Corps School to get my rate."

Greg pulled back in mock surprise. "You mean you're new at the doc game?"

"*Brand*-new. I ended up getting assigned here out of

Corps School instead of the usual six months' ward duty in a hospital. But, hey! Why do you think it's called the *practice* of medicine?''

Greg laughed. "Now I'm scared."

"You should be. Anyway, they have me kind of marking time here until I can get assigned to a combat platoon."

"You're eager to get back, huh?"

Tangretti made a face. "I'm not sure *eager* is the right word. Don't get me wrong. There's nothing glorious about combat, and the most exciting thing about it is the fact that you can end up dead. But, yeah, I guess I want to go back."

"How come?"

"I'm a SEAL. Combat is what they trained us for. It'd be a waste to have me pushing pills for the rest of my hitch, wouldn't it? Okay, tell me, Twidge. Did they explain to you how you were supposed to report injuries during training? How you weren't supposed to try to cover them up and keep going anyway?"

"Yeah, I guess."

"You guess?"

"Okay. They told me. A lot."

"I heard about one SEAL trainee," Tangretti said, "who busted his leg during BUD/S. Just a hairline fracture, but it must have hurt like nobody's business. He told himself it was just a sprain and kept on going. Running on the damned thing. I don't know how he did it. It was three weeks before his leg got so swollen and black and blue and purple that they finally got him to sick bay and checked it out."

"Man! What happened?"

"A few months in the hospital and corrective surgery. Then he went through BUD/S again. He made it, too, I understand. The point is, he could've lost the leg."

Greg felt a stab of cold fear. "You're not saying *this* is broken, are you Doc? I mean . . . if I get yanked out of Class 42, I'll get put into the queue and have to take Phase One all over again." He suppressed a shudder. *Another* Hell Week; maybe another set of idiot mind games with Ferraro. He didn't think he could go through that ordeal again.

"I don't think it is," Tangretti said. He leaned against a counter, arms folded. "Just to make sure, you're going to see Dr. Graham—he's the duty doctor today—and we'll take some X-rays. If it is busted, well, there's not a lot we can do. If not, I think we can work something out.''

"It's *not* busted," Greg said, with a fierce determination that challenged the universe to try calling him a liar.

"We'll see. . . .''

An hour later, Tangretti walked out to the waiting area where Greg was thumbing through some three-year-old *National Geographic*s. Greg leaped to his feet, then sat down again as the pain hit his ankle.

"Stay put," the corpsman said.

"What the doctor say? How are the X-rays?''

"Relax, Twidge. It's not broken.''

Greg hadn't known such relief since the Saturday morning after Hell Week, when it had finally sunk in that the hard part was over. "Oh, wow! Thanks, Doc.''

"Hey, don't thank me." He was frowning, hands in the deep pockets of his lab coat. "Dr. Graham is still recommending that you be put on light duty.''

"Light—You mean, *drop out of the program?*''

"Relax. We had a long talk . . . and he knows how you tadpoles are. Here's what we're gonna do. You'll have the rest of the day off. Keep ice packs on that ankle, and see if the swelling goes down. Starting tomorrow, I want you to soak it in hot water, every chance you get. I've got an Ace bandage for you. I'll show you how to keep it wrapped up tight.''

"Okay.''

"Now, here's the important part. That ankle's gonna hurt.'' He pulled his right hand out of the lab-coat pocket. He was holding a small, brown plastic bottle with a white lid. He shook it, rattling the pills inside. "When the pain gets bad, and I mean, really bad, take two of these. And *only* two. I mean it. They're strong. They'll knock you on your ass. You're not to drive or operate heavy machinery within six hours of taking these things, and I think I'd stay away from things like the rappelling tower and the rifle range, too.''

He accepted the bottle. He couldn't make out the writing

on the label. "I might not have a lot of choice there, Doc. . . ."

"Well, use your judgment. But be careful of these. And, ah, don't leave this bottle around, okay? Where other guys can see it?"

"Oh, right. What is it, codeine?"

"Stronger."

"Morphine?"

"Let's just say it's the very latest thing in pharmacological treatment of sports- and exercise-related injuries. If you need more, come back and see me. I'll see what I can do."

"Man, *thanks*, Doc!" He pocketed the precious bottle.

"Thank the Navy," Tangretti said with a shrug. "They feed you, house you, educate you, clothe you, and give you free dental and medical care. I'll want you to come back in a week, and we'll take another look at that foot. We can also issue you a crutch or a cane, so you can keep the weight off. Okay?"

"O-*kay*! Doc, I don't know how to thank you!"

"You can thank me by letting someone know when you hurt yourself."

"You got it, Doc. See you in a week!"

"Good luck, Twidge."

Tuesday, 8 October 1968

Basic Underwater Demolition/SEAL Class 42
Classroom 227
Coronado, California
0910 hours

"Military intelligence," Lieutenant Baxter said solemnly, "is an oxymoron. That, gentlemen, is a word or a phrase that contradicts itself. Like 'good grief' or 'civil war.' "

The class chuckled appreciatively.

"But my lecture here today is supposed to cover certain aspects of military intelligence, how it works, and how you people are going to make it work for you, once you're in the field."

Baxter looked from face to face, trying to get a feel for

what he saw there. Class 42 was down to twenty-one men
and, short of injuries or something really unprecedented, the
chances were that all twenty-one were going to make it
through. They were hard, tough, smart, and *eager*. Good material. Good men.

NAVSPECWARGRU had sent a directive through a few
days ago. There were slots open in the Pacific command for
ten UDT personnel and twenty-five SEALs; chances were,
four or five of this class would end up going to the UDT,
while the rest became SEALs. The differences between the
two were felt only in the final stages of training, when future
SEALs were sent to San Clemente Island and elsewhere to
participate in light infantry training and tactics, while the
UDT people learned more about beach surveys, demolitions,
and SCUBA work. Not that the two weren't interchangeable
sometimes. A SEAL platoon had recently assisted in the demolition of a barricade across a major canal in the Mekong
Delta, while there were plenty of cases of UDT frogmen
getting into firefights with VC. The two were very close in
most ways. Baxter personally felt that the day wasn't far off
when SEALs and UDT would merge completely.

In the meantime, though, he knew that most of Class 42
was going to end up as SEALs. A new platoon, Delta Platoon, was being formed up now, and would probably be deployed to Vietnam early next year.

He desperately wanted to tell them, to show them, to make
them know and feel what it would be like. Some of what he
said might well save lives; if he said it wrong, it could cost
lives, and Baxter didn't want to carry that on his conscience.

"The important things to remember about intelligence
work in the Nam," he continued, "aren't too hard to remember."

He began ticking the points off on the fingers of his left
hand.

"If it comes from a Vietnamese government source, it is
probably too late, it's probably wrong, and the enemy definitely knows that you have the information. The higher the
rank of your informant, by the way, the more certain it is
that he's dirty, that he's taking money from everything from

the black market to Communist agents, and that *whatever* he tells you, it's designed to cover his ass.

"If it comes from an American military source, like MACV, it is probably too late, is probably wrong, and the enemy *almost* certainly knows that you have the information. The higher the rank of your informant, the more certain it is that he's politically motivated, and that whatever he tells you, it's designed to cover his ass.

"If it comes from an American *civilian* source . . . and by that, of course, I mean the CIA, the Christians in Action, as we called them over there, the information is *possibly* late, *possibly* wrong, the enemy *might* know about it already, and you have to watch your back because the Agency could be running some sort of screwy double-blind op where they feed you misinformation as a part of some deeper and darker plot. Whatever they tell you, the truth is probably something else.

"Now. If your source is a local civilian, some guy you meet in the street every day, maybe, you've got an interesting problem. He *could* be VC, which means his information could be completely wrong or even bait for a trap . . . and, of course, the enemy knows what you know.

"On the other hand, you've got the guy right there. You can have him lead you to the spot. You can cross-question his friends, family and relatives. You can question lots of other guys like him and start to build up a picture of what's going down in that neighborhood.

"And if the guy in question is not Vietnamese at all, if he's Nung or Montagnard, things really start to get interesting. The Nung are ethnic Chinese, or mostly so. Mercenaries. Terrific fighters. You *don't* want to get on their bad side, believe me. The Montagnards are a hill people who were never assimilated by the Viets.

"We have whole PRUs over there now, most of them up near the Cambodian border or in the Central Highlands, that are composed entirely of Nung, Montagnards, and a few other tribes that have always held themselves apart from the general Vietnamese population. The Viets don't like them and have persecuted them, off and on, for a good many years. So, of course, they don't like the Vietnamese. But they seem to hate the Communist Vietnamese more than they hate our

Vietnamese . . . and, for the most part, they like Americans.

"Give 'em half a chance, and they work very well with us. Some of you may have heard about the fighting at a town called Chau Doc, on the Mekong River right across the border from Cambodia, during Tet. We had some SEALs up there, and they took part in the fighting, as did Army Special Forces. What usually doesn't get reported, though, was that the brunt of the fighting was born by a Nung CIDG unit under the command of a CORDS advisor stationed up there. They kicked Charlie's ass right out of town. The CORDS guy pulled a Medal of Honor for that action.

"The Nung and the Montagnards, especially, already have decent intelligence networks set up, and if you can make good contacts with these people, you'll be able to tap into those networks and get some very good intel out of them. The Nung have networks that extend through much of the south, especially in the cities where there is a sizable Chinese population. The Cholon district of Saigon is a good example. The Montagnards don't have much use for cities, but they keep an eye on everything that goes on in their stretch of mountain and forest. Nothing moves out there without them knowing about it. If you can make friends with some of them, you'll have good, timely intel on enemy movements down the Ho Chi Minh Trail and into the rivers of the Delta almost before Charlie does.

"The upshot of all of this is that the SEALs have been having to learn how to set up and run their own intelligence service. We establish networks everywhere we go, networks of informers, agents, mercenaries, whatever. Some of these agents are just ordinary folks who help us because we don't bash them around like everyone else does. Some of them are mercenaries whom we pay for information. Quite a few are self-admitted double agents. They can't make ends meet working for the Communists, so they sell stuff to us. Just because a guy is working for the other side doesn't mean he's necessarily a bad guy, when it comes to being an intel source. We've had some informants who turned out to be very highly ranking VCI indeed.

"What the Teams need most in Vietnam right now are what we call 'operators.' These are guys who can go into an area and really work it, get it to pay off in terms of useful intelligence.

"Don't get me wrong. Hunters and shooters are great. We *need* guys who can swim ashore in the middle of the jungle, hike overland for ten klicks, and wait for two days beside some trail in order to nail the local tax collector. But it's the operators who turn up the information about where and when that tax collector is going to show up, so we can have some shooters there to whack him.

"It is absolutely imperative that you learn to be operators over there. Like the old-time cop on the beat, you get to know the people in your area. Make friends with them. Find out what they know. You'll find the medical personnel with your unit, the hospital corpsmen, to be especially useful in that regard. We've had some damned fine intel come in from people who were grateful that our docs came through regularly, giving shots, passing out pills, and sewing up or bandaging wounds.

"One doc I worked with held regular sick call at a whole string of villages in our AO. And while he was swabbing out wounds and shooting 'em up with bicillin, they'd be telling him about where the VC had stashed some weapons, or when the local tax collector was due to show up. Once they told him where and when Charlie was planning on ambushing us, as we motored up a river in our LCM. That time, we off-loaded the platoon a couple miles downstream, hiked overland, and caught Charlie from behind just as he was drawing a bead on that empty Mike boat.

"If you don't take anything else out of this classroom, take this. Most of the villagers you meet, the ordinary people, are just that, ordinary men and women who want nothing more in this world than to be left alone to raise their crops and their families. They don't much care who runs their country. What they want is for the war to end and for soldiers—whether ARVN or VC or NVA—to stop taking their crops and their sons. Some of them have been taught to hate Americans, either by the enemy, or by stupid Americans. Others look to us to end the war and drive the VC away. You'll get a lot of good intel about local VC activities from people who have reason to hate the VCI in their neighborhood, maybe because of the high taxes the Communists are imposing, maybe because the local VC cadres are bullies and shoving the people around, maybe because the VC took your informant's son from the village last night at gunpoint and nobody knows when they'll see him again.

"When I was over there last, the Teams were starting to get a lot of mileage out of the Hoi Chanhs, the VC deserters who turned themselves in under the South Vietnamese Chieu Hoi, or 'Open Arms' program. It sounds a little weird, I admit, having your former enemies guide you to good targets, but ninety-nine times out of a hundred, these people provide good, hard intel, definite targets, and a solid payoff. Some of the Hoi Chanhs are so good that, after they've been out a time or two, we started letting them carry weapons."

There was an uncomfortable stir among the trainees.

"There *is* historical precedent," Baxter went on. "Anybody here think of an example?"

Two hands went up, Casey's and Halstead's.

"Halstead?"

"Yes, sir. Indian scouts working for the U.S. Army."

"Exactly right. The situation in the American West seventy or a hundred years ago was a lot like what we have in Vietnam today. The enemy doesn't go in for large military formations, as a rule. He doesn't have a lot of armor. He can't grab air superiority. He has no Navy, no helicopters, and his mobility is limited to what he can do on foot. However, he has rugged terrain to hide in, and he knows that terrain well, like the American Indians.

"People today say the VC are the best guerrilla fighters ever. That's a lie. The best guerrilla fighters, bar none, were probably the Apache Indians of the American Southwest, back around the turn of the century. *That* war was a lot like Vietnam, though most people have forgotten. Geronimo and the other Apache leaders would strike some town without warning, then vanish into the hills. The U.S. Army would go charging in after them, and nine times out of ten wouldn't find a damn thing. That tenth time, they'd get ambushed, usually with disastrous results.

"What finally ran Geronimo to ground was the Army's use of Apache scouts, Apaches who'd turned themselves in and, for one reason or another, were willing to fight against Geronimo's guerrillas.

"Maybe in memory of that, the ex-VC working for our side are called Kit Carson Scouts. Now, it's true you have to watch your tails. You plan your operations so that your Kit Carsons know what's going to happen to them if they're setting you up for the bad guys. Sometimes, in-country, during a snatch operation, we'd have our Hoi Chanh with us when we broke into the hooch he'd fingered for us. He knew that if he was the first guy through the door, he was going to get zapped if Charlie was warned and waiting for us.

"In all my time over there, I had several sets of intel from VC defectors that were obviously mistaken—usually they'd underestimated the strength of the force we were trying to hit—but it never appeared to be a deliberate setup. I've known Kit Carson Scouts who fought as bravely and as determinedly as SEALs when we came under fire.

"When you think about it, that's only natural. The bad guys over there have a standing rule about traitors that they manage to recapture. The poor bastards are tied or nailed to trees and disemboweled alive, sometimes with their own genitals stuffed in their mouths. Anyone who tries to help them is also killed, and usually it takes them a long, long time to die. They fight hard because they most assuredly do *not* want Charlie to capture them again.

"Usually, your NILO will be willing to work with you on that. He'll ask you for your source on a particularly juicy bit of intel, you'll tell him the source is confidential but reliable, and he'll let it go at that. Usually. Or you can claim the info came from some PRU, when it was actually that B-girl you chatted up in Saigon. Or you can say it was from a villager who was killed by the VC when they found out he was talking to Americans. The NILO won't press you too closely about that, and I think most of them are getting used to the idea that SEALs don't like to compromise their sources. Of course, the fact that our system works, that it's been working since we started setting it up, is the best guarantee we have. As long as we produce results, most of the people on the next rung up the intelligence ladder over there will smile and nod and leave well enough alone. If we look good, they look good, and they're not going to screw with that. The problems come from the idiot desk jockeys and pencil-pushers farther up the ladder, who either want to grab some of the glory and credit for themselves, or who just can't resist tinkering with a good thing. You'll have nothing but headaches from them, and all you can really do is keep a low profile and watch your ass.

"After a while, you'll be able to build up a good, reliable intelligence network of your own. I tell you now, gentlemen. Treat it like it was pure gold. Don't give the names of your sources to *anybody* else—Army, Army Intelligence, CIA, whoever—if you can possibly help it, because, damn-near guaranteed, the day after you let someone back at MACV know who the spies are in your district, the next morning you'll find 'em nailed to a tree with their nuts in their mouths and their guts strung out on the ground.

"I'm not kidding about this, people. I've seen it happen. You'll hear a lot of wild stories about VC and NVA atrocities, stuff so wild you'll be tempted to call it all bullshit. It's not. It's just that our news media, in its ever-vigilant enthusiasm to be fair and unbiased, doesn't report things like that. I remember one bad case, down in the Rung Sat, where Bravo Platoon operated for a long time. There was a small town with a Catholic girl's school, run by a nun. The VC figured out we were getting information from that village, so they decided to make a point. A political statement, if you will.

"They raped the nun and hung her from a tree outside the school, upside down with her legs spread wide apart. They cut off her head and stuck it up there in her crotch, looking down at the ground in front of her body. They took the little girls at the school—twelve or thirteen of them, I think— killed them all, lined them up in neat rows in front of the nun's body with their heads stuck in their crotches, looking back up at her. Thus endeth the lesson. Don't talk to the Americans, or the same'll happen to you.

"The astonishing thing is that horrors like that haven't so terrified the civilian population to the point where they kill every American they meet. In fact, behavior like that usually just reinforces their hatred of the VC and everything they stand for. They won't help you if they think Charlie will find out. But they'll help you any way they can, in secret.

"And in secret is how you SEALs are going to be operating over there. You materialize out of the darkness, the men in green faces, kill the bad guys, and vanish back into the night, like ghosts. The Scarlet Pimpernel has nothing on us, gentlemen. A lot of those villagers see us as real, genuine heroes, come to town to rescue them. They trust us and will do anything in their power to help us.

"*Don't* betray that trust."

Baxter checked his watch. It was almost time for the class to end, but he'd wrapped it a little earlier than he'd expected. "Any questions?"

There was no immediate response. After a moment, though, Casey raised his hand.

"Mr. Casey."

"Yes, sir. I don't have a question about your lecture. But I wonder if I could ask you something else."

"Go ahead. We have a few minutes."

"I think all of us are wondering, sir, about how the war is going over there. What's *really* happening. Sometimes . . ." He shrugged. "Maybe this is a question about intelligence after all. I'm not sure we're getting the straight dope here, either through the newspapers and TV, or from government news sources. Sometimes the sources are, uh, questionable. Know what I mean?"

Baxter pursed his lips. "Yup. Do you believe your commander in chief when he tells you there's a 'light at the end of the tunnel'? Or do you believe Walter Cronkite when he says the war's in a stalemate? Leaves the poor fighting man kind of hanging in the middle like a wet pair of undershorts, doesn't it?"

They laughed.

"I'll tell you the truth . . . at least as far as I understand it. SEALs don't lie to SEALs . . . but understand that I'm not exactly up there in the higher echelons of military decision-making." He tapped his collar tab. "I've just got railroad tracks, not a star. But I can tell you what I've seen.

"Last January and February, as you know well, the Communists launched an all-out offensive throughout South Vietnam. They hit all the major cities, including Saigon, the government capital, and Hue, the spiritual capital. The attack caught everyone by surprise . . . though I should mention that the Teams had been bringing in solid intel about a major offensive for several weeks before it happened. Things like stockpiles of North Vietnamese Army uniforms down in the U Minh Forest, squirreled away so that NVA regulars could slip south in civvies, without being spotted.

"Despite the surprise, the VC and NVA were beaten at Tet. I know that that's the official line from the Pentagon, and for that reason, a lot of people are inclined to doubt it. But it's true. The only real success the VC enjoyed during Tet was the complete takeover of Hue, and the fact that we had to damn near level the Old City's Imperial Palace to winkle them out. That took twenty-six days. But we did get them out, and from all indications, the VC infrastructure was badly, badly hurt all throughout South Vietnam. We started getting lots of intel after Tet indicating that the NVA were having to step in and take over more and more operations that had been VC before. There were some entire VC regiments, we found out, that were sixty and seventy percent NVA regulars after Tet.

"In early May, the Communists launched another offensive. A big one. It was supposed to be even bigger than Tet, but somehow they weren't able to coordinate their attacks nearly as well, and a lot of it simply fizzled. They'd timed the attacks to give us something to think about with the beginning of the peace talks in Paris. They were scheduled to begin 13 May, I think. The attacks concentrated on the eastern part of I Corps, up around Dong Ha, in the Central Highlands, and in Saigon.

"We dubbed the May Offensive 'Little Tet.' The NVA failed, at extremely heavy cost, to get a foothold in Saigon or to carry off a single one of their objectives.

"At the same time, I should point out that American casualties in May were heavy. For those of you who like numbers, I can say that in one week of the fighting in May, from the fifth to the eleventh, there were almost three thousand American casualties, including about six hundred dead. Compare that to the week from 27 January to 3 February—Tet.

We had about twelve hundred casualties—I don't remember the exact figure—with about two hundred of them killed. Mr. Prescott?''

"Yes, sir. How many bad guys got capped?"

"Your guess is as good as mine, Maverick. And those figures don't include ARVNs who got killed. The point is, the Communists have been throwing everything they had at us, and we've been swatting them down damn near as fast as they come. Sooner or later, those losses are going to tell. They pulled still another offensive throughout South Vietnam in August. MACV estimates they lost twenty thousand more men on that one.

"One place the enemy is being especially hard hit is among the cadres—that's what the VC and NVA's trained leaders are called, cadres. Their best and most experienced men have been getting picked off. They're having to replace them from lower-level, less-well-trained men. In some ways, this makes our jobs tougher, because the cadres we capture over there seem to know less and less. On the other hand, they tend to be less well indoctrinated and more willing to spill the beans on their comrades, even turn Chieu Hoi and lead us right to them. There's some evidence that various programs aimed at targeting the VCI to kill or capture their best people is beginning to have an effect, too. And as for their main forces, more and more of them are turning out to be some poor farmer that got yanked out of his ville or rice paddy, was handed a rifle and told 'go get 'em, tiger.' Remember what I said earlier. Most of these people don't want any part of the war, but lots of times the VC drag them in.

"From where the SEALs sit, it looks like the Communists are starting to run out of men, while the Americans are running out of time. It's a race, and it's going to be a squeaker to see who can outlast who. And it looks like, with the November elections coming up, we're going to have kind of a referendum on the war. Now, as U.S. military personnel, we're not supposed to have any opinions on politics." The class chuckled. "I guess it won't hurt to state the obvious, though. Humphrey, whatever he says, is pretty much stuck with LBJ's policies. Nixon's supposed to have a plan to get us out of the war, though he says it'll compromise national security if he says what it is." The class chuckled again, louder.

"It's taken us a long time, but we've learned how to fight this war, how to fight the VC and the NVA on their own terms, and win. They hate us, and they fear us even more. I saw some intel, an interrogation report, that said one whole VC battalion simply packed up and moved out of an area, because they heard a SEAL platoon had just moved in.

"What we don't know is whether or not the politicians are going to give us the time to do our job . . . and just maybe make a difference over there. . . ."

0930 hours

Greg listened to Baxter with a growing, burning excitement. At long last, all of the training, all of the bullshit, all of the preparation were starting to come together. The twenty-one remaining members of Class 42 were keyed up and ready to go, weapons primed and ready to be loosed at the Communist forces in Vietnam. Lieutenant j.g. Casey, especially, fit that description. Sometimes, when a class discussion or an after-hours bull session turned to Vietnam and combat and killing Communists, there was a cold light burning in Casey's eyes that was inspiring—or frightening, depending on how you looked at it.

Greg was ready to go, though he wasn't as sure of himself as Casey seemed to be. Casey, in Greg's opinion, was a born warrior; Greg was a forged one, a college student transformed in the crucible of BUD/S into a deadly fighting machine.

He decided he wanted to look up that SEAL corpsman again, Bill Tangretti. His ankle was fine now, thanks to those near-magical pain pills he'd given him. He'd been wanting to thank the guy, when he had a chance, maybe by buying him a few some Saturday night over at the Golden Neptune. And maybe he could get Bill to open up a bit about what it had been like in Vietnam. That booby-trap incident, for instance, that had hospitalized him. There had to be more to the story than the guy's simple assertion that he'd been stupid.

Baxter had been there, in combat, but he was an officer and an instructor and he seemed downright unapproachable, standing up there at the front of the classroom, talking about intel and sources and VC atrocities. Bill had been there, too, but he was a *buddy,* a fellow enlisted SEAL. Of course, he was a bit close-mouthed about what had happened in Nam. One interesting twist of psychology that Greg was beginning to recognize was the fact that people who'd been in close combat, SEALs especially, tended not to talk about it much. You could always spot the wanna-bes in a bar ashore by how loudly they boasted of their kills or their combat records. SEALs pretty much kept to themselves and said little, even to one another . . . and to outsiders, they said less.

Yeah. Bill might have a lot to say, if he could be approached right, and Greg wanted to hear *everything.* Like Doc Tangretti, he'd been trained to fight; he knew he was going, and he wanted to know everything about what he was getting into that he could.

Chapter 27

Saturday, 21 December 1968

Jenner, California

The two sailors grabbed their bags out of the bus's cargo compartment and started off down the sidewalk. At the first intersection they turned to the right, heading away from Main Street. They were an unlikely pair, one blond and at least six or seven inches taller than the other, who was dark-haired, but a closer inspection would have revealed a resemblance. There was something about their demeanor, their bearing. Even in their dress blue uniforms they revealed a physical and mental hardness, a toughness that marked these two as something special. They were both U.S. Navy SEALs.

"We could've gone to the store first, Doc, and asked Jerry to give us a ride home," one of them said. "But I thought it'd feel good to stretch our legs after that bus ride. It's not far. Besides, you remember what I told you happened the last time."

"Hey, this is great, Twidge," the other said. "After thirteen hours on that contraption, I'm ready for a ten-mile run. How 'bout you?"

"I'm game" was the response. Twidge broke into an easy run. Doc was startled, but then he grinned and followed. Despite the inequities in their heights, the two ran as one, pacing each other. Ten minutes later they turned onto Pleasant Avenue.

"There's my house," Twidge said, pointing.

They didn't stop running until they got to the front porch, but neither one was breathing hard. Twidge pushed the door open and called out, "Anybody home?"

Two women came bursting out of the kitchen, both talking at once.

"Greg! When'd you get in?"

"Did Jerry drive you? Dad didn't call."

They enveloped the taller man in hugs and questions. Eventually Greg was able to disentangle himself long enough to make introductions.

"Mom, Pat, this is my good buddy, Hospitalman Third Class Bill Tangretti. Bill, my mother, and my sister Pat."

Bill reached out his hand. "Glad to meet you, Mrs. Halstead. I really appreciate your letting me barge in on Christmas."

"Oh, it's our pleasure, Bill," Ellie Halstead said warmly. "Greg's written us so much about you. We're delighted to get this chance to get to know you in person."

Bill then shook hands with Pat. "Hi, Pat. I almost feel like I know you already, from all Twidge here has said about you."

"Twidge? When did Greg become Twidge?" Pat looked at her brother, a twinkle in her eye.

"Oh, just about everybody in the Teams has a special

handle,'' Greg said. ''Bandit, Slinger, Maverick, Squirt.''

''But how'd you get to be Twidge?'' Pat persisted.

''Well, ETs are called twidgets, you see,'' Bill said helpfully.

''Well, that's a big help!'' She grinned. ''What's your handle, Bill?''

''Aw, come on, Pat, you should know that! He's a corpsman.''

Pat hit her forehead with the heel of her hand. ''Of course. Well, delighted to make your acquaintance, Doc,'' she said with a curtsy.

Bill responded with a bow. ''Enchanted, my dear Miss Halstead.''

Ellie had been watching the byplay with amusement. ''Don't tell me you got all those fine manners with the SEALs!''

''Why, certainly, ma'am,'' Bill said, winking at Pat. ''SEALs are trained to operate anywhere, including fancy-dress balls.''

Greg picked up the joke. ''That's right, Mom,'' he said with a perfectly straight face. ''Commander Hargrave was our etiquette instructor, and he was tough. I remember once when I used the wrong fork on my salad. *Man*, I thought he was going to keelhaul me for sure!''

''Keelhaul you!'' Ellie exclaimed.

Pat put a hand on Ellie's arm. ''Mom, they're kidding.''

Ellie looked at the two grinning sailors, so different and yet so much alike, and smiled. ''You boys are incorrigible! Now why don't you two go upstairs and get comfortable. Pat can show you where to get towels and things. I've got my dishes to wash.''

Dinner that evening was quite festive. Ellie was obviously enjoying having a new person to make a fuss over. She kept urging Bill to have some more roast beef, another helping of mashed potatoes, some more green beans. Pat didn't say much, but Greg noticed that she frequently had her eye on Bill. For that matter, Doc seemed quite taken with his sister.

''All right, Greg, what are you grinning at?'' Pat demanded.

''Oh nothing,'' he replied innocently.

David wiped his mouth with his napkin. "So, Bill," he said. "Tell us some more about yourself. Greg said you come from a Navy family."

"That's right, sir. My father and my brother are both in the Navy. Both SEALs, in fact."

"Three SEALs in the family! That's quite something," Ellie said.

"Yes, ma'am."

"How long has your father been in?" Grandpap asked.

Bill ran a hand through his hair. "Let's see, it must be getting close to thirty years now, sir."

"Then he was in during World War II."

"Yes, sir. He started out as a Seabee—that's the Construction Battalion, ma'am—and ended up with the UDT."

"The UDT!" David exclaimed. "Then he was in the Pacific. I might have met him."

"I know he was at Kwajalein for a time. Then he was with the CDUs on D-Day in Normandy, and then he was back in the Pacific later in '44."

"He certainly got around, didn't he?" Ellie sounded impressed.

Bill grinned. "Yes, ma'am, he sure did."

"Do you remember the names of any of his ships in the Pacific?" David asked.

"The *Callahan* and the *Badger*."

"Hmm. Don't know them."

"Dad was on the *Blessman*," Greg put in.

Bill looked up. "Were you on her when the kamikaze hit, sir?"

"It wasn't a kamikaze, Bill. It was a Japanese bomber. And yes, I was aboard. The UDT men were incredible that night. And not only the men from the *Blessman*. The *Gilmer* came up close aboard and sent some UDT men across to give us a hand. I heard later that it was Commander Coffer himself who led the boarding party."

"Who's Commander Coffer?" Pat asked.

"He's the guy who practically started the UDTs in the first place," Bill told her.

"When did your father become a SEAL, Bill?" Ellie asked.

"He was actually the very first SEAL ever, ma'am, when President Kennedy signed an executive order to create the unit back in '62. He was just a lieutenant, but he was put in charge of the unit." Bill grinned. "Dad always said that that was the brass's way of making sure they could keep control of this new special warfare unit."

"I don't understand," Ellie said. "How would putting your father in charge help the others keep control?"

"Lieutenants are lowlife scum, Ellie, when it comes to commanding a unit," David said. "I imagine the brass thought that a mere lieutenant could be controlled . . . manipulated."

"Exactly, sir," Bill said, nodding. "Only this time their plan sort of backfired on them. My dad . . . well, let's just say he doesn't manipulate all that easily."

Ellie looked thoughtful. "That must have been difficult for you, Bill. I mean, having a father like that to have to live up to."

Bill shot her a sharp glance. "You're right about that, ma'am. I usually try to avoid letting people know I'm related to *that* Tangretti."

"What's your brother's name?" Pat asked. "Does he feel the same way about having a famous dad?"

Bill laughed. "He doesn't have the same problem, 'cause he has a different last name. His name is Hank Richardson, same as his father, his *real* father. He's actually my half brother. And my stepbrother. It's kind of confusing. His father was my dad's best buddy during World War II. He was killed on D-Day about a month after he and my mother were married. Later after the war was over and Hank had been born, my dad married her and they had me."

"How has your mother been able to handle all this, Bill? She must be a wonderful person. I'd love to meet her someday," Ellie said.

"It has been hard on her, that's for sure. It's not easy being married to a Navy man under any circumstances, and being married to a SEAL is ten times worse. She knows that his job may take him away from her at any time, and with little or no warning. It's not a comfortable way to live."

Bill polished off the last of his apple pie, scraping the plate clean. "Of course, it seems like there's always some girl crazy enough to take on a SEAL. Hank just got hitched this fall, a nurse named Lisa that he met over in Nam."

"So, Bill, what are your own plans?" Grandpap asked. "Are you just going to serve your four and get out, or have you thought about going career?"

"Have another piece of pie, Bill," Ellie put in.

Bill grinned. "Thanks, ma'am. Don't mind if I do. We won't be seeing great food like this over in Nam, eh, Twidge?"

"You're the one who should know, Doc."

"I'm really not sure, sir," Bill said, returning to Grandpap's question. "When I joined up, I just knew I had to be a SEAL, and I didn't think things through any further than that."

"I'm not surprised you felt compelled to be a SEAL, Bill," Pat said, "with your family background. Was Hank already a SEAL when you joined the Navy?"

Bill nodded, his mouth full of apple pie. "Mmm-hmm," he mumbled when he could speak again. "He was already a second class by then. I did have some ideas about using G.I. Bill money for college when I got out, but nothing more specific than that."

"What decided you on Hospital Corps School, Bill?" David asked.

"David, dear, is it really necessary to grill him this thoroughly?" Ellie looked concerned. "He's done nothing but answer questions since he sat down."

"I don't mind, ma'am, really." Bill smiled warmly at her. "To answer your question, sir, it started when I was at NNMC Bethesda after my last tour. I'd gone to BUD/S without a rating, and I knew I had to get rated pretty soon. I got to talking with some of the corpsmen on the ward I was on, and it sounded like a good idea. I'd always been good at science in high school, so I figured I wouldn't have too much trouble with the classroom part of it. I mentioned it to my doctor, and sure enough, as soon as I was discharged, I found myself heading for Great Lakes."

David shook his head. "I kept hoping Greg would opt for Corps School, but no such luck."

"Come on, Dad," Pat said. "You know what Greg was like in science. He was abysmal!"

"Hey!" Greg protested. "I wasn't that bad!"

"Who was it that got you through chemistry, brother dear?"

"Well, just because you were the super science whiz kid, that doesn't mean I was a dunce!"

"Do you enjoy being a corpsman, Bill?" Ellie asked, waving at her two children to try to settle them down.

"Now, Ellie," Grandpap put in. "I thought we were going to stop quizzing the poor boy." He turned and winked at Bill.

"Yes, ma'am, I do," Bill replied, grinning. "In fact, I've been thinking lately about maybe going to medical school. I can get college credit through USAFI, and then I could get the Navy to pay for med school with a promise to serve as a Navy doctor. I'm not sure yet, but that might be a good way for me to go."

Once everyone had assured Ellie that they'd had more than enough to eat, she bustled the men off to the living room while she and Pat did the dishes. Bill swapped war stories with David and Grandpap, while Greg listened in delightedly. Pat joined them after a while, and then Ellie. Eventually Ellie reminded the others about church in the morning, and she and David and Grandpap went upstairs.

Pat stayed and talked with Bill and Greg for what seemed like hours. The three of them finally went upstairs to bed around midnight. Greg and Bill shared Greg's room; Bill lost the toss and got the trundle bed. While the two of them were getting ready for bed, Greg asked, "So. What do you think?"

"About your family?" Bill replied. "They're great folks. I really appreciate being able to spend the holidays with them."

Greg bopped him over the head with a pillow. "I'm talking about my sister, you twit. Even a blind man could see she was making eyes at you."

Bill flushed. "Aw, c'mon, Twidge, she was just being nice."

"Nice? Nice, he calls it." Greg shook his head in disbelief. "Well, let me tell you something, Doc. You'd better be just as *nice* to her, or I'll break your arm."

Bill hesitated. "You . . . you wouldn't mind?"

"You should've seen the last twerp she hung around with. Believe me, even *you* would be a big improvement on Andy!"

There was silence for a moment. Then Bill started whistling. It might have been the "Rambling Wreck from Georgia Tech" anthem . . . but was more likely the "Demolitioneers." Greg chuckled, another pillow went flying, and the whistling stopped. "Sweet dreams, Bill."

"Same to you, Twidget."

Thursday, 2 January 1969

Bill looked out of a living-room window and sighed with satisfaction. The past two weeks had been among the happiest of his life. Greg's family had taken him in and made him feel at home right away. Greg's mom had told him in no uncertain terms that she was expecting letters from him. "I need to keep track of my boys," she'd said. Greg's dad had delighted in showing him around the pharmacy and had asked him if he had considered pharmacy school. And then there was Pat . . .

He'd spent a lot of time with Pat over the holidays, though not as much of the time as he would've liked had been with just the two of them. If Greg wasn't with them, then Ellie was, or else the whole family. Today was probably his last chance for some time alone with her. Fortunately the timing was working out so that Pat could take the same bus to San Francisco that he and Greg were planning to take. Her classes didn't start till Monday, but she said she didn't mind going back a few days early in order to have some more time with them. He wondered if it was just her brother she wanted to spend time with, or . . .

"Hi, Bill. What're you looking so thoughtful about?"

He turned at the sound of her voice. Such a beautiful voice. "Oh, nothing. Just thinking about what a great time I've had here."

"It's been great having you here," Pat said with a smile.

"It's so good to know that Greg will have a good friend in his platoon."

Bill looked down at the carpet, trying to come up with the words he wanted to say. "Um, Pat?"

"Yes?"

"I was wondering . . . I mean, would you like to go for a walk with me?"

Her smile lit up her face. "I'd be delighted. Just a minute. Let me go change."

She really was back in less than a minute, jeans and sneakers on and jacket in hand. The two of them started out the door just as Greg came downstairs. "Hey, where're you going, guys?" he asked.

"Nowhere that need concern you, brother dear," Pat said with a wave of her hand. "See you later."

As soon as she was on the front porch, Greg gave Bill a wink. "Way to go, Doc!" he whispered.

Bill grinned foolishly and followed Pat down the walk. They walked in companionable silence for a while. Fortunately the weather was nice, a bit nippy but not too cold, and not windy at all. He stole occasional glances at Pat, watching her blond hair bounce around her small face. Once she caught him looking at her and grinned. "Whatcha looking at, sailor?" she asked.

He flushed and mumbled something incoherent. Fortunately, she didn't pursue her question.

"Bill," she said after a while. "Can I ask you something?"

"Sure. Anything."

She smiled. "Anything? That's a rather rash promise, don't you think? No, I was just wondering about . . . what it's going to be like over there. You've been to Vietnam before. I just wondered . . . what you and Greg were going to be getting into."

Ah, so that was it. She just wanted to get him alone to quiz him on behalf of her brother.

"Well, the weather's atrocious, of course, hot and humid all the time, though really you don't notice it much after a while. The food . . . well, it's Navy food. Some of the guys like to eat Vietnamese food. That way the VC can't smell you coming.''

"Smell you! You're joking.''

"Nope. Americans are heavy meat eaters, and they can smell it. Almost as bad as smoking cigarettes for giving you away to the enemy.''

"I've heard a lot about drugs in Vietnam. Is it hard to stay away from?''

"Same thing, only more so. Any SEAL who was dumb enough to do drugs, well, first of all, he wouldn't have made it through Hell Week, and second, he'd be dead on his first night patrol. We depend on stealth, and marijuana is a dumb way to be inconspicuous.''

"I see.''

There was another long silence, while Bill tried to think how to direct the conversation along more personal lines. They ran out of sidewalk and continued along a dirt trail up a gentle slope. After a while they came to a clearing with a fallen tree providing a bench. Pat straddled the tree, and Bill sat facing her.

"Bill,'' she said, hesitantly. "I've been wanting to ask you something.'' She looked up at him as though she was asking permission.

"Okay.''

"You're a SEAL. You're trained to kill people, right?''

"Yeah.''

"And you're a corpsman. You're also trained to patch them up, to heal people.''

"Ah.''

"So how do you reconcile those two things? You know, it's funny. When Greg first started talking about wanting to become a SEAL, I kept wishing he would go to Corps School like Dad and Grandpap. That way, he wouldn't have to go to Vietnam and he wouldn't be put in a position where he would have to kill people.''

"And look who turns up as his best buddy, but a guy who's a SEAL *and* a corpsman,'' Bill said. "Yeah, it's kind of strange.''

"So are you a . . . a split personality?'' She smiled to take the edge off the question. "Or do you have some way of reconciling the two?"

Bill was silent for a while, thinking about her question. "I'm not sure I've got it all figured out, Pat. I wasn't a corpsman when I was in Nam before, and I've got to confess I've been wondering how I'm going to handle it. On the other hand, it was a SEAL corpsman who saved my life over there. I guess one way of looking at it would be that I'm there to kill the enemy and heal my buddies, but it's not really that simple. When we took prisoners, if any of them were wounded, Doc Randolph would patch them up, same as he'd do for any of us. So . . ." He looked at Pat, at her deep blue eyes looking back at him. "So I guess I don't have a good answer for you. Not one that would make any sense."

"Well, it wasn't an easy question, Bill. It probably wasn't even a fair one. But it's enough to know that you're thinking about it, that you're aware of the problem, that you *care*."

Her voice almost cracked on that last word. Bill wondered if the timing was right. He moved closer to her on the log, reached out and took her hand. "I *do* care, Pat. I care an awful lot."

She kept her eyes down, but she didn't pull her hand away.

"Will you write to me, Pat?"

She looked up at that and smiled. Her eyes were glowing. "I'd like that, Bill. I'd like that very much."

He leaned closer, and she didn't turn away. He kissed her, gently at first, but then harder as he felt her response. She lifted her arms around his neck, one hand gently stroking his hair. He wrapped his arms around her waist and held her tight as their kiss deepened. Yes, this was definitely the best leave he'd ever had!

Chapter 28

Hong Fat Restaurant
Waverly Place, San Francisco
2135 hours

The Chinese restaurant had been Pat's idea, a place she'd discovered during her sojourn at San Francisco State. The three of them, Greg, Bill, and Pat, had caught a bus together back to San Francisco, a way to extend by a few precious hours the time they were spending together.

They'd arrived downtown at just past four in the afternoon, Bill and Greg in their dress blues to take advantage of the serviceman's special fares, Pat in a blue, miniskirted dress that showed off her long legs to good advantage. A bus would be leaving for San Diego at twenty-three hundred—"eleven in the PM, for you civilian types," Bill had explained to Pat—so they'd stored their luggage at the Greyhound terminal, then caught a cab for Chinatown.

They'd started the evening with visits to several bars, and by the time they arrived at Hong Fat's, they all were feeling well lubricated. It was just as well that it was as late as it was by the time they got there. There were few other patrons to be disturbed by the noisy party in the booth in the back corner.

"So *this* guy," Greg was saying, jerking a thumb across the booth table at Bill, "tells me he's got this really powerful super drug. I mean, the way he talked about it, I thought it was raw opium, straight from the Golden Triangle!"

"Now, come on!" Bill said, pretending to be wounded. "It wasn't as dramatic as all that!"

"No? Listen, Pat. There I am with my ankle a disaster area, couldn't even walk, and he's, you know, kind of looking left and right as he pulls these pills out and slips them to me. I mean, real hush-hush stuff. And the thing of it was, they worked!"

"Well?" Pat asked. She looked at Bill. "Don't keep me in suspense, guys! What were they?"

"APCs," Bill admitted.

"ABCs?" She wrinkled her brow.

Bill thought she looked awfully cute when she puzzled up her nose like that. "No. APCs. Acetylsalicylic acid."

"Aspirin, Pat," Greg explained in patient tones. "*Aspirin.* 'Now, if the pain gets bad,' " he went on, mimicking Bill's somber warning tones, " 'you take *only* two of these. They're strong. Don't drive or operate machinery, and stay away from the rifle range.' "

"*Aspirin?*" Pat squealed with laughter, holding both hands over her mouth and nose.

"Well, hey," Bill said, spreading his hands and assuming an expression of purest innocence. "They worked, didn't they?"

"Yes, damn you. But you still tricked me!"

"You tricked yourself, Twidge." Bill looked at Pat. She was smiling at him, and the sight made him feel very warm. "You know, it is astonishing what recuperative powers there are just in the power of suggestion. I swear that all of the medicines known to modern medical science can't do a tenth of what our own body can do all by itself." He winked at Greg. "*If* it's properly motivated!"

"The embarrassing part of it," Greg explained, "was that they worked great. My ankle was a little sore and swollen for the next few days, but I just picked up with the program and kept on going."

"So how did you find out?"

"Well, this quack had me thinking I was using some kind of dangerous, controlled substance. I didn't want anyone else in the class to get ahold of them. And I didn't want some snoopy instructor to think I was abusing. So, after a few weeks, the ankle was fine and I still had five little white pills left. So me, like a class-one chump, I go back to the sick bay and try to turn the leftovers in! That's when I found out what this guy pulled!" He pointed a finger at Pat. "Let me tell you, sis. *Never* trust a Navy corpsman! They either poke you, stick you with needles, or lose your health records and make you get all your shots all over again! They are *not* to be trusted!"

Pat rocked back in her seat, arms folded across her stomach, laughing hard. The waiter chose that moment to arrive with a huge tray. Sweet and sour shrimp for Greg. A spicy concoction called General Tso's Chicken for Bill. Chicken with cashews for Pat. A big bowl of steamed white rice for them all. The waiter, an older Chinese gentleman, smiled at them. "Enjoy, please," he said.

"*Hsieh hsieh,*" Bill said, smiling. He pitched the first word higher than the second.

The waiter's smile broadened and he bowed deeply. After he'd left, Greg leaned forward. "Don't tell me you speak Chinese!"

"Not really. But I do try to pick up lots of useful words and phrases. *Thank you* and *please* are the best words you can memorize in any language. They'll do in a pinch even if you don't know anything else."

"I like that!" Pat said.

"Know any Vietnamese?" Greg asked.

"A little. I can tell you to come here and put up your hands. Throw down your weapon. Things like that."

"Where'd you get that?" Pat wanted to know. "A Berlitz phrase book?"

"Actually, I got an LDNN to teach me some useful phrases, when I was over there last."

"LDNN?"

"South Vietnamese SEALs," Greg told her. "Only VN military types worth a damn, from what I've heard."

"It's not that bad," Bill told him. "But it does seem that way, sometimes."

"I heard they've got a language school going for Vietnamese," Greg said. "Some of the SEALs going over to work with the PRUs and as LDNN advisors are being put through.''

"Good idea," Bill said. "You can't help 'em if you can't talk to 'em."

They started in on their meals, helping themselves to rice, and ignoring their silverware in favor of the chopsticks that had been brought with the food, wrapped in individual paper wrappers. Pat and Bill were able to manage with the chopsticks quite well. Greg, however, fumbled the two pencil-length, tapered wooden dowels between the thumb and the first two fingers of his right hand, trying to snag a shrimp. "C'mere, you sneaky little VC!" He looked up at the others. "That stands for vried chrimp!" The chopsticks slipped, loosing his victim.

"Maybe you should try a hook and line," Pat suggested. "Or a fishnet!"

"You know, don't you," Bill added, "that your incompetence with chopsticks could well bring on a diplomatic incident in our host country."

"So? What are they going to do, start a war?"

"No, but they might send you to remedial chopstick class. I think there's an A school for that."

"That's a Navy rating, right?" Pat asked.

"Absolutely," Bill told her. "I knew this one CH1 . . . uh, that's 'chopstick handler, first class,' and he was tellin' me—"

"If this is another of your sea stories," Greg said, "I'm outa here!"

"You know," Pat said, "that's really a good idea. They should teach you the customs of where you're going."

"Oh, they do," Bill assured her. "They do! They tell us all about how people are ambushed in Vietnam. Also, how to call in artillery fire. How to secure a landing zone. How to *properly* hold and throw a hand grenade . . ."

"Pinky extended," Pat suggested.

"Exactly," Bill said. "To be sure! And, ah! Don't forget the etiquette of the sneak-and-peek!"

Greg nodded. "And the proper deportment of a wham-and-scram."

Pat shook her head, brow furrowing. "Sneak . . . scram . . . what?"

"The graceful art of the SEAL, sister dear," Greg told her. "The sneak-and-peek is a recon operation. That's reconnaissance, the . . . uh . . . the *sine qua non* of the special warfare commando."

"Shit, Twidge," Bill said, sounding disgusted. "I didn't think you used that kind of language! 'Specially around pretty women!"

Pat twinkled at him. "My brother can be full of surprises." She looked at Greg, grinning. "So, reconnaissance is 'sneak-and-peek'? What's wham . . . uh . . . that other one?"

"The wham-and-scram, ma'am," Bill told her. "That's where we add some dirty demo to the sneak-and-peak. We sneak in and break the bad guy's toys. Makes a dreadful mess, and usually ruins his whole day."

Greg tried with the chopsticks again, and again he acquired his target, only to lose it just short of his mouth. "Shit!"

Bill reached over and picked up Greg's fork, lying beside his plate. "Allow me to introduce you to a new and exciting piece of modern technology," he said. "It's called 'the fork.' "

"Yeah, but they don't have forks where we're going!" Greg said, laughing. "You know, Doc, I think you're absodamn-lutely right! We really should have been taught the finer points of etiquette and proper table manners! Look, here we are, on our way to darkest Vietnam, and they haven't taught us how to use chopsticks yet, for chrissakes!"

He tried again, losing most of the rice and shrimp halfway to his mouth.

"Nope, nope, nope!" Bill said, laughing. "Look! This evolution *will* be carried out in an orderly, proficient, military manner!" He dropped one chopstick, held the other just above his plate for a moment as though hunting a moving target, then stabbed, lightning fast, skewering a single piece of chicken from the rice and transferring it to his mouth.

"Honestly!" Pat cried, laughing so hard that tears were rolling down her face. "I can't take you guys *anywhere*!"

"No, no," Bill said. "*He's* the one with the spastic chopsticks. I get along with them quite well, thank you!"

"Oh, for cryin' out loud," Greg said. He took both chopsticks and stabbed them vertically into the pile of rice on his plate, leaving them standing on his plate. "These things make *great* decorations. Like parsley."

"Uh, Greg—" Bill started to say. Just then, one of the Chinese waiters walked toward them, a fresh pot of tea in one hand. He was wearing a smile, but as he reached the table, the smile froze uncomfortably in place. Swiftly, Bill reached across the table and pushed Greg's standing chopsticks over, laying them flat.

"Everything . . . okay here?" the waiter asked. "More tea?"

"Yes," Pat said. "Thank you."

The waiter took the old teapot and left the new. His face was stiff and uncommunicative as he walked away. Bill sat there a moment, looking after him. "Shit."

"What?" Greg asked. "What's wrong?"

"I'll be back in a sec," he told them. Rising, he followed the waiter to the door to the kitchen.

Greg looked at Pat, his eyebrows raised in question. She shrugged. Bill was talking to the waiter, who shook his head, then made a shrugging, dismissive gesture. Bill suddenly gave a short, sharp bow. The waiter returned it. He was smiling now.

"What the hell was *that* all about?" Greg asked as Bill slipped into the booth again.

Bill sighed. "Twidge, let me pass on a small tidbit of advice. What you did a moment ago with your chopsticks? Standing them up that way?"

"Yeah. . . ."

"That is a very uncool thing to do *everywhere* in the Far East. It's kind of an insult."

"Why?" Pat asked.

"Chopsticks standing up in your food like that look like the little incense sticks they have burning in front of a body at a funeral. Definitely bad luck to see that in your place of business."

"So when that waiter came by . . ." Pat began.

Bill nodded. "About like handing a white rose to an Italian restaurant owner with Mafia connections," Bill said. "Or, hell, I don't know. Tossing a dead cat on the table in an American restaurant. A dead *black* cat. Bad omens, y'know?"

"Damned superstitious nonsense," Greg said.

"Maybe. But they're real to the people who believe in them." He grinned. "Like those pain meds I gave you."

Greg blinked. "Ouch."

"Anyway, I always figured I probably have some customs and ways of doing things that are pretty damned strange to other folks. It doesn't do to antagonize people unnecessarily."

"This from a Navy SEAL?" Pat said. She laughed. She had, Bill thought, a beautiful laugh. "So what did you do with the waiter, anyway?"

"I apologized for all of us," Bill said. "I explained that some of us weren't familiar with his customs, and I asked him to overlook the clumsiness of Western barbarians."

"Barbarians!" Greg said, eyes widening.

"The Chinese have a civilization that goes back three thousand years," Pat reminded him. "They must think we're newcomers."

Bill looked at Greg, head cocked. "I thought you were the historian in the family?"

"I think I've taught her too well!"

"Anyway, I still feel bad, because he lost face."

"Why?"

"Because *I* lost face, in his establishment. By assuming responsibility for you."

"I see," Greg said. "So then you bribed him."

"No, I didn't want to make him lose even more face by offering money," Bill explained. "But I do think a nice tip would be in order."

"I'll take care of it," Greg said. He shook his head ruefully as he fished his wallet out of the hip pocket of his blue pants. "You know, maybe a course on Asian social customs wouldn't be such a bad idea after all!"

"Well," Bill said thoughtfully, "killing a guy is one

thing. That's just business. But it's something else entirely to insult him!''

Waverly Place, San Francisco
2205 hours

They walked down the street arm in arm, laughing. Bill liked the feel of Pat's arm around his waist, and he liked the way she snuggled in under his arm when he draped it around her shoulder. It was late, well past dark, and the street outside the restaurant was deserted.

"Okay, you guys," Pat told them. "Can SEALs sneak-and-peek a cab?"

"No," Bill said with mock seriousness. "But we can hi-jack one."

"I've got a better idea," she said. She pointed up the street. "That's Sacramento. We're sure to find a cab there."

Laughing, they started up the street, still arm in arm.

"Well, lookee here!" a deep voice said behind them. "Looks like a goddamn pig convention!"

"Hey!" another voice put in, filled with menace. "Baby-killers!"

"More like faggots in little-boy sailor suits," yet another voice said.

"Hey!" one of them cried. "You pigs! We're *talkin'* to you!"

Bill turned, releasing Pat as he did so and stepping a little away from her, giving him freedom to move quickly if he had to. Several street toughs were stepping out of the black mouth of an alley they'd just passed.

He went cold inside, the same way he'd felt just before a firefight in Vietnam, when the enemy was in sight and things were about to get hot. There were five of them, three of them big and husky, all of them cruising for trouble. They had the look of bikers about them, despite the peace signs and other hippie paraphernalia hanging from their costumes. Several had long hair, tied back in ponytails; others had short hair, but all carried themselves with the same swaggering arro-gance of men confident in their ability to do damn near anything they wanted. One chugged a hefty swallow from a nearly empty bottle of cheap whiskey.

Instinctively, Bill went into ready mode. His position didn't change, and his hands were still at his side, but inwardly he was as hard and tight-coiled as a steel spring. His weight was on the balls of his feet, and his knees were slightly bent.

He guessed the leader was the biggest one of the bunch, a six-two monster with a massive beer gut and unkempt, dirty blond hair. He wore a heavy-looking peace sign around his neck and a filthy leather jacket.

"Well, well, well," the leader said, looking Pat up and down with a greasy leer as he walked closer. "They're not *all* pigs! I kinda like the look of this one!"

"Hey, baby!" a skinny kid with a scraggly beard said, crowding past his partner. "Don't waste your time with these faggots!"

"Yeah, sweet tits," the one with the bottle said. "You need some *real* lovin', from some real men!"

"Lay off," Greg said, stepping in front of Pat. "We don't want any trouble with you people."

"Ha!" the leader said, turning his head toward the others. "He don't want no trouble, he says!" Spinning back to confront Greg, he jammed a stubby forefinger at the SEAL's face. "Maybe, sailor-boy, you just found yourself a shitload of trouble!"

"Get that filthy thing out of my face before I bite it off," Greg said in a low voice that stopped just short of being a growl.

"Ooooh!" the skinny kid said. "I'm afraid, now! I'm shaking!"

The street toughs started closing around them, spreading out, moving closer. "We was lookin' for some Chinks to rumble," one of them said. "I think this is gonna be a lot more fun!"

"I *like* that dress!"

"Maybe she'll give it to you, Skitter."

"Nah. I want her panties!"

"Free love, man. Let's take her back to the pad and, you know, make love, not war!"

"Yeah! We'll show you what *real* men can do for you, babe!" the skinny one said. He smirked at Bill. "Sorry, but you boys ain't invited. Just the lady, here. You guys ain't our type!"

" 'Course," the leader said, "we'll relieve you fairies of your wallets first, just to show there ain't no hard feelings!"

"Hard feelings! Here, I got hard feelings!" One of them grabbed his crotch, thrusting his hips forward and leering. "We're gonna have a gang bang!"

"I don't think so," Bill said. "Why don't you boys go play someplace else?

"Fuck it," the one with the bottle said. With a sharp flick of his wrist, he shattered the bottle against the brick wall of the building beside him. Glass shattered, the pieces spinning away and tinkling across the pavement. The harsh light of a streetlamp gleamed from the jagged edges of the glass remaining in the tough's fist. "Let's waste these pig-creeps and do the chick, y'know?"

The leader's hand twitched, and a switchblade snicked open in his hand. "Sounds like a plan, Gonj. Me, I'm gonna carve me some smart-mouthed faggot dick and feed it to 'em."

"What," Greg said, deliberately provoking him. "A pus-gutted pencil-dicked fart-breathed asshole like you?"

The leader's face darkened. "*Yaaah!*" He lunged, leading with a wild stab of his blade.

Greg sidestepped left, touched the inside of the tough's wrist with his right hand, and slammed the heel of his left squarely into the elbow; Bill heard the joint snap just as he brought the tip of his Korfam dress shoe slashing up into the bottle-wielder's groin, then caught the hand, breaking it inward until the glass crashed on the pavement. As Gonj doubled over, Bill's heel came up, connecting with the guy's nose in a scarlet splatter of blood.

Greg had pivoted above the screaming gang leader, sweeping the feet out from under Skitter and sending the skinny kid hurtling facefirst into a telephone pole, losing his white hat in the process. Bill touched a nerve in the fifth thug's wrist and plucked a switchblade out of his hand, before ramming a rigidly stiff thumb deep into his right eye. Skitter was just getting up off the pavement; Bill pivoted hard, slashing with the liberated switchblade and laying the guy's bare upper arm open almost to the bone.

The leader had dropped to his knees, cradling his broken arm and yowling. Greg slammed his knee into the man's face, sending his head slamming back into the wall, stunning him. Skinny was trying to get up; Bill drove a Hwrang-do knuckled fist straight-armed into his temple, dropping him cold, then dropped into a coup-de-grâce roundhouse kick to the bleeding Skitter's head. Greg drove his elbow into the back of the last thug, who was clawing at his savaged eye.

Greg, Pat, and Bill were the only ones left standing, Pat with her back against the wall, the two men with their backs up against each other. "Clear!" Greg called.

"Clear," Bill replied.

"My . . . *God*!" Pat said, eyes wide. Perhaps three seconds had passed since the gang's leader had made that first lunge with his knife. Neither of the SEALs was even breathing heavily.

"Nice to know that martial arts stuff works for real, huh?" Greg said, turning. "Man, what a mess!"

Bill stooped, checking pulses.

The leader of the gang was trying to sit up, his back against the brick wall of the building behind him. Blood was dribbling from his misshapen nose. Greg took the metal peace sign that was dangling from the tough's neck and carefully positioned it against his forehead. With a sharp, sudden blow, he drove the heel of his hand forward, slamming it against the emblem and driving it hard into the man's forehead. The gang leader's eyes crossed, then rolled up in his head.

"Peace, brother," Greg said, peeling the broken-cross peace emblem away from the bloody impression stamped into the skin of the man's forehead, then tearing it from his neck. He looked at the others and grinned. "Always wondered if that trick of the Phantom's really worked. With the skull in his ring, marking bad guys, y'know?"

"Shit," Bill said, looking at the bright red wound. "I think you branded him for life."

"Nah. Just a hickey. A very *strange*-looking hickey."

Greg picked up a discarded switchblade, rammed it as hard as he could into a telephone pole, then yanked the handle sharply to the left, snapping the blade with an audible *ping*. Bill found the other and gave it the same treatment.

"Are we . . . should we call the police?" Pat asked.

"I don't think so," Bill told her. He pointed at Skinny, then at Skitter. "I'm afraid those two bought it. I don't think we're going to want to hang around answering a lot of questions, y'know?"

"I'm sorry, Pat," Greg said. "Those two guys kind of rushed me. I didn't have time to be gentle, you know?"

She touched his shoulder. "Greg, you don't have to apologize to *me*!" She shuddered, looking at the sprawled and bloody bodies on the pavement. "They deserved what they got. And Bill's right. Let's just get out of here before someone calls the police."

The two SEALs straightened their blue jumpers, and Greg retrieved his white hat from the street.

Arm in arm, then, but with a more subdued manner, the three of them walked away up the street.

Chapter 29

Tuesday, 4 March 1969

SEAL Compound
Cam Ranh Bay, Republic of Vietnam
0930 hours

"Hurry up, man," Rodriguez called, sticking his head in through the barracks door. "Looks to me like the show's ready to start! I ain't seen so much brass since the last time a seventy-six-trombone parade marched past."

"Hey," Bill Tangretti said. "They want to see SEALs, they should inspect us in battle dress. What the hell do they want to see us in dress whites for, anyway?"

"Reporters, man, reporters," Rodriguez said.

"Yeah," DM2 Robert Cain added. "The brass just wants to make sure that everyone knows we're Navy!"

"Is that so?" Greg Halstead said, straightening the square knot in his black neckerchief and trying to get the ends to hang with the proper crisp flair. "Fuck, and here all along I thought we were in the Marine Corps."

"Watch your language, Twidge," Tangretti said with a knowing grin. "Someone's liable to gig you for 'conduct unbecoming.' "

"Unbecoming to what? I'm no officer, and I *sure* as hell ain't no gentleman!"

It was hard to keep whites looking properly pressed and crisp in the perpetual damp of the sauna that was Vietnam, but at last the members of First Squad, Delta Platoon were shipshape enough to spill out of the barracks door and into the bright tropical sunshine of Cam Ranh Bay.

Bill Tangretti blinked in the light and took a deep breath of salt-tasting air. This was a long way indeed from the swamps of the Rung Sat—less than two hundred miles by air, but in terms of geography and the facilities themselves it could have been on another continent. Tangretti remembered Nha Be and the Rung Sat Special Zone as steamy hot and muggy, always wet, always muddy. The base at Nha Be had reminded him of a junkyard, and living conditions there had been downright primitive. Most of the barracks at Cam Ranh Bay were fairly new cinder-block constructions, clean and air-conditioned. Some of the older buildings looked a bit ramshackle, and many had sheet-tin roofs, with sandbags placed in rows to hold them down during the occasional typhoons that blew in off the South China Sea, but overall the facility was modern, looking more like a naval base Stateside than a run-down marina in some third-world banana republic.

Cam Ranh Bay proper was an enormous naval facility; the harbor was the best in Vietnam—possibly the best in all of Southeast Asia—and always crowded with shipping, both commercial and military.

The SEAL facility, though, was off by itself, tucked in alongside the LDNN SEAL training compound on about fifteen acres above a broad, half-kilometer-long beach of fine, white sand.

This was one of the main LDNN schools in the country. It wasn't large; at any given time, there were seven American SEAL advisors stationed there, along with thirty to forty Vietnamese trainees. The setting had made Tangretti a little nervous the first time he'd seen it. The base was located about a quarter mile back from the bay, well clear of the other base facilities. A large tank farm was positioned nearby, protected by nothing more than a wire mesh fence. Rising above the rear of the LDNN compound was a steep, thickly wooded hill from which an enormous, flat, rock outcropping protruded. Someone had turned that boulder into a billboard, painting—in enormous, white letters across the rock—LDNN SEAL.

It made him feel vulnerable and exposed. They might just as well all go around wearing large bull's-eyes painted on their chests and backs.

Other than that, though, duty here was pretty good so far. There was no mud to be found anywhere around, and that and the constant breeze off the sea meant fewer mosquitoes. That breeze meant the heat and humidity weren't as intolerable as they often were south of Saigon in the swamps, and the air didn't stink. The uniform of the day was personal choice unless they wanted to go over to Mainside where the *real* Navy lived, and usually that meant swim trunks everywhere but the mess hall. The beach was a short run down the hill, past an enclosure set aside for the training of German shepherd patrol dogs—the K-9 Corps, as the SEALs called them.

Tangretti was fascinated by the dogs. The word was that they were used in small boats to patrol the water approaches to Cam Ranh Bay, with noses so sensitive they could detect the smell of NVA combat swimmers from the bubbles released by their SCUBA gear. Tangretti wasn't sure he believed that story, but he liked having the dogs nearby. Most Vietnamese didn't like dogs, not as pets, anyway. They were used to animals small enough to eat . . . not large enough and ferocious enough to eat *them*.

Most of their time since they'd arrived had been taken up with indoctrination. All of the SEALs had been sitting in on classes held by the LDNN SEAL advisors, learning all they could about the land, the people, and the tactics employed by their enemies. Tangretti had been particularly interested in the classes on VC booby traps, run by a Navy SEAL chief named Holbrook. The old fear that he might be paralyzed by indecision his next time out had returned, growing stronger each day he was back in Vietnam.

He hadn't told anyone about it, however, not even Twidge, who'd become his closest friend. He hardly dared admit it to himself.

In most other ways, though, he found he was actually happy to be back in Vietnam. He was fitting in well with Delta Platoon, and with First Squad, which had taken on the unofficial nickname of "Casey's Commandos." Morale was high, and excitement about coming to grips with the enemy was keen. The only thing to intrude on that happy mood were the occasional "bullshit evolutions" . . . like these inspections. Tangretti's theory was that *someone*, an unseen presence higher up on the Navy food chain, had the idea that SEALs needed to be reminded every once in a while that they were still members of the United States Navy.

Otherwise, they might spend the rest of their tours in swim trunks . . . or wearing face paint and playing with noisy toys.

The platoon fell in on the grinder outside of the barracks, drawn up in two squads, First Squad in the front, Second in the rear. They were wearing dress whites, unusual garb for SEALs, but appropriate to the occasion of a full-dress inspection. Tangretti had had to run over to the base ship's store Mainside the day before, however, to make sure he had all of the service ribbons he was required to wear on his dress uniform. He'd really not been expecting this sort of bullshit nonsense, and he'd left the originals back in the States. He was just happy this wasn't supposed to be full dress, with medals instead of the little ribbon bars that represented them. Those damned things were expensive, and he'd left all of his back in the World, too.

He only had eight service ribbons in all, a top row of two centered over two rows of three, a light load compared to SEALs who'd been in for a while. Chief Ramsey, for instance, wore four rows of three. He was a spectacular sight in full dress, with a mass of bronze and colored ribbon that looked as heavy as an M60. The joke had gone the rounds that he didn't need a Kevlar flak jacket when he wore his medals, as opposed to the ribbons, not with that much metal over his chest.

At the top of Tangretti's rack were the Bronze Star, with the V for Valor that indicated he'd won it in combat, and the Purple Heart, for the wounds that had landed him in Bethesda. The others were ranked beneath. Vietnam Service. The Republic of Vietnam Service, his one foreign decoration. The National Defense Service Medal—usually referred to as the "gedunk ribbon," since it was handed out to everyone who'd served in the military during the Korean War period or since 1961. "Gedunk" was Navy slang for snacks or junk food, and sailors joked that they'd been awarded the gedunk ribbon because they'd volunteered rather than running away to Canada. Expert Pistol Marksman and Expert Rifle Marksman, which Tangretti had qualified for during his duty period at Coronado.

The ribbon that he was actually proudest of was the blue, yellow, and red horizontal stripes of a Navy Presidential Unit Citation—awarded in mid-January to SEAL Team One by President Johnson as one of his last official acts in office.

"Medals," his father had told him once. He could still hear the derisive snort. "What the hell good are they? They won't even buy you a cup of coffee." Most SEALs felt that way, though there was the inevitable warm and friendly bitching about the system when one guy picked up a medal for precisely the same sort of derring-do that some SEAL did routinely and without official comment, every time he went into the bush. One story still circulating through the Navy Special Warfare community told of an enlisted SEAL who'd been put in for the Congressional Medal of Honor the previous March and had it bumped down to a Navy Cross because the first SEAL to get the CMH *would* be an officer.

Fuck the officers. Fuck the high-level brass that had nothing to do but make up silly-ass rules and yank the chains of enlisted pukes.

Out of the corner of his eye, Tangretti could see the coterie of officers approaching, most in dress whites, some in green fatigues. Several of the men in utilities had a less than military look about them, with cameras draped around their necks. *Reporters*.

Fucking reporters, Tangretti amended to himself, a little bitterly. These were the people who reported on the war, brought the war home to America every night on the evening news. He was beginning to suspect that these were the people who were doing more for Charlie's cause than Charlie himself. He watched their approach with dark suspicion.

"Platoon!" Casey bawled in his best parade ground bellow. "Atten-*hut!*"

Tangretti snapped to rigid attention. He was standing in the front rank with First Squad, fourth from the end. He could see the officers and reporters out of the corner of his eye to the right, slowly coming toward him, stopping to chat for a moment with each SEAL Team member. All of the attention was focused on one man who led the pack, a short and feisty-looking man in green fatigues and a billed cap. Tangretti felt a shock of surprise as the man drew closer; he was wearing three stars on his collar flap . . . a vice admiral, no less. Tangretti didn't even know a vice admiral had been assigned to Vietnam. Generally, he thought, that particular breed of brass seemed to stay pretty close to its natural habitat . . . Washington, DC, and the Pentagon.

No one had passed the word about an inspection tour by a vice admiral out here. Bill wondered if Casey had been told and not had time to tell the men, or if he was as surprised by this as the rest of them were.

The admiral was in front of Greg Halstead, immediately to Tangretti's right. "Where are you from, son?" the admiral asked.

"Sir! Jenner, California, sir!" Greg fired back in best kaydet fashion.

"No kidding?" the admiral said, cracking a grin. "I'm from San Francisco, myself. Just down the coast a ways. I've been up in your neck of the woods a number of times. Real pretty country.''

Then the admiral was in front of Tangretti, looking up at him with piercing eyes that could easily have been those of a hawk, or some other bird of prey. The man was young, Bill realized, probably in his forties, which made him *damned* young for three stars. Most of the captains and commanders following along in the admiral's wake were older than he was.

For some reason, Tangretti thought about the movie that had been shown at the Mainside theater just a week before . . . *The Dirty Dozen*, a '67 war flick starring Lee Marvin. There'd been a scene in that movie, which the SEALs had loved because of its acid commentary on both military authority and the hierarchy of rank, when a private had impersonated an American general, carrying out an inspection just like this one.

It suddenly dawned on Bill that this had to be some kind of a joke, maybe someone at the Cam Ranh Bay Naval HQ jerking the newbies' chains. This guy *couldn't* be an admiral!

"What's your name, son?" the impostor asked him.

Tangretti broke into an innocent grin and stuck his hand out. "My name's Bill. What's yours?"

The admiral stared into Tangretti's eyes for a moment, then pursed his lips, grinned, and took Tangretti's hand. "I'm Elmo." He shook hands, then moved on down the line. One of the captains in the entourage shot Tangretti a deadly look, and one of the camera-draped reporters was shaking his head, but nothing else was said.

The inspection was completed moments later. The admiral spoke a few quiet words with Casey, then received his salute. "Very good, men," the admiral said. "Carry on!"

"Platoon," Casey called as the admiral and his staff walked away. "Dis—*missed*!"

Casey was in Tangretti's face a second later. "What the *fuck* are you trying to pull, Doc?"

"What's the problem, Lieutenant?"

"Do you have any idea who that man was?"

Tangretti grinned. "You mean 'Elmo'?" The grin that had started to form on his face froze then, with a sudden, biting realization. *Elmo* had seemed like such an unusual name . . . confirmation that the guy was an impostor, carrying out an unlikely joke for the newbies' benefit.

But as Casey glowered at him, he remembered a name, a very famous name in Navy circles.

Elmo Zumwalt.

Vice Admiral Elmo R. Zumwalt, Jr., was something of a legend throughout the Navy, a fiery, opinionated, and undeniably brilliant officer determined to cut through red tape and bureaucracy wherever necessary, to streamline procedures, and to make the Navy *work*. Before Zumwalt had been named COMNAVFORV—commanding officer of all naval forces in Vietnam—the Navy's role in that war had increasingly been one of static defense and patrol . . . and a dead end for any officer who intended to build a naval career. He'd changed all of that, beginning at the end of September in 1968. He was already notorious for his "ZWIs," or "Zumwalt's Wild Ideas"—innovations at streamlining naval operations and bureaucracy.

And Tangretti had forgotten all about him. "Oh . . . *that* Elmo."

"It's a damn good thing for you he likes SEALs," Casey said. "Otherwise your next duty station would be Adak, Alaska. Counting penguins."

"There aren't any penguins in Alaska, sir," Tangretti said miserably. He looked off in the direction in which Zumwalt had gone. *That* Zumwalt? . . .

"I knew about the inspection yesterday," Casey said, "when I passed the word to you clowns. I didn't find out it was *him* until this morning. Seems he happened to be in the area, heard there was a new SEAL platoon in, and requested, no, *demanded* to come inspect it. Damn it, Doc. Don't you have better sense than to mouth off to a three-star?"

Tangretti opened his mouth to say that that was obviously his father's genes. The elder Tangretti was mildly notorious throughout the SEAL community for his occasional offhand attitude toward rank and brass hats. But Bill, afraid that mentioning the relationship would look like he was seeking special privilege, had been careful to avoid bringing up his famous UDT-SEAL father. "Ah . . . I guess not. Sir."

"Get out of here, and be glad you're not on report!"

Only later, back at the barracks, did Tangretti wonder whether Zumwalt's presence at Cam Ranh Bay meant something more than a simple glad-hand-the-troops public-relations visit. More often than not, the appearance of high-ranking brass in an AO meant that something big was going down, and soon.

He wondered what it might be.

Friday, 7 March 1969

SEAL Compound
Cam Ranh Bay, Republic of Vietnam
1920 hours

Greg sat in the bull pen with three of the other newbie SEALs in Casey's Commandos: Bandit Rodriguez, MM3 Joseph "Slinger" Amadio, and DM2 Robert "Boomer" Cain. Bandit, of course, was a fellow survivor of Class 42; Cain and Amadio had both come out of Class 41, but this was their first combat rotation to Vietnam. The "bull pen" was the SEAL facility's briefing room, which they'd taken over temporarily because it was a room that could be sealed from the outside. Security conscious, as always, they'd decided to prep for the upcoming mission here, where unfriendly eyes wouldn't be able to see their activity and figure out that an op was under way.

They'd pushed a couple of big, folding tables together to create a work area, and all three were busily stripping and cleaning their weapons. Bandit had been designated as the squad's sixty-gunner, and he had his M60 partly disassembled and was swabbing out the bore with an oiled patch. Slinger was carrying one of the new M-16/M203 combos, an upgraded descendent of the XM-148. SEALs had already field-tested both weapons in Vietnam, but only now was the combo becoming standard issue. Greg was cleaning his Mark 23 Mod 0 Stoner Commando. Maintaining the weapon had become a kind of daily ritual with him, comforting in its familiarity and repetition. The Stoner weapons system had been invented by Eugene Stoner, the man who'd originally invented the AR-15 . . . the weapon that had gone on to become the ubiquitous M-16. Outside of the SEALs, no unit within the U.S. armed forces had bought the Stoner system, which was reputed to jam easily and which was not very forgiving when it came to mud or dirt in the receiver.

SEALs, however, knew how to take care of their weapons and did so religiously, with the same constant devotion that they'd developed in BUD/S, when the care and cleaning of their IBS was the first thing trainee boat crews had learned. With proper care and field maintenance, the Stoner was one of the best weapons systems in Nam. Most SEALs loved them, and only the legendary AK-47, which could be dragged through the mud or lost for days on the bottom of a river and still fire without being cleaned, was more reliable. The weapon was light—a bit over eleven pounds—easily handled, and accurate. The only real down-grudges so far as the SEALs were concerned were an occasional tendency to go full-auto when set to single shot, and the annoying fact that the individual links for the 5.56mm ammo, which allowed the weapon to be belt-fed from a 150-round box, were eternally in short supply; SEALs had quickly learned to collect their expended links, even in the middle of a firefight, because requisitioning new ones from the local supply depot was always a chancy proposition at best.

Conversation, strangely enough, did not center on the upcoming mission. They'd been given a warning order at about fifteen hundred hours that afternoon, followed by a briefing. In another two hours, they would be boarding a Seawolf helicopter for the flight to their patrol zone, on the coast off the South China Sea, and the tangled expanse of forest along the Cai River near Dong Trang.

There'd been some initial speculation, of course, over whether or not the raid had anything to do with Admiral Zumwalt's presence at Cam Ranh. There were rumors floating about that the admiral had violated some rather stiff regs on at least one occasion to sit in on a riverine raid near the Cambodian border; people with the sort of security classification he had—and the knowledge of highly classified information—normally weren't allowed anywhere near an AO that might get hot. Zumwalt, though, had the rep of being a

sailor's admiral, the sort of man who wouldn't order anybody
to do something he wasn't willing to do himself.

In any case, the op was going to be a routine patrol, with
the goal of taking on targets of opportunity. The upper Cai
Valley had been a solidly held Communist bastion for as
long as anyone could remember. Like the Rung Sat, south
of Saigon, or the U Minh Forest west of the Mekong, it was
a largely impenetrable and mostly unexplored region that
could hide entire armies.

Delta Platoon's orders were to move in and let Charlie
know that the SEALs were here, and that there were no priv-
ileged sanctuaries for them anymore along this part of the
Vietnamese coast.

But outside of a sentence or two about Zumwalt's possible
connections with the mission, earlier on, none of the SEALs
seemed willing to talk about it. Talking shop was one thing
. . . but discussing an upcoming op, outside of the formal
setting of a briefing, was distinctly something else. Combat—
and what might happen in combat—were intensely private
matters, rarely discussed even among brothers.

"So," Greg was saying as he carefully cleaned the receiver with an oily rag. "You think the leaflet programs do
any good?"

They'd been discussing psy-ops techniques, and the talk
had turned, inevitably, to the massive numbers of leaflets
dropped from helicopters and other aircraft across the length
and breadth of South Vietnam.

"Well, they do use them to come through the lines,"
Boomer said. "You know, like a white flag."

"Yeah, but the Chieu Hoi program gets most of its people
from prisoners," Slinger said. "I always had the impression
that when Marvin ARVN got through working a POW over,
they gave him a choice. You know, 'work for us or you're
history, man.' "

"That's not what I heard," Greg said. "Sure, lots of prisoners turn to save their own hides, but a hell of a lot of VC
have just plain decided they didn't want to fight anymore.
Becoming a Hoi Chanh is the only hope they have to eventually get back home, see their families."

"Yeah," Rodriguez said darkly. "If they still have a home or a family when they get back."

Greg chuckled. "I heard one story. This is the truth, too, no shit. Guy in Personnel told me, over at Mainside, and he got it from one of the guys involved. Seems there was this one Army helo crew who'd been assigned to drop leaflets over this one part of the jungle. The trouble was that they kept taking a lot of fire from the ground, and it wasn't exactly healthy to just hover up there while they emptied the leaflet sack, which was this big bag, like a seabag, about so tall, and weighing, I don't know. A hundred pounds, maybe. So this one time, they decided to save time and just chucked this whole bag full of leaflets out the door, then yelled at the pilot to get the hell out of Dodge.

"A few days later, this VC turns himself in at the base. Seems he was out in the jungle with his best buddy when this goddamn big mail sack just fell out of the sky, right through the jungle canopy, and *whop*! Hit his buddy standing right next to him and squashed him like a bug. Scared the poor son of a bitch so bad he decided to give up, right then and there."

"Man, do the strategic bombing guys know about this?" Boomer wanted to know. "Might put a whole new twist to the bombing campaign up north!"

The others laughed. "Yeah," Rodriguez said. "That's what it takes, though. *Kill* the fuckers. *Sat Cong!* And I don't mean talk 'em to death."

"I wonder how much they read that shit anyway," Greg said. "We don't believe their propaganda, when they broadcast it over loudspeakers, or get Hollywood movie personalities to front for them. Why should they believe ours?"

Rodriguez nodded as he slipped the trigger assembly home in the M60 and locked it. "That's what I'm sayin', y'know? The only thing that works is when you put the fear of God in 'em, show 'em what's gonna happen if they keep fighting you. Demoralize the bastards, any way you can!"

"Speaking of demoralize," Slinger said suddenly, looking toward the door. A pair of apparitions was just coming in, and Greg had to look twice to convince himself that it was Tangretti and Chief Ramsey. Their faces were coated with paint so thick they did not look human; Tangretti's face was entirely green and black; Ramsey's face was mostly green and black, but it had some smears of red-brown as well, breaking up the green outline of his face and subtly rearranging and blurring his features, so that when his eyes moved, there was a small shock of recognition: *Oh, those are* eyes.

"What the hell is it?" Rodriguez asked.

"I'm not sure," Greg replied, "but it's green and it's pissed."

"If it's pissed at *us*," Slinger said, "I'm outa here!"

"Awright, SEALs," Ramsey growled. "I want to see you mugs in full war paint in thirty mikes, max. How's the armory business going?"

"Just about done, Chief," Rodriguez said.

"Okay. I'll say it again. This is a first combat patrol for most of you. You've been through the drill back in the World, but you'll hear it from me again. No dog tags. Your buddies know who you are, and your buddies will drag your body out of the bush, no matter what happens. Check all your clothing for tags, ratings, anything that will identify you.

"Next anything, anything at all that might click or clink or rattle or make noise, you take black electrical tape and wrap it up. Anything shiny or bright-colored in your gear, you cover it or you paint it." He pointed at Slinger, then at Greg. "You . . . and you. I want the both of you to pack a LAW each on this one. Haul ass over to the arms bunker and draw a couple of those babies out. Then go to the supply shed and get a spray can of black paint. On the sides of those LAWs is a fucking bright red label, put there by REMFs back in the World to annoy my ass. Spray paint the fuckers black. Got it?"

"Sure thing, Chief," Greg said. He was beginning to realize that there was likely to be a lot to combat that they hadn't told him back in Coronado . . . and that even the grueling, exhausting, and dick-dragging nightmare of Hell Week wouldn't be able to fully prepare them for combat—even though that was precisely what Hell Week was supposed to be for.

"The Wheel has just posted the march order for this op," Ramsey continued. "Wheel" was SEAL slang for the officer in command of an op. "Normally, selection of clothing and personal gear is up to you guys, but the Man says that everyone, and I mean *everyone*, will wear floatation jackets tonight. Rodriguez, since you're humping the pig, you're gonna want two of 'em."

"Aw, Chief—"

"Don't give me 'aw, Chief!' On May 6, last year, a PO2 David Devine of SEAL Team One stepped off a PBR in a river and fucking *drowned* because he was carrying an M60 and was loaded too heavy. You were all drown-proofed in BUD/S at great expense to the American taxpayers, and I want you to *stay* drown-proof! I don't want any of you ripping Uncle Sam off for that money, y'hear me? Halstead, two jackets for you, too. You're humpin' the radio." He looked at his watch. "Assembly on the helo deck at twenty hundred hours. I'll give you and your gear a final check then. That is all."

"Hey, nice paint job, Chief," Greg called out as the chief started to walk away. His heart was hammering beneath his sternum. *This is it!*

"You'd better learn to do the same, rookie," Ramsey replied. "Doc, here, can show you people how. When you're out in the bush, you've got to know how to become a bush. Or you ain't gonna make it."

"Here endeth the lesson," Boomer intoned as Ramsey strode out the door. "Welcome aboard, Doc. Pull up a chair."

"What the *hell* do you have there, Doc?" Bill asked. Tangretti was carrying a paper bag from the Mainside PX, which he dropped on the table, along with several waterproofed canvas pouches, before unslinging his Stoner and setting it upright against the wall.

"Just stocking up, gentlemen," Tangretti replied, grinning. Opening the paper bag, he removed several packages of a popular commercial brand of sanitary napkin, stacking them in neat piles on the tabletop.

"Whoa," Rodriguez said. "Hey, man. I heard of buyin' nylons for the ladies, but not *those* things!"

"You pass those out to your girlfriends, Doc?" Slinger asked. "Or is there somethin' about you we don't know?"

"Well, you know how it is," Tangretti said. "You just never know what kind of medical emergency you may run into." Whistling tunelessly, he began opening up the pouches, each of which was packed with medical supplies—gauze pads, paper tape, rolls of gauze, hemostats, scissors . . . all of the tools the team medic might need in the field. Into each kit, he stuffed as many of the sanitary napkins as he could.

"No kidding, Doc," Slinger said. "What's with the Kotex?"

"It's a trick I learned from a SEAL corpsman I knew once. I use these instead of regular bandages. They're more absorbent than the issue stuff. Soak up blood like you wouldn't believe, and they're easier to handle. They don't slip and slide around when they get soaked through, either."

"Yeah, but are they sterile?" Greg asked.

"Believe me, Twidge. For field first aid, as long as it's cleaner than the wound—and *toilet* paper is cleaner than your typical or garden-variety battlefield wound—it's okay. Clean enough for government work, anyway."

"Man, you know, I think we got us a first-class quack, here," Rodriguez said, shaking his head.

"Nah," Tangretti said, still packing the napkins away. "I'm only a third class." He tapped the sleeve of his greens, which was empty of any rank. "One stripe, see?"

"Very funny."

"Didn't they teach you guys anything about improvising when you had to?" His eyebrows, almost invisible in his painted face, moved up. "Surely you remember the old UDT hands and the condoms!"

The others laughed. Greg had actually heard the story first from Bill, though the instructors had mentioned it in demolitions training as well, back at Coronado.

During World War II, when the original Navy Combat Demolition Units had been training at Fort Pierce, Florida, a frequent problem had been wet fuze igniters—the pull-ring triggers that set a fuze burning. According to Tangretti, his father and his best friend, Hank Richardson, had solved the problem by encasing the igniters in rubber condoms, which kept them dry even in the surf or underwater. The trouble had started when the NCDU trainees kept buying up every condom from every drugstore in the area . . . which naturally further boosted the horny reputations of the demolitions trainees. Richardson, according to Bill, had been the "Condom King," because he'd been so good at locating and cumshawing impossible supplies of the things.

"So you're the Kotex King, now," Greg said, laughing.

"I still don't want you sticking those things on any of *my* wounds," Bandit said.

"How about in his ugly mouth instead?" Slinger suggested.

"Now there's an idea."

As the others joked, Greg went back to assembling his Stoner, then broke out two more boxes of 5.56mm ammo and began making up another 150-round belt, carefully feeding the rounds into each belt link and clipping them together.

He caught himself thinking again about Pat.

She'd been writing him ever since he'd left for Vietnam, at least a letter a week, and sometimes more. His letters had been a little more scattered than hers, with writing time squeezed out of his personal time—which included taking care of his uniform, cleaning his weapon and combat gear, and taking care of his own grooming needs—and he'd been feeling a bit guilty about that. He'd been thinking about her a lot; he glanced at Bill Tangretti and smiled to himself. He wondered if Bill thought about her as well. Certainly, her letters had been filled with questions about Bill. The guy'd made a mighty big hit with her in San Fran, that was clear. He wondered if she was in love with Bill.

The thought seemed shockingly incongruous, at first. Pat? The antiwar demonstrator? In love with a *SEAL*? That was just too weird to be believed. In fact, he wondered what she would think if she could see Bill right now, his face smothered in green and black paint as he cheerfully stuffed paperwrapped feminine sanitary napkins into his medical kits.

Bill had also laid out a couple of prisoner-handling kits—sets of plastic ties used in place of handcuffs to control any prisoners the squad might take, and the manila tag that the captors would wire to the POW's clothing, listing the time, date, and circumstances of the capture. The antiwar types back home were screaming about inhuman treatment of prisoners . . . and they would likely have something to say about the unit's corpsman being responsible for Vietnamese captives . . . or hauling around a Stoner assault rifle, for that matter. There were a good many murky areas in the current rules and regs for medical personnel, and SEALs tended to blur those areas even more than most.

The thought of antiwar demonstrators raised again the memory of Marci. He wondered where she was now, what she was doing. Damn, they'd had something good together, the two of them. In some ways, the Vietnam War was becoming as much a civil war for Americans as it was already for the Vietnamese. If it hadn't been for the war, he was sure he would have asked Marci to marry him; certainly, they would have been living together by the time they were through with college. Even before he'd decided to join the Navy, he would have seen her a lot more often if she hadn't always been running off to one demonstration or protest or another.

He missed her. Even now, he missed her.

Greg dragged his thoughts back to the here and now, furiously stringing Stoner links together as he fed rounds into the growing belt. Pat had asked him once, an age or two ago, whether he would be able to aim his weapon at someone and pull the trigger. That particular question had been looming quite large in his mind lately.

Somewhat to Greg's surprise, he didn't doubt that he would be able to shoot someone. His training had been long and exacting, and a large part of its purpose had been to break down certain civilian notions of decency, civilized behavior, and fair play, and to condition him to be able to kill . . . from ambush, no less. According to some articles he'd read Stateside, one of the hardest things for American boys in the military, it turned out, was having to launch ambushes on unsuspecting people. There was a deeply ingrained sense that shooting people in the back was wrong . . . just as it was wrong to shoot women or children.

Yet it was entirely possible, he knew, that in this ugly

little war he would find himself aiming his Stoner at a
woman or at a child. Lieutenant Baxter had told them all,
back in Coronado, about an op where they ended up capturing a female VC officer. There were women and there were
girls and there were nine-year-old kids over here . . . and he
would be expected to pull the trigger on them because they
were the enemy, because they were armed and would do their
best to kill him, if they had the chance, and because it was
what he'd been trained to do.

Baby-killer!

He knew he would be able to do it, to aim, squeeze, and
cut them down. There was no question about that.

What he didn't know—and what scared him most—was
how he would feel afterward.

Chapter 30

Friday, 7 March 1969

**Seawolf helicopter
Cai Song Valley
2115 hours**

The Seawolf transport carried them low across the landscape,
barely clearing the tops of the trees, then dropping to within
a few feet of the surface of the river as they skimmed west
toward their target. It was almost full dark, though a linger-
ing light in the west and a pale glow in the sky up ahead
marked the very end of the brief and fiery tropical sunset.

In the darkness of the blacked-out chopper, the seven men
of Delta Platoon's First Squad sat silently, already all but
invisible in the darkness.

Greg leaned out of the open door, feeling the wind snap

past his face as he peered ahead out of the helo's port-side door. He'd done helocasting before, in training back in California, of course, but this was the first time he'd done it for real . . . in a situation where there were so goddamn many unknowns. There was light enough from the sky for him to see the water rushing past beneath the Huey's starboard-side skid, but how deep was it? How muddy was the bottom? Factors like that were carefully considered during training. Out here, anything could happen and probably would.

The chopper was skimming along about twenty feet above the water. They were traveling at a speed of something less than thirty knots, but their low altitude and the darkness contributed to the sense of exhilarating speed. When Greg raised his eyes to the horizon, he could just make out the blur of trees that was the southern shoreline of the river.

The Cai Song Valley wound through fairly rugged ground; mountains rose to north and south, with the valley between them flat-bottomed and covered with jungle vegetation.

"Two minutes!" Casey called out. "Everyone, check your buddy." Greg had been teamed with Slinger. Carefully, Greg went over the other SEAL from head to toe, then turned him about and went back to the head, checking that buckles were snug, loose or rattly pieces of equipment taped down, grenades snug and the pins taped, and his M-16/M203 combo tightly strapped to his back behind his right shoulder, muzzles down and capped. Then it was Slinger's turn to check Greg's gear, making sure everything was secure, his Stoner properly strapped down, the squad's PRC-77 radio snug in its waterproof satchel. They exchanged thumbs-up, then waited while Casey checked them both a second time.

"Just like at Coronado," Casey said as he grabbed the back of Greg's neck and gave a playful squeeze.

Then there was nothing to do but wait. Greg's heart was pounding harder now. In a few minutes, he would be on his first operational combat mission. He found, somewhat to his surprise, that he was less worried about getting killed or wounded than he was about doing a good job. Was he going to screw the pooch? To fuck up? Worst of all, was he going to let the other guys down? Somehow, his rating of ET had qualified him in their eyes to hump the radio. If it got smashed up, it would be *his* fault.

He wasn't even certain what was scaring him more right now . . . the fact that he was going into combat, or the fact that this was his first combat helocast. *One thing at a time,* he told himself. *Get through the helocast . . . then worry about the rest.* He took several deep breaths to steady himself.

What is the lieutenant thinking? he wondered then. *What's going through his head right now? This is a first for him, too.* It was impossible to read Casey's face through all of that green goo, but Greg could remember the determination in those eyes back at Coronado, during Hell Week.

And at that moment, he knew that he was going to be all right.

Casey's hand slapped Ramsey's shoulder, and the SEAL CPO leaped into the darkness. Slinger went at the same moment, de-assing out the starboard side of the Huey. Next it was Doc and Boomer, and then Casey slapped Greg's arm and he stepped out into space with hardly a thought about what he was doing. *Son of a bitch!* he thought. *Training works!*

There was a moment's stomach-twisting fall, with his arms crossed and his legs tight together; then he hit the water with a savage shock, plunging beneath a cloud of bubbles.

The water was deep and surprisingly warm. Greg tugged at the pull rings for his floatation vests, and seconds later bobbed to the surface.

By the time his head emerged above water, the thunderous roar of the helicopter had dwindled away to almost nothing, a clattering in the distance, quickly fading. Any VC in the area would have heard the Huey's passage, of course, but they would not have heard the telltale change in the pitch of its rotor noise as it hovered to let off troops. Few Vietnamese paid any attention at all to a single helicopter, and it was unlikely that they would investigate the passage of this one. In seconds, the jungle was silent again, save for the chirping of insects and the trickling noises of the river. The Huey's rotor noise was swallowed up completely by the night, and Greg felt very much alone. He couldn't see the other SEALs of his squad, but in an odd way, that was comforting. If he couldn't see or hear men who were only a few yards away from him in the river, it was unlikely that any chance VC in the area could see them either.

Looking around, he got his bearings and started swimming. A few moments later, his coral shoes brushed a muddy bottom . . . and then he was crawling ashore at the tangled foot of an immense and moss-covered tree.

The other SEALs of First Squad were coming ashore, too, silent, dripping shapes emerging from the water like shadows, all but lost against the blacker shadows of the forest. No words were exchanged. Every man knew his job and what was expected of him. In minutes, all seven men had formed up in a line, with Slinger on point, and begun moving north, away from the river and deeper into the forest.

The mission this night was a trolling expedition with a twofold purpose. In general, Delta Platoon was to announce its presence, to let the enemy know that the Navy SEALs were in town. Chances were, the enemy knew that already, but tonight's raid—if it went down as planned—would hammer that point home. More specifically, however, Lieutenant Gillespie, the platoon's NILO, had been given information by the naval intelligence detachment at Cam Ranh Bay.

Xa Dinh was a village hidden in the jungle north of the Cai River, about ten klicks from Dong Trang. According to Gillespie, it was the headquarters for a big-shot VC tax collector in the area, a man named Nguyen Dinh Ca. The name "Ca" was supposed to mean "eldest," but pronounced slightly differently, it meant "fish," and that was what Ca was known as to the locals.

The Fish also had a reputation for being extremely cagey. The word was that ARVN units had been sent out to track him down several times and failed. An Army Special Forces A-team had tried as well, without success.

Now the SEALs were going to have a try at it. They didn't have a Hoi Chanh to point the Fish out, but they did have a photograph, taken in Nha Trang the year before. He looked a lot like his namesake, with protruding eyes and a mouth that must be set in a perpetual, fishy pout.

Nailing the Fish would be a great way to announce that

Delta Platoon and the SEALs had just hit the beach.

Silently, they moved through the forest, staying off the trails that crisscrossed the area, stopping periodically to listen to the night sounds around them, and twice even doubling back on their own path, ready to ambush anyone who might have picked up their trail.

By 2310 hours, however, despite the double-backs and delays, they were outside the village of Xa Dinh. Slinger Amadio held up his hand, then turned, holding the hand in front of his face, his fingers splayed like claws. *Enemy in sight!*

Carefully, everyone but Boomer, who was charged with rear security, moved up to the edge of the forest, looking down into the ville. The clearing was in a bowl-shaped depression, surrounded on three sides by the forest and on the fourth, to the north, by a steep, tree-covered slope. The SEALs were on the crest of a hill. It would be difficult to approach Xa Dinh without being seen; the slope leading down to the village was clear-cut and open, covered with short grass and at least fifty meters wide . . . a long, long way to move without any cover at all save the night.

Greg glanced at the Wheel. Casey was studying the town carefully through the squad's AN/PVS1 nightscope, the green glow from the eyepiece circling his eye like a brilliant bull's-eye. At this distance, the light should be invisible, but Greg knew he was going to be nervous until the thing was switched off. Only Casey would use the scope tonight, and then only with his left eye; it would take a long time—thirty minutes or so—to get his night vision back in the eye exposed to the nightscope's light.

Casey, of course, had already checked this site out from the air, flying over in a single helicopter yesterday. He'd given the other SEALs a pretty good idea of what to expect, during the briefing that afternoon, and they'd gone over maps of the ville back at Cam Ranh. Xa Dinh consisted of only about a dozen buildings, lightweight thatch and nipa-palm structures, together with as many sheds, pens, and outbuildings. The place had a curiously dead and vacant look about it; according to Gillespie, the villagers had been forcibly removed several months before, as part of an ARVN plan to pacify the entire region behind the central coast.

After a long time, Casey switched off the scope, then silently signaled the others. No life, no sign of the enemy.

Moving stealthily, the SEALs slipped along the treeline, working their way around to the north side of the ville. There, they could scramble up along the steep, wooded slope overlooking the village clearing and get a closer look at their objective.

If most of the buildings in Xa Dinh looked deserted and unkempt, one did not, a large, almost barnlike structure located at the edge of the town, quite close to the forest and almost directly under the SEAL squad's position. Greg thought it looked like a barracks, and it might well be a temporary stopover and home away from home for Communist troops on the move east through the Cai Song Valley.

The SEALs took up their positions, then settled down to wait.

SEALs were very good at waiting.

They had several options for this type of situation. They could have slipped into the town, even into the barracks itself, checking for the enemy . . . or they could have opened up an indiscriminate attack, targeting the probable barracks. Either course of action, however, was risky, because with little intelligence on enemy strength in the area, without even a sure knowledge of whether there were troops down there, or how many, First Squad could easily blunder into what was euphemistically called "a situation." Greg remembered reading a report on a SEAL platoon action during the previous year . . . the notorious one, in fact, where an enlisted SEAL chief had been put in for the CMH, but had it knocked down to a Navy Cross. During that action, a SEAL team had actually entered a barracks filled with sleeping VC; unfortunately, something had gone badly wrong and a firefight had broken out at point-blank range.

The Wheel was taking the patient route, keeping the objective under surveillance.

Greg remembered what he'd been taught in the tactical segments of BUD/S, deliberately squatting in an uncomfortable position in order to stay awake. The trick here was to be more patient than a very patient foe; the seven men were prepared to wait through the rest of the night and all of the following day as well, with a helo extraction planned for the next night.

He thought about the villagers who'd once lived in Xa Dinh, forcibly removed from their homes, away from the graves of their ancestors, and herded like cattle into concrete-and-barbed-wire enclosures someplace, perhaps many miles away.

It was easy enough to understand the rationale behind the order. The Central Highlands dominated this part of South Vietnam, from here through the rugged interior of Dac Lac Province and on to the Cambodian border, and that land of mountains, plateaus, and highland forest had been a VC stronghold since early in the war. Intelligence believed that the VC were bringing troops and supplies down the Cai River into Nha Trang . . . worse, that it would be an invasion route soon. Recent VC/NVA offensives had concentrated on the far north of the country, up in Quang Tri Province, and the area around Saigon to the southwest. Future thrusts might well be aimed right down the center, striking out of the Central Highlands and snapping the slender country in two by seizing the coastal area between Qui Nhon and Cam Ranh.

Xa Dinh, then, an isolated village in a remote valley, had suddenly acquired considerable strategic importance, and one day its entire population had simply been relocated elsewhere. Greg wondered where they'd been taken, where they were now. Their absence made the SEALs' job simpler—anyone in Xa Dinh was automatically an enemy—but it was unsettling to think of an entire community simply whisked away, probably to an internment camp or "strategic hamlet," which from what he'd heard would be little better than a concentration camp.

What a lousy, fucking war. . . .

By 0530, the sky was swiftly growing light. Greg didn't see the figure enter the clearing; suddenly, he was simply there, a lone man in black pajamas and a coolie hat, carrying a weapon of some kind. A second figure emerged cautiously behind the first. Greg felt a jolt of recognition. They were *women*!

He glanced at Casey, almost completely invisible in the brush to his right. The Wheel would signal the start of the ambush by opening fire with his M-16, but he was obviously waiting for more VC to show themselves. Charlie often sent decoys ahead of his main body, and often those decoys were women.

Women. *Shit*! He'd known about the possibility, of course; BUD/S lectures had frequently dwelt on the possibility that he would have to fire on women . . . or even on people who in the sane world of the United States would be classified as children. He didn't like it. He licked his lips, tasting salt and the oily crayon taste of camo paint.

One of the women signaled, and more figures emerged from the forest. Greg could feel the tension rising among the hidden men; there were at least twenty-four people down there in all, most in peasant garb, a few in the khaki uniforms and pith helmets of NVA regulars. He could only see a few AKs in the group; most carried SKS or M1 carbines; several appeared unarmed, though they were carrying heavy packs or A-frame loads, or slinging crates along between poles balanced on the shoulders of two men. Likely, they were villagers from some nearby town pressed into service as beasts of burden. Perhaps twelve of the people, altogether, were armed.

It was still a powerful force, and Greg wondered whether Casey was going to hit it . . . or let it go.

He saw the Fish.

Even thirty yards away and in the poor light of early morning, the man's bulging eyes and fishlike expression were obvious. He was talking to two of the NVA troops, pointing toward the west, obviously enjoying a position of some authority.

And still the SEALs waited, as the crates and packs were piled up outside the large barracks, two VC were posted to guard it, and the rest began filing inside. Some of the unarmed people were dispersing to other hooches; it was possible, though by no means certain, that the armed Communist troops were staying together in one building, separate from the rest. This was probably a unit infiltrating from the Ho Chi Minh Trail in Cambodia through the Central Highlands to the coast . . . and the Fish, who would have an excellent knowledge of the local geography, must be serving the unit as a guide.

Greg let the sights of his Stoner rest on the Fish, following him as the man walked across the ville's central clearing. Their operational orders were to capture the man if at all possible, but to get him one way or another, and Greg was measuring his chances of crippling the man with a burst into his legs. If the guy was serving as a guide for incoming troops and supplies from the Ho Chi Minh Trail, he was even more valuable than Intelligence had thought, because he would have a good picture of rendezvous points, schedules, countersigns, and waypoints that would be of tremendous value in any future ops aimed at shutting down the flow of supplies from the North to this part of Vietnam.

Still talking, the Fish led the soldiers into the large hooch. Greg squinted over the sights of his Stoner, trying to slow the racing thud of his heart. When the Fish was out of sight, Greg acquired a new target—one of the guards at the supply dump. The Wheel had full go/no-go authority on the ambush. Was he going to fire? Damn it, *was he going to fire*? ...

The burst of gunfire from Casey's rifle was startlingly loud, its echo ringing back from the hillside, followed within a heartbeat by the thunderous chatter of the rest of the SEAL squad's weapons, all going full rock and roll. Greg's finger clamped down on his Stoner's trigger, loosing a short burst. The man he was aiming at spun to the left, arms flailing ... but it could have been anyone's fire that had marked him down. The second guard was down before he could acquire the target.

The unarmed porters were scattering in confusion, screaming, or simply standing in dumbfounded paralysis. Several VC soldiers who were still outside raised weapons to shoulders, but their heads were pivoting wildly back and forth as they tried to spot where the deadly fire was coming from, and then they were down, too. Another man smashed out through the hooch door, stumbled, and went down.

"Call the cavalry, Twidge!" Casey snapped, as the gunfire let up. There were no more targets visible.

Greg picked up the mike for the PRC-77 and keyed the transmitter. "Viper One! Viper One! This is Bushmaster!"

His voice sounded a little too loud, a little too strained, to his own ears. He tried to control it, but his heart was still thumping hard. "Do you copy? Over!"

"Bushmaster, Viper One," a calm voice replied over the speaker. "Go ahead."

"Viper One, Snakebite! I say again, Snakebite! Over!"

"Ah, roger that, Bushmaster. We have Snakebite. ETA ten mikes."

"I copy. Bushmaster, out." He looked at Casey. "On their way. Ten minutes."

The ready-helo force had gone back to the airstrip at Nha Trang to await First Squad's call, rather than flying all the way back to Cam Ranh Bay, which meant it was only a few minutes away.

Casey nodded, then gave the signal. *Go! Go!*

Heart still pounding furiously, Greg rose from ambush and started down the hill.

Saturday, 8 March 1969

Xa Dinh
Cai Song Valley
0532 hours

Casey led the way into the village, jogging up to the half-open barracks door. Slinger and Twidge dropped to their knees, facing outward, forming a defensive perimeter, while Doc began checking the bodies lying on the ground. Rodriguez and Ramsey made it to the hooch first, taking up positions on either side of the door. Ramsey held an M26 grenade, ready to toss if there was any sign of resistance, but the hooch remained death-silent. Casey gave a signal, and the two SEALs rolled into the building, Ramsey first with his sawed-off Ithaca shotgun, Rodriguez just behind with the M60.

"Clear!" Ramsey yelled from inside.

With swift efficiency, the SEALs outside began rounding up the civilians left behind by their VC comrades. Most had fled into the woods with the first volley, but four had remained behind, and the SEALs began securing them for transport, binding their hands behind their backs with the plastic ties from their prisoner-handling kits.

"Hey, Lieutenant?" Ramsey called from inside. "You'd better have a look!"

He stepped into the cool darkness of the barracks hooch. There were hammocks strung from palm-log roof supports, and numerous mattresses and piles of mosquito netting scattered about the floor. The place stank of *nuoc mam* and gun oil. There were no bodies inside . . . no sign at all of the dozen or more people who'd filed inside a few minutes ago, just before the SEALs went rock and roll. *Damn!*

"Look here, Skipper," Ramsey said, pointing. In the building's north wall, down near the floor, was a man-sized flap, cut from the wall and reattached with leather hinges. "They had a back door."

"Probably scooted through as soon as they heard us," Casey said. "What's out back?"

"A ditch, heading off into the woods, underneath a feed crib for the animals and some piles of wicker baskets. Bandit's checking it out now. My guess is that they dove out the back and crawled into the woods as soon as we opened up."

"Okay," Casey said, accepting the news. "Helos're inbound. We'll go to the backup."

"Right. I'll pass the word."

Casey began rooting through the possessions left behind, mindful of booby traps, but looking for documents or anything else of value. There wasn't much . . . a paper-bound book written in Vietnamese that appeared to be a copy of a U.S. Army manual on claymore mines. Something that might be a watch list or K.P. manifest. He pocketed them, then left the building as the roar of approaching helicopters thundered out of the eastern sky.

They circled low above the village, two Seawolf helicopters, one providing an armed overwatch, the other checking out the LZ, then settling down in the clearing in the center of the ville. Tangretti, Amadio, and Halstead led the prisoners toward the grounded chopper, picking them up bodily and tossing them aboard when they faltered or held back. Casey doubted if any were actual VC, but right now he needed a show for the ones that had managed to get away.

Casey trotted over to the helo and spoke for a moment to the pilot, shouting up at him through cupped hands against the rotor noise. The man nodded, and Casey moved back, signaling the other SEALs.

The helicopter's roar increased as it started to lift off. Casey gave the assemble signal. They were going to have to work smooth and fast now. . . .

"Ready to rock 'n' roll, sir?" Ramsey asked.

"Let's do it."

Chapter 31

Saturday, 8 March 1969

Xa Dinh
Cai Song Valley
0544 hours

In the center of the village, all was confusion, shouting, and noise. More SEALs—the members of Second Squad under Ensign Charles Dubois—leaped off thundering helos and noisily fanned through the village, searching huts, shouting orders, even performing some recon by fire, cutting loose with long bursts from their automatic weapons at random into the jungle, as though trying to elicit a response from the VC who must be hiding there. Some men went through the supplies piled outside the hooch, gathering up what they could—ammo and weapons, mostly—and tossing thermite grenades on the rest. A supply of rice was found in wicker baskets stashed in one of the other huts, and that was burned as well. In a few seconds, a black cloud of smoke was curling into the sky above Xa Dinh as rice, uniforms, web gear, and medical supplies burned.

Eventually, though, the SEALs reboarded the helicopters, some squeezing aboard the first aircraft with the prisoners, the rest waiting for the second chopper to touch down after the first had dusted off.

And then the second Seawolf was rising into the sky. It gave a final, defiant turn about the village, then wheeled off toward the east, leaving the dust suspended in the morning sunshine like a thin, golden cloud hanging above the silent center of the village. A pillar of smoke marked the burning supplies; some rounds of ammo continued cooking off as the fire burned, like fitful echoes of the departed Americans.

Five minutes passed ... then ten. A single man, clad in black pajamas and an ancient helmet of French manufacture, stepped into the village, his SKS carbine shifting uncertainly this way and that. Satisfied that the invaders were gone, he waved, and moments later a dozen of the Viet Cong who'd fled into the forest reappeared. They were nervous at first, almost mincing into the clearing ... but when they saw the village was empty, they became more animated, laughing loudly and calling to one another.

It's okay! The green faces are gone!

Clumsy Americans! ...

They busied themselves for a time, dragging the bodies of their comrades aside for later burial. They were not particularly dismayed by the raid; the loss of several hundred kilos of supplies laboriously hauled south down the Ho Chi Minh Trail was a nasty blow, but not an insurmountable one. There were plenty more where those had come from, and more still to be captured from the Americans, or even purchased from corrupt ARVN officers.

As always, men were the critical asset, the war matériel not easily replaced, and the only losses in that regard were a few peasant conscripts and some porters who knew little about the war and who cared less.

After a final, thorough search of the village, two of the VC soldiers took their places outside the large, central hooch, while the others opened the door and began filing inside.

In the forest, on the steep hillside above the village, there was the slightest of movements. ...

Gunfire ripped out, a savage, staccato brawl of noise as

five automatic weapons opened up as one. There was a sharp, teakettle's hiss, and a LAW rocket streaked down out of the night, slamming into the large hooch and detonating with a thunderous roar.

One of the guards went down at once; the second spun wildly, bounced off the front of the hooch, then sagged to the ground as the building at his back jumped and vibrated with the multiple impacts of hundreds of rounds. The door burst open again and someone came running out, arms circling wildly, collapsing in a heap before he'd gone five steps. A second LAW round streaked into the building, blowing out the entire north wall.

Casey held up his hand, palm down, fingers out, moving it in a sharp cutting gesture. *Cease fire!* The gunfire stopped almost as suddenly as it had begun, and now someone could be heard in the bullet-riddled hooch below, screaming in agony. Slowly, four of the SEALs rose from cover and moved down the hill. Halstead stayed behind, talking on the radio.

Bill Tangretti was stunned at the sheer power of that onslaught, which couldn't have lasted more than eight or ten seconds. The hooch had been partly stripped of thatching and nipa-palm–log walls, and the walls still standing had been riddled by bullets, shrapnel, and blast. A pile of wicker baskets stacked behind the hooch had been shredded, the fragments strewn across a quarter of the compound. Bodies were lying everywhere, inside the building and out. Some were still feebly moving.

Halstead waved the radio handset at Casey. "Choppers on their way back, sir!" he yelled. "ETA five mikes!"

"Get your ass down here!" Casey called back.

It was a trap already worked by other platoons in Team One, and generally with considerable success: hit the village, make a lot of noise, call in the choppers for a conspicuous dust-off . . . and in all of the confusion, leave a small stay-behind force to keep an eye on the objective. The ambush had not been particularly clean, since most of the targets had been out of sight inside the less-than-bulletproof hooch. Of twelve men who'd come back out of the forest, seven were dead, five wounded.

Tangretti entered the shattered frame of the hooch, probing

the smoky shadows with his Stoner. A light haze of smoke filled the air, creating a medium for dozens of shafts of sunlight lancing through the bullet holes and blown-out panels of the east wall. It was a charnel house in there, with limbs and less identifiable body parts scattered about like the bloody debris of a hurricane. Blood lay splattered everywhere, and the air had a coppery taste to it, mingled with the stink of feces.

He stopped dead, staring at one body, forcing himself to follow its lines and curves. It was a woman, her blood-matted hair spread out on the ground like a black-and-red oriental fan, her blouse ripped open to show her breasts and the trio of ugly bullet wounds that had mangled them. Another woman lay facedown nearby, her body unmarked except for the fact that the back of her head, from ear to ear, was missing.

Swallowing hard, Tangretti made himself keep moving. There were wounded men here who would be dead soon if he didn't do something fast. As the other SEALs spread out and began searching the area, he started checking the injured VC. Two, miraculously, were only slightly hurt, one with a bullet through his upper arm, the other with a bleeding cut in his scalp; they sat on the hooch floor, looking up at him with dulled expressions, stunned by the suddenness of the violence that had briefly whirled around them, unresisting even though several weapons lay within reach. Tangretti kept them covered as Slinger and Ramsey gathered up the weapons and took them outside, then gave each of them a Kotex napkin and showed them how to hold them against their wounds to stop the bleeding.

Two more of the wounded, Tangretti was certain after only the briefest of checks, were not going to make it. The scalp of one had been peeled back and his skull cap shattered; the top of his brain was exposed, a wet gray-pink and red mass that pulsed slightly with his fading heartbeat. He was unconscious, mercifully enough. The other was missing his right leg, and his torso had been torn from groin to navel; he was the one who'd been screaming moments ago, though by the time Tangretti reached him, the screams had dwindled to a feeble, whimpering moan. Tangretti tried to stop the *pump-*

pump-pump of bright red, arterial blood from the man's groin, but his body was too badly torn. He could do nothing but give the man some morphine to ease the pain as he bled to death.

The last wounded man was the Fish.

The VC guide and tax collector was in a bad way, gutshot. He'd taken a round or a piece of shrapnel that had sliced across his belly, opening him up like a hideous, blossoming flower. Bill could see his stomach and the dark, red-brown shroud of his liver exposed inside; his small intestines were spilling out, a glistening wet, uncoiling mass that threatened to spill out onto the dirt floor as the wounded man moved. He was obviously in agonizing pain. His bare feet were plowing furrows in the soft earth, and he was writhing back and forth, both bloody hands clutched over the obscene, gory horror of his bowels. His mouth gaped open, soundlessly screaming; no sound at all emerged save a dry, rattling whine . . . like the whimper of a mutilated puppy.

Swiftly, Tangretti knelt beside him, breaking open a medical kit and extracting a morphine syrette. He uncapped it, stabbed the needle deep into the man's biceps, and squeezed the tube empty. There wasn't a great deal he could do about the wound, not here. The faster they got the Fish to a field hospital, the more likely it would be that he could be fixed up . . . but that would take a full-fledged OR and a surgical team, not one SEAL medic in the middle of the jungle.

The emergency field first aid rules for belly wounds like this one were simple enough. You gave the patient nothing by mouth, you checked for bleeding, you treated him for shock. When his guts were spilling out in the dirt like this, you didn't try to put them back—and complicate the surgeons' job by including sticks, dirt, and God alone knew what else. Instead, he covered the exposed organs with his largest surgical dressing, then covered that over with a sanitary napkin, using several rolls of gauze bandage to wrap the whole tightly and securely.

"Is he going to make it, Doc?" Casey asked.

Still working, Tangretti shook his head. "Damn, I don't know. If we can get him to a hospital OR fast, yeah. He should."

"I have a feeling this guy's a prize, Doc. See that he makes it."

Tangretti was about to snap off a sharp reply, something about taking care of all of the wounded, but he said nothing. It had occurred to him, while he was bandaging the man, that it could have been a round from *his* Stoner that had sliced the Fish open; certainly, he'd been firing straight into those thin walls, sweeping the weapon back and forth to search out every corner. But then, so had all of them. There was no way of knowing who had hit whom.

It was a strange feeling, though, to be on both the killing and the healing end of things. The current rules for medical personnel in Vietnam actually forbade them from carrying weapons, though SEAL corpsmen ignored that rule routinely. When you only had seven operators to begin with in a squad, *everyone* humped weapons and fuck the rules, just as everyone carried a medical kit and could carry out emergency first aid on himself or on a buddy if he had to.

He kept working on the wounded man, trying desperately to save his life. By this time, the morphine was having its effect and the man was quieting some; Tangretti filled out a manila tag, listing the time he'd given the man morphine and a brief description of what he'd done, then wired it to his shirt collar. Finally, he used a grease pencil to mark the prisoner's forehead with a large, red M—a warning to the medical personnel who would see the man back at Cam Ranh that he'd already had morphine, a safeguard against overdosing him into a coma.

It was, Tangretti thought, a fascinating bit of irony. A few minutes before he'd been doing his best to kill this guy.

Now he was doing all he could to save his life.

0610 hours

For Greg, the scene in Xa Dinh held a mingling of horror and utter fantasy. This had been his first time in combat . . . the first time he'd killed someone. He kept telling himself that the man he'd fired at *could* have been hit by any one of the SEALs firing from ambush, but something inside kept telling him that the thought was an empty attempt at rationalization. He thought about the old idea of a firing squad, where the men are told that one of their rifles is loaded with a blank cartridge so that they will always have some small measure of doubt about whether or not it was *their* shot that killed the prisoner. There was a basic fallacy built into that palliative, of course; the man firing a blank didn't feel the kick of recoil, while those with loaded weapons did.

And Greg recognized the fallacy here as well. He'd aimed at the guy and felt his Stoner buck and thunder in his grip; the target—how impersonal that word seemed now!—the target had thrown up his arms, twisted in a grotesque parody of dance, and fallen. Perhaps others had hit the man as well, but Greg had no doubt that his rounds had contributed to the man's death.

It was far worse as he entered the ruin of the thatched barracks. The heaviest building materials in the entire structure were sheets of plywood in the walls and some sheet tin in the roof; most of the walls were thatching and palm log, bamboo and nipa-palm leaves, which were about as effective at keeping out that sudden, sleeting storm of lead as tissue paper. The SEAL ambush had riddled the flimsy structure and chopped down everything inside.

Following Bill into the wrecked hooch, he stopped when he saw the bodies of the two women, stopped and swallowed hard to keep the rising lump in his throat in place, then moved on. He'd known they were in here . . . and did it really matter what their sex was? They'd been carrying weapons; if they'd had the chance, they would have shot him down without a second thought.

Well, you wanted to be a goddamned SEAL. . . .

He very much wanted to talk with Pat, wanted to write her another letter at the very least. He wanted desperately to believe that what he was doing was right, that it would make a difference in ending this war, that it was saving American lives, that there was some *reason* for this bloody business.

He was pretty sure that his father would accept what had happened here. *War is war, and war means killing.*

His mother, well, she wouldn't want to think about such things, but she would tell him she loved him and that he was her son and that sometimes you had to do things you didn't like.

What really mattered to him, however, was what Pat would think. He knew what her antiwar friends would say. *Baby-killer! Murderer!* What, though, would *she* say?

He found that it mattered a very great deal.

Greg saw Bill bending over one terribly wounded VC. Moving closer, he was surprised to see that the wounded man was the Fish. The lieutenant, he thought, would be happy about that. Prisoners were always better than corpses, and Casey had been eager to take the Fish alive. What did Bill think about this slaughter, though?

"Need a hand, Doc?" he asked him.

"Nah," Tangretti replied, distracted. "Thanks anyway." Then he nodded at the two lightly wounded men, who were sitting just outside a blown-down wall, with Slinger standing guard over them. "You can go check those guys, and make sure they're keeping those pressure bandages in place."

"Sure thing." He started turn away. "God, what a mess."

"War is hell, man."

"Yeah. I'm starting to realize that. Especially when it's up close and personal, you know?"

Tangretti ripped a strip of gauze roll, then tied the end tightly, holding the dressings in place on the Fish's abdomen. "No push-button warriors here, Twidge."

He was right. That was part of what was bothering him, Greg realized. He'd been able to come to grips with the idea of killing someone—a faceless enemy, a tiny and indistinct shape above his rifle sights at a range of three hundred yards.

But these people had faces—most of them, anyway. He didn't know their names, but he could think of them as people. Not "gooks." Not "dinks." Not "targets." Not "casualties."

People. . . .

0616 hours

With the patient as stable as he could make him, Bill Tangretti then saw to the other seriously wounded prisoners, making sure that both stayed flat on the ground to avoid the

effects of delayed shock. By the time he was done, the helicopters were back, one circling on lookout, the other gentling to rest in the village clearing, where Rodriguez had
tossed down a colored smoke grenade to bring the birds in.

The man with the missing leg died before they could load
him aboard a chopper; the one with the savage head wound
died during the flight back. The Fish, however, lived, though
Bill still wasn't sure if he was going to make it or not. Belly
wounds were always problematical on airborne medevacs; as
the aircraft went up, air pressure dropped, expanding gas
trapped in the bowels and threatening to eviscerate the patient completely as internal pressures increased. Tangretti
tried to counter that by threading a stomach tube down the
man's throat and past the pylorus, and by warning the helicopter pilot not to fly too high. Then he slid an IV needle
into a vein in the man's arm, taped it in place, and attached
a plastic bag of serum albumin which he held high, letting
the golden fluid trickle into the man's system. If he could
avoid having him go into shock, maybe . . .

The other SEALs in the helicopter with him watched his
efforts to save the wounded man with expressions curiously
detached and remote, though both Slinger and Halstead offered to help. They were tired, and postbattle letdown was
setting in. Tangretti had to force himself to hold his focus
on the job of keeping the prisoner alive. Exhaustion dragged
at him like a great weight slung from his back and shoulders.
After a time, there was nothing more that could be done,
save hold the albumin bag high, and keep an eye on the
patient's color and breathing.

In less time than Tangretti had imagined possible, the Seawolf was circling over Cam Ranh Bay, flying north and then
east of the peninsula for the final approach to the facility's
Mainside airbase. With a roar of rotors and a swirl of dust,
the helo settled down on its landing skids on the base airstrip.

The SEALs began piling out. Bill stayed with the patient,
however, as a pair of Army medics arrived, reaching up into
the cargo area to take the stretcher down from the Huey.
Holding the IV bag aloft with one hand and steadying the
slap-slap of the Stoner slung over his shoulder with the other,
he hurried along beside the stretcher toward a truck marked

with the Geneva red cross. The wounded man looked up at him, the protruding eyes glassy with pain, shock, and drugs. With one blood-smeared hand, he reached up and grabbed Tangretti's combat vest.

Tangretti grinned at the man, still not knowing if he spoke any English at all. "Don't worry, friend," he told the Fish. "You're gonna be okay. You! *Anh*! Okay! *Tot lam*! *Anh tot lam*! Understand?"

"*Cam on!*" the man said. "*Cam on rhat nieu!*" Tangretti felt the emotion behind the man's thanks.

"We got him now, Doc," one of the medics said. They'd reached the ambulance and were loading the POW aboard. One of them took the IV bag from Tangretti's hand, and he was left standing alone on the tarmac.

Almost alone. A man in OD utilities and a baseball cap was standing a few feet away, watching Tangretti with a curious expression. He had several cameras hanging around his neck by their straps. "You're 'Doc'?" the man asked.

"They call me that," Tangretti replied. "Who are you?"

"Doug Benson," he replied. "Associated Press. I'm here with the admiral."

Dimly, Tangretti realized that Benson must mean Admiral Zumwalt. He was pretty sure that this guy, complete with cameras, had been part of the admiral's entourage the other day, during the inspection.

"I'm real happy for you." Tangretti started to walk back toward the other SEALs, who were filing out of the Huey.

"Just a moment, Doc," Benson said. "What the hell's that thing on your back?"

"Huh?" Tangretti blinked. He hadn't even felt the weight of the Stoner and had to think for a moment to realize what the man was referring to. "Oh. That's my Stoner."

"What *is* it?"

"The Stoner Mark 23 Mod 0 Commando is a 5.56-millimeter belt-fed, gas-operated machine gun, a variant of the Stoner 63A weapons system, with a rate of fire of seven hundred fifty rounds per minute and a—"

Benson had been signaling for several seconds. "Whoa! Whoa there! I got 'machine gun.' It's a machine gun?"

"That's what I said."

Benson reached into one of his canvas pouches and extracted a small cassette tape recorder. "Do you mind? What's your name?"

"Bill," he said.

"Ha! That's right! I remember you from the inspection the other day! You're the guy who shook hands with the admiral!"

Tangretti was surprised that Benson had recognized him through all of the face paint. "Look, I'm pretty tired right now, Mr. Benson—"

"Hey, this won't take a moment! What is your rate, anyway?"

"I'm a third class. E-4."

"No, no. That's your rank! I mean your *rate*!"

"I'm a SEAL. SEAL Team One."

"That medic called you 'Doc.' Doesn't that mean you're a hospital corpsman?"

"Oh . . . yeah." Tangretti shrugged. "I guess so." Hospital Corps School, Great Lakes, seemed about a million miles and a million years away, just now. SEALs, he'd found, rarely even thought about their formal ratings.

Benson shoved the tape recorder a little closer. Tangretti could see the tape inside the cassette slowly turning.

"Well, help me out here, Doc. What are you doing carrying a machine gun? I mean, the Geneva Convention clearly states that medical personnel are *not* supposed to be armed and are not supposed to engage in combat. I think there's a provision for a sidearm, for self-protection, but that monster you're hauling there is a bit more than a sidearm, don't you think?" His eyes narrowed. "You know, I believe the Geneva Convention also requires medical personnel to wear prominent Geneva red crosses on their uniforms. Now, you're not wearing a helmet, but surely you should be wearing an armband with—"

"*Are you fucking nuts?*"

Benson's jaw dropped, and he blinked rapidly several times, shaking his head as if to clear it. "I . . . uh . . . beg your pardon?"

"Do you think there is fucking *anyone* in this fucking

country who gives a fuck about the Geneva fucking Convention? . . ."

"But you're not allowed to carry a machine gun!"

Tangretti took a step toward the man, his voice dropping to an intimate growl. His fist closed on the front of Benson's fatigue shirt, drawing him closer to Tangretti's paint-smeared face. "Mister, if you can get Charlie to abide by the *rules*, I'll consider it! But red crosses make great bull's-eyes out there, and that's about all they're fucking good for!"

"But—"

"When Charlie hits an American patrol, he's looking to cap three guys first . . . the CO, the radioman, and the medic! As for the weapon, I just wish to hell I could carry three of these things out there, and maybe a sawed-off shotgun to balance the load!"

The reporter seemed to be recovering his composure. Carefully, he disentangled himself from Tangretti's grip on his collar. "Look, uh, Bill. I really would like to—"

"Excuse me," another voice said. A hand reached past Tangretti's shoulder and snatched the tape recorder out of Benson's hand. "I'll just take this, sir, *if* you don't mind."

Benson gaped. "Wha! . . . Hey! You can't—"

Then he saw who was speaking, and his mouth snapped shut. Tangretti turned and found himself face-to-face—once again—with Admiral Elmo Zumwalt.

"Mr. Benson, you are not authorized to be in this area."

"I most certainly—"

"You are *not*!" The admiral popped the tape cassette out of the machine, dropped it in his shirt pocket, and handed the recorder back to the reporter. "Furthermore, you are not to talk to these men. You have never met these men. In fact, these men do not exist. They are not here. They were *never* here. Do I make myself clear?"

Benson opened his mouth to say something, then closed it again. The other members of Casey's Commandos had seen that something was going down and had walked over, surrounding Benson, Tangretti, and the admiral in a ring of savagely painted, grim, and heavily armed men.

"You will come with me, sir," Zumwalt concluded.

Benson took another look at the firepower and hostile attitudes surrounding him, and nodded. "Yes, sir."

Zumwalt turned away, the reporter following after him. Abruptly, Zumwalt stopped, turned, and looked at Tangretti. "Doc," he said, his voice showing wry exasperation, "*don't* talk to reporters!"

"Aye, aye, sir!" Tangretti rasped.

Zumwalt grinned at him, then strode off, the reporter trailing behind.

"I'll be a son of a bitch," Tangretti said quietly.

"Good thing you have friends in high places, Doc," Greg said. "That reporter was out for blood!"

"Yeah," Bandit added. "Yours."

Tangretti walked back toward a waiting truck that would take them back to the SEAL compound, feeling somewhat bemused. It was only now occurring to him that he'd not thought once during that operation about booby traps, the secret terror he'd once feared would paralyze him the next time he was in combat. He'd been too busy, first operating with the squad, then saving a man's life, to worry.

Maybe I'm going to make it after all.

He wondered, though, what Pat would think about this strange, dual nature of his, killer and healer together in one package.

He wasn't sure he knew himself what to think. More than anything else, he needed a hot shower and some rack time.

All of the rest could take care of itself.

Chapter 32

Camp, Ham Tam Island
Nha Trang Bay, Republic of Vietnam
0730 hours

Nguyen Chi Lam emerged from the bunker, looking up into the incessant drizzle. This was the dry season near Saigon, but the seasons were different up here, in the central part of the country, along the coast. Here, the dry season ran from June through October; the wettest time started in late October and ran through November, with rain falling nearly every night and most mornings. Generally, March was a clear month on the coast, but days like this reminded Lam of the fact that he was far indeed from his home. The difference in rainy seasons—inexplicable, so far as Lam was concerned— helped hammer home his intense feelings of homesickness.

Lam had been born and raised in Hoc Mon, a town located just a few kilometers northwest of the sprawling airport at Tan Son Nhut, on the outskirts of Saigon. His father had been a woodcutter; his name "Lam," in fact, meant "forest."

The war had not intruded much in Lam's day-to-day life while he was growing up. This close to Saigon, there was little overt Communist activity . . . though everyone in the village knew that VC cadres passed through the region regularly. Hoc Mon was almost exactly halfway between Tan Son Nhut and the town of Cu Chi; and it was common knowledge, at least to the residents of Hoc Mon, that there was an extensive tunnel network at Cu Chi, one so vast, it was whispered, that it reached clear to Cambodia.

"It's wet." Phan Nhu Hung was standing nearby, his AK-47 slung muzzle down behind his shoulder. "Not a good day."

Lam shivered. He looked up toward the forest canopy, turning slowly in place as the drizzle spit and misted against his face. The jungle here was thick enough it was impossible to realize that they were on an island. The cliffs that divided the island in half were visible through the trees a few hundred meters to the north, but in every other direction there was only the impenetrable green of the forest. "It is *never* a good day, Hung. Not here. I do not like this place."

Hung chuckled and nodded, the motion jarring loose a small shower of water droplets beading along the rim of his gray sun helmet. "I know what you mean, Lam. I wish we could both be home."

"Do you have a cigarette?"

Hung glanced both ways, then reached into his tunic, extracting a pack of Russian cigarettes. Cadre discipline frowned on smoking while on duty. It was well-known that the Americans could be *smelled* while they were still hundreds of meters distant by the cigarette smoke that clung to them incessantly . . . and much farther than that if they were smoking marijuana. The others were inside, however, and on the other side of the compound. Lam accepted the cigarette gratefully; Hung lit it for him, cupping the flame carefully in his hand to shield it from the drizzle, then lit one of his own. For a long time, they stood together, simply sharing the comfort of each another's company.

They were unlikely friends, these two, for Hung was both from the North and from a city at that, the great port of Haiphong on the Cam River, just one hundred kilometers from Hanoi itself. Lam had met him only six months ago, when he'd arrived as a replacement for poor Trung Van Be, who'd died of malaria. Despite their differences, they'd become friends.

In Lam's experience, the Northerners tended to be stiff, proud, and arrogant, and *all* city people looked down on farmers and woodcutters and other people who lived and worked in the countryside. He'd mistrusted them all, as he'd always mistrusted anyone from farther away than the next village, but Hung was different. He'd been friendly, and perhaps a little lost and vulnerable when he'd first arrived at Lam's encampment. One night, sitting by the campfire, Hung had told him a little about his life in Haiphong before he'd "volunteered," about how the girls he'd known had teased him, about the agonizing trip south that had taken him over six months to complete. He told of the B-52 attack, and how the jungle had flashed and shaken, and he told of his feelings when he saw the people he'd been traveling with—his new friends—torn into bloody, unrecognizable shreds by the fury of the American attack.

Lam soon recognized in Hung a kindred spirit, a man who'd been through many of the same things Lam had experienced, and more. Certainly, he knew the same pains, the same longings and homesickness. They both hated their leaders, both hated the orders—sometimes wildly inappropriate, or even nonsensical—that seemed to be issued without regard to human feeling or failing.

Both men wore leather bands about their left wrists. One of the special dreads for Vietnamese in this war was the fear that they would not be properly buried. Many of the men wore these bands so that, if they died in battle, their comrades could use wire hooks to reach out, snag the band, and drag their bodies away into the forest rather than leaving them to rot or be impiously disposed of by the government troops or the Americans. Hung's wristband had been Lam's first indication that this man might not be like the other Northerners. He thought of himself as mortal and feared what might happen to his corpse if he were killed.

He'd known that Hung was much like him almost from the beginning. He'd decided that he actually *liked* Hung, however, the day the Northerner admitted to him that he hated the jungle . . . and Lam had confided in reply, "Who doesn't?" The moment had created a bond for them, a shared secret that excluded the Party and the cadres and the Ten Oaths of the Soldier and all of the political education officers of the National Liberation Front.

In truth, no Vietnamese liked the jungle. The joke was that the Americans assumed that the Communists *liked* it there and lived in it by preference, that the Americans thought of the NLF and their Northern allies as superb jungle fighters. Lately, it seemed, even the cadres seemed to have picked up this particular bit of idiocy and begun believing in it. "We rule the jungle," Captain Ngai liked to tell them in their weekly political meetings, "as we rule the night! The Americans are the elephant, blundering through the forest, extremely powerful, yes, but blind and helpless to the stealthy approach of the tiger. We are the tiger, unseen within the jungle that is our home, who will strike at the elephant's feet and flanks time and time again, until the beast succumbs at last and is bled to death. . . ."

And that was simply so much buffalo piss. The People's Front did not rule the jungle. No one could rule such a place. You either survived the jungle, or you died . . . and there were so many things lurking there, waiting to kill you. The snakes were the worst. Lam had always hated snakes, and snakebite had taken a fearful toll of NLF troops, who generally went barefoot or wore rubber-soled sandals. Malaria was bad, too; Lam had heard that more comrades had been killed by that debilitating specter than from all other causes combined, including enemy action, and nearly everyone was subject to periodic chills, fevers, and malaise.

Sometimes, though, Lam thought that the worst part of life was simply the boredom. Nothing ever happened, especially at a remote and secret camp like this one. Though he'd not been eager to leave his home and join the Communists, he'd held some of his darker fears at bay by promising himself that at the very least he would enjoy some excitement. Battle, after all, was supposed to be exciting, was it not? The thrill of gunfire, the glory of striking down enemies. . . .

Lam had been in combat only a handful of times, and only twice had he actually *seen* the enemy . . . both times a patrol of ARVN soldiers. One of Lam's secret shames was that he couldn't remember whether he'd actually *fired* at them. On both occasions, his magazine had been empty afterward, but, try as he might, he could not remember actually taking aim and squeezing the trigger, as the comrade instructors had taught him to do.

So far, he'd found less excitement in combat than he'd found pure, stark terror.

"So," Hung said after a long and companionable silence. "Did you hear what happened at Than Phu?"

Lam looked up, inhaling the warm, throat-scratching smoke. "No."

Hung shook his head. "It's not good. I heard they've found comrades dead in the night, their faces streaked with green paint."

Lam's eyes widened. His breath snagged in his throat. "The Men With Green Faces!"

"Several of our people are missing there, as well." He tossed his head, indicating the command bunker, unseen beyond the trees. "They say a new American commando unit has just arrived at Cam Ranh Bay, the Soldiers Who Fight Beneath the Sea. They say that they are going to be operating throughout this whole area."

Lam's right hand moved involuntarily to his side. "I've . . . I've heard terrible things about these . . . commandos."

Hung's eyes flicked to Lam's hand, resting on his side, then back to Lam's eyes. "I've heard the stories, too. I don't know if they're true, Lam. Sometimes, it's hard to know what is true and what is lie."

Lam had heard many stories about the Men With Green Faces, how they were not men at all, but supernatural horrors that emerged at night from the hated jungle to devour comrades, how they could see in the dark, how they were skilled at certain incantations or mental disciplines that allowed them to make themselves invisible, how they liked to eat the livers of their victims.

That last particularly horrified Lam. Stories circulated through every NLF camp, each more outrageous than the last, but wide-eyed soldiers more than once had told of comrades found dead in their huts. Guards posted just outside had seen and heard nothing, yet the victims had been found horribly mutilated, their faces streaked with green paint, their bellies slit open with surgical skill, and their livers removed and laid upon their chests . . . each with a large, ragged bite taken out of the organ.

There was a particular, retching horror in that, the stuff of endless nightmares. A man whose liver had been eaten could never enter Nirvana intact. Some said the green paint on the face was just to let the living know who'd done the deed; others claimed that it was part of the black magic, that the victim's soul would become a slave to the enemy's demands for all eternity.

Lam had made a decision during the past few days . . . a decision that had been gnawing at him all that time as he wrestled with the problem of how to tell Hung. The problem was there was no good way to say it, even though he was pretty sure his friend would understand. Wordlessly, Lam reached into a pocket and extracted the leaflet.

Hung's eyes widened, and again he glanced in both directions, as though fearing that the jungle itself was watching. "It is dangerous to have that on you, friend. If Ngai caught you . . ."

"Are you going to turn me in?"

For answer, Hung reached into his own blouse and pulled out an identical leaflet. Lam could not read, but he knew well enough what the writing said. It was both a call to members of the National Liberation Front to rally to the legitimate government of Vietnam, and a safe-conduct pass, requiring members of the Army of the Republic of Vietnam to allow the bearer to enter government lines unharmed. It told of the "Open Arms" program, the Chieu Hoi, and promised that those who rallied would be well treated.

"We have no promise that the government troops won't kill us anyway," Hung said. "The cadres say the Saigon puppets torture their prisoners."

"I wonder if their torture is worse than the torture of remaining *here*?" Lam asked.

There seemed to be no answer to that. They stood there for a time listening to the jungle.

"So," Lam said finally. "When are we going to do it?"

"It can't be too soon for me," Hung replied. He shook his head in disgust. "Troung has been riding me lately about ridiculous things. I want out of here."

"Me too. I just—"

"What?"

"I wonder if it is the right thing to do."

Hung gave an unpleasant smile. "You care for the revolution that much?"

Lam shrugged. "So long as the government left me and my family alone, I never saw that much reason to support a revolution. Revolution against what? I would have fought against the Americans, of course, had they come and tried to take my land or family . . . but all we heard about the Americans was that they came to fight the NLF."

"If it weren't for the revolution, the Americans would not have come," Hung agreed. "So what worries you?"

Lam gave a short bark of laughter, but it was ragged with fear. "What doesn't worry me? If we are found out, if we are caught, we will be disciplined. Perhaps severely."

"True enough." They both knew the penalty for desertion. If they were lucky, it would be a bullet in the back of the head. If the cadres decided to make an example of them . . .

"But why should the government troops, or the Americans, honor these scraps of paper? We could come out of the jungle and they could shoot us down where we stand."

"Again, true. But the alternative is to stay here. Sooner or later, the Americans will come for us."

"The Men With Green Faces?"

"Perhaps." He shook himself. "I don't like thinking about them."

"Nor I."

"They will not shoot us, however, if we can provide them with payment. Something in exchange for our lives."

Lams snorted. "I have no money. Besides, they could take what they want."

"Actually, I was thinking of a different type of coin. We can offer them this camp."

"You mean . . . work with them? Lead them back here?"

"Exactly. It's not as though we would be betraying friends or family." He made a sour face. "I have no one here, except you."

The admission made Lam feel warm.

"The best time to make our move," Hung continued, after a moment's thought, "will be two days from now."

"Why then?"

"Because the sapper company will be on the mainland that night. Something about a raid in the interior. Only Ngai and a few of the cadres will be here, besides us. The camp will be poorly guarded. That means it will be easy for us to slip away without being seen, and easy for the government forces to come and capture the documents Ngai and the others have hidden in the cave."

"That makes good sense." Lam felt troubled, though. He had no love for Ngai or the others, especially, but they were still his comrades in hardship, and he would hate to be the one responsible for their deaths. "You are with me, then?"

Hung clapped his shoulder. "With you! Whatever comes!"

"You know, once we have won our freedom," Lam said, "and we return to our homes, I will miss you."

"I will not be leaving."

"I thought you missed your home, in Haiphong?"

Hung laughed. "It will be difficult for you to make your way home, my friend. For me, such a journey is out of the question! Imagine! There I am, a deserter, no papers, no orders, walking north along the Ho Chi Minh Trail! I would be arrested at once. At best, they would assume I'd been lost and put me into another battalion. More likely I would be shot.

"And even if I managed to elude capture, to sneak all the way back to my home in the North, what then? I would still have to face the women. The young men, if they are still there, would remember me. The old people would certainly remember me and wonder why I had returned. If I was missing a leg or two, perhaps that would suffice. But I am still too healthy and too much in one piece to look convincing as an invalid!"

"But then . . . where will you go?" Lam was mortified. He'd not fully thought out the consequences of his friend's situation. He'd simply assumed that both of them would be going home.

"I will find a place to live," Hung said. "Perhaps I will lose myself in the city. Saigon is a very big place, and I understand there is lots of work available there.''

"With the Americans.''

"Yes, with the Americans.'' He grinned, nudging Lam in the ribs. "Perhaps I will become rich!''

Clearly, there was a lot to consider that Lam had not thought about. If Hung couldn't go home . . . what about him? His family, he thought, would be glad to see him and would not consider him to be a traitor for having deserted from the NLF, but others in the village were Communists, he knew, and the Communists were always traveling through the town, on their way between Cu Chi and Saigon.

"Perhaps you could come home with me,'' he said uncertainly. "Or it may be that you have the better idea. Perhaps I will come to Saigon with you.''

"We will be rich together! Brother!''

They laughed.

"In two days, then,'' Hung said. "We will wait until Ngai and the rest have gone, then slip out while one or the other of us is supposed to be on guard duty. That will give us six hours.''

"Longer,'' Lam volunteered. "If we arrange our schedules so that I'm on first, and you are to relieve me . . .''

"Perfect! We leave together, as soon as your watch begins. With luck, they won't even realize we both are missing until the next day.''

"I'm just worried about one thing.''

"What is that, Lam?''

"Suppose we meet the Men With Green Faces before we leave? They will never believe that we were going to surrender anyway!''

"A risk that must be taken, Lam. I doubt that they even know this base is here. That's what makes it a valuable bargaining tool for our purposes.''

"Perhaps,'' Lam said, half-seriously, "we should pray to them, that they stay away until after we have left!''

"Somehow,'' Hung said, his brow creasing, "I never thought of the Men With Green Faces as spirits that could be reasoned with. Most demons can be placated with the proper ceremony or offering, but these . . .''

Lam shuddered. "I know. The devil of the Westerners would be more sympathetic."

"With luck, we will not have to deal with them."

Lam took some comfort from that thought.

Chapter 33

Thursday, 13 March 1969

SEAL Compound
Cam Ranh Bay, Republic of Vietnam
1620 hours

The SEALs of Delta Platoon had been trickling into the bull pen for several minutes now. Casey watched them with considerable pride. They'd been on a number of ops now throughout the Cam Ranh AO and had proven themselves . . . and their training.

Those ops had started paying off big-time, too, in terms of intelligence gathered . . . especially in their picture of how the VCI was set up and working in Khanh Hoa Province.

He watched Bill Tangretti walk into the room, exchange a friendly jibe with Twidge Halstead, and take a seat. Throughout the past month, Casey had found himself relying heavily on those members of his platoon with previous combat experience, men like Tangretti and Ramsey, but the Doc had pulled off a real coup five days ago when he'd saved the life of that VC bigshot up at Xa Dinh. They'd gotten him to the hospital at Cam Ranh in time, and the Naval Intelligence boys had been with the guy ever since he'd woken up after surgery. Someone a little further up the chain of command than Casey—he wasn't sure, but he privately wondered if it had been Zumwalt himself—had arranged for

Nguyen Dinh Ca, a.k.a. "the Fish," to remain under Navy jurisdiction, rather than having him turned over to the ARVN.

Delta Platoon was starting to "operate," building up a solid intel picture of its AO. And now that intel was about to pay off.

As the last SEAL sat down in one of the folding metal chairs, Lieutenant Gillespie walked to the front of the room. A large-scale map hung there, showing the tangle of islands and promontories along the broken and deeply indented coastline around Nha Trang.

"Good afternoon, gentlemen," Gillespie said. "We've got a hot one for you today."

There was a rustle of movement among the listening SEALs. Some were leaning forward, intent and eager.

The NILO pointed to the map. "Nha Trang is located on the coast just thirty miles north of Cam Ranh Bay," he continued. "It's located along one of the nicest beaches in Southeast Asia."

"You can say that again, Lieutenant," someone called from the audience. A ripple of laughter circled the room. During the past month, the SEALs had been getting to know Nha Trang well. The place was famous for its seafood, for its five-kilometer-long sandy white beach, and for the girls—mostly locals, but with a few round-eye nurses or relief workers appearing from time to time—often in skimpy bikinis. Delta Platoon SEALs had reconned the beach on several occasions, bringing back stories of various levels of unbelievability about the action that followed.

Gillespie waited for the noise to die down, a disapproving frown on his face, then pushed ahead. "Offshore . . . here, and in the mouth of the Cai River to the north . . . here, are a large number of rocky islands. Some of them are quite steep and difficult. Good cover, but treacherous ground in places.

"Late last night, gentlemen, two VC defectors came in. They're sick of the war, and I gather they're pretty shook by the idea that the Men With Green Faces have just popped up in their backyard. They brought us some very interesting information."

He pointed out a particular island in Nha Trang Bay, between the city and the large island of Tre off the coast. ''This is Ham Tam Island. It's not very large, and it's dominated on the north side by this hill. That hill is like a rock wall coming up out of the sea three hundred fifty feet high, and it limits the usable ground on Ham Tam to this small area south of the cliffs. It's a good defensive position. One lookout up on this hilltop can see the whole bay, and a camp down here in the forest at the foot of the cliffs has its back to the wall, literally. It only has to defend against an approach from the south.

''Our informants say that the local VCI has an intelligence team on Ham Tam. Only five men, but they run a much larger intelligence apparatus that extends throughout this entire part of Vietnam. We're not sure, but this net has most likely penetrated every ARVN and government base, organization, and unit in Nha Trang, and possibly in Cam Ranh, Ninh Hoa, and as far south as Phan Rang. We think this organization controls all of the VC and NVA intelligence for Khanh Hoa Province . . . and possibly for Thuan Hai Province as well. They are also behind a number of sapper raids in the Nha Trang–Cam Ranh Bay area.

''Thanks to the good work by First Squad the other night, in the raid on Xa Dinh, we can corroborate a lot of what these two defectors are telling us. We know the VCI is pretty strong through this area and that they have solid logistical lines feeding off the Ho Chi Minh Trail. The prisoner you people brought back, the gutshot guy, told us an awful lot about the local political setup, and it corroborates a lot of what our Hoi Chanhs are telling us.

''For this op, we want to make a covert insertion on Ham Tam Island. Find the base and hit it. We want documents and we want prisoners.

''There's a time limit on this one. Our defectors were part of the intelligence team's security. According to them, it's not unusual for them to be gone for as much as twenty-four hours at a time, off in Nha Trang or elsewhere, but if they're gone much longer, the VC intel team is going to assume they've defected or been captured. They'll leave Ham Tam, probably for a backup site on some other island in the bay

. . . or possibly squirreled away up in the Cai Song Valley. Either way, if that happens, we'll be back to square one. This is the best opportunity we've ever had to catch the local VC spooks and get a good look at their side of the intelligence picture. I don't need to remind you of what a treasure trove the load of documents they must have stashed on that island must be. Pay and personnel records for VC agents. Tax lists. Code books. Radio call signs and protocols. Recognition passwords. Directives and instructions from Hanoi. Maybe copies of orders sent to all of the agents throughout the province.

"You've all heard, I'm sure, about SEAL Two's Tenth Platoon's big score at My Tho in May of last year. Intelligence was able to grab the names of every VC agent working inside ARVN and U.S. military bases in the province. The bad guys were shut down completely, and the arrests of those agents probably blinded them in the My Tho area for six months or more. That's what we're hoping to do here. Charlie hasn't been seriously challenged out here. With Market Time and some of the other naval ops going on along the coast, we've pretty much kept him on the run at sea, but he's been sitting fat and happy ashore, holed up in places like the Cai Song Valley and thumbing his nose at us. If we can hit Ham Tam before the VC spooks pull a fast fade, and especially if we can grab their records, we should be able to shut them down cold throughout the Khanh Hoa District.

"So, in order to take advantage of this opportunity, we need the raid to go down tonight, predawn. There won't be time for a preliminary scouting of the objective. You'll go in after dark. First Squad will take the insertion. Second Squad will provide backup." Several members of the Second Squad groaned at that, and Casey grinned. The competition for combat ops could be pretty keen at times.

"Your insertion will be by SEAL Team Assault Boat," Gillespie continued, ignoring the interruption. "Your support unit will be a second STAB that will be operating nearby, close enough to move in and lend a hand if you need it. Primary extraction will be by Seawolf helicopter when you have the camp secured. Emergency extract, if you run into something you can't handle, will be by STAB.

"You shouldn't run into any problems, however. Our defectors were certain that no more than five men will be on the island tonight, and they won't be heavily armed. Occasionally, more show up for a special powwow, or when there's going to be a major sapper operation, but that's pretty infrequent. For obvious reasons, Charlie doesn't like large numbers of people going in and out of Ham Tam. Doesn't want to attract attention."

He pulled down another map, one showing the island in greater detail. "The defectors have identified two possible sites where these bad guys hang out. Here, at the main base . . . a camp, really, tucked in close to the south face of the cliff. And here, about a hundred meters away, near the south beach. There's a building there, near a small pier. We're calling it the barracks, but it's probably just a storage shed for fishermen or other temporary visitors on the island. Over here, about two hundred meters from the other two sites, is a clearing, big enough for a Seawolf to set down. That will be your primary extraction site.

"So, here's the drill. Standard operational orders. Force members will choose their own weapons and kit. The insertion force will be First Squad, plus one LDNN liaison officer—that will be Mr. Vinh—and the two defectors, of course." Gillespie looked up at the sudden unsettled creak and scrape of chairs in the room. "I'm told the defectors are completely cooperative and are quite eager to help us. They will lead us to the island, show us precisely where the VC camps are, and point out the people we're most interested in.

"You'll have your choice as to the approach. Mr. Casey, I'd like to see an operational plan from you by eighteen hundred."

"Sure thing."

"Find the bad guys and neutralize them. Take 'em prisoner if you can. Search both sites for documents, explosives, weapons. Move to the LZ and call in your extraction bird. Questions?"

Greg Halstead raised his hand.

"Yeah."

"Sir, aren't the water approaches to the island pretty open?

How come these VC agents are able to go back and forth between the island and the mainland without being seen?''

"Fair question. The trouble is that there's a hell of a lot of coastal traffic in the bay, and it's just not practical to stop or search every damned sampan, junk, and canoe. Any of you people sample the local bird's nest soup?'' A couple of hands went up. ''It's a delicacy, or so I'm told. The nests are built by a certain kind of sea swallow, high up on the rocky hills and cliffs on most of the islands in the area. Hunters climb around all of these islands quite a bit, gathering nests which they sell for soup, and for a medicinal tonic. I'm told the white nests fetch a fair price back in Nha Trang, but the red and pink ones are damn near worth their weight in gold. That means lots of coming and going by the locals, though I don't think you boys will run into any of them at zero-dark-thirty. But it does explain how the VC can come and go as they please, disguised as nest hunters. Hell, they probably bring their share of nests in and sell them in the Nha Trang marketplace, just like the real hunters.''

"I wonder how Charlie keeps the local nest hunters from popping in at Ham Tam?'' Ensign Dubois asked.

"I think word gets around,'' Gillespie replied. "The locals know there are some places around here you don't go. Unless, of course, you don't care about coming back again.

"Tonight, though, it's going to be Charlie who runs into trouble. Good luck, men. Bring us back some VC spooks!''

Friday, 14 March 1969

**Off Ham Tam Island
Nha Trang Bay
0140 hours**

They went in at 0100 hours that night, tooling slowly through Nha Trang Bay in a STAB—one of the sleek, low-slung assault craft that had arrived in-country last year. It was a clear, moonless night, the stars overhead carrying that special brilliancy seen only in the tropics, and only far from the nearest sky-choking cities.

The island was an enormous black shadow against stars

and Milky Way, rising from a black sea to the south as three of Casey's Commandos—Slinger, Boomer, and Ramsey—slipped over the side, one by one, entering the water with scarcely a ripple to mark their entry, and began swimming toward the shore. The other four—Casey, Tangretti, Rodriguez, and Halstead—scrambled into a seven-man IBS, along with Vinh and the two Hoi Chanhs, while the STAB boat crew held the raft steady close alongside. They passed down the heavy gear once the SEALs were aboard, including Bandit's M60, the two LAWs, and the PRC-77, which Greg slung over his back like a field pack.

Keeping low, partly to maintain low silhouettes, partly to keep a low center of gravity in the heavily loaded rubber boat, they started paddling toward shore, each of the SEALs and Vinh wielding a paddle; the defectors weren't given paddles mostly because none of the SEALs trusted them to be able to use them without making loud splashing noises . . . or flashing them carelessly in the dim starlight.

Casey was studying the rugged-looking crest of the island's hill as he paddled. "Mr. Vinh?" he asked quietly.

"Yes, sir."

Vinh's rank was the equivalent of an American first class, but the man's unfailing politeness had engendered an answering politeness in the men working with him, and he was never called anything except "*Mr.* Vinh."

"That hilltop there would be a great place for an OP. Do these boys know if the bad guys ever post anybody up there?"

Vinh talked to the two Vietnamese quietly for a moment, then shook his head. "They say, Mr. Casey, that there is often a man posted up there . . . but not tonight. With most of the VCI ashore on the mainland, there are only five, and they will probably all be either in the main camp or in the barracks."

" '*Probably,*' " Casey repeated. He didn't like it. Plans had a way of turning with the vagaries of Mr. Murphy, and he was worried that someone might be up there even now, watching the stealthy approach of the raft.

They kept stroking. Casey was reminded of that Hell Week race in the IBS around North Island and into San Di-

ego Bay . . . and the even longer return trip. There was sure
as hell no shortcut they could take this time. The island continued to grow, blotting out more and more of the stars.

Because of the mountain, they basically had two options
on this one. They could have made the approach from the
south, on the same side of the mountain as the Communist
camp . . . but it would be harder to come ashore undetected
there. The defectors had told them that the southern shoreline
was frequently patrolled, and there were always sentries in
the jungle, usually posted at different places in order to keep
a watchful enemy from detecting a pattern that could be util-
ized.

The alternative was what Casey had decided on, that afternoon back in the safety and comfort of the SEAL platoon's bull pen. Approaching from the north side of the
island gave them a good chance of sneaking in by an unguarded back door. The only trouble was the reason the back
door was unguarded—the mountain, 350 feet tall and much
of it straight up. The platoon was going to have to climb that
thing in pitch-darkness, reach the top unobserved—itself a
chancy proposition if the bad guys had a lookout up there—
then climb down the far side. If they made it, they would be
coming down almost on top of the enemy camp, and from a
totally unexpected direction.

But so goddamned many things could go wrong.

A red light winked on against the shoreline . . . winked off
. . . on-off-on-off. That was Ramsey's signal that the scouts
had made it ashore and that the coast was clear. They began
paddling in that direction.

Minutes later, the IBS grounded on sand in shallow water,
as the men aboard sprang out, grabbing the carry ropes to
haul the craft ashore. Ramsey was there to meet them;
Slinger and Boomer were already inland, manning a defensive perimeter. It took only a few minutes to hide the raft
beneath a heavy layer of nipa-palm fronds. No words were
spoken; orders were passed by hand signals and touch alone.
Casey himself went over the area carefully as the column
formed up and got ready to move, making certain that the
area was sanitized . . . no dropped cartridges or gear, no drag
marks or footprints in the sand, no disturbed vegetation that

would lead a chance enemy patrol to the hidden IBS. Their goal loomed high against the night, rising above the trees only a few tens of meters inland from the beach.

The hill that divided Ham Tam Island in half rose 350 feet above the beach, a near-vertical wall of red-brown rock that by day and from a distance looked smooth but up close, even in the dark, showed dozens of fractures, crevices, and hand-and footholds. Casey took some time at the bottom, studying the rock carefully through an AN/PVS1, observing the entire route they would be taking, picking out the best paths, and places to avoid. Very quietly, then, he discussed the route with Boomer, who would be leading the way.

Then, he went from man to man in the squad, making sure that everyone's gear and weapons were secured . . . and he waited while Chief Ramsey checked him. Finally, with a silent nod to the others, he signaled Boomer to start climbing and followed.

Ham Tam Island
Nha Trang Bay
0215 hours

Greg found himself enjoying the climb. Despite the near-vertical slope of the cliff face, the footing wasn't bad, and there were plenty of handholds along the way. He'd been concerned, at first, when he'd seen the cliff, not because he was afraid the SEALs couldn't make it . . . but because they had the two defectors in tow, and they didn't look like they were used to this sort of thing. Both men were small, skinny, and obviously terrified of what might happen on the island. He wasn't certain of their ages but thought one was probably a teenager, while the other was either in his late teens or early twenties. *Kids.* . . .

But they seemed willing enough to accompany the SEALs up the cliff, and they seemed positive that there would be no one waiting for them at the top.

Boomer was in the lead as they climbed. He seemed to have a pretty good feel for finding the best way across un-familiar terrain in the dark . . . an unlikely talent for a former Navy draftsman. He'd admitted to enjoying free climbing as a hobby, however, and was infamous in the Teams as the SEAL who'd once climbed six floors up the *outside* of a hotel in San Diego, from the third floor to the ninth, so that he wouldn't be seen by anyone in the hallways—a smart move, since he'd been naked at the time, and the woman's husband had just phoned from the lobby and was on his way up. The escapade had threatened him with a different sobriquet than "Boomer" for a time; "Drafty" could refer either to his Navy rating or to his condition during his ascent, but he tended to get angry when people used it.

For this night's climb, at least, Boomer wore pretty much the same as the rest of the SEALs—blue jeans and camo shirt, black coral sneakers, and a black load-bearing vest. Floatation jackets had been left hidden with the IBS. As always, headgear ran the gamut from Doc's boonie hat to Boomer's olive drab head scarf.

He kept climbing.

Greg had had a class in free climbing—*balance* climbing, as rock climbing without ropes or mountaineering gear was properly known—in BUD/S, even though everyone in the class had known that they were going to Vietnam and would be far more likely to end up wading through rice paddies than climbing a mountain. He was damned glad for the class now. There was the acronym they'd taught him, a litany of what to do, and what *not* to do, while balance climbing: CASHWORTH.

Conserve energy.

Always test holds.

Stand upright on flexed joints.

Hands are kept low; handholds should be waist-to-shoulder high.

Watch your feet.

On three points of contact at all times, without using knees or elbows.

Rhythmic movement, never awkward or out-of-balance.

Think and plan ahead.

Heels kept lower than toes, and pointing inward.

The part about standing upright was always a problem for Greg. There was a natural tendency to try to hug the rock, as though it was possible to get as far from the emptiness at his back as possible, or somehow to become a part of that rock face itself, especially when, like now, he was carrying a load on his back that tended to shift his center of gravity backward a bit.

In fact, leaning forward while climbing made it harder for his shoes to maintain a good grip on the rock he was standing on. He had to remind himself to keep his body back a little from the rock, upright, with at least three points of contact— two feet and a hand, or two hands and a foot—at all times.

He found himself thinking about the U.S. Army Rangers at Pointe-du-Hoc, during the D-Day invasion. *History,* he thought wryly. *I'm climbing a mountain on an island in Vietnam, and I'm thinking about military history.*

It fit, though. Those men had had to scale sheer cliffs rising one hundred feet straight out of the sea . . . and in broad daylight, with Germans at the top of the cliff firing machine guns and hurling grenades down upon them all the way. The Rangers had made it, though, with a stubbornness that had seemed nothing short of suicidal at the time. The fact that their mission ended in failure—the big naval guns they'd been sent up those cliffs to capture were not in place but had been moved several miles inland—did not detract in the least from their accomplishment, or their memory.

Still, Greg hoped that this climb would not be similarly empty. They had no real evidence that the VC were still on Ham Tam. In fact, the chances, he thought now, were against there being anyone on the island at all. Once the VCI had realized that two of their rank and file had vanished, they would have evacuated the island in a hurry. There was a strong possibility, even a probability, that the VC were long gone from Ham Tam.

The toughest part of the climb was near the top, where the men had to employ a lie-back hold—literally walking up a steep slab of rock with an offset crevice running up the face, by pushing down with the feet while hanging on to the lip of the crevice with their hands and leaning back to maintain friction for the climb. Above that, the pitch of the rock face became even steeper, and they had to employ a shoulder stand to pass it—one man standing still while the next scrambled up onto his shoulders, then performed a mantel to press himself up and over the top of the escarpment before turning and offering a hand to the man below.

It was an exhausting climb, but they made it at last ... with most of the delay being several long waits for the two Hoi Chanh. At the top of the hill, they lay in the shadows of a clump of boulders while Ramsey crawled off into the darkness, checking the naked crest.

Bill Tangretti lay on the stony ground, recouping his strength, taking small sips from one of his canteens, and studying their surroundings. The view, even in the middle of the night, was spectacular, for the sea caught and mirrored enough of the light from the stars to make it visible, a softly luminous floor beneath the glorious heavens. *My God,* he thought, looking back toward the north and west. *We were down there. If they'd had anyone up here . . .*

But then, the guys on the other side weren't SEALs. That wasn't something to plan combat strategies on, but it was comforting, nonetheless.

He thought about Pat.

It would be awfully good to have something stable, a relationship . . . something beyond the Teams. For a long time, now, he'd thought that he didn't need anything else besides his friends in the SEALs, but he was beginning to question that now.

There were things that he couldn't really talk about with the other SEALs, and he felt as though he needed to share them with someone. Pat, for instance. It wasn't that he felt closer to Greg's sister than he did to the other SEALs. Hell, these guys were like brothers—closer, even. But so much simply wasn't said, was taken for granted, was tacitly assumed and never discussed. He could *talk* to Pat.

He decided to write her another letter as soon as he got back from this op.

Ham Tam Island
Nha Trang Bay
0240 hours

A soft twitter, like a bird's sounded in the night . . . Ramsey's signal. A moment later, the chief materialized out of the night, crawling flat on his belly. *All clear*, he signaled.

Casey gathered the others with his eyes and pointed, the gesture just visible in the starlight. *Let's go.*

This was the chanciest part of the infiltration plan. They'd made it to the top of the Ham Tam hill, but now they had to descend the southern face, every bit as steep in places as the cliff they'd just climbed. They had to traverse it in the dark and they had to descend in complete silence and without knocking any rocks loose, for there would be guards in the forest below, alert to just such an attempt as this.

There was a trail of sorts, a path leading down the south face of the cliff. SEALs, by preference, avoided trails—the things were too likely to be booby-trapped—but there was little choice this time, since the alternative was to slide down huge slabs of rock that might very well end, in the darkness, in a precipice opening into thin air. If they'd had ropes and climbing gear, Casey would have considered going straight down, but the path was really their only alternative. They proceeded slowly, this time with Slinger in the lead, checking the trail ahead at every step for possible trip wires or triggers.

The descent was actually considerably easier than the climb, since they did have a trail to follow this time. Casey was pretty sure that the path must be what the VC used when they posted sentries on the top of the hill.

He just hoped they didn't meet anybody coming up.

Less than a hundred feet above the base of the cliff, the hillside broke suddenly in a broad, wide ledge almost thirty feet wide, a perfect spot to stop and reassess their final approach. Unfortunately, it was also a good spot for a VC sentry. Slinger called a halt as the column neared the ledge, silently signaling the presence of one enemy soldier. Casey could see him in the dim light, a solitary VC in black pajamas and coolie hat, an SKS carbine slung over his shoulder.

The other SEALs looked at him; silently, he pointed. *Tan-*

gretti. Halstead. Go. They were best positioned . . . farther
down the trail and at a spot where they could easily descend
to the ledge without making noise.

The two SEALs quietly removed their packs, weapons,
and heavy equipment, leaving them with the others, then
slithered off the descending path and vanished into the night.

Ham Tam Island
Nha Trang Bay
0308 hours

There was no cover at all on the ledge itself. It was bare,
flat rock furrowed by erosion, with clumps of grass or weed
here and there growing from the patches of sand that had
accumulated in the rock's grooves over the centuries. They
stayed invisible by hugging the ground close to the vertical
rock wall at their backs, moving slowly and sticking to the
shadows. The VC sentry was not looking in their direction
in any case. He seemed content to walk slowly back and
forth, staring out over the jungle and the sea to the south.

Bill Tangretti led the way, with Greg following a few feet
behind, timing their moves for the moments when the VC
was walking away from them. They'd practiced this sort of
thing hundreds of times in BUD/S; "sentry stalking" was
what they'd called it. Silently, Bill drew his knife, a UDT-
issue K-Bar with a black, Parkerized blade, and the two men
waited for a small eternity as the sentry reached the end of
his circuit, paused a while, then slowly started walking back.
He didn't seem particularly alert; most likely he was bored
and wondering why it was necessary to go through the mo-
tions of guard duty in such an out-of-the-way location as
Ham Tam.

As he walked toward them, Bill lowered his eyes, staring
at the rock in front of him, aware of the sentry's position
solely by peripheral vision. Old hands in the SEALs almost
to a man insisted that if you looked directly at a target, he
would look back . . . and see you; worse, they swore that you
could feel someone staring at you, and it would put you on
your guard. Bill wasn't sure whether he believed in a literal
sixth sense or not, but the old SEALs certainly did, his father

among them . . . and the only reason they *were* old SEALs was the fact that they'd survived long enough to become so. He was not about to test the theory now.

The sentry walked closer, and Bill concentrated on being a rock. That was another bit of wisdom from the SEAL community. Some men claimed that by imagining yourself to be a rock or a bush or something else innocuous, you could literally make yourself invisible. Again, Bill wasn't sure how much he believed in such things, but he'd heard plenty of stories to support the idea. Whether it made sense or not, perhaps this was a very good time to imagine himself to be a rock . . . a rock . . . a rock . . .

When the sentry was only five feet away, he stopped again, staring out to sea, turned so that Tangretti could glimpse his profile out of the corner of his eye. Tangretti waited . . . waited . . . and then just as the man was turning away to begin his walk back the way he'd just come, the SEAL leaped forward and up, his left hand reaching around to clamp down over the man's mouth, his right hand bringing the K-Bar up hard, slashing across the throat to lay trachea and jugular vein alike wide-open in a grisly red flower, then angling the tip of the blade in and up, driving hard into the base of the man's skull.

The man's feet snapped out in a wild kick at empty air . . . but Greg was there just an instant behind Tangretti, tackling both of the man's legs and helping to ease the lifeless body, rifle and all, to the ground without the slightest clink of metal to stone. The attack had lasted no more than a second or two and had been carried out in utter death-silence.

After checking the ledge carefully—this was a good spot for several VC sentries, after all—Greg gave a hand sign. Moments later, the other SEALs joined them, slipping like green-faced ghosts out of the night. Casey crawled on his belly to the edge of the cliff, turning the AN/PVS1 night-scope onto the jungle below. After studying the lay of the land for a long time, he went into a low-voiced consultation with Ramsey, Vinh, and the two Hoi Chanh.

Tangretti, meanwhile, checked the man he'd just killed, then dragged the corpse back into the shadows at the side of the cliff. The guy wasn't very old . . . maybe in his late teens.

The only papers he had on him appeared in the carefully shielded beam of a penlight to be some personal letters . . . and a small and badly faded photograph of a pretty young Asian woman.

Shit. He wished he hadn't seen that. It was so much better when the enemy remained impersonal . . . and inhuman.

He pocketed the documents. Any papers taken from the enemy had potential intelligence value, but he hated himself for doing so.

He was beginning to wonder if he was really cut out for this stuff, and that thought jarred him.

He wondered if the others had the same sorts of doubts, and hoped very much that they did not.

Chapter 34

Friday, 14 March 1969

Ham Tam Island
Nha Trang Bay
0316 hours

Greg Halstead had felt a savage rush of adrenaline with that short, sharp action with the VC sentry. He remembered that news program he'd seen with his sister, the one with the chanting students. *Ho! Ho! Ho Chi Minh! The NLF is gonna win!*

He shook his head at the thought. *Nah, I don't think so.* Some of the SEALs in Delta Platoon, he knew, speculated openly that they were on the wrong side . . . that the VC and the NVA were far better soldiers—more dedicated, more professional, braver, more prepared for combat, better trained—than their opponents with the ARVN. He'd heard

Chief Ramsey say more than once that he felt that he had more in common with the NVA regulars than with any of the South Vietnamese troops he'd seen yet, with the possible exception of some of the LDNN SEALs, like Vinh.

But the National Liberation Front was doomed to certain defeat. That much was obvious to him, now that he'd finally reached Vietnam and seen the reality up close. The enemy might be good fighters, but they were poorly fed, poorly armed, and they looked good only when matched against the incompetence of Marvin ARVN or, paradoxically, against the cumbersome and clumsy bull-elephant lumberings of the U.S. Army.

Success would come when the American military learned that guerrilla forces could best be fought by specialists trained in the way the guerrillas fought and thought. Specialists in counterinsurgency ops like the Army Special Forces and Rangers.

And, of course, the Navy SEALs.

Casey held a quiet conference with the three Vietnamese, with the Hoi Chanhs animatedly pointing out various landmarks in the forest below. A few moments later, the lieutenant assembled the rest of them near the face of the cliff, as Vinh stood guard nearby.

"Okay," Casey whispered, speaking just loudly enough for the six of them to hear. "I can see the VC base camp, almost directly below us." He pointed past the edge of the cliff. "About . . . there. I could see the paths, and they look clear. We'll split up, Plan One. Check your gear."

That meant weapons, and it meant radios. Besides the PRC-77 that Greg was carrying, the squad's sole link to their fire support and the helicopters that would come in to lift them off this rock, each man carried his own TR-PP-11, an FM transceiver in a splash-proof case that had a range of only three or four kilometers, but weighed just five pounds and was frequency compatible with the Prick. The SEAL platoons operating in Vietnam were increasingly finding the importance of maintaining good radio communications among the various members of the tactical unit. Close coordination between separate members of the team translated into greater efficiency, surprise, and striking power when and where it counted.

Details of the approach had been worked out the previous afternoon. According to the two Hoi Chanhs, there were two paths that led off this broad ledge, angling down the south face of the cliff, one toward the east, the other to the west. They came out in the forest on the island's southern half, on either side of the VC base camp. The defectors had reported that the paths were occasionally booby-trapped, though the fact that the bad guys had a sentry up here might reduce the risk of that.

Plan One called for the squad to split up now. Casey would take Doc Tangretti and Slinger, along with Mr. Vinh and the two defectors, and make their way down the west path. Greg, Bandit Rodriguez, and Boomer Cain would follow Chief Ramsey down the east path. The double envelopment would let them come in on the VC base camp from two directions; if one force flushed the enemy, the other would be in a position to catch them as they fled. Ramsey's group would also be responsible for checking out the barracks and pier area on the south coast, while Casey's group was responsible for checking and securing the helicopter LZ.

As a final precaution, all of the SEALs would remove their coral shoes. The remaining parts of the path were smooth, and the forest floor was soft, even muddy in places. They would move more quietly barefoot—a practice many SEALs had adopted as standard operating procedure when moving in muddy or wet terrain.

"Everybody clear?" Casey whispered. The others nodded. Casey gestured then. *Go!*

Greg caught Tangretti's eye and gave him a grin and a jaunty thumbs-up. Bill merely nodded, obviously worried about something.

Well, there would be plenty of time to see what was bugging him, once they got back to base. Hefting his Stoner, he set off down the eastern path.

Ham Tam Island
Nha Trang Bay
0322 hours

After checking their radios and weapons, they discarded their coral shoes on the ledge and separated into two parties. Bill Tangretti led the way, followed by Casey, then the Vietnamese, and with Slinger bringing up the rear. This part of the descent was much easier than the earlier climb, with a clear and easily navigable path zigzagging down the southern face of the cliff through several steeply angled switchbacks. They were less than fifty feet above the forest floor now and would probably be in position to assault the VC base camp in another ten minutes or so.

He refused to let himself hurry, however. They'd been warned during the mission briefing of the possibility of booby traps here, and for Bill, each barefooted step forward brought a tingling anticipation, a mingling of fear and the adrenaline rush of imminent fight-or-flight.

He was afraid. He knew that . . . *accepted* that, though he was ashamed to admit it. Almost worse than the fear itself, however, was the added terror either that the other SEALs in his squad would find out, or that his fear would make him screw up.

He thought about Lucky, his old squad mate back in Bravo Platoon. He'd nearly been killed by Bill's *last* screwup with a booby trap. It was a real bitch that he'd survived the grenade explosion in January, only to be KIA four months later.

Concentrate on the damned mission! . . .

Step . . . step . . . step . . .

When they'd stalked the VC sentry a few minutes ago, he'd been thinking about the paranormal talents that old-hand SEALs believed in so emphatically. There was something like that operating now, he thought, an extension of his own senses that amounted to a sixth sense, reaching out ahead of him with each step. There was something wrong here . . . something he couldn't quite grasp. . . .

He moved his head slightly, bobbing left, then right . . . and the change in angle showed him the trip wire, barely visible by the pale light of the stars. Dropping to one knee, he held up his hand, halting the column, then carefully followed the trip wire from its tie point at the side of the ledge back across the path to a crevice in the rocks perhaps four inches wide.

He used his penlight to explore the crevice, being careful to shield the beam to avoid giving away their position. Inside the crevice was an American M26 hand grenade, the pin already pulled, the arming lever held shut by the pressure of the crevice walls. The wire was wrapped around the grenade's body; a careless step would yank the grenade out of the crevice and onto the path, and the wire would keep it from bouncing off the ledge. Three seconds later, it would explode, the perfect intruder alarm system.

His mentor with this sort of trap—quite similar to the one that had nailed him last year—had been Bravo Platoon's Lucky Luciano: *Always carry some spare grenade pins with you when you're on patrol.* With a silent thanks to Lucky, he plucked a cotter pin from the canvas headband of his boonie hat, reached into the crevice, and safed the grenade. Then he removed the wire.

Casey patted his shoulder. *Well done.* Slinger eased his way past both of them, taking point. Bill had just wrecked his night vision by switching on the penlight, and they needed someone in the lead who could still see in the dark. He extracted the grenade, slipped it into one of his pouches, then let Vinh and the two Hoi Chanh edge past him on the path. He would take up drag, the rear guard.

The entire incident had lasted only a few moments, and everything was done without hesitation or loss of time. It was several moments before the realization of what he'd just done—facing his first booby trap since he'd been wounded fourteen months ago—hit him.

He smiled.

Ham Tam Island
Nha Trang Bay
0343 hours

As Slinger led the way for his group down the western trail, Casey kept an eye on the VC base camp, which was not visible in the dark but wouldn't be more than ten or fifteen yards away from where the trail angled sharply down across the face of the cliff. There still was no sign of life from the camp; likely, that sentry they'd taken out was the only man awake.

Soon, they reached a ledge well below the uppermost branches of the trees, a vantage point from which they could see the place, looking down into the VC camp itself. There wasn't much to it—a scattering of small, thatched huts that were little more than lean-tos, and the glowing remnants of a fire that cast just enough illumination to reveal the shapes of artificial structures. Pausing on the trail, Casey used the AN/PVS1 once again to scan the area carefully. He could see blankets inside one of the lean-tos, and what might be someone sleeping on top of them. An AK-47 leaned against the structure's bamboo frame. There . . . on the far side of the camp. He could see two, no, three hammocks slung between trees, and people lying inside the hammock nettings.

Good. The VC hadn't fled the island, then. He was feeling quite pleased with the way the mission had proceeded thus far. If the defectors were right and there were only five VC on the island tonight, the odds had just been pegged back a notch with the death of the sentry on the ledge. Four men left that he could see, and all of them, it looked like, sound asleep. Perfect.

Casey took a moment to check the approaches to the camp, picturing how best to carry off the op. A sudden rush, he thought, overpowering the sleeping VC all at once. That would do it. Four prisoners, all VCI and all with knowledge of Communist intelligence operations throughout this province. Intelligence ought to love that.

It was not exactly the sort of tactical situation that he'd imagined as a kid, playing war games with plastic guns with the other kids in the neighborhood. There were no heroes here, and damned little glory. Nor was it what he'd imagined when he'd pictured fighting the Communists, payback for what had happened to his dad in Korea. It wasn't even what he'd pictured when he'd heard about the SEALs; there were rumors of SEAL ops going into countries like Cuba and even the Soviet Union, yeah, but a SEAL accepted the assignments offered him, and what he had was Vietnam.

Fair enough. This type of sneak-and-grab raid, however, was fast becoming the most effective SEAL operation going, with each successful snatch nailing someone higher on the enemy's command pyramid and winning a better, clearer picture of what they knew and how they were operating.

It was kind of hard to square what he knew about Communists, though, with those skinny little kids who'd turned themselves in yesterday, turning Hoi Chanh in exchange for the promise of going home. These were the cagey masters of jungle warfare, guerrilla fighters supreme, the vanguard of Ho Chi Minh's army of liberation? They looked like hungry, scared teenage kids to Casey. He wasn't about to underestimate them . . . hell, he had more respect for the VC and the NVA than he had for most ARVNs he'd met so far, but it was good to put this struggle in its proper perspective. The real enemy was in Hanoi . . . no, in *Moscow*, and these children were puppets twitching to the whims of their unseen and distant masters.

But if the only way to get at the masters was through the puppets, so be it. Casey started to move farther down the track, feeling his way barefooted across the rocks.

A flat stone the size of a dinner plate shifted suddenly under his foot. He shot his right arm out to the side, trying to catch himself on the rock wall beside him; his hand missed the surface, plunging instead into a foot-wide vertical crevice, smashing something rough, crunchy, and yielding, like a large pine cone.

In the next instant, the crevice erupted in a swirl of shrieking, squawking birds that exploded into the night air around his head and shoulders. He regained his balance and took a step back, unhurt, but feeling a flood of horror and what could only be called embarrassment. Birds circled and shrieked; sea sparrows, the same sea sparrows that built the nests so prized by the people of Nha Trang, proved to be splendid lookouts, sounding the raucous alarm.

From the ground a dozen yards below, someone cried out. *"Cuu voi! Cuu voi!"* A burst of automatic fire followed, and bullets clipped the leaves of the trees just below Casey's feet.

Above and behind him, Tangretti returned fire with his

Stoner, a steady slam-slam-slam of full-auto fire hosing into the encampment. Ahead, at the bottom of the trail, he heard Slinger's M203 cough, and a moment later an explosion ripped through the trees, catapulting the sleepers out of their hammocks.

Somehow, Casey managed to get his feet back under him, managed to hang on to his rifle and bring it to bear. He fired a burst, then sat down atop a large and gradually sloping boulder that appeared to offer the fastest way down off this exposed ledge. Giving himself a shove, he started sliding; the burst he fired as he slid down the boulder on the seat of his pants was pure bravado, with no hope of connecting with anything, but it must have added to the confusion in the VC base camp. Suddenly, the rock was gone from beneath his legs, and for a stomach-wrenching instant he was falling through the air.

Then he hit another ledge, still some twenty feet above the floor of the forest, legs flexing to absorb the jolt, taking a step back to keep his balance as he dropped into a crouch. Bullets shrieked and howled from the boulder down which he'd been sliding a moment before. Scrambling forward again, he clattered down on a loose pile of scree and talus, then rolled behind a sheltering boulder.

One thing was instantly clear. There were a hell of a lot more than five bad guys down there, and they were *not* "lightly armed." He could hear the bullets as they snapped and whined, and they were coming from several different directions. Damn . . . there must be ten or twenty of them down there at least, and not just in the base camp, either. He could hear them running through the woods now, coming from the direction of the barracks.

And his missed step had just stirred up the whole goddamned hornet's nest, bringing the enemy out in angry swarms.

Ham Tam Island
Nha Trang Bay
0403 hours

Tangretti had been picking his way along a particularly narrow stretch of the trail when the Wheel had slipped up ahead of him, releasing the cloud of screeching birds. The gunfire from the camp had erupted an instant later, sweeping up toward the cliffside. He'd ducked as ricochets sang off the rock nearby; he'd nearly lost his footing and plunged the forty feet or so to the ground below.

Where was Casey? He couldn't see the SEAL lieutenant, but he was pretty sure he'd seen him fall. The path ahead was blocked by Vinh and the two defectors, cowering now in a huddle on the trail. Rather than trying to squeeze past, Tangretti elected to take the shortcut to the ground, scrambling over a boulder, then letting himself slide down a steeply canted incline of dirt and loose rock.

He slid about thirty feet before landing in a pile of loose rock and earth, the impact knocking him to the side and sending him sprawling.

The lieutenant ought to be *that* way, to the right. Muzzle flashes flickered and flashed among the trees ahead, however, and bullets continued to shriek off the rock in wildly random ricochets that were as dangerous as the aimed fire.

He saw an answering burst of fire—an M-16—stutter from the darkness ahead . . . and high up. That would be the lieutenant. He must still be up on the cliff.

Tangretti hurried in Casey's direction.

Ham Tam Island
Nha Trang Bay
0404 hours

Casey worked himself farther down the trail, still delivering bursts of fire whenever he thought he glimpsed movement or the flicker of a muzzle flash among the trees below. His initial surprise had given way to frustration and anger . . . frustration that his carefully worked-out plan of approach had been blown completely by something as stupid as a loose rock and a flock of nesting birds, anger that the volume of fire coming from the ground was clearly a hell of a lot more than that possible from five lightly armed men. He glanced back up the side of the cliff but couldn't see the two Hoi Chanhs . . . or Vinh or the other two SEALs, for that matter. He wondered if this was some kind of elaborate trap, a way of luring the Men With Green Faces into a box from which there was no easy escape.

The more he thought about it, the likelier it seemed. They'd been strung out along the rock wall of the cliff like targets in a shooting gallery, while the enemy was out of sight in the forest. He fired another burst, holding the trigger until his M-16 clicked dry. Then he dropped the empty mag and snapped home a fresh one, closing the bolt with a snap to chamber the first round.

He would shoot the false Hoi Chanhs himself . . . if he got the chance. Right now, he had to get his people down off the wall.

"Doc!" he yelled. "Slinger! I'll cover you! Get down off this rock!"

He leaned against a boulder, firing in short, precisely triggered bursts. Damn, the volume of fire coming up out of the forest was a lot heavier than they'd expected. It sounded like there was a whole damned company down there. He was below the tree canopy now, but it was dark, darker than it had been up in the starlight, and he couldn't be sure of anything he saw.

He thought he saw a better vantage point, twenty feet farther down, among a tangled spill of loose boulders along the foot of the cliff. It looked like heavy construction down there; every rockslide and avalanche off this weathered cliff since the island's beginnings had landed there in a clutter of boulders ranging in size from as big as his head to as big as a house.

He saw movement—a shadow slipping from behind a tree, making for that same spill of boulders. He raised his M-16, led the darting shadow by a hair, and triggered a long burst. The shadow flopped to the ground; whether the target had been hit or was shamming, there was no way to tell.

Rounding the boulder he'd been sheltering behind, Casey slipped over the edge of the trail and slithered on his butt down a long, steeply sloping surface that dropped away suddenly as he fell, dumping him in a pile of rocks and loose gravel. Another shadow moved, and he fired again; the shadow fired back, and bullets sparked and ricocheted from a boulder a few feet away.

Damn, this was no good, no good at *all*! SEAL squads weren't intended to engage in long stand-up fights, not when the odds were this one-sided.

The sharp staccato of a Stoner ripped through the night from his left. "Lieutenant!"

It was Tangretti, letting him know that he was down off that damned cliff.

"Cover me!" he yelled. If Doc and Slinger could lay down enough of a barrage, he was in a pretty good position to work his way forward, toward the winking muzzle flashes that he now estimated were about a hundred meters ahead. If he could work his way left, directly in the lee of the cliff, he might be able to get on the bad guys' flank. . . .

Something gave a sharp and metallic clink against the rocks above him and to his left. He spun, thinking someone was coming down the cliff and behind him, but the object bounced again on the rocks near his feet, clattering less than a yard away. *Grenade*! . . .

Chapter 35

Friday, 14 March 1969

Ham Tam Island
Nha Trang Bay
0405 hours

Casey had no time to react, no time to move or even think before the hand grenade, a Russian-made RGD-5 antipersonnel grenade, detonated, 110 grams of TNT exploding in a savage blast that lifted him bodily and hurled him backward through the air. His back slammed into the rock of the cliff wall behind him, and the blow nearly ripped his consciousness from him. He fell to one side, missing the ledge he'd been standing on, then tumbled several feet more before coming to rest, crumpled and broken, on a jagged pile of talus and avalanche debris directly beneath the cliff.

For a long and strangely tranquil moment, Casey thought the battle had stopped. The gunfire, that thunderous, incessant din that had been filling the night ever since the VC had spotted them, was magically gone. He heard nothing but a high-pitched, persistent ringing that grew louder moment by moment. Dazed, he shook his head, then started to get up. For some reason, he was having some trouble with his right leg. He looked down, and saw . . . no, that *had* to be someone else's leg, or what was left of it. He felt nothing and could not for a moment identify what he was seeing as something that was actually attached to his body. The bare, charred, and blackened foot was turned inward at an impossible angle; much of the skin and muscle of the lower calf had simply been shredded, leaving splintered white bone and bloody tendons. He tried moving again, saw his knee move and the ruined leg dragging with it, suspended by a few tatters of flesh.

Though he still couldn't feel it, the sight struck him with an emotional shock that equaled the physical shock of the grenade's detonation. He felt violently, wrenchingly sick to his stomach. The ringing in his ears was growing louder . . . and still louder, and now he could hear the gunfire of the battle again, tough distantly and muffled. The blast, he realized, must have deafened him, at least temporarily, but his hearing was returning now.

But his leg . . . God, his *leg*! . . .

Ham Tam Island
Nha Trang Bay
0405 hours

Tangretti had seen Casey firing at the enemy camp, had seen the blast of the grenade and a shadow that must have been Casey's body tumbling off the cliff. Now he was scrambling across the boulders as bullets sang and chirped around him, trying to find the lieutenant, praying that he was still alive.

There he is!

Scrambling down the last of a shallow, rocky slope, Tangretti reached Casey's body. At first, he thought the man was dead, but then the lieutenant opened his eyes, startlingly white in that black- and green-painted face, and blinked . . . and he tried to move his leg.

Tangretti's stomach churned unpleasantly at the sight of the horror that had been Casey's lower right leg, but he went right to work. "It'll be okay, Lieutenant," he said . . . but Casey's eyes were vacant, and he wasn't sure the man could hear him. Tangretti checked first for spurters, severed arteries pumping blood with every beat of Casey's heart. It was dark enough that he couldn't be sure—he had to do part of his exploration entirely by feel—but he was pretty sure there weren't any. There was a lot of blood, of course, but it seemed to be welling out rather than coming out in jets. He crammed several Kotex deep into Casey's leg up under the knee, wedging them against the bone and tying them in place with a long strip from a gauze bandage roll.

Another explosion thundered nearby, and Tangretti heard a yell. Looking up, he saw a VC running straight toward the two of them, an SKS carbine leveled in his hands.

The man fired as he ran—a terrible habit to get into since it was almost impossible to hit anything except by accident, but Tangretti heard the hiss and snap of the bullets as they seared past his head. The muzzle flashes lit the VC soldier's face each time it flared in the darkness.

Smoothly, scarcely missing a beat, Tangretti scooped up his Stoner and pulled the trigger, sending a stream of 5.56 rounds hosing across the VC's belly, doubling him over, spinning him back, and slamming him to the forest floor.

Then he dropped the Stoner and kept working on the lieutenant's leg.

Gunfire continued to slam into the cliff. . . .

Ham Tam Island
Nha Trang Bay
0405 hours

Greg Halstead had been heading east down the cliff face and was on the far side of the VC camp when he heard the firing break out to the west. Ramsey muttered something unpleasant under his breath.

"Sounds like they were spotted," Greg whispered.

"Fuckin' right," Ramsey replied. "C'mon, SEALs!"

The four SEALs quickened their pace, scrambling down off the cliff and across the spill of rock at the hill's base. Fanning out, Ramsey, Halstead, Rodriguez, and Cain moved in open fire-team formation through the forest, angling back toward the camp. Moments later, they could see the lean-tos . . . and several running shapes.

"Man, I think we got us more than five lightly armed guys, Chief," Rodriguez said.

"Bandit! Quit flapping your jaw and work your way over to that log! Lay us down some fire!"

"You got it!"

"The rest of you, with me!"

They charged toward the camp.

Ham Tam Island
Nha Trang Bay
0406 hours

"Nice . . . shooting . . ." Casey said, as Tangretti finished tying off the dressings packing the shattered leg.

"Thanks, L-T! How you feeling?"

"Not too bad, considering . . ." He sounded weak, but alert. His initial lack of response had suggested that he was either deaf or pretty far gone in shock, but he seemed to be rousing now.

"Any pain? I can give you something for it."

"A little," Casey said. He tried to move, gritting his teeth with the effort. "Not . . . too bad." He closed his eyes, then shook his head. "No drugs."

"Well, you change your mind, let me know."

"We walked into a trap."

"There's a hell of a lot of the bastards," Tangretti replied. "More than five, anyway."

He needed a splint, or what was left of Casey's leg was going to just rip free the next time he tried to move. The best splint available was Casey's M-16, lying on the rock pile a few feet away. Tangretti emptied the clip through the simple expedient of blazing away at the unseen enemy until the chamber clicked empty. Then he dropped the magazine and set the rifle against Casey's leg, butt down, and used a roll of gauze to wrap leg and rifle tightly together, from ankle to hip.

After that, there wasn't a lot he could do, except try to make Casey comfortable, and elevate his other leg a bit to reduce the possibility of shock. He wasn't sure how Casey was continuing to function with a wound like that.

Another grenade went off, several yards away. Bill threw himself partway over Casey's body, as rock and gravel rained momentarily from the sky. From the right, Slinger's M-16/M203 fired a long burst, then gave a short, harsh thump; the 40mm grenade struck somewhere in the middle of the enemy camp, the flash lighting up the night.

"You'd better get that Stoner in action," Casey said, levering himself upright. "Slinger can't hold that bunch by himself."

"You stay lying down, sir."

"Don't tell me what to do, Doc. Just get that Stoner working!"

Officers! He picked up the Stoner and opened fire.

Ham Tam Island
Nha Trang Bay
0407 hours

The pain in Casey's leg was growing worse, a throbbing, insistent fire that threatened to work its way up his thigh and torso and explode inside his head. He reached for his radio, pulling it out of its pouch slung from his combat vest high on his left shoulder, and thumbed the transmit key.

"Rattlesnake Two, this is Rattlesnake One," he called. "Over!"

"Rattlesnake One, this is Two," Halstead's voice replied. "Go ahead!"

"Looks like we kicked over the anthill, Two. What's your position? Over!"

"Just east of the base camp, Lieutenant. Getting ready to hit them! It doesn't look like they've seen us yet. Over!"

"Tell the chief to find a good spot and sit tight. They've already tried rushing us once and been knocked back. I think they're gonna try again. If we can hold them, I think they'll break, and when they do, it will be right past your position. When they come, cut 'em down! We'll try to backlight them for you and provide a crossfire. Over!"

"We copy, One. Sit tight and let them come to us. Over!"

"Good. If it looks like they're going to get the best of us, I'll call you in and you rush 'em from behind. Stand by! Rattlesnake One out."

"Here they come, Lieutenant," Tangretti said.

Casey pulled himself up a bit farther; the ends of his shattered tibia grated together and he almost screamed with the pain, but somehow he gritted it down. He could see two . . . no, three shapes in the darkness, moving from tree to tree, trying to slip closer to their position.

"Okay, Doc. You're a SEAL now, not a goddamn pecker checker. Hit 'em!"

Tangretti opened up with the Stoner, firing with the rifle resting across a convenient boulder. One of the running shapes stumbled and fell. A moment later, another of Slinger's 40mm grenades burst among the trees, sending one trunk slowly tippling to the side. Someone was screaming out there in the woods. More gunfire was stabbing down from the cliff above his head . . . Mr. Vinh, joining the fight at last.

The Stoner ran dry, its box empty. Then something moved, coming fast, coming up the spill of loose rock.

"Doc! Watch out!"

But it was already too late. . . .

Ham Tam Island
Nha Trang Bay
0407 hours

Bill Tangretti was just reaching for another belt of 5.56mm ammo for the Stoner when Casey's warning sounded; he saw the movement at the same instant, a short, wiry shadow vaulting over the boulder he was sheltering behind.

He twisted, trying to bring the empty Stoner up as a club, but the shadow hit him with surprising force and mass, knocking him back. His attacker was carrying an SKS carbine with a fixed bayonet. As Tangretti sprawled backward, the man reared up, rifle held high, ready to lunge.

Three harsh coughs sounded from close by Tangretti's ear; Casey had drawn his 9mm Hush Puppy and was firing up at the VC. Pain, shock, or both made the shots wild, but at least one hit their attacker, staggering him, but failing to knock him down.

At the same moment, Tangretti slid his K-Bar from its sheath and lunged upward, surging to his feet, colliding with the Vietnamese, batting the rifle aside and slamming the knife point hard into the man's diaphragm, just beneath his rib cage. His momentum carried them both over the boulder, and he and the VC toppled together onto the ground on the other side. As they hit, he yanked out the knife and stabbed again, smoothly sliding the blade between the third and fourth ribs. He wrenched the blade free again, and the man gave a spasmodic shudder, his chest seeming to deflate. As Tangretti rose, yet another VC materialized out of the night, this one with an AK-47.

Unarmed, save for the bloody knife, Tangretti moved forward, just as a flare exploded overhead. For a paralyzed instant, SEAL and Viet Cong stared into each other's eyes from a distance of three or four feet, Tangretti with his hideous green face and dripping knife, the Vietnamese with the AK.

Tangretti bared his teeth, knife raised; the VC screamed as the flare's light shivered in the night sky, then fired a single shot. The bullet struck Tangretti's head, a hammer-blow that knocked him back a step . . . but somehow he kept on his feet. He could feel blood pouring down the left side of his face, now, and he couldn't see out of his left eye. There was no time to worry about that, though. The Viet Cong was staring at him with wide, horror-stricken eyes. Somehow, Tangretti took a step forward, and put everything he had into a bellow. "Hoo*yah*!"

The VC screamed again, then dropped the rifle, and ran. Tangretti lunged for him and missed. He dropped to the ground, supporting himself on all fours. His head was pounding now, and even when he wiped the blood away, he was blind in the one eye.

Fuck it. He picked up the discarded AK. A quick check by touch confirmed what he'd suspected. The AK-47, though an excellent weapon, had a single, serious design flaw. The fire selector switch moved from safe to full auto to single shot, in that order . . . making it likely that in the heat of combat, a soldier would snap the selector all the way down to semiauto fire when what he wanted was full-auto. The mistake had just saved Tangretti's life. If the rifle had fired on full auto, it would have torn his head off.

He snapped the selector to full-auto and sent a burst after the fleeing Viet Cong, but he could no longer see the man. Another flare exploded fifty meters in front of him, a blinding, dazzling coruscation of raw, white light.

He couldn't see anyone now . . . though he could *hear* them, crashing through the forest ahead.

Running away. . . .

Ham Tam Island
Nha Trang Bay
0408 hours

"Again, Slinger!" Casey yelled. He was still clutching the Hush Puppy in one hand and yelling into his radio with the other. "Keep firing flares!"

Slinger's M203 could fire 40mm flares, as well as high-explosive thump-gun rounds, though he was delivering them in a somewhat unorthodox manner. Normally, illumination flares were fired high into the air, where they burst after a five-second delay and floated to earth on a parachute, burning all the way. Slinger was firing his grenades straight into the woods, where they exploded, igniting the underbrush and creating an eye-searing dazzle of light.

And the VC were fleeing. Casey didn't know whether it was because they'd broken in their last rush, or because they thought the flares were some new and terrible weapon, but they were fleeing.

Directly back toward Ramsey's waiting SEALs. . . .

"Keep . . . firing . . ."

Dizziness swirled about him in bloodshot, whirling darkness. . . .

Ham Tam Island
Nha Trang Bay
0408 hours

Greg lay on his belly, his Stoner aimed toward the base camp. Another flare exploded . . . and still another. Slinger was firing 40mm M583 flares into the woods on the other side of the VC base camp.

The middle of a forest, even an open one such as this, was not the preferred environment for illumination flares, but as one flare after another burst in a line among the trees, they cast a savage backlight, one that turned the fleeing Viet Cong into black, fast-moving silhouettes.

"Fire!" Ramsey barked.

Greg leaned into the heavy, slamming recoil of his Stoner Commando, walking the fire across the line of running silhouettes. From the right, fifty yards away, Bandit Rodriguez opened up with his M60, the heavier machine gun spitting a stream of bright red tracers low across the forest floor, sweeping into the running shapes, bowling them over. Greg could see the tracers streak rapidly toward the enemy, where they seemed to slow, thanks to a trick of perspective, then plunged into the encampment; some struck rocks and sailed off at odd angles. Most extinguished themselves in the forest.

At the same time, Ramsey and Boomer were firing as well, laying down overlapping fields of fire that caught the VC in a bloody kill zone . . . a death trap from which there was no escape.

"Cease fire!" Ramsey yelled. "Cease fire!"

There were no more targets. Greg could hear someone screaming in the distance, an agonized shriek that went on and on. There was a single, sharp pop, a gun firing, and the scream stopped with chilling abruptness. Had that been one of Casey's SEALs? Or a VC putting a comrade out of his misery? Greg tensed, ready to fire again. He thought he could see movement. . . .

"*Chieu hoi!*" a high-pitched voice cried. "*Khong ban! Chieu hoi!*"

Open arms. A plea for surrender.

"Bandit!" Ramsey called. "Boomer! Cover us!" The chief looked at Greg. "Let's check 'em out, Twidge."

"You got it, Chief."

"Rattlesnake Two! This is Rattlesnake One!" crackled over Greg's radio. It sounded like Doc, though the voice was ragged, and a little weak.

"One, this is Two. Go!"

"You guys okay?"

"We're fine. I think they're giving up in the camp."

"Okay. Ah . . . we're going to need a medevac, fast."

Greg felt a stab of alarm. "Bill! Are you okay?"

"It's the lieutenant. . . ." Static hissed over the open channel.

"The lieutenant's down," Greg told Ramsey. "And I think Doc's hit, too."

"Let's go. No . . . Twidge, you stay put. Get on the horn and yell for pickup. Boomer, you're with me."

The two SEALs moved toward the base camp, illuminated now by the guttering light of failing fires, ignited by Slinger's flare barrage.

Greg began calling on the radio.

Ham Tam Island
Nha Trang Bay
0412 hours

Pain. . . .

Casey lay flat, willing the pain to recede, but he was losing the fight. He couldn't make it go away. . . .

"Doc?"

A hand squeezed his. "I'm here, L-T."

"It . . . hurts . . ."

"You want me to give you something?"

He considered this. "Nah. Not as bad . . . as BUD/S."

"Nothing's as bad as BUD/S, Lieutenant. You survive that, you can survive *anything*."

"What happened? I don't hear any firing."

"It's all over. Ramsey's people are in the camp now."

"We won?" It was very dark. At first, he thought it was just the night, but there was a haze across his vision, making it difficult to see.

"We won."

"How many . . ."

"We bagged five prisoners. Slinger says there are seven enemy KIA. There might be some more bodies or wounded in the woods we haven't found, though. And some might have escaped to the sea."

"I mean, how many did we lose?"

"You and me wounded. No KIAs."

"Thank God." He swallowed. He was very thirsty. "I'm dying. . . ."

"Nah, they can't kill SEALs like you, L-T. You're too tough."

"My leg?"

There was a hesitation. "I don't think they're going to be able to save it, sir. It's pretty badly mangled. But you're gonna be okay."

"Of *course* I'm going to be okay, Doc. Shit, I'm going to take up skydiving when I get back to the World!"

"I believe it, sir. But right now, you just rest. Medevac chopper's inbound."

"That's good. Tell Ramsey to . . . to . . ."

"The chief knows his job, Lieutenant. He's running the squad, now."

"You wanna know something, Doc?"

"What?"

"I didn't think I was gonna get through BUD/S, either."

"But you did, L-T. And that's why you're gonna get through this."

Casey smiled as he slipped into oblivion.

Ham Tam Island
Nha Trang Bay
0435 hours

By the time the first Seawolf gunship was circling the island, nearly twenty minutes later, it was beginning to grow light. Slinger and Boomer had checked both the barracks-pier area and the LZ and pronounced them clean. Five dispirited Vietnamese sat in the base camp, hands tied behind their backs, blindfolds over their eyes, as Vinh roughly questioned them.

Greg ignored the interrogation, hurrying instead to the clearing nearby, where Rodriguez waited to guide the evac choppers in. Doc and the lieutenant were there. The wounded would be the first off the island, followed by the prisoners and the enormous mound of documents they'd found stashed in a cave at the base of the cliff.

"Doc!" he called. "You okay?"

Tangretti looked up at him and managed a tired smile. "I forgot to duck." Someone had pressed a Kotex pad to the left side of his head and over his left eye and tied it in place with a roll of gauze. The blood had seeped through pad and gauze alike; Tangretti looked horrible.

"Maybe you should lie down."

"I'm okay. It just grazed me. It looks a lot worse than it is."

Greg nodded toward the lieutenant, who appeared to be unconscious. His leg, horribly mangled below the knee, was held rigid by the M-16 splint. "How about him?"

"He'll make it." Tangretti frowned. "He'll be out of the program, though. He won't like that."

"Oh, damn. . . ." It was almost as bad as hearing that a buddy had been killed. Or crippled. *Out of the Teams.*

Back to the fleet? No, with a wound like that, he'd be out of the Navy.

Greg sat down heavily, the euphoria of a moment ago

gone. Lieutenant Casey, invalided out. His friend Bill, wounded . . . and he seemed unwilling to talk about how bad the wound might be.

"I hear we struck it lucky," Tangretti said.

"Huh? Oh, yeah. Ramsey says we got something like three seabags full of documents. Intel on every dink operator in the province. That ought to keep Intelligence busy for a while."

"Might generate some new ops for us. Higher up the ladder, you know?"

"Yeah. . . ."

But Greg wondered if it had been worth it.

With a thunderous roar, a sound of pure beauty that could stir the heart like nothing else, a Seawolf angled in toward the LZ.

Chapter 36

Monday, 17 March 1969

SEAL Compound
Cam Ranh Bay
Republic of Vietnam
1030 hours

Bill Tangretti walked into the SEAL bull pen and slumped into a folding chair next to Greg.

"How's it going, Doc? How are you?"

The question had more than purely social overtones. "The eye's fine," he said.

It was only a small lie. In fact, vision in his left eye was markedly blurry now, where it had been perfect twenty-twenty before he'd been hit . . . but it wasn't enough to incapacitate him in any way, and it sure as hell wasn't going to get him kicked out of the Teams. He had too much invested in the SEAL program now to risk letting some half-assed Navy doctor tell him he couldn't be a SEAL anymore. He could see well enough to cheat on the eye exams, anyway, and that was all that counted.

"The eye's just fine," he said again. Tangretti lightly touched the bandage that wrapped around his forehead, holding a large surgical dressing in place. "But those bastards aren't going to clear me for an op until this thing comes off."

"Well, it figures, doesn't it?" Greg replied, grinning. "That white bandage wouldn't go very well with green-painted skin."

"They make olive drab bandages. Nah, they're afraid I have a concussion or something."

"What, would that make you crazy in combat?"

"Hell, I'm for that. We should try it."

"Maybe it's not such a good idea. Here." Greg extracted a letter from his shirt pocket and handed it to Bill. It had a Jenner return address. "Read that instead."

Pat . . .

He tore the letter open, eager.

"They had mail call while you were down at the sick bay. That came for you."

"Thanks." He was already reading. It wasn't a long letter; after he'd told her how much he liked getting mail frequently, she'd started writing him short, newsy letters every couple of days. In fact, there'd been times when he'd gotten two letters from her in one day. He felt he was getting to know her very well. It was amazing how much you could learn about someone from letters. Still, he wished he could talk to her in person. It would be over four long months before he'd be back Stateside. He'd have to ask her for a photograph in his next letter. Not that he'd ever forget what she looked like, but he'd really like to be able to look at her picture every day.

"So," Greg asked as Bill carefully folded the letter and put it away. "How's things in the World?"

"Oh, fine. Fine. Pat sends her love to you."

"She *used* to send letters to *me*."

"She said she had one in the works. It'll probably be along in a day or two." He grinned. "What's the matter, Twidge? Jealous?"

"Not really. Just so long as you don't alienate my sister's affections."

Bill was thoughtful for a time. When he didn't reply immediately, Greg added, "Hey, I was kidding."

"Huh? Oh, sure. Listen, Twidge. How do you feel about it?"

"How do I feel about what?"

"Uh, you know. Pat and me."

"What about Pat and you? Remember, I didn't get to read the damned letter."

"C'mon, Twidge! You know damn well—"

Greg laughed. "Doc, I can't think of anybody else I'd rather trust my sister to. It's like keeping it in the family, y'know?"

Tangretti smiled, nodding. "Sure, Bro. Like they say, vice is nice, but incest is best!"

"I'll tell you once, Doc. Pat is very special to me. She's good people and she deserves the very best of the best. If you ever hurt her, I will, I swear to God, hunt you down and kill you. But otherwise, well, as far as I'm concerned, good luck, man!"

He stuck out his hand. Gravely, Tangretti accepted it, shaking it firmly. "I really don't know what's gonna happen yet, Twidge. But I love her. *God*, I love her." He tapped the letter in his pocket. "And, well, I think she loves me, too."

"I approve. It couldn't happen to a nicer SEAL!"

Bandit Rodriguez dropped into a nearby seat. "Hey, dudes," he said. He was cultivating a bushy, drooping mustache, the ends definitely curving past the corners of his mouth in a decidedly nonregulation manner. The SEALs, so far at least, had had few problems with Navy grooming standards. "Doc! You put in for another Purple Heart?"

Tangretti made a face. "Nah. It's just a scratch. And after what happened to the lieutenant, well, it didn't seem right, y'know?"

"I read you, buddy. I heard tell one SEAL platoon just

doesn't even put in for the things. No one's been seriously hurt, y'know? And they have a kind of a superstition against it."

"Maybe we're not so different from the Vietnamese," Greg offered. "With the superstitious shit, I mean."

Tangretti shrugged. "It's human. Them and us, we're both looking for ways to control one hell of an out-of-control world around us. If superstitions give you a handle on things, hope for the future, whatever, so be it."

"You'd better check in to sick bay," Bandit said. "That whack you took upside the head scrambled something, turned you into a philosopher."

"He's already been," Greg said.

"Yeah? How is it?"

"I'm fine," Tangretti said.

"Concussion," Greg said. "He's too crazy to go into combat."

"Fuck, you have to be crazy for that!"

"Yeah," Tangretti said. "Look at you two."

"You don't have to be crazy," Greg said.

"But it sure helps!" all three chorused in unison.

"Damn shame about the lieutenant, though," Rodriguez said.

"Yeah," Tangretti said. Frank Casey's leg had been amputated below the knee shortly after he'd been medevacked back to Cam Ranh Bay. The word was that he was going to be fine. He'd probably be fitted out with a prosthetic leg in a few months, back in the States. The experts predicted that he would walk again; Casey had loudly proclaimed that he would run in a marathon and skydive. That was SEAL spirit.

The only trouble was that he wouldn't be able to stay in the Teams. In fact, he would probably be out of the Navy. A *civilian*.

"Hey," Rodriguez said. "Did you hear the skinny? The lieutenant got put in for the Medal."

Tangretti's eyes widened. "What ... the Medal of Honor?"

"The little blue button. I heard Zumey was in on it. I bet it clears and he gets it."

"Well, he *is* an officer," Greg said. "They were waiting

for a SEAL officer to do something stupid enough to win the CMH. I guess Ham Tam qualifies, huh?''

"Where'd you hear this, Bandit?" Bill wanted to know.

"Guy I know in Personnel. We're gonna have officers snooping around in the next week or two, asking questions. Having us write reports.''

"Reports!"

"Just the usual after-action shit. Only they'll want to know what Lieutenant Casey did.''

"How do you like that?" Greg said, shaking his head. "And I went through BUD/S with the guy. Medal of Honor, huh?''

"That's the word. Of course, it could get bumped down the pyramid. Navy Cross or Silver Star.''

"Nah, that won't happen," Bill said. "He'll get it.''

"What makes you so sure?" Greg asked.

"Because this fucking war needs heroes," Bill said simply. "Heroes mean good news and brave deeds and great victories to the folks back home.''

"Ho, Ho, Ho Chi Minh," Greg said, shaking his head. "*That's* what folks are saying back home. Remember?''

"Not all of them. And the military is going to want to remind people that there *are* heroes out here. Medal-of-Honor-type heroes." Bill winked at Greg. "Including heroes who don't get medals.''

"Who needs medals?" Greg said, grinning. "They don't even pay for a fucking cup of coffee. . . .''

"Attention on deck!" someone called, and everyone in the room stood up. Lieutenant Gillespie walked in, followed by Lieutenant Victor Elliot Connolly, Delta Platoon's new comanding officer.

"As you were, gentlemen," Connolly said.

As they sat down, Tangretti studied Connolly closely, as did every other SEAL in the room, most likely. He looked young, with the suntanned good looks of a Southern California boy. They'd flown him out from Coronado on a special flight just as soon as the word came through that Casey had lost his leg and would no longer be the Wheel for Delta Platoon. Ensign Dubois, in Second Squad, it was felt, was too junior to boss a platoon, so a replacement had been brought in.

NAVSPECWARGRU-VN was eager to have Delta follow through on the success of its intelligence raid on Ham Tam Island, and they didn't want it to operate at anything less than full strength. Tangretti, for one, felt a certain amount of suspicion about the new man. He wasn't Casey, after all, and Casey had been in combat.

Still Vic Connolly was a SEAL, a graduate of BUD/S Class 41. If he held together all right on a combat op, he would probably be okay. . . .

Tangretti wondered if the guy would get a handle in Vietnam. The word was they'd called him "VC" back in San Diego, but that was a name that wasn't likely to last long here.

"Good morning, men," Connolly said, standing at the front of the room. "I know we haven't really had a chance yet to get properly acquainted. That, I assure you, will come. In the meantime, we've got a job to do . . . and that is to make the intel you guys grabbed at Ham Tam pay off. And it's going to pay off, big-time, starting now!

"All I'll say right now is that I'm glad to be aboard with Delta Platoon. I know Lieutenant Casey left me a good unit. I know we're going to rock 'n' roll together with the best of 'em, because we are the best! Mr. Gillespie?"

The NILO stepped forward. "Thanks, Lieutenant. Okay, men. Here it is. The stuff you grabbed on Ham Tam included lists of every goddamn VC intelligence agent, official, and collaborator in Khanh Hoa Province. There's a bonus, and we're going to take advantage of it now, before the situation changes. It turns out that two key members of the local VCI are staying in a ville up in the mountains called Khanh Son. It also turns out that one of those Hoi Chanh who accompanied you guys to Ham Tam knows both men, and since he's been to Khanh Son a couple of times on assignments, he knows what hooch the targets are likely to be staying in."

That *was* a bonus, Tangretti thought. Intelligence had decided that the two Ham Tam defectors might have been mistaken about the timing for the return of a large force of VC sappers to the island, but that they were not double agents.

That meshed with his own assessment of them, that they were little more than scared kids.

Gillespie unrolled a map, showing the interior of the province.

"Here's the op, gentlemen. . . ."

Khanh Son
Khanh Hoa Province
Republic of Vietnam
1420 hours

It would be the first raid carried out by Casey's Commandos since the assault on Ham Tam, three days before. The intel from Ham Tam had identified Ky Xuan Dai as a key member of the provincial VCI, an NVA colonel who'd taken over the administrative and intelligence duties for the district after his Viet Cong predecessor had been killed during Tet. Another VCI bigshot in the area was Nguyen Ba Tang, the district political officer in charge of both propaganda and recruitment.

Part of First Squad was going in to get them.

This type of operation was relatively new, something begun by the Teams only in the past few months. Called a *parakeet op*, for reasons still unclear to Greg, it was fast becoming one of the more powerful weapons in the SEAL inventory.

Greg sat in the Seawolf, his Stoner Commando balanced across his lap. He wore fatigues with the Vietnamese tiger-stripe camouflage pattern, a combat vest loaded with extra ammo, grenades, and equipment, boots, and boonie hat. His face had been painted green, as much for effect as anything else. The paint wasn't that useful as camouflage in a raid carried out in broad daylight and at close range, but it certainly had a psychological effect far out of proportion to the effort needed to achieve it.

Phan Nhu Hung sat next to him, looking out of the Seawolf's open side door. They still weren't letting the NVA Hoi Chanh have a weapon, but he seemed willing enough to continue providing information to the Americans. As Greg understood it, the guy couldn't go home . . . not when his home was near Hanoi. All he could do was keep serving his new masters until the war was over.

Maybe then, Greg thought, with a final victory for the south, Hung might be able to see his home again.

The others in the rear of the helo included Mr. Vinh, as translator, Boomer, Bandit, Ramsey, and, of course, Lieutenant Connolly. They were flying slowly over the village, as Hung stood in the door, studying the cluster of hooches and small buildings below.

"Remind him that we have to be sure," Connolly told Vinh. "I don't want this going off unless he's sure we have the right damned hooch."

"I will tell him," Vinh said.

Greg watched Connolly as the LDNN spoke rapid-fire Vietnamese with the Hoi Chanh. The new lieutenant seemed competent enough. He was a SEAL, after all. Still, Greg missed Casey, missed him a lot. There was something special about serving in a platoon with some of your BUD/S classmates, men who you'd literally been through hell with, and something special, too, if one of those men was your CO. You knew you could trust him, knew the way he thought, the way he planned. Hell, half the time you knew what he was thinking. Greg hadn't gotten a handle on this newbie yet.

That would come, he imagined.

But damn, he wished Frank Casey was still the platoon's Wheel. Since Delta Platoon had been assembled under his command, he naturally fit in in a way that no newcomer could.

That wasn't reason enough to dislike the new guy. The worst of it was that Greg couldn't shake the feeling that if he and Bandit hadn't worked so hard to keep Casey from dropping out on the last day of Hell Week, the guy would still have both legs. It was an unpleasant thought. The Navy, especially a tight-knit organization like the SEALs, never allowed you to escape the responsibility of your actions. *Never.*

Maybe that was why the Navy was the ideal place to turn children into men.

The Hoi Chanh pointed suddenly, jabbering quickly. Vinh

turned to Connolly. "He says that is the house. There."

"Bring him up forward."

Connolly, Vinh, and Hung all somehow squeezed up against the narrow space between the pilot and copilots' seats. As the Seawolf swung around, Hung reached up and put his finger on the pilot's windscreen, precisely identifying the one hooch in the entire village that they were interested in.

"Everybody get set!" Connolly yelled to the other SEALs in the helo. Boomer grinned at Greg, and the two exchanged winks. *This is it!*

"Lock and load!"

Greg dragged the charging handle of his Stoner back, chambering the first round.

Then the Huey descended with a stomach-fluttering swoop, dropping out of the sky directly in front of the target hooch. Greg heard the helicopter's pilot talking to Gold Arrow, the flight of four Seawolves flying shotgun for this parakeet op.

The key to the parakeet op was the oft-observed fact that Vietnamese villagers never paid attention to *one* American helicopter. One helo by itself might be many things—a medevac chopper, a mail flight, even a reconnaissance flight, but it was never a full-fledged attack.

The assault chopper, then, carried a snatch team of four or five SEALs, a Hoi Chanh, and an intepreter; the Hoi Chanh would point out the specific hooch where the target could be found and the helicopter would deliver the snatch team to the front door . . . or to the roof if there wasn't room to set down out front. At the moment the assault chopper made its descent, four Seawolf gunships, which had been loitering out of sight behind a nearby hill or treeline, would suddenly pop up, giving the villagers something to worry about besides the Huey that had suddenly touched down in their midst.

The snatch team would smash into the hooch, grab whoever they'd come for, and leave. Depending on the situation, the prisoner would be bundled aboard the helo or taken into the jungle; generally, the snatch team would E&E on foot.

Surprise was riding with them, as powerful a weapon as

the rocket pods and machine guns mounted on the Seawolf's sides. Though most SEALs preferred operating at night, most parakeets were pulled at midday. Like SEALs, the Viet Cong were nocturnal beasts and likely to be roaming far afield in the night; at midday, however, they were usually sacked out.

Suddenly, it was time. The helicopter dropped to within a couple of feet of the ground, raising great, swirling clouds of dust with its rotor wash. Greg was first off the chopper, leaping out and hitting the ground running. He kicked in the thatch door of the target hooch and stormed in, Stoner Commando at the ready. Bandit and Connolly were right behind him, while Boomer and Ramsey mounted guard outside. Inside were two men, one groggily rising on a straw mat with rice-husk-stuffed pillows, the other squatting on a mat in the middle of the room, holding a bowl and a pair of chopsticks. A pair of AK-47s leaned against the far wall of the hooch, out of reach.

"*Anh dang lam gi do?*" the man on the sleeping mat said. Then he got a good look at the green faces above him, his eyes widened, and he screamed.

"Surprise!" Greg called. He grabbed him by his shirt collar and flung him facedown to the dirt floor, dropping one knee to the small of his back and pinning him there long enough to secure his hands with a plastic tie, then swiftly pat him down for weapons. Bandit had the other man down on his belly, and was tying his hands at the same time, as Connolly covered them both.

Vinh and Hung entered as the two prisoners were yanked upright and gagged with strips of cloth. Hung said something, pointing at both men. Vinh nodded. "He say these are the men." Vinh gestured at the man Greg was holding. "That is Colonel Ky Xuan Dai," he said. He pointed at Bandit's man. "That is Nguyen Ba Tang; Hung is certain of their identities. He said both men were often at Ham Tam."

"Okay, gentlemen," Greg said. He stood, dragging Dai along like a sack of grain. "Let's go!"

This time, the Seawolf had remained just outside the hooch, its rotors still turning. Stooping low, Greg trotted up to the starboard-side door and tossed Colonel Dai aboard. Bandit threw Tang aboard next, then stepped aside as

Boomer scrambled on with them, carrying the two AK-47s that had been found inside the hooch. He would be escorting the prisoners back to Cam Ranh. Hung and Vinh climbed aboard next, and then the other SEALs backed off, waving to the pilot. The Seawolf pilot tossed them a salute, then hauled in on the collective, sending the Huey into the sky, clearing the tops of the hooches and roaring away low over the forest to the east.

Greg jogged back inside the hooch, where Connolly was checking for documents. He'd found two metal ammunition boxes for American .50 caliber rounds stashed in one corner, underneath a pile of woven mats.

"Careful, Lieutenant," Greg warned.

"Damn straight," Connolly replied. He cracked the lids of the boxes gently, checking for wires or signs of tampering. Finding none, he opened them both.

"Jackpot," Connolly said. One was filled with Vietnamese money. The other contained papers and maps. "Looks like we're gonna party."

While money was supposed to be turned in when it was recovered, most SEALs routinely kept all or most of it, putting it into their operating fund to pay informants . . . and sometimes to fund a beach party, complete with beer and girls. Their higher-ups either didn't know or looked the other way. SEALs, after all, got results, and even the slowest brass hats were starting to catch on to the idea that the best way to keep getting results was to let the SEALs operate.

Connolly packed up the ammo cans again, and stood up. "Coming?"

"In a sec."

"Make it snappy."

Greg paused after Connolly had left, examining the interior of the hooch. A calling card of some sort would be nice, like the stripes of green paint sometimes left on the bodies of victims . . . something that would take advantage of the Vietnamese fears and superstitions, something to let them know who had done this, and to serve warning that joining the Viet Cong was definitely hazardous to your health.

There were no bodies this time, however. There was just

the shocking absence of two men who'd been there just a moment ago. Perhaps that was enough.

Then Greg saw the bowl left where a moment before Tang had been looking up in terror as the SEALs had burst in. It was half-filled with rice and chopped up bits of fish, including one fish head the size of Greg's open hand. The pungeant aroma of *nuoc mam* hovered above the bowl like an acrid cloud. The chopsticks lay on the dirt floor nearby.

He smiled. There *was* something he could do.

Moments later, he emerged into the dusty sunshine outside. The Seawolf with the two trussed-up prisoners and the Hoi Chanh on board was long gone. The SEAL squad was forming up to exit the ville, slipping away into the woods to the north. They would extract by Seawolf helicopter at a clearing about ten klicks away, after sweeping their own trail a time or two, and setting an ambush for any Victor Charlies dumb enough to try chasing SEALs.

He doubted that they would try.

The gunships, meanwhile, crisscrossed protectively overhead as though daring the VC to strike back. Their orders were to open fire on anyone behaving in a threatening manner, and their rules of engagement gave them a fair amount of latitude on that point. Still, the villagers of Khanh Son did not appear eager to interfere with the green-faced SEALs. Those who hadn't fled into the bush at the first appearance of the assault team were keeping their distance, watching from the edge of town or staying inside their houses. Connolly gestured at Greg. *Take drag.*

The SEAL squad began filing out of the village, plunging into the bush. Greg was the last man out, walking backward, his Stoner ready to engage anyone who made a hostile move.

Greg's SEAL calling card remained behind inside the objective hooch, the food bowl sitting all alone in the middle of the floor, the two chopsticks stuck vertically into the mound of rice.

Like a pair of incense sticks . . . a memorial to the dead.

He thought the villagers left behind in Khanh Son, including the VC living with them, would get the point.

Chapter Epilogue

March 1970

The Congressional Medal of Honor

For conspicuous gallantry and intrepidity at the risk of his own life above and beyond the call of duty on 14 March 1969 while serving as a SEAL Team leader during action against enemy aggressor (Viet Cong) forces in the Republic of Vietnam. Acting in response to reliable intelligence, Lieutenant (j.g.) Casey led his SEAL Team on a mission to capture important members of the enemy's area political cadre known to be located on an island in the bay of Nha Trang. In order to surprise the enemy, he and his team scaled a 350-foot sheer cliff to place themselves above the ledge where the enemy was located. Splitting his team into two elements and coordinating both, Lieutenant (j.g.) Casey led his men in the treacherous downward descent to the enemy's camp. Just as they neared the end of their descent, intense enemy fire was directed at them, and Lieutenant (j.g.) Casey received massive injuries from a grenade which exploded at his feet and threw him backward onto the jagged rocks. Although bleeding profusely and suffering great pain, he displayed outstanding courage and presence of mind in immediately directing his element's fire into the heart of the enemy camp. Utilizing his radioman, Lieutenant (j.g.) Casey called in the second element's fire support which caught the confused Viet Cong in a devastating crossfire. After successfully suppressing the enemy's fire, and although immobilized by his multiple wounds, he continued to maintain calm, superlative control as he ordered his team to secure and defend an extraction site. Lieutenant (j.g.) Casey resolutely directed his men, despite his near-unconscious state, until he was eventually evacuated by helicopter. The havoc brought to the enemy by this very successful mission cannot be overestimated. The enemy who were captured provided critical intelligence to the allied effort. Lieutenant (j.g.) Casey's courageous and inspiring leadership, valiant fighting spirit, and tenacious devotion to duty in the face of almost overwhelming opposition, sustain and enhance the finest traditions of the United States Naval Service.

—Richard Nixon